Dear Reader:

I hope you will enjoy the first installment of the *Pure Ones* saga on the following pages. You will soon see that much more is yet to come.

Every story has many points of view, many different interpretations and versions of the truth. So what about the perspective from the Dark Ones' POV?

Email me at megami771@yahoo.com to find out more. And follow me on https://www.facebook.com/AjaJamesAuthor and https://aja-james.blog/. I will have free chapters and other goodies on my upcoming release *Dark Longing*, as well as Book 3 *Dark Desires*.

I love hearing from you!

Enjoy!

Aja James

Glossary of terms

Awakening: test of courage and strength of spirit which leads to the subject coming into his/her Gift, a supernatural power, if he/she passes the test.

Bonding Ritual: symbolic ceremony whereby a Pure One pledges his/her devotion to his/her Eternal Mate, or when the Healer unites with his/her Consort. The binding pledge, delivered by the Master of Ceremonies, contains the following verses:

> *In Darkness and Light, in Life and Death*
> *Two souls will join to share One Path*
> *With heart and mind, and every breath*
> *You become each other's present and past*
> *What the future holds only the Goddess can see*
> *Paved by the choices you both shall make*
> *Step by step toward your Destiny*
> *In Bond Eternal that none shall break*

Cardinal Rule: Sacred Law number three, thou shalt not engage in sexual intercourse with someone who is not thy Eternal Mate. See Sacred Laws.

Chevalier: a combination of Pure and human warriors who stand as the first line of defense against rising vampire Hordes and human menace.

The Chosen: six royal guards of the New York-based Vampire Queen.

The Circlet: five royal inner council members of the Pure Queen.

4

Consort: temporary Mate for the designated Healer of the Pure Ones. For thirty days during the Phoenix Cycle, the Consort will provide the Nourishment to supply the Healer's reserve of energy for the next ten years. See Phoenix Cycle and Healer.

Cove: base of the New York-based vampire hive, with dominion over the New England territories in the U.S.

Decline: condition in which or process of a Pure-Ones' life force depleting after he/she Falls in love but does not receive equal love in return. The Pure One weakens and his/her body slowly, painfully breaks down over the course of thirty days, leading ultimately to death unless his/her love is returned in equal measure.

The Dozen: see Royal Zodiac.

The Elite: six royal personal guards of the Pure Queen.

Eternal Mate: the destined partner to a given soul. Each soul only has one mate across time, across various incarnations of life. Quotation from the Zodiac Scrolls describing the bond: "His body is the Nourishment of life. Her energy is the Sustenance of soul."

Fall/Fallen: process or condition of a Pure One having infused his/her partner with life force through sexual intercourse in the act of falling in love. If the love is unreturned in equal measure, the Pure One will enter into Decline and die within thirty days.

Gift: supernatural power bestowed upon Pure Ones by the Goddess. Usually an enhanced physical or mental ability such as telekinesis, superhuman strength and telepathy.

The Goddess: supernatural being who is credited with the creation of the Pure Ones. She is a deity to which Pure Ones devote themselves. She protects the Universal Balance.

Healer of the Race: the one Pure One with the Gift to heal others, even bring people back from the dead in some rare cases. The Healer is typically a Pure-female, and she requires the Nourishment of a Consort to provide her with enough energy to heal others. She selects her Consort through the Rite of the Phoenix and takes Nourishment from him during the course of the thirty-day Phoenix Cycle. The bond between Healer and Consort is the only exception to the Sacred Laws.

Hive: society of vampires with a matriarch, the Queen, at the head.

Horde: small groups of vampires with no Queen, typically composed of Rogues who band together for ease of hunting.

Jade Lotus Society: society of females devoted to healing arts.

Nourishment: the strength that Mated Pure-females take from the Pure-males' body and blood. Once Mated, the Pure-female becomes dependent upon the Pure-male for sustaining her life. If her Mate dies before her, she too will perish. In equal exchange, the Pure-female provides Sustenance. See also Sustenance.

Orb of Prophesies: orb that harnesses powers of precognition, interpreted or channeled through the Seer.

Phoenix Bonding Ritual: bonding ceremony between Healer and Consort. Similar to the bonding between a Pure One and his/her Eternal Mate. Difference being that the bond between Healer and Consort is temporary, with no promise of the future. See also Bonding Ritual.

Phoenix Cycle: thirty-day period in which the Healer rejuvenates her powers through her chosen Consort. The Consort would become her sole source of Nourishment for the duration and provide the reserve she would need to carry out her role as the Pure Ones' Healer for the next ten years.

Phoenix Mate: another name for the Healer's Consort. The Healer's temporary Mate. See also Consort and Healer of the Race.

Pure One: supernatural being who is eternally youthful, typically endowed with heightened senses or powers called the Gift. In possession of a pure soul and blessed with more than one chance at life by the Goddess, chosen as one of Her immortal race that defends the Universal Balance.

Rite of the Phoenix: process by which, every ten years, the Healer of the Race chooses a new Consort.

Rites of Passage: decadal three-day trial in which six chosen unmated, qualified Pure-males undergo three final tests to apply as the Healer's Consort. The first day tests the Pure-males' strength and vitality. The second day tests their endurance for pain and ability to heal. The third day tests their sexual compatibility with the Healer.

Rogue: lone vampire who does not belong to an organized vampire society or Hive.

The Royal Zodiac: twelve-member collective of the Elite, the Circlet and the Queen of the Pure Ones.

Sacred Laws: One, thou shalt protect the purity, innocence and goodness of humankind and the Universal Balance to which all souls contribute. Two, thou shalt maintain the secrecy of the Race. And three, thou shalt not engage in sexual intercourse with someone who is not thy Eternal Mate. Also known as the Cardinal Rule.

Sanctuary: physical seat or residence of the Healer during the time she presides over the Jade Lotus Society.

Service: the contract between the Healer of the Race and her Consort. The Consort's provision of Nourishment to the Healer over the course of the thirty-day Phoenix Cycle.

Shield: referred to as the base of the Royal Zodiac, wherever it may be. Not necessarily a physical location.

Sustenance: the strength that Mated Pure-Males take from the Pure-females' spirit. Once Mated, the Pure-male becomes dependent upon the Pure-female for sustaining his life. If his Mate dies before him, he too will perish. In equal exchange, the Pure-male provides Nourishment. See Nourishment.

Universal Balance: underlying order that is essential for the continuation of time. The idea that everything exists in cycles or pairs—good and evil, darkness and light, past and future, right and wrong, male and female, life and death, etc. Disruption to this balance leads to destruction, chaos, and eventually, the implosion of time and space.

Vampire: supernatural being who prefers to live in the night and who gathers energy and prolongs his/her life by feeding off the blood, and sometimes souls, of others. Vampires are made, not born. Some vampires are Pure Ones who have chosen Darkness rather than death after they break the Cardinal Rule. See also Glossary in *Dark Longing*.

Zodiac Prophesies: events yet to come, foretold by the Seer of the Pure Ones through the Orb of Prophesies.

Zodiac Scrolls: events past, recorded by the Scribe of the Pure Ones.

Prologue

He's still following me. Crap.

Oh well, it's not like I can lose him when he's been trained for all this top-secret-shadowing stuff while I'm just a normal college student trying to get to class on time.

Hi, let me introduce myself. My name is Sophia Victoria St. James. A mouthful, I know. And rather hoity-toity sounding if you ask me. Brings to mind an Italian heiress or protagonist from a Jane Austen novel or something.

It's hard to live up to. I don't feel like a Sophia or a Victoria. I'm neither wise nor victorious, if my barely-average grades and constant losing battle with my wayward hair are any indication. So you wouldn't have guessed that someone like me would have a twenty-four/seven bodyguard, right?

Yeah, it's not all it's cracked up to be.

Today is the first day of classes Freshman year at Harvard. Before you get the wrong idea—I don't really know how I got into Harvard. It's not like I'm one of those really smart or rich or famous kids who got in on their own merits or because of their parents' money and influence.

I got into Harvard because I'm weird.

Eccentric, if you want to put a slightly more positive sheen on it. Eccentricity is almost synonymous with individuality, and we're in the U.S. of A. Don't we celebrate that stuff here? Apparently, Harvard appreciates applicants with my sort of rambling background (even though I can barely pass eighth grade algebra), and surprisingly, they thought that my application essay about vampires and the ultimate battle between Good and Evil was highly entertaining—"indicative of an active imagination and a wellspring of creativity," the admissions officer had written in my acceptance letter.

Go figure.

So here I am, terrified that someone will find out that I'm nowhere near as imaginative or as creative as other students enrolled, those who actually deserve to be here. And everyone puts all sorts of glorious titles on their résumés, like "President of Asian American Association," "President of Alpha Beta Phi," "President of Student Council" and so forth and so on. All very important sounding titles. Makes me feel like the future leaders of the world are collected on one campus in Cambridge, Massachusetts.

In contrast, all I can say is that I'm the Queen of the Vampires. Though I wisely left that out of my application. Well, actually I'm not the Queen of the Vampires, but if anyone asked, it's easier to explain if I said that, except I'd have to kill them afterwards. Or more likely have my bodyguards do it. No one is supposed to know.

The truth is: I'm the Queen of the Pure Ones.

Why did I mislead you into thinking I was something snazzier like the Queen of the Vampires? Because there's blood-sucking involved in this race that I rule, and whenever there's blood-sucking, if you Google it, you get vampires.

Actually you don't, you get "hematophagy," but that's beside the point. If you ask anyone on campus what's the first thing that comes to mind…

Anyway, the Pure Ones are not vampires. It's an unforgivable insult to be called one. Matter of fact, we're at war with the vampires. Hence my application essay about vampires and the battle between Good and Evil. It's what I live every day, so I didn't feel inspired to write about much else.

And here I am. At Harvard. Someone in the admissions office must be having a riot at my expense. Oh well. I'll enjoy this ultra-expensive and exclusive education while I can.

Crap. I've been going the wrong way.

My first class in ancient Chinese history got moved to the Kennedy School of Government campus due to the remodeling in the East Asian Studies complex. I forgot about that. Now I'm going to be at least fifteen minutes late hauling ass across Harvard Square!

Ha, maybe I can ditch my tail through some nimble maneuvering...

Back to the Pure Ones. I don't know much, but I do know the Cardinal Rule. It's hard to miss. Basically, if a Pure One falls in love and has sex with anyone who isn't their Eternal Mate, they die a slow, excruciating death within thirty days.

Kinda puts a damper on your sex life.

Finally! Made it to class. And the professor didn't even notice my extreme tardiness because the lecture hall is overbooked. Who knew so many youngsters these days would be interested in ancient Chinese history. And my tail? Still there.

Of course he is. If there's anyone more in need of a reprieve from the no-sex rule... just saying.

Val would probably turn me over his knee if he knew I'm thinking this. He's "old school." *Waaaayyy* old. I mean, with a name like Valerius Marcus Ambrosius, you're pretty clued in he's not from the twenty-first century.

But it's more than that. He's more reserved physically than anyone I know. Hates being touched. He never touches anyone and is very adroit at avoiding physical contact from others. Which is why his chosen weapon is the chained scythe. He's unbeatable in distance combat. And pretty lethal in short distances too, for that matter.

Val is one of The Elite, the six warriors that compose my personal guard. They are the bravest, toughest, awesomest fighting machines of the Race. Word is that Val's body count is the highest among the six. I guess that makes sense. He's been around for at least a couple thousand years, his human origin dating to sometime in ancient Rome. No one knows the exact year, month and day, including himself.

Val is always in control. But I can see his self-restraint cracking.

My Gift is the ability to see Pure souls as well as read the intentions of all living beings. Val's intentions are kinda confusing, but they center around maintaining discipline and distance, especially whenever he encounters one of my inner council members, one of the Circlet—Rain.

Just Rain. One-word name, like Rhianna or Gisele.

Rain is the Pure Ones' royal Healer. Before that she was (and is) the most powerful Healer of the Race. I personally recruited her from Hangzhou, China. When I was seven. So, okay, I had a little help from Ayelet, my Guardian. Don't recall the details, but I do remember the very strong sense that Val's first encounter with Rain was rather... explosive is not the right word.

Momentous. Game changing. So intense that the air around them whenever they're in the same space together seems charged with electricity, singeing everyone within a five-yard radius.

Maybe I'm making it up. I'm continuously fine-tuning my Gift. Sometimes the feelings come to me in a garbled foreign language I can't decipher. Val and Rain have known each other for ten years now (though they never seem to be in the same room together for any length of time). So you'd think they've gotten used to each other.

But lately, especially with the Rite on the horizon, I get the tingly sensations again (could also be due to the fact that vampires have escalated their murdering rampage or the fact that I ate some suspicious sushi last night before bed)—I feel—

Like the mother of all tsunamis is about to break.

Chapter One

10 years ago. Hangzhou, China.

He felt her before he saw her.

Every muscle tensed as Valerius braced himself against an unseen force.

The soft tinkling of bells announced someone's approach. A relatively tall, graceful woman garbed in a traditional-looking oriental dress emerged from the inner chamber where their hostess remained hidden from view. On her forehead, just below her hairline, was what appeared to be a tattooed plum flower. Around her ankle was a simple chain of small golden bells.

She was not the one.

Valerius released the breath he didn't realize he was holding and relaxed. Only slightly.

He stood back while the members of his convoy, Ayelet the Guardian and Sophia the new Queen, greeted the woman with deep customary bows, right hands pressed flat over their hearts. The woman returned the gesture, bending forward at a precise ninety degree angle from the waist, straightened from her bow and smiled welcomingly at Ayelet.

"Dear friend, it has been too long," she said in a lilting, softly accented voice. She stretched her hands toward Ayelet, and the Guardian clasped them without hesitation.

"Wan'er, it is good to see you again," Ayelet returned, giving the woman's hands an affectionate squeeze. She turned to include Sophia and Valerius in their circle.

"May I introduce to you our Queen, Sophia Victoria St. James? Sophia, this is Wan'er of the Jade Lotus Society. Wan'er is handmaiden to our esteemed hostess, Rain." Ayelet gently guided the seven-year-old Queen a few steps into the foreground as she made the official introductions.

Wan'er dipped deeply into an elegant curtsy on one knee, reserved only for their sovereign, right hand over heart. "My Queen," she acknowledged with serene respect.

Sophia, who, up until a month ago, had been oblivious to this significant new role she was destined to take on, fidgeted a bit with the belt of her formal royal robes and glanced at Ayelet how to proceed.

Ayelet gave a nod of encouragement, and Sophia bent forward with small hands outstretched, gently lifted Wan'er by the elbows, gesturing for her to rise.

"Thank you, Wan'er of Jade Lotus, for your hospitality," the child Queen said, stumbling ever so slightly over the words that took many hours to memorize.

Ayelet smiled with her eyes at her Ward and stepped back to introduce Valerius. "This is one of the Elite Guard, Valerius Marcus Ambrosius. He is our Protector on this journey."

Wan'er and Valerius bowed to each other. Once straightened, Wan'er gazed up at Valerius with a subtle nod and slow blink. It was the unspoken acknowledgement that Valerius would go wherever the Queen went. No chamber would be closed to him, save one during the duration of their stay, even though, as a rule, the Jade Lotus Society did not allow males into their sanctuary.

The Society was founded by the incumbent Healer of the Race, Rain, over two thousand years ago as a sanctuary for women who struggled with the social confines of their time.

Women poets, scholars, musicians, women who didn't want to marry into the traditional contract between families. Concubines who wanted to escape the intrigue and politics of the royal harem. Wives who wanted refuge from their abusive husbands. Women, in short, who sought better lives for themselves, who wanted to express their individuality and passions.

The Society was led by nine Pure-females , but its members were mostly human females. Over time, as Rain nurtured and honed her Gift of healing, the Society became known as a center for healing arts. It combined deep knowledge of ancient Chinese medicines and herbs with the studied practice of harnessing *qi*, one's spiritual energy, to soothe, regulate and optimize health and wellbeing. Though the members were female only, men and women from far and wide, Pure Ones and human alike, traveled to the sanctuary to seek solutions for their ailments.

Patients were typically received on island pavilions above the underground sanctuary, whose main entrance was located beneath the Baochu Pagoda just north of the famous tourist hotspot, West Lake, on top of Precious Stone Hill. The sanctuary spanned several square miles of underground passageways, chambers and halls, some stretching directly beneath the West Lake itself, connecting to the islands dotting the surface of the lake through underwater tunnels.

As times changed, as the modern world opened new doors, members of the sanctuary mingled more easily with society at large. Instead of banding together as refugees and outcasts, they drew strength from one another for a common purpose—the mission of healing. The members were still female only, and they remained the only occupants of the hallowed sanctuary halls.

Today, however, was an exception. Not just because of the new Queen's attendance, but because it was the first day of the decadal three-day Rite of the Phoenix that opened the sanctuary to unmated, qualified Pure-males from around the world.

At the end of the three days, Rain the Healer would select her Consort.

As Valerius also straightened from his bow, his jaw flexed involuntarily as he prepared to meet their hostess.

All Pure-males knew about the Rite of the Phoenix, and given their limited numbers, Valerius knew personally several past Consorts of the Healer, three of the Elite Guard for example. It was a position much revered and intensely vied for. Only the strongest, most disciplined Pure-males need apply. And it was the only exception, outside of Mating, to the Sacred Law of Celibacy.

For nine months during the year of the Rite, Pure-males from far and wide gathered to present themselves before the Healer. They never met her unless they were chosen as one of the final sextet.

The initial interviews were conducted by the Healer's handmaiden while the Healer herself observed the proceedings, hidden from view. She would then give her handmaiden a jade ring or an onyx ring to extend to the applicant. Only six jade rings were given out. As the days of the Rite approached, the six chosen Pure-males would return to the sanctuary for the final selection.

Then there would be three days of Rites of Passage.

The first day tested the Pure-males' strength and vitality. The second day tested their endurance for pain and ability to heal. The third day tested their sexual compatibility with the Healer. For ultimately, the chosen male would become her sole source of Nourishment for thirty days and provide the reserve she would need to carry out her role as the Pure Ones' Healer for the next ten years.

At the end of these three days, one ring of Tiger's Eye would be given to the Consort to wear over the course of his Service.

Valerius had never put himself in the applicant pool, though he knew his personal choice did his people a disservice. He was one of the most qualified Pure-males in existence. Not only because he was one of the oldest and, through experience and combat training, one of the strongest, his very Gift was the ability to heal faster than any other Pure One.

Pure Ones healed ten times as fast as humans, a source of their eternal youth. Valerius healed thrice the rate of his fellow warrior-class males. The Nourishment he would be able to provide would be thrice as potent as any other male. The Healer could in turn harness that power to save many more lives, especially as the Pure Ones entered the critical new millennium.

But he could not bring himself to do it.

Although he knew without a doubt that he would best all other males in the first two Rites of Passage, he was equally confident he would fail the third and final test.

If he had a choice, he would have continued to avoid the Healer at all costs—better that she never knew he existed, so that his decision to abstain from the selection process would remain his own. But this journey was unavoidable, and he was the best choice as royal escort. He could not fail Sophia and Ayelet in his protection, nor could he fail the Healer when they brought her back with them on the return journey. He couldn't countenance that level of selfishness.

Now, finally, he would meet her. The Healer.

Rain.

Wan'er guided them through a long, torch-lit hallway into the inner chamber of the Healer. Despite the lack of windows, as the sanctuary was deep underground, the passageway was brightly decorated with Chinese scrolls that depicted mountains, lakes, pagodas and exotic animals so real, they seemed to come to life beneath the flickering warmth of the torches.

Valerius paused briefly before a painting as the phoenix inside seemed to stretch its neck and turn its bright eyes toward him. His right hand went reflexively to the scythe handle at his waist as he peered more closely.

His eyes widened when he saw that the waterfall in the background was actually flowing, making a soundless splash into the lake beneath. He shook his head and looked again. The phoenix was facing away from him once more, looking into the distance. Perhaps he had imagined it all. But somehow he thought not.

The entrance to the inner chamber was an elaborate hexagonal opening, gilded with intricate designs that were carved out of the framing wood. It was about ten feet tall and twelve feet wide, and it led to a vast, but not cavernous, well-lit hall in which the centerpiece was a large raised dais shielded by semi-transparent wispy silk curtains gathered together in a sort of tent around and over the area.

Valerius' eyes were immediately drawn to the feminine outline behind the curtains.

Contrary to his training and protocol, he barely registered the surrounding area, the ornate yet elegant furniture, the walls covered entirely with natural scenery that looked just as real and alive as the scrolls in the outer passageway, the whimsical splattering of multi-colored round paper lanterns across the ceiling, giving the chamber a cheerful glow.

To his utter confusion and dismay, his heart doubled its tempo, and every nerve in his body became overwhelmingly sensitized. He suddenly felt drugged by the faint, elusive fragrance of lilies and jasmine, and in reaction, blood rushed to his groin, hardening him in an instant. His neck and face got what was left as he flushed deeply in mortification and anger at his total loss of discipline.

In his two thousand plus years of existence as a Pure One, he had never, *never*, lost control. Why his self-restraint deserted him now he couldn't begin to fathom and didn't have the luxury to even try, for he suddenly found himself not two feet before the Healer, sitting above him on the dais on a soft pedestal of pillows. He executed a bow by rote, as if his body had developed a mind of its own.

Valerius stopped short of raising his gaze to meet hers, however. He knew that keeping his eyes lowered was a sign of submission which he'd never before allowed in himself, no matter the odds he faced. But he swallowed his pride and locked his jaw, because somehow, somewhere deep within, he knew that meeting her gaze would change his world forever.

Instead, he peered through the filter of his lashes at the shape of her chin, and the enigmatic, fleeting smile that tilted the corners of her full, sensuous mouth.

"Warrior," she greeted him softly, pausing a heavy beat after greeting Sophia and Ayelet.

When he continued to withhold his gaze, the corners of her lips tilted ever so slightly more, as if she were amused by his reticence.

But it wasn't shyness that kept Valerius' eyes lowered; it was self-preservation.

"Healer," Ayelet began as Valerius backed away from the softly illuminated dais into the background shadows, "you know why we have come."

It was not a question, but an understanding.

The woman on the dais dipped her head elegantly in acknowledgement, a small smile still hovering on her lips.

"Then you consent to come back to the Shield with us?" Ayelet tried to ascertain, referring to the Pure Ones' home base, not a permanent location but the moniker for the place where the Queen and her inner circle resided at any given time.

The Healer shifted in her seat, raising a pale, slim-fingered hand to brush aside a wisp of silk as she leaned in with her reply. But it was not Ayelet or the Queen she set her gaze upon, but the warrior's tense, steely frame in the shadows behind them.

"Would it please you to have my consent?" She gently pushed the question toward Valerius, who tensed even more, if that were possible, at her query.

She could not see his eyes in the shadows, but she knew when he finally looked upon her. There was an instant recognition and a blast of energy radiating from his body toward her, so forceful she had momentary whiplash from the dazzling currents.

Interesting.

Ayelet, Sophia and Wan'er looked to and fro, surprised by the redirection in the conversation. Sophia, in particular, seemed dazed by the explosion of awareness between the Healer and the Protector. She blinked rapidly and squeezed her little brows together in concentration as if trying to decipher an unspoken exchange between the two.

What could he answer, Valerius thought grimly as time stretched between them in excruciating slowness and clarity.

Their troop of Chevaliers, a combination of Pure and human warriors who stood as the first line of defense against rising vampire Hordes and human menace, was rapidly dwindling in number, leaving the remaining few exhausted and weighed down by countless injuries new and old after each battle.

They needed the Healer in their midst, within reach. They needed her strength and comfort, needed her to heal and invigorate and give them hope. For the future of his people, for the humans and the world the Pure Ones protected, how could he say no?

But for himself, his peace of mind, his wildly-beating heart, and the inevitable, exquisite, punishing pain that he knew his future held with her in it, how could he say yes?

As he took in her ethereal visage with starving eyes, he realized that his time had run out.

Swallowing the lump in his throat, he took a deep breath and replied in a low, rumbling voice, raspy from the emotions he tried to contain:

"Aye."

And without a backward glance, Valerius walked out of the chamber as fast as his long strides could carry him.

*** *** *** ***

"Aye," he'd said.

It was the first and only word he'd uttered in her presence, Rain reflected. Though she'd never met the Protector, she was well aware of his reputation. With a couple thousand Pure-males in existence at any given time, and less than a fourth being of warrior-class, the Elite guard to which the Protector belonged was widely talked of, highly revered — even legendary. Rain had previously met each of the six members. Except the Protector. Never the Protector.

Two thousand years was a long time to evade her. Rain couldn't help but feel that he did so by choice. Though she would never presume to question his motives, it still stung her pride to be so diligently avoided. So she satisfied her curiosity with the occasional news and tidbit about the Elite. From what she knew of Valerius, she'd expected to be impressed.

She was not disappointed.

His deep, husky voice sent shivers up and down her body. How poetic that such a voice should be housed within such a body. The sound was like a warm blanket that calmed her, while at the same time it was a roaring fire that ignited her.

The warrior was starkly beautiful in his minimalism and brusqueness. He stood six feet six, over a foot above her own height if they were standing toe to toe. He was endowed with incredibly wide shoulders, deep chest, lean hips and long, muscular legs.

His attire was entirely black, made for ease of movement, hugging his form only when he was in action. When he stood still, his clothes were part of his camouflage, worn not to be noticed but to discourage attention and blend into the shadows.

His shaved head showed the shadow of dark hair roots that indicated a full, dense head of hair if it were allowed to grow out. Rain abruptly wondered how his hair would be— curly, straight or wavy. Intuitively, she guessed it would be wavy, tousled, even wild, antithetical to the strict manner in which he held himself.

His face was intensely masculine, all sharp angles, hollows and edges, his nose a narrow blade with a bump on the bridge. And yet he was undeniably beautiful, deeply sensual with his heavily lashed light green eyes and full, wide mouth.

But it was obvious that the warrior himself didn't think so.

It was as if he consciously tried to disguise his beauty, or even closer to the truth, that he was ashamed of it. Ashamed of his body, uncomfortable in his own skin, except when the presence of danger demanded that his warrior instincts preclude all else.

Ninety-nine percent of the time, Rain had no doubt that he was warrior to the bone, confident and in control, but she glimpsed in this introductory meeting a rare flash of vulnerability and self-doubt.

Probably why he'd removed himself from the room. He couldn't stand that she witnessed—no, more than that, *felt*—his hidden shame.

She didn't understand the whys, but her heart responded to his obvious pain with empathy. Absently, she placed a hand over her heart to soothe it, turning back to her visitors.

"You have my answer then," she confirmed for Ayelet, implicitly answering the question the Guardian posed.

She unfolded herself lithely from her seat, stepped down from the dais, and sank into a deep curtsy before Sophia.

"At the end of this Phoenix Cycle, I will come with you, my Queen, wherever it may lead me."

Startled, Sophia rushed forth to raise the Healer from the floor, clasping her forearms with surprisingly strong little hands.

"Please rise, my lady. I am honored to have you by my side."

She looked again to Ayelet for support.

Ayelet nodded with a mix of gladness and relief.

"Indeed, Healer, your presence now completes the Royal Zodiac—the Queen, the six Elite guards, and the five Circlet council members. It is a crucial step in fulfilling the Prophesy of our age. We cannot predict how the future unfolds, but we know that we will be immeasurably stronger with your support."

Rain smiled briefly, wondering what the Balance would require.

Every action caused a reaction. If she added strength, did that mean that someone else would become weaker? Was that someone the Protector? Was that why she'd glimpsed his vulnerability?

Wan'er stepped forward to guide Sophia and Ayelet to the guest rooms as Rain trailed behind them with parting words.

"Please feel free to enjoy our sanctuary for the next thirty-three days," she said invitingly, then paused before continuing until her guests stopped walking and looked back at her.

"But you will not visit this chamber again until we prepare for departure at the end of the Cycle," the Healer stated firmly, waited for the nods of assent from Ayelet and Sophia, then smiled again. "I will not accompany you often during this time, but we shall see one another at midday meals if it pleases you."

Sophia broke out of royal character and clapped her hands. "Yes, please! Can we have dumplings and *baozi* and pearl milk tea?"

Rain and Wan'er simultaneously raised their hands over their lips and chuckled softly at the child Queen's enthusiasm.

"But of course, my Queen," Rain responded with easy affection.

Ayelet grimaced as if an unpleasant reminder suddenly came to mind.

"We will, of course, also convey your message to Val." It was understood among the three women which message Ayelet referred to—the Healer was not to be disturbed during the Rites of Passage and the Phoenix Cycle.

The Guardian added, rather embarrassed and more than a bit confused, "please accept our apologies for Val's rudeness just now. He's not usually—"

"Please don't trouble yourself," Rain smoothly cut in, taking hold of Ayelet's hand. "I am sure the warrior has his reasons and that they are good ones. I take no offense."

She let go of Ayelet's hand with a reassuring squeeze and smiled wryly.

"Perhaps we could have met in a different time, but I suppose Fate will lead us where it will. It certainly does not like being denied."

Both Ayelet and Sophia wore similar expressions of puzzlement and acceptance, as if Rain's words rang true, yet they were sure they didn't quite understand the full story.

Rain stopped escorting her guests at the hexagonal entryway. Remaining inside the chamber's threshold, she bid Ayelet and Sophia farewell for now.

Wan'er led the way down the hall of scrolls to their guest chambers, chatting warmly with Ayelet. Sophia looked back once in their progress and saw that a man had emerged from one of the rooms further down the opposite end of the passage. She watched curiously as he strode into the Healer's inner chamber and suddenly the glow of light within snuffed out all at once, as if a door had been shut in his wake. But Sophia had seen no door when she'd entered the Healer's chamber before.

How strange.

She skipped a little to catch up to her Guardian and the handmaiden.

"Why is the Healer's hair all white?" she asked when she reached them.

Ayelet frowned a little and was about to chide her for her impertinence, Sophia knew that look well, but Wan'er answered with a smile, "Because she needs Nourishment."

Sophia nodded, but still looked confused. "Does that mean if she eats some dumplings her hair will be black again like yours?"

Ayelet sighed softly, a sign that she'd given up on intercepting the young Queen's questions. After all, Sophia needed to learn about all aspects of her people.

"She needs more than human food," Wan'er responded patiently. "She needs the Nourishment of her Consort."

Sophia tilted her head, trying to understand, barely noticing that Wan'er had ushered them into a large, lushly furnished chamber that held three canopied beds, one for each of the three guests.

As if sudden comprehension dawned, Sophia asked brightly, "Is her Consort like a Mate? Like Tristan is for Ayelet?"

Wan'er clasped her hands before her and gave the Queen her full attention.

"Yes and no," she said slowly, as if considering how best to reply. "A Mate is forever and a Consort is for a short period of time. But during that time, the Healer and her Consort will cherish each other as if they were Mated."

Sophia nodded, catching on.

"And Rain will be choosing her Consort over the next three days?"

At confirming nods from both women, she continued, "But why does she need three days? She should just choose Val and we can all go home."

Both women drew back in shock, as if Sophia had spouted horns. She looked from Ayelet to Wan'er and wondered why no words were emerging from their mouths though said mouths opened and closed several times.

Finally, it was Ayelet who responded, "Val is not for consideration this time. He and Rain have just met."

She looked to Wan'er for support, but the handmaiden was looking away, as if deep in thought.

"But they like each other," Sophia persisted, "I can tell."

Ayelet could not say she agreed. If anything, she sensed the opposite was true, though the feeling of antagonism was one-sided, only from Valerius, and she was confounded as to why.

Wan'er raised her head from her private contemplation.

"Perhaps next time," she suggested. "The warrior would assuredly be qualified."

Sophia frowned but didn't question further. It seemed a monumental mistake to her that Valerius wouldn't be the Healer's Consort, now and in the future. She didn't completely understand, but it just felt wrong.

She shrugged with a seven-year-old's limited attention span, changed the subject to Chinese lanterns and silk dolls, and climbed on top one of the luxurious beds.

What did she know? The adults obviously had everything under control. She had more important things to dwell on—like which flavor of *baozi* she should prioritize for tomorrow's midday meal.

Chapter Two

Present day. Boston, MA

Valerius curled tight, drawing his knees to his body, tensing his leg muscles and transferring a surge of power to his thighs as he leapt ten feet into the air, tucked and rolled in mid-flight, and landed with precision on all fours on the next brownstone's roof, fifteen yards away.

Without skipping a beat, he sprang back up and was within striking distance of his quarry with two long leaps.

Mid-stride, Valerius reached for the handle of the chained scythe at his waist and released the weapon with a sharp whistle at his target.

The titanium chain whipped unerringly through the night air, a flash of silver in the dark, moonless sky, and wrapped around its prey once, twice, its momentum generating enough force to choke its victim like a python.

The vampire gurgled out a broken scream and fell to his knees like a rag doll, clawing in futility at the unforgiving chains, which increased pressure the more he struggled.

Valerius flashed in front of the male, stopping three feet away, close enough to hear if the vampire managed to speak, but too far to reach, not that the blood-sucker had enough strength to do damage at this point.

"Where is the Horde?" Valerius demanded in a low rumble, tensing the chain further to ensure the vampire's undivided attention.

The male shook his head frantically, his eyes all but bulging out of their sockets from the tight squeeze of the chains.

Valerius knew that he would get no information from this male, not because the vampire was refusing to tell, but because he didn't know anything to tell.

With a flick of his wrist, the scythe on the end of the chain, all but forgotten on the ground behind the vampire, snapped like a pendulum sideways and upwards in an arc, cleanly slicing the vampire's head from his shoulders on the swing back around. Almost instantaneously, the severed body disintegrated into a pile of ashes, and a gust of wind swept it unceremoniously off the roof as if the creature never was.

One less bloodsucker roaming the streets of South End.

And one less rapist, too, from what Valerius had seen ten minutes ago before he'd given chase.

His upper lip curled slightly on one side in a low growl. That clean beheading was too good for the vampire. If Valerius had time to spare, he would have returned the violence upon the vampire tenfold. As the Protector of the Pure Ones it was his duty to hunt down rogue vampires who abused and tormented innocent humans.

He recalled the scythe to its original position with a curled pull of his forearm and secured the handle on his weapon belt. With two large bounds, he leapt off the roof and landed in the alley below without a sound.

A homeless woman curled on the steps of the townhouse next door looked up from the beer bottle she nursed, as if sensing his presence, instinctively pulling back against the wall in case there was any threat to her habitual spot. Watching Valerius' long-legged strides as he walked past her, she shrugged, not giving him a second thought. Clearly, he was a resident who just came out of the brownstone and was used to her taking up that corner, though strangely, she hadn't heard the door open and close.

Valerius strode purposefully to his awaiting Hayabusa, also known as the Suzuki GSX1300R, the fastest motorcycle ever built. He'd had it fitted specifically for his long, lean, muscular form and had the exterior painted entirely in black with selective silver accents to blend seamlessly into the night, the perfect stealth vehicle for hunting vampires.

As he rounded the corner of Draper's Lane and Ivanhoe, the Hayabusa in sight, he stiffened a split second before he caught the glint of a *spatha*'s blade out of the corner of his eye just as it swung with deadly force from his right side.

Reacting on pure instinct before the danger registered fully, Valerius curved his torso to the left and twisted out of range.

But not before the blade glanced his hip, slicing through his black leathers like butter, leaving a six inch gash in its wake.

Valerius leapt back, fully prepared now to take down his ambushers. He sensed three in the shadows in front of him and one approaching from behind.

He broke into a sprint before his enemies could close in, but he ran in the opposite direction of his ride, back down Draper's Lane toward the intersecting alley with Upton Street.

He wasn't ready for the hunt to end this night. With a vengeance, he wanted to take down the four vampires rapidly gaining on him.

Valerious led his pursuers into a dead end alley. As he reached the end, he increased the length and power of his strides and leapt onto the fifteen-foot brick wall barring the exit. He used his momentum to spring backwards with a solid push from his right leg against the wall, back curving in a long, deep arc to propel his body swiftly in the opposite direction.

As if in slow motion, he released the chained scythe while his body arched in midair two feet above three of his vampire foes just as they reached the dead end. With a snap and a jingle, the scythe and chain whipped across two vampires simultaneously, beheading one and falling the other.

With his head angled back at the height of the backward somersault, Valerius saw an upside-down image of the fourth vampire running toward them.

On his way down to the ground, now facing the dead end again, he jerked the chains back and effectively sliced through the shins of the third vampire, literally cutting his legs out from underneath him.

The vampire howled in pain, a startling screech in the silent darkness. With two vampires down for the count in the dead end alley and one already disintegrated, Valerius twisted fluidly to confront the fourth one just as one flying dagger whistled past his face and the second struck him in his left side, barely missing his kidney.

At the impact, Valerius compensated by going down on his right knee even as he pulled the scythe back and whipped it like a boomerang toward the approaching vampire, tautening the chain at the precise moment when the curved blade of the scythe reached behind the vampire's neck, pulling the weapon back to him with the vampire's neck severed on the return journey.

Valerius made short work of the vampire with the severed legs, but wrapped the lightning chains around the last remaining vampire in a suffocating squeeze.

"Where is the Horde?" Valerius asked quietly, willing his patience to last a little longer. "Who is your Master?"

This last bloodsucker was no yellowtail, unlike Valerius' first prey of the night. He hissed menacingly at the Protector like a cornered cobra, baring his elongated fangs, dripping with saliva from the adrenaline of the fight.

These four were trained assassins, Valerius reflected back upon their combat maneuvers and stealth. They'd almost succeeded in their ambush. It occurred to him that the first vampire could have been bait. He didn't just happen to encounter these vampires by accident.

Someone had orchestrated this attack with foresight. And he had been targeted for a reason.

Without wasting more words, Valerius tightened his hold of the chains, pulled out the dagger still embedded in the flesh of his side and whipped it in a sideways arc toward the immobilized vampire, cleanly beheading the male.

Four piles of ashes fluttered in his wake as Valerius walked out of the alley, barely breaking stride despite his wounds. They should be healed in a few hours at the most. He could already feel the tissues knitting together in his side and the skin starting to pucker around the gash at his hip.

With single-minded efficiency, the Protector reached his Hayabusa, yanked on his helmet and gunned the engine to life, racing out of South End toward the bright lights of Prudential Tower, where the Shield was based, well hidden beneath the Christian Science Plaza.

*** *** *** ***

"You need Nourishment," Wan'er said with a concerned frown as she ran the fine-tooth ebony Changzhou comb through Rain's knee-length silvery white hair, each strand glinting like a moonbeam in the soft lamp light.

It was actually an easy task to comb the requisite one hundred strokes through the silky length, for each strand of hair had a life of its own, flowing through the teeth of the comb and arching in pleasure like a feline getting a rub along its spine.

Indeed, the Healer never needed to arrange her hair, despite its thickness and length, for each individual silken tendril knew its place precisely.

When she relaxed, as she did now, Rain's hair flowed loosely down her back like a river of diamonds. When she needed ease of movement, her hair obediently twisted itself into a fishtail braid, lying like a thick long rope down her back or coiling into an intricate bun at the base of her neck.

The Healer's hair was her unique Gift.

There was only one Healer at any given time among the Pure Ones, and Rain's predecessor had a different Gift. Rain's hair served as both a healing instrument as well as a deadly weapon when she required.

As a healing instrument, it spread around her and her patient like a suspended web before tensing into micro-thin needles that inserted into the patient's pores where needed, in the manner of acupuncture needles. The difference was that each strand of hair also served as a conductor of energy from the Healer to her patient, soothing the pain and ultimately mending the wound, as well as invigorating the recipient with renewed energy.

In exchange, the strands drew out the pain from the wounded into the Healer, where she used her inner *qi* to ameliorate and dissipate the pain. However, some remnant of the sting would remain, making the process occasionally difficult to bear for the Healer. But Rain had over two and a half millennia to practice, succeeding most of the time in sealing away the pain, only to be released every ten years during the Phoenix Cycle.

As a weapon, the braided rope had the tensile strength of steel cables, but was far more flexible. Rain seldom engaged in combat, but if she were ever endangered, she could more than adequately handle herself, provided she was near her full physical strength.

She used her roped hair like a whip against her opponents. One flick of her braid did more damage than a swipe from a samurai sword, for the whip blazed a trail as wide as its circumference. Other times, she'd break a few inches off a couple of strands and throw them like needles with deadly accuracy into the exact nerves that would immobilize or incapacitate her attackers.

Rain never dealt the lethal blow, however. It went against her very essence to kill.

Normally, her hair flowed behind her like an elegant long cape, and when she moved, there was a slightly delayed reaction for every action, as if her hair was suspended in water rather than air. For the most part it behaved like any other part of her body, an extension of Rain's person.

But sometimes... sometimes it had a mind of its own.

"The Rite begins in two days, followed by the Cycle," Rain calmly responded to her handmaiden's urging, "I shall recover very shortly. Do not worry yourself so."

Rain referred to the thirty day reenergizing period which would begin after she chose her new Consort from the Rite of the Phoenix.

Over that time, her body and soul would replenish their strength like a reservoir filling with nourishing rain after an extended drought. Her silvery hair would gradually turn back to its midnight blue-black, and her complexion would transform from the translucent ice it was now to a less fragile, richer porcelain tone. Her body would fill out slightly with deeper curves, but she would never be voluptuous.

More than once, she'd wondered whether *he* preferred a woman with curves and, therefore, found her too unappealing to apply for. Currently, she was so drained she looked rather like a ghost of herself, her wrists so thin they were smaller than a child's. No wonder he never looked upon her.

Rain smiled wryly, silently chiding herself for her petulant thoughts.

As if reading her mind, Wan'er huffed with indignation on her lady's behalf.

"The Protector should beg to be your Consort, but I suppose he's too full of his own importance to apply to Serve you. If he had been the one who provided your Nourishment ten years ago, your strength would surely not have faded to the extent that it has."

True enough. Valerius' strength would have surpassed Rain's last Consort ten, twenty times.

Qualified Pure-males were more and more difficult to come by, and Rain refused to take the same male as Consort more than once. Though she tried her best to make it easier, those thirty days of Service were exhausting at best, torturous at worst. No male needed a repeat experience—not that they didn't volunteer.

But more than that, Rain did not want to risk too much attachment. She could not afford to repeat the past.

"If he had been my Consort, what would I have to look forward to?" Rain teased with a mischievous smile, enjoying her handmaiden's momentary sputtering.

More solemnly Rain replied, "It is his choice to apply or not. Perhaps it's for the best that he doesn't, for he is much needed in other spheres, especially in these urgent times."

Wan'er gave the glistening white mass one last stroke and sighed.

"Very well, I shall not belabor the point, as you will certainly defend him to the end."

Rain looked at her handmaiden in the mirror and gave her a cajoling smile, attempting to improve her mood.

Wan'er moved away to fold her lady's day dress discarded on the bed, arranged a few things more neatly, bowed a bit more stiffly than usual, and left the room.

Rain waved her handmaiden goodnight and looked back at her reflection in the mirror. The only points of color from head to toe were her sleek black brows, eyes and rose-red lips.

She looked like a Japanese Kabuki doll, she thought with a weary sigh. Not a very attractive vision unless one tended toward the macabre.

She glided slowly to her bed, crawled beneath the satin coverlet, and lay still on her back, her hair fanned out around her sides, not a single strand beneath her.

Rain closed her eyes, took a relaxing deep breath and wondered whether she would see him again in her dreams.

She hoped so. It was the part of her day she looked forward to the most.

*** *** *** ***

The next morning Valerius struggled to rise, his body weighed down by an invisible force. He pulled himself to a sitting position by sheer force of will and ground his teeth against the burning pain in his side and hip.

This did not bode well.

He should have healed completely by now. Checking both wounds, he saw that the skin had already closed perfectly, but angry blackish-purple bruises remained, indicating clearly where the *spatha* had grazed his hip and where the nine-inch dagger had pierced through his side.

He staggered to his feet and pulled on a loose black shirt and trousers, his fingers barely able to tie the drawstring at his waist. He shook his head to banish the pain to a corner of his mind to reexamine when he had more time. Right now, he needed to brief the Dozen.

As he strode briskly down the hall directly underneath the Christian Science Plaza's long rectangular pool, he saw through the one-way glass ceiling that served as the bottom of the shallow pool that the sun had already reached its zenith.

How had he slept half a day away? And still his wounds had not completely healed.

Squaring his shoulders, he determined to ignore his body's protests. He entered the throne room where the Circlet and four of the Elite gathered just in time to see three Pure males he did not recognize go down on one knee before the Healer.

Though he normally would have turned about face and walked right back out before anyone noticed his presence, desperate was he to avoid being in the same room with the Healer, he found himself rooted to the floor.

"We would be honored to Serve you, my lady," the three Pure males said in unison.

Rain gestured for them to rise and nodded to each of them in turn.

"The honor is mine," she replied, briefly touching her hand to each of the jade rings on the third fingers of the three males' right hands, flattened against their hearts in solemn pledge.

Valerius bristled all over at the ephemeral touch as if every fiber of his being protested against the Healer having any contact with a male other than—

Valerius ruthlessly shoved the rest of that thought away and willed his body to calm down.

What possessed him? He had no claim whatsoever on the fragile Healer. He'd made that abundantly clear by not applying to Serve her.

Again.

He watched stoically as the Pure Ones' Consul, Seth Tremaine, spoke with the three qualified males in low tones. He didn't hear anything that was said, the roaring in his ears drowning out everything else. All of his concentration zeroed in on Rain, hungrily taking in her graceful form.

His heart squeezed painfully at her too slender curves, too narrow shoulders, and too thin hands. He hated himself in that moment.

If only he weren't so selfish. If only he could overcome his demons. She did not deserve to wither away like this while he had the Nourishment she needed.

He could not move as the conversation with the guests subsided and Wan'er led them toward the throne room's exit, the Healer following close behind.

As she passed, the handmaiden speared him with a lethal look but otherwise ignored his presence. The three Pure males regarded him with curiosity and even wariness at the animosity he unconsciously radiated toward them.

Rain passed by him last, meeting his feverish gaze with widened eyes.

He had always avoided looking at her directly. She was obviously not expecting him to now. Her initial surprise quickly turned into a look of concern, however, as her brows knitted slightly as if she couldn't figure something out.

It was all he could do not to sink to both knees in front of her and beg to Service her needs.

His teeth hurt from how hard he was clenching his jaw; sweat beaded in a fine sheen over his entire body as he struggled not to reach out to her.

At something one of the applicant Pure males said, Rain reluctantly turned away and progressed down the corridor to the inner chambers.

Finally uprooting himself from his frozen stance, Valerius shut the throne room double doors with a resounding slam and came upon the startled royal council with a few furious strides.

"Only three," he ground out without preamble. "And even our trainees could best those striplings."

The first to recover from his surprise, the Consul drawled, "You could always volunteer yourself, Val."

Valerius pierced him with a ferocious look and spat, "You know nothing."

Seth's eyebrows elevated a fraction, but he chose not to respond.

Ayelet interceded with a soothing hand on Valerius' forearm, trying to calm the incensed warrior.

"There were few options this year, Val. You know as well as I we have been losing too many good males to the war."

"Then you," Valerius pointed in turn to the three unmated Elite males, "should offer your Service again. Any one of you is ten times as strong as those three boys."

In the back of his mind he knew he was being abominably selfish for even making the suggestion, when he had not even Served the Healer once. But he felt helpless and angry.

Desperate. Like the walls were closing in.

The Spartan Leonidas folded his arms over his massive chest and responded, a challenging glint in his eyes, "We have made the offer. Many times. Over many centuries. But you know full well that the Healer does not take the same Consort more than once. You can no more convince her to bend that rule than bend your own."

Valerius knew all of this. Why did he even bother mentioning it? He almost wished he'd grown out his hair so he could yank it out now in frustration.

No, it was more than frustration. It was fear.

He feared for his people's well-being, feared for the Healer's strength and endurance, feared for his own sanity if anything should happen to her while knowing that he could have prevented it.

Determinedly, he shook off those feelings. There were other pressing matters to attend to.

"When will our Queen and Tristan be back?" he suddenly changed topics, intending to brief the council when all twelve, save the Healer, were together.

A frown flickered on Seth's face at Valerius' use of "Queen." The warrior was seldom formal about rank as it pertained to Sophia unless there was serious issue at hand.

As if conjured by his words, Sophia entered with Tristan at her side from the East wing, apparently coming in straight from classes, shoulder bag with her laptop and books dangling casually on her arm.

"That was fun," Sophia said with sarcasm and a roll of her eyes by way of greeting, "Next time, Tristan, can you please find a place to wait outside the classroom? Preferably outside view of anyone? I don't appreciate the disruptions during what could have been a stimulating lecture and wasting my time waiting for hormonally charged girly girls to back off you at the end of class. Geez!"

To emphasize her displeasure, Sophia struck a pose of annoyance with hands on hips.

Tristan scratched the back of his neck in embarrassment and pulled off an apologetic sheepish look. Frankly, he didn't enjoy getting mauled by teenage girls either.

He made straight for his Mate Ayelet and gave her a full kiss on her amused mouth and wrapped an arm around her shoulders.

The young queen rolled her eyes again at her Elite guard for the day in the universal code for "whatever" and directed her attention to the gathered Dozen.

"So what's up?" she asked, looking first to Ayelet, then to Seth. "Looks like something serious if all of you are here in one place in the middle of the day. Nothing amiss with the Rite, I hope? Is Rain okay?"

But it was Valerius who answered, though he brushed aside her last two questions, "I was ambushed during the hunt last night."

That got everyone's attention immediately.

Leonidas was the first to respond. As the Pure Ones' Sentinel, it was his duty to ensure the safety of the Royal Zodiac.

"Do you know which Horde? Who was their Master?"

Valerius shook his head grimly.

"They were professional assassins. The civilian vampire they used to bait me was uninformed."

He tilted his head in a sudden flash of recognition. "They were old. At least a thousand years. Their weapons were of the ancient world. One of them used a *spatha*."

Leonidas took in that piece of information contemplatively, rubbing his chin with thumb and forefinger. He exchanged a knowing look with Aella, the Strategist, who narrowed her eyes in calculation.

Valerius spoke of a straight sword measuring about three feet, used throughout first millennium Europe and the territory of the Roman Empire until the seventh century, mostly in war and in gladiator arenas. Whoever their Master was, she was very old, and therefore very powerful.

It was not definitive that the Master was a female, but it was very likely. Female vampires were generally older and more powerful. Though they might not have been the first vampire, they were the earliest vampires.

Some believed that females craved love and the rarest of Pure Ones' treasures, children, and were therefore more prone to take risks finding the right Mate, while males more stoically focused on the Pure Ones' Cause.

Others believed that because females fed from males in the corporeal sense, and males drew from the spiritual, it stood to reason that the first Pure Ones to deviate from their Path, taking the blood of humans, were females.

However, the latter belief was less widely held because vampires also took human souls. And any modern feminist might also reject the first belief as well.

Whichever the case, vampire society mirrored that of Pure Ones, meaning that it was a matriarchal society led by one Queen for each Hive. Dominant male vampires tended to run solo or at most at the head of a small, loosely formed pack, called a Horde. Aside from that, they were seldom found in the company of others of their breed. Those males who did not serve a Hive or belong to a Horde were called Rogues.

Which meant that the well-organized assassins who attacked Valerius more likely reported to a female Master than a male, though both were possibilities.

Aella did a quick mental survey. The closest Hive was in New York City, and Jade Cicada was its Queen.

As if hearing her thoughts, Seth voiced out loud, "Jade would not make a move that all but declares war on us. Not when she's trying to rein in the rogue vampires herself. She would have disguised the assassins if she truly wanted to take one of us out without discovery."

Aella nodded in agreement. "True. But there is no other I know of in the vicinity who has the power to control vampires that old. And if they could ambush Valerius with close success, they were damned well organized and disciplined."

Dalair, the Paladin, spoke from his position leaning against one of the twelve marble columns that ran from floor to ceiling in a semicircle in the center of the room.

"Perhaps we should send an emissary to the Cove to inform the vampire queen of this development and ascertain her position."

"It would have to be either Rain or Seth," Ayelet determined, "the rest of us would get an antipathetic reception at best."

"The Healer is too weak." Valerius rejected that avenue immediately. "She should not take on any mission before she recovers her full strength at the end of the Phoenix Cycle."

"I guess that leaves me," the Consul drawled with an exaggerated sigh, "though your faith undoubtedly exceeds my abilities, Ayelet."

Ayelet smirked good-naturedly. "Somehow I doubt that."

"Where did the attack occur?" Tristan asked, bringing the focus back to Valerius.

"South End, Draper's Lane and Ivanhoe," the Protector answered.

He then quickly gave the group a rundown of the encounter, first the civilian vampire, then the four assassins.

The Elite frowned as one.

The Boston faction of vampire rogues was getting restless, willing to take more risks, expanding their territory. Thus far, they had mainly kept to the North End, also known as Little Italy, a bit farther from Boston center. But with this maneuver, if they were the culprits, they'd effectively encroached upon the heart of Boston. If this wasn't dealt with soon, there could be countless casualties.

But there was no guarantee that this was the same Horde the Elite had been fighting and gradually eradicating over the past several months. In fact, recently, the North End Horde had been relatively quiet, constantly changing their hideout and adopting discretion in favor of the flamboyant kills they perpetrated when they'd first rolled into town.

This ambush stank of something far more sinister and deadly.

"They know our routines," Valerius continued, "my sense is that I wasn't the sole target. Perhaps the first, but not the last."

"Why you were the first might give us a clue," Orion the Scribe interjected. "I concur with your instinct that this is just the tip of the iceberg, the first salvo in a full-scale campaign."

The Mesopotamian tapped his chin in thought. "When we adjourn, I will consult the Scrolls. The exact words elude me, but I recall having read a passage that disturbingly echoes your battle last night, Protector."

"I will go with you," Eveline the Seer nodded in his direction. "No doubt there will be insights from the Zodiac Prophesies we can glean."

As keeper of the Zodiac Prophesies, Eveline held the key to the Pure Ones' future, while Orion, the keeper of the Zodiac Scrolls, held the key to the past. Because Universal Balance dictated that all things moved in Cycles—Death, Life, Good, Evil, Yin, Yang, Past, Future—history had an uncanny habit of repeating itself. By comparing the Scrolls and the Prophesies, the Scribe and the Seer could better prepare the Pure Ones for battles to come.

One thing that did change—people could learn from mistakes of the past.

Like a constantly rolling sphere, the Cycle of Life did not necessarily follow a straight line; it could curve into a better, brighter Path, or a darker, bleaker Path, based on the force of choices made.

"Meanwhile, we should pair up on hunts and alter our normal schedules," Alexandros, the General, proposed, eliciting nods of assent from the group.

He turned to Valerius with discerning eyes.

"You look worse for wear, Protector," the General noted, gesturing to the sheen of sweat on the warrior's skin, visible to all under the bright chandelier, even as Valerius weaved slightly on his feet, dangerously close to losing his balance.

"I'm fine," Valerius growled through clenched teeth, a wave of nausea washing over him while the fire in his side and hip blazed hotter, as if little vampire devils were roasting his flesh and jabbing it with pitchforks.

Leonidas gave him a doubtful look, in turn, but didn't argue, saying instead, "Nevertheless, Xandros and I will take over the hunt for now."

At Valerius' glare, he added, "To shake up the routine, if nothing else. You will be back out there before you know it."

When Valerius looked as if he'd still like to argue, Leonidas firmly stated, "We need you here to protect the Dozen in my absence, especially Sophia and Rain during her crucial time. This is not a request, warrior."

Dissatisfied with the outcome but knowing the wisdom of it, Valerius gave one nod of acceptance.

As the Royal Zodiac adjourned, the Seer and the Scribe heading off to the Vault two levels below, Tristan escorting Sophia to her chambers to retrieve books for her late afternoon classes, and the rest remaining in the throne room to debate their next move, Valerius made his way to his room in the West Wing of the stronghold, barely keeping his feet from stumbling over each other.

As if his legs were suddenly cut from beneath him, he staggered over the threshold of his chamber and crumbled to the floor.

His body shaking with the effort, he rolled onto his back and blinked hard, trying to keep his eyes open. The ceiling zig-zagged in and out of focus for a few seconds, then faded out of sight completely like the flash of a TV screen shutting off.

Valerius' last thought was of Rain before oblivion engulfed him.

Chapter Three

That evening, after Rain had spent the better part of the day hosting and getting to know the three applicant Pure males better, she bid them goodnight and made her way down the corridor to her own chamber.

It was barely seven o'clock, right after they'd finished a light, early dinner. Rain had left Wan'er to escort the three candidates to their rooms, while she sought out Ayelet to catch up on the afternoon's events.

Troubled with the news she was given and worried about Valerius, she made a left, turning down a different corridor, the one that led to his chambers in the West Wing, before she even realized what she was doing.

Pausing indecisively in front of his door, she raised her hand to knock but pulled back again.

Valerius had made no secret that he didn't like being in her presence. There was a palpable aura of push-back from him whenever they were in the same space together. She could almost feel the repelling energy projecting from his body whenever she was near. Unconsciously, she'd always stepped a few steps back to give him wider berth when they passed each other.

He would not welcome her attendance now, she thought with a weary sigh. But that was too damned bad. Because she was here to help and—

The door creaked open slightly as the central air in the underground complex kicked into gear. It wasn't locked.

This time, Rain did not hesitate and rapped smartly on the door before entering, without waiting for the room's occupant to give her leave. Head held high in defense of her intrusion, she didn't notice the body on the floor until she tripped over a muscular calf.

With a gasp, she tumbled down on top of Valerius and sprained her wrist awkwardly in an effort to break the fall.

When she realized the severity of the situation, she straightened quickly to kneel beside him, hands out before her over his prone body to assess the damage, the pain in her wrist forgotten.

Harnessing the full force of her power, fingers extended, hair stretched around them both in a silver halo, the Healer honed in on the source wounds and realized that the poison had already spread throughout the warrior's body.

The poison roared back at her like demons guarding the gates of hell, so strong was its venomous energy that Rain had to brace herself from physically staggering back. Instead, she redoubled her efforts. Tendrils of her hair tautened into spider-web-thin needles, inserting lightning quick through the thin layers of fabric into her patient's skin beneath.

A pained whimper escaped her lips despite her best attempt to withhold it as the fiery poison coursed from Valerius into herself.

Eyes closed in concentration, she knew that she and her patient were shrouded in a dark vacuous cocoon. Encapsulated in a protective bubble, even though anyone who came upon them could see their bodies, they would not be able to interfere with the healing process. If someone approached, the energy field Rain erected around Valerius and herself would stun them back with an electric shock.

Rain's veins raised through her skin as the poison coursed through her, dark green and black lines moving like tree roots across her face, neck, and arms as if they had a life of their own.

She did not utter another sound despite the overwhelming pain she drew from Valerius' body into her own. Her lips, one of the only remaining spots of color on her person, turned blue from the exertion. Her skin took on a grayish hue, and breath exited her nostrils and slightly parted mouth in icy puffs, as if she were climbing to an impossible mountain peak in the middle of the Arctic.

Summoning all of her strength and training, she squeezed her eyes tightly for one final draw. Then, as if two powerful magnets were forcibly wrenched apart, she withdrew from Valerius the needles of hair, the soothing warmth of her hands and fell back against the floor in a lifeless crumble.

*** *** *** ***

In the suburbs of Boston, surrounding a forgotten strip of underground train tracks, an elaborate catacomb stretched like termite teeth marks into the dark unknown.

Though cold, damp and sometimes a little odiferous, the catacomb lacked no modern comfort.

It even had its own karaoke and dance bar.

In a corner chamber along one of the spoke-like corridors, an exquisitely beautiful vampire idly swirled blood-red wine in an antique crystal goblet.

Gently inhaling the subtle fragrance of the vintage liquid, the vampire breathed a satisfied sigh. It surveyed the chess board on the carved stone table at its feet and picked up one of the white diamond pieces.

A Knight.

What a handsome piece, it mused, as ruby red eyes glowed with appreciation. Long, elegant fingers smoothed over the perfect chess piece with loving care, its thumb rubbing the thigh of the warrior, sitting astride a rearing stallion.

It felt its loins ignite with arousal as its thumb brushed back and forth, back and forth across the hard, smooth thigh, as if vicariously rubbing its own genitals, now filling with liquid heat.

The other long-fingered hand languorously slid down its chest, stomach, inner thighs, to rest delicately over the pleasure area, one perfectly manicured nail dragging over its arousal.

Aahh.

It leaned more deeply in the sheepskin-covered chaise, deeper into the goose down pillows as pleasure hummed throughout its body, pooling inexorably in its lap as its other hand rubbed more urgently over the chess piece, faster and faster until hot black fluids seeped through the satiny white robe tied loosely at its waist.

Draped lazily across the chaise like a well-satisfied feline, it examined the black stains with mild curiosity.

Time to feed.

As if summoned by the thought, a soft rap sounded at the door.

"Come," it beckoned, then giggled coyly behind a raised hand.

How clever, it made a pun.

A male vampire entered but stayed behind the chaise in the dimness.

"It is done, Master."

Stretching out an arm so that its visitor could see its curling finger from around the chaise, it purred, "Perfect. Now come here into the light, shy one, but make sure you are properly un-attired."

The male shed his clothes as he came before his Master and knelt within reach.

Idly discarding the chess piece back on the board, innocently knocking over a bishop on its way down, the vampire reached greedily for a different piece to play with.

*** *** *** ***

Valerius came to abruptly with a gasp, as if he'd been yanked from the jaws of death, but just barely.

He knifed into a sitting position and kneaded his eye sockets with the seat of his hands.

Rays of dawn filtered through the tiny square skylight overhead. To unsuspecting humans above ground, the squares were decorative patches of glass embedded in the streets they walked on.

Valerius felt disoriented, as if he were drugged, but otherwise awake and invigorated. The agony of the past day and night seemed a distant memory.

A sudden awareness infused him at the thought. How was he able to heal himself?

It was only then that he noticed Rain on the floor beside him.

Forgetting his own rules, he grasped her roughly and hauled her into his lap, examining her ashen face and cold form with panicked eyes. He cupped her face with one large, calloused hand, the other holding her body tightly to him, and smoothed a thumb urgently over her cheek.

"Rain," he called to her, the first time he'd ever used her name in the ten years of their acquaintance.

"Rain!" he could not keep the alarm from his voice as she remained lifeless in his embrace.

He shook her a little, set his face close to hers to detect her breathing. The barest of breath relieved him so much he shuddered from head to toe.

"You little fool!" he cursed her, furious that she'd used what scarce energy she had remaining to heal him.

He thrust his wrist against her lips and urged, "Take it. Bite me, damn you!"

Though there was no movement, he felt her stirring, her breath a little stronger against his skin. She opened her mouth and formed words, but they were uttered so softly he could not hear.

He bent closer until their foreheads were touching.

"What is it sweetheart? What do you need?"

In a raspy whisper she breathed, "I'll not take from the body I just healed."

"Stupid girl," Valerious berated her, though his deep tone of concern was at odds with his words. "I would have healed eventually on my own. Your energy is wasted on me."

He thrust his wrist against her lips again, forcefully enough to scratch the skin against her canines.

"Now feed," he commanded in a voice that brooked no argument.

Amazed at her own strength, Rain suddenly pushed back from his embrace and off his lap. She scooted back against the foot of the bed and let her head flop against the bedframe.

"You are not my Consort. This is not the Cycle," she whispered weakly but resolutely. "I will have no other but my Consort."

"Then choose me!" Valerius exploded, uncaring of the consequences he'd spent two thousand years avoiding.

"It is the least I can do to repay you—"

He broke off at a resounding slap against his cheek. Though lacking in force to bring any pain, the sound it made nevertheless reverberated in the silent room.

Stunned, he could only gape at her.

"I am not a pity fuck," the Healer ground out in a low, trembling voice with shocking vehemence. She was too weary and in too much pain to carefully choose her words as she was wont to do.

"You think I don't know you've done everything possible to avoid me these past ten years? You think I don't notice you leaving a room whenever I enter? How you cringe away from even the hint of an accidental touch?"

Confronted with the blunt words coming from the delicate female's mouth, so small and slight she was like a child, Valerius could only continue to gape, not that Rain paused for his interjection.

"I don't need you to be the sacrificial lamb at my altar. The Phoenix Cycle is trying enough without the Consort Nourishing against his desire. You wouldn't be able to handle it."

At that, Valerius stiffened until his back was ramrod straight.

"Oh put aside your umbrage," Rain said on a disgusted huff. "Nothing you do or say can convince me that you'd enjoy thirty days of blood-letting and orgy, not when a simple brush tenses you up more effectively than a torture rack."

To demonstrate, she lightly swept a hand down his neck and chest as she spoke, and to her satisfaction for making her point, tempered with keen disgruntlement, he reflexively jerked away from the brief touch, as if burned.

Valerius gritted his teeth in shame and fury at himself for unwittingly proving her right.

Rain struggled to stand, and Valerius moved to aid her. But a fulminating glare put him back in his place, his extended arms falling empty at his sides.

Weaving slightly on her feet, Rain said in a bone-weary voice, almost too low to hear, "I repel you so much you would rather die a slow, painful death than come to me for healing. If I found you even an hour later, I do not think I could have defeated the poison."

When he would have argued, she silenced him with a raised hand.

"I know you heal faster than others and are ten times as strong. But you knew you couldn't heal yourself this time. You *knew*."

Valerius could not bring himself to lie to her; she would not have forgiven him.

"So consider that we are even." Rain went on relentlessly, "You insult me with your blatant avoidance and I healed you against your will."

She moved slowly but determinedly to the door, and stopped him in his tracks as he made to follow her with the blast of her parting words.

"The Rite will begin tomorrow, and I will select from the three qualified males in attendance. My chosen Consort will satisfy me in every conceivable way until I overflow from his Nourishment."

Valerius' heart thudded heavily, painfully in his chest, as if it wanted to burst through its cage and release its agony.

She paused at the threshold, and without turning around, splintered him completely with—

"He will fill me and fulfill me in ways you never could."

*** *** *** ***

Back in her own room, Rain encountered a worried Wan'er who grasped her hands the moment she stepped inside, leading her to the bed.

"My lady, where have you been?" Wan'er fussed, close to tears. "You have not slept in this bed all night. I was of a mind to raise alarm just as you came."

"Hush." Rain silenced her companion more sternly than she meant to.

Softening her tone, she said, "I was with a patient and forgot the time when I rested afterwards. It's nothing. I just need a good long nap."

Knowing she was being dismissed but too concerned to move, Wan'er hovered over the Healer, helped her get settled, tucking the coverlet around her.

Rain sighed.

"Please, Little Sparrow," she coaxed her handmaiden with the fond nickname, "let me rest for now. I have three long days ahead of me. You would not have me preside over the Rite less than at my best, would you?"

Wan'er shook her head. On a whim, she bent down and kissed her lady's cheek, giving her a brief hug before shuffling out the door and closing it behind her.

Rain breathed deeply as she tried to calm her roiling emotions, thinking back on her exchange with the Protector.

What had possessed her to speak in such a manner? To attack him with those ruthless words and physical assault besides! She'd offended his pride, his sensibility, his very masculinity.

She could feel the hurt and torment coming off him in great waves as she left the room. She doubted he knew how clearly she could read him. It was part of her Gift to understand and manipulate energy. He'd already been in pain whenever she was in his presence, but at her unprovoked bombardment, his anguish had magnified a hundred times, until it consumed his entire being.

And she, the Healer, had visited that suffering upon him.

Tears of shame and remorse welled in her eyes and leaked down her cheeks.

She did not understand him after all. She did not understand herself. She wanted him desperately. Had craved him for ten years, ever since she'd first looked upon him in the sanctuary. She hated that he hadn't applied to Serve her, hated that he didn't apply again. Furious that he only offered himself to settle a debt.

It took every ounce of willpower she had to stop herself from caving in to the ambrosia he offered.

How dared he press his vein against her lips, against her teeth.

How dared he tempt her to forget herself!

How hard she struggled to leash her desire to burrow deep into his warmth, sink her fangs into his wrist, his throat, his thighs, his groin—fill herself to the brim with his Nourishment over and over and over again.

She was beside herself with starvation. She knew that full well.

What she didn't know was whether she craved the Nourishment or whether she craved the man.

*** *** *** ***

Valerius sat on his bed, elbows on his thighs, hands in front of his face, palms up as he examined his wrists in wretched silence.

He was deluding himself to think she would want to take Nourishment from him.

Not from these veins. Not from this body.

He could barely stand to be in his own skin, much less expect others to bear his presence.

He wouldn't have been surprised if the blood in his veins ran black instead of red, so dark was his heart and shuttered his soul. The only time he felt free was when he hunted vampires. Amidst the rage, brutality, and vengeance, he could be himself and unleash the demon within.

It was his only purpose in this world—to kill.

Pain was the only thing he understood...

Sometime before 200 B.C. Outskirts of Rome.

The gladiator spun around and raised his shield a moment before his opponent's axe struck it with resounding force, pushing him back several steps, his shield arm throbbing from the impact.

Only momentarily fazed, he swung his sword in a sideways slice, spinning as he did so, using the momentum of his torso to increase the power of the stroke.

His opponent leaped back but not in enough time, as the blade swiped a deep gash through his unprotected side.

Bellowing from the pain, the other fighter staggered back and almost lost his footing, quickly growing weak as blood poured freely down his legs into the dirt ground beneath him.

With a roar to anticipate his final blow, the gladiator took two large rapid steps forward, swinging his sword in an unstoppable downward arc.

The opponent didn't even have time to scream before the deadly spatha carved through his skull, splitting his face in half and exiting the other side through his neck. He fell first to his knees, his torso followed with a clang and a thud, the sounds unheard over the roaring of the spectators in the makeshift arena.

The gladiator strode in a circle around the stage of his victory, arms held high, shield and sword in hand. He played to the cheering crowd as a shower of coins were tossed down at his feet.

He'd put on a good show. He knew that his master's coffers would be full tonight.

Circling a final time, he exited the arena through an underground passage into the pits where other gladiators, slaves, prisoners, and animals were kept.

Where his fourteen-year-old son was waiting with a sleeve of wine.

"Ha!" he exclaimed in a booming voice, still energized by the fight. "Your old man still has it in him, eh?"

He ruffled the boy's hair affectionately and tossed him two gold pieces he'd picked up from the arena grounds. That should represent his cut of the winnings. Enough to send home to his wife and daughter to buy them a month worth of grains, meat and spices, enough still to pay for a new suit of armor and a real sword for his son, who excelled at battle with an almost unnatural talent.

The gladiator's chest puffed with pride at the boy, who beamed up at him in return with awe and admiration.

In his day, the gladiator was a fearsome warrior, undefeated across most of Rome and its surrounding cities, but the endless battles had taken its toll, and age had finally caught up with him. Victory these days were more and more difficult to come by, but this old tiger still had some teeth.

He laughed and parried with his son as the boy practiced with an ancient, rusted sword, for the moment ignoring the numbness in his shield arm that was spreading slowly but relentlessly to his shoulder...

Later that night, as the gladiator soaked in a hot, steaming bath, his son hard at work scrubbing his back with a wash cloth, he counted his remaining days in the arena with foreboding.

As if reading his thoughts the boy asked, "Sire, when can I fight? I defeat all the other trainees easily, and sometimes even the seasoned gladiators. I know I am not yet as big and strong, but I am much faster and nimbler, and I think on my feet. Didn't you tell me that's most of the battle? The ability to anticipate your opponent's moves?"

"Aye," the gladiator answered, sighing in pleasure as the boy kneaded his aching shoulders with just the right amount of pressure.

"But your old man has yet a few years left, never fear. Enough time for you to hone your technique and become truly unbeatable."

He grabbed one of his son's hands to get his attention.

"You have to plan your campaign, Valerius. You cannot enter the arena before the right time. You have to take care to build your reputation, until your reputation becomes myth, and myth becomes legend, and you become the greatest gladiator of all time. Then you will be a rich man in your own right, and you can buy your freedom, your mother's and sister's too, and take a decent woman to wife, raise and support your own family and hold your head high as a full Roman citizen."

"And your freedom too, Sire," Valerius answered the usual way.

It was a recurring conversation between father and son, a dream they both shared and nurtured, each taking steps toward making it a reality.

But Valerius was impatient. He wanted everything for his family today, not tomorrow. And despite what his father said, he knew he was ready, at the tender age of fourteen, to enter the battlefield of men.

"One more fight," the gladiator said, his eyes closing with the onset of sleep. "One more fight and I'll retire to leave the charge to you. My son."

Valerius circled his arms around his father's neck in a brief embrace, a deep and abiding love washing over him.

A gladiator's life was brutal at best, bleak and terrifying at worst. But his father was a good fighter, and an even better man. He was generous with his affection, though Roman men eschewed public displays, and the softer emotions in general. He was generous with his time, teaching his son not only how to be the fiercest fighter that ever was, but also how to be a real man.

A man upheld his responsibilities. To his dependents, his superiors, but most of all, to his own sense of right and wrong. He never cheated, never lied, and always defended those weaker than him. He respected his father and mother, his sister, his friends and, one day, his woman. He would woo her, protect and provide for her, and cherish her above all others, above himself.

All this Valerius learned at his father's knee, and occasionally when he strayed, by the flat of his father's sword. They were worthwhile lessons to learn.

Valerius helped the gladiator out of the washtub, briskly toweled him off and half led, half supported him to the awaiting straw cot.

His father was asleep before his body hit the mattress. With a sigh, Valerius pulled a thin blanket over his pater and lay down on his own ragged pallet beside the cot.

He immediately fell into a deep sleep, dreaming of the arena, and amidst the deafening cheers, his freedom...

One week later, their master decided that Valerius' sire had one good show still left in him. He arranged for the gladiator to take on a wild beast, a chariot with archers and three prisoners of war in a well-orchestrated spectacle.

They'd agreed on the plan of attack ahead of time, the tricks that the master would pull to tip the advantage to his prized gladiator, so there was limited danger save unexpected human and animal reactions in the heat of combat.

Despite Valerius' entreaties, his father decided to take the risk and entered the arena with his favored shield and sword— one last battle before his retirement from the field, one more win to secure his family's freedom.

As the gladiator took to his stage from the south entrance into the arena, a lion, chained by his back paw, was released from the west through an underground tunnel.

Like a graceful dancer, the gladiator pivoted to his left and faced the beast with sword ready to strike. He slashed and stabbed with methodical strokes, beating the lion back towards the tunnel. The crowd seemed pleased with his efforts, but there were also jeers of boredom.

Not enough bloodshed.

Before the Lion had fully retreated into the tunnel, a chariot drawn by a team of two war-trained stallions entered the area from the north gate, holding one driver and two archers with full quivers of arrows, bows drawn back with deadly aim.

Momentarily stunned by the appearance of the second foe before the first had been fully subdued, the gladiator stood rooted to his spot, arms lax at his sides.

This was not the plan.

Quickly, however, he regrouped to face the second opponent, shield held closely before his torso.

But these were not stage archers, letting fly arrows mostly for show. These archers aimed for his legs and feet where he was unprotected and one arrow pierced his right calf.

"No!"

The gladiator barely registered the shout of anguish from his son. He was too taken aback.

This was not the plan!

Crouching down so that most of his body was covered behind the shield, he hobbled backwards toward the south gate.

It was time to retreat. Though this was supposed to be his final victory, though he'd planned the show down to each and every move with his master, something had gone terribly wrong. Vaguely, he considered that his master might have betrayed him. But for what purpose?

Suddenly, the lion pounced from his left, and he turned just in time to block the claws and jaws with his shield. But the weight was unbearable, and his shoulder and forearm exploded in pain, then completely lost feeling in a matter of moments.

Involuntarily, his grip on the shield relaxed, the metal barrier falling with a clang to the arena grounds as his left arm fell limp against his side.

Another arrow pierced his back right between the shoulder blades. The gladiator fell forward to his knees, the shock and the pain from his wounds muting all of the sounds around him, his eyes blurring as they tried to focus on his opponents.

This was the end, he thought, even as he heard the trap door to the underground tunnel from the east open and the last of his opponents arrive.

This was all wrong. He was supposed to have defeated them one at a time, yet now they charged at him all at once. He could hear the men's shouts of battle, their only goal to cut him down. Either his life or theirs.

He managed to get to his feet in time to parry a blow from one of the men, barely avoiding another arrow that jabbed into the earth beside his foot.

This was not a fair fight by any stretch of the imagination, he knew, but he took a deep breath and roared his own battle cry, charging at the men with every last ounce of strength.

He would not go down meekly, he thought. He would give the audience their money's worth. With his glorious death, perhaps he could still free his family. If this was what his master required to fulfill his blood debt, then by the gods he would deliver.

And then he was not alone.

Someone was pushing back the lion with a long spear. He could see the quick, efficient movements of the lion tamer out of the corner of his eye. When the lion had been beaten back into the tunnel, his aide took down one of the archers with a powerful spear toss.

As the archer's dead body fell over the side of the chariot, the wheels struck it awkwardly as they rolled over it, and the driver lost control of the reins. The chariot swerved dangerously, and the remaining archer struggled for balance. He lost his aim and concentration, instead gripping the sides of the chariot to stay inside the vehicle.

The gladiator watched in a daze as his shield got picked up by the newcomer, who gained momentum with a few quick steps and let fly the circular metal shield like a discus at the stallions' front legs. The horses stumbled upon impact and crashed hard into the dirt ground. The sudden stop jolted the chariot like a catapult, and the two remaining riders shot out with bone-breaking velocity.

It all happened so fast, the gladiator only caught a blur of movement as his aide stepped in front of him, effectively intercepting a blow from one of his remaining opponents' club. The gladiator's vision was steadily receding, and he blinked hard to keep his foes in sight.

"Get back!" the young warrior who defended him shouted amidst the jarring sounds of battle.

Valerius?

The gladiator could only shake his head in confusion as he realized belatedly that his rescuer was indeed his fourteen year-old son. The boy was fighting three grown men bare-handed and winning!

Valerius managed to dodge a thrust from one of their swords, turning sideways at the last moment and using the forward momentum of his attacker against him to pull him effortlessly to the ground.

He leapt onto the fallen back of the first attacker and used the body as a springboard to engage the other two men while simultaneously cracking some bones underfoot and ensuring that the fallen opponent stayed down.

With a series of turns, twists, well-aimed elbow and knee jabs, body throws and nimble maneuvering, Valerius made short work of the other two opponents until all three men lay defeated on the dirt grounds.

The crowd went wild with cheers and applause at the incredible display. But Valerius didn't notice as he rushed to his father who had sunk to the ground, lying motionlessly on his belly, bleeding profusely from his wounds.

"Sire!" Valerius gathered him close and tried to ascertain the damage.

His father pushed his searching hands away, saying gruffly, "This is your moment. You must play to the crowds. Leave me be. Rise and walk your victory rounds."

Valerius was shaking his head before his father had finished speaking, but the gladiator clutched his arm urgently and plunged ahead, "You will do this, my son, for both our sakes. You are the new champion, and they love you. You must secure the crowd's affection and approval so that they shower you with coin. This is a stage, and you are a player. We are all players. The crowds are the gods of your destiny. Go and appease them. Go!"

The gladiator shoved his son away and watched as Valerius briefly hesitated before turning to their audience in the stands, raising his arms and letting out a long cry of victory.

The crowd roared with approval, sending a shower of coins to rain on the arena grounds. The gladiator watched with pride as Valerius strode around the arena, getting the crowds to cheer louder, establishing himself as the undisputed champion.

He'd done it, the gladiator thought. He'd secured the crowd's favor. Surely there would be enough coin from this win to pay off his entire family's debt, and his own defeat only added to the drama and suspense.

The gladiator sighed a long, weary breath.

It was time for him to retire, he thought as his eyelids grew too heavy to lift. And what a glorious way to do so, being able to witness his son's induction into manhood, resplendently victorious in his youth and might.

My son.

Yes, it was time to retire.

The gladiator embraced his long-awaited rest with a smile.

Chapter Four

Rain bid farewell for the day to the third qualified Pure male and watched him slowly and painstakingly make his way beyond the threshold of the Rite Enclosure.

She closed her eyes and released a pent up breath.

It had been a long second day in the three-day Rite of the Phoenix, a day she looked forward to only slightly less than the third and final day. Today, she had pushed the males almost beyond their endurance. She was surprised they hadn't decided to withdraw their application.

The Phoenix Cycle would be much worse.

As she prepared to leave the chamber, Wan'er came forth with a nonplussed expression.

"My lady," her handmaiden said haltingly, "it appears you have one final applicant."

"What?" Rain responded reflexively.

She heard her handmaiden perfectly well, but the words didn't make a lick of sense.

Wan'er shifted a bit nervously, as if indecisive about how to break some bad news.

"Your final applicant is waiting in the antechamber." She bit her lower lip and blurted, "It is my lord Valerius."

Rain's eyebrows shot up in shock. Surely she had not heard correctly.

"Shall I show him in and prepare him for the test?" Wan'er asked tentatively, uncertain of her lady's mood.

Without answering her handmaiden, Rain marched angrily to the antechamber and threw apart the double doors.

"Just what do you think you're doing?" she demanded of the warrior leaning against the back wall.

She braced herself against the welcome sight of him in full health. She'd been on tender hooks all the previous day, wondering whether she'd been able to heal him completely, whether she should have checked on him. She could barely concentrate on the first day's tests, she'd been so distracted. But now that he appeared fully recovered, her anger overrode all concern.

He straightened from the wall and stood tall and alert before her.

"Applying to Serve you, Healer."

"I will not allow it," Rain retorted immediately. "We have had this conversation and that was my final word."

"I don't believe you can disallow an application," Valerius said quietly, slowly, as if giving her time for the words to sink in. "I can fail the tests, but I have every right to apply."

"Well, you are disqualified," Rain pushed back. "You missed the first day of the Rite. That is an automatic fail."

Wan'er cleared her throat behind her, interjecting awkwardly, "Actually, my lady, the Protector does not need to attend the first day since he is one of the Elite and, therefore, already proven in his strength and vitality."

Rain turned toward her traitorous handmaiden with a sharp glare.

Wan'er bowed her head at the force of Rain's displeasure, but did not back down.

"Shall I prepare him for the test?" she repeated the offer, all but taking the decision out of Rain's hands.

Rain turned back toward the warrior with narrowed eyes.

"You will fail," she assured him ominously.

Then, as if she couldn't bear to be in their presence a moment longer, she spun on her heel and retreated to the inner chamber to await Wan'er's preparations.

The handmaiden sighed exhaustedly and led Valerius to the Rite Enclosure.

"I hope you know what you're doing," she muttered as she closed the double doors behind them.

Ten minutes later, Valerius stood with legs spread wide, all but nude, save a thin towel that Wan'er had given him to wrap around his waist, between two thick steel poles that extended from the floor, his hands cuffed to the handle bars on top of the poles, his ankles secured to the bottom.

Thus restrained, he awaited alone in the silence and dimness of the Rite Enclosure for the Healer to begin her trials.

Valerius closed his eyes and breathed deeply.

He'd promised himself a long, long time ago that he would never let himself be tied down, never be vulnerable and helpless again. Yet here he was.

Exposed. Powerless. At the mercy of someone else.

The only saving grace was that in this instance, he *chose* his fate. He chose to be here, to submit himself to Rain.

He did not know what the trials involved, but he was certain he could pass any test for pain and endurance. He'd gone through enough hell in his human lifetime to last an eternity. And that was before he had the magnified healing abilities as a Pure One.

What he fought against was himself.

His aversion—no, *phobia*—of being touched. If the trials did not involve direct contact with the Healer, it would be simple endurance. But if they did...

Valerius' jaw clenched as he fought off a wave of nausea.

He could not fail. He would not fail.

The Healer entered with Wan'er a few steps behind. Without looking at him, head held high, back ramrod straight, she stepped before him until she was merely two feet away and closed her eyes.

Without warning, she stretched out her arms until her palms faced his chest and blasted him with a shock of energy so powerful, he would have fallen on his ass if not for the restraints. Even as his torso felt as if it'd been struck by lightning, relief washed over Valerius in a soothing rush.

No physical contact. He could do this all day.

And then the Healer seemed to levitate from the ground, supported in a magnetic field that radiated from her body. Her loose robes flowed in the air, rippling with the currents of energy around her. Her hair stretched away from her face, each tendril extending outward until it formed a white semi-circular halo behind her back.

She floated closer to him, her extended hands almost touching his skin, the pressure and electric shock she exerted increasing until Valerius felt as if every nerve was on fire.

His breath quickened as he tried to free his mind from the pain, and just when he thought he'd disciplined his senses, the countless needles of her hair inserted deeply into his skin.

He felt torn asunder.

Never had he suffered such acute, incredible pain.

Not like this.

This was continuous, ever increasing, mind bending agony. And it went on and on and on.

Just when he thought he'd break his jaw from clenching so tightly against the screams that were building in his throat, he heard a distant gasp.

"My lady!" Wan'er entreated, watching horrified as the warrior endured ten times the level of pain Rain had ever used in the Rites for already twice as long.

Abruptly, the needles retracted and the pressure released, leaving Valerius doubled over in a fit of coughing as he tried to find his center of balance again, as his nerves sucked in oxygen and his muscles slowly unclenched.

Rain descended slowly to the ground and lowered her arms to her sides.

Eyes still closed, she ordered her handmaiden, "Leave us."

Wan'er looked at her with alarm.

This was simply not done. The handmaiden always attended the Healer in the Rite, more because of tradition than anything else. But given where Rain had taken this particular trial, Wan'er was seriously worried for the warrior. Surely her lady would not go too far, she thought, but just the same, she'd like to ensure—

"*Now*," Rain issued the command with enough force to send apprehensive shivers down the handmaiden's spine.

Wan'er took one last look at the Protector, who had recovered enough to stand tall once more between the two steel poles, and decided that she could not interfere even if she wished to. This was between Rain and the warrior.

It was their time of reckoning.

When the handmaiden left them and closed the doors behind her with a soft click, Rain opened her eyes and gazed fully upon the Protector.

"It is no surprise you surpassed the other applicants in this test," she said quietly. "I would expect nothing less."

Holding his gaze, she closed the short distance between them until they were almost toe to toe, barely an inch separating their bodies.

Had Valerius not been secured to his position, he would have stepped back immediately. As it was, his heart began to pound harder, faster, his breath breaking into rapid bursts, as if he couldn't get enough air into his lungs.

And then he felt her palms on his chest, lightly grazing his ultra-sensitized skin.

The thick muscles jumped reflexively, and Valerius could not hold back a gasp at the contact, his face contorting in a different kind of pain.

"But we both know the test you would fail," Rain continued as if they were having a casual conversation. "So why wait until tomorrow to meet your fate? Let us end the madness today."

Her eyelids lowered in a sleepy swoop, and her hands spread wide on his pectorals. Slowly, leisurely, they roamed over his naked flesh, around his shoulders, his collar bone, his throat, jaw, cheeks and brows. By the time they were winding their way back down again, Valerius had forgotten how to breathe.

It did not escape Rain, as she delved into a detailed exploration of the Protector's body, that he was in excruciating pain. His body gave off waves of anguish far greater than when she'd literally set him afire.

But she would not relent. This was not simply a point to prove. It would be better for them both if he withdrew his application.

She didn't know why, but she feared the consequences down to her very soul if he didn't.

Methodically, her small hands glided back over his sweat-dampened chest, her thumbs pausing to rub softly over his pebble-hard nipples. His stomach sucked in at the touch, then pushed back out as he released a shuddering breath.

She drew a path over his ribs, counted the iron ridges of his abdomen, trailed a finger down the deep groove bisecting his middle to his navel and further down to the fold of towel tucked low around his hips.

Like a hunted animal caught in a trap, Valerius' pupils dilated with fear and pain, but he could not shut his eyes against his impending doom.

He could not fail. He *would* not fail. Please, Goddess, don't let him fail!

With a gentle pull, his last covering fell away, and his body was bared completely before her. There was a moment of hesitation as she drank him in, and then her hands were back on his body, one hand sliding up his torso to the back of his neck, the other resting lightly on his hip.

"Shall I give you a taste of what's in store?" Rain asked softly, her breath warm against his skin. "Will a glimpse of your life for the next thirty days convince you to retreat?"

The hand on the back of his neck exerted only the smallest pressure, but it was enough to bend his head down closer to hers.

"Shall I show you what it means to Serve me, warrior?" she whispered against his ear, as the hand at his hip curved inward to grasp his penis, already painfully erect.

Valerius could not prevent the moan that escaped.

He was on fire. He was on ice. His body vibrated with tension as he struggled to control it. His muscles strained so hard the steel restraints creaked in protest.

She stretched upwards until she was on tiptoes and brushed her lips against his throat, once, twice, wetting the throbbing vein there with her breath.

"It is not too late to back out," she tempted him, grazing her elongated fangs over his tender skin the same time that she squeezed his staff firmly in her fist and pumped it once hard.

Valerius' breath came in harsh bursts, and to his utter shame and defeat, his eyes blurred with tears.

They would not fall, he thought fiercely. He would not fall!

"Just tell me to stop," she urged him, the hand at his neck kneading the bunched muscles there in silent persuasion. "You can end your torment right now."

He never knew what it cost him, but somehow he turned his face closer to hers, pushing the vein at his throat tighter against the sharp tips of her fangs.

"No," he answered her, his deep voice quiet but firm.

He would not back down. Not then, more than two millennia ago, and not now.

"So be it."

The words hissed from her lips a moment before her fangs penetrated his skin, inserting deep into his vein. With her first long pull, Valerius' body began to transform.

His muscles seemed to enlarge and tighten, standing out in stark relief, each sinew and line sharply defined. His veins pushed out against his skin, as if vying for her attention, volunteering to be drawn upon. His penis elongated and thickened further, to the point that he was sure he would explode from the pressure within.

It pushed against the slender fingers that held it, the fingertips far from meeting around the swollen girth, as if fighting against the confinement, yet begging to be held even tighter. He felt a trickle of moisture seep out of the narrow slit in the enormous head, and despite himself, his hips bucked awkwardly, desperately, against her hand.

She seemed to know what his body wanted, even as his mind struggled to distance itself, horrified by what was happening to him. She gripped him tighter and brushed her thumb slowly, continuously over the head of his penis, back and forth, back and forth, until his entire length was wetted and the tip became so sensitive he had to bite his tongue on a plea for her to end this merciless torture. All the while she drew steadily from his vein, at once draining his strength yet filling him with renewed vigor.

The undeniable drive to Mate.

Abruptly she withdrew her fangs and licked the two small wounds closed, though her hand increased the friction around his penis.

"Shall I see what else you have to offer, warrior?" she asked on a languorous sigh, like a feline awaking from a long, satisfying nap.

His helpless gaze followed her as she went down before him on her knees, now both hands gripping his staff covetously.

His monstrous erection jerked in anticipation, his body shuddered in fear, and his mind recoiled against the vision of her before him.

Please. Please *please* let him withstand this, he begged the Goddess.

He could not fail. He *would* not fail.

But memories of the past assailed him, as real as physical blows. He closed his eyes briefly and prayed for strength, then opened them wide and stared at the woman between his legs.

It was Rain, he reminded himself.

She needed him. He could see that even a few draws upon his vein had brightened her countenance, infusing her cheeks with a rosy glow. It was in his power to revive her completely, return her to her original vitality. She wouldn't have suffered as she did if he'd been her Consort ten years ago. For the past few years, he'd stood by and watched her slowly waste away. He could have prevented her pain. He'd been too selfish. Too cowardly.

No more. He would not fail her again.

"Take me," he urged in a rough, husky voice, pushing his hips forward, the wetted head of his cock grazing her closed lips.

Stunned at the blatant offer, Rain raised her eyes to meet his.

This was Rain. His body shuddered in recognition. He was giving himself to Rain.

As the thought washed over him, his muscles began to relax, his inner battle subsiding, and a potent musk filled the air.

Rain's pupils dilated, her nostrils flaring at the sudden fragrance that filled her senses, permeating her very pores. It was a combination of sunlight and earth, fresh rain and clean man. She grew heady from the scent and felt her core throb in recognition.

This was Valerius. The warrior she had wanted for so long, the Nourishment for which she starved. On a sigh of relief, she gave in to her deepest desires.

With both hands she brought his cock to her lips and opened her mouth around the plump, hot head. His gasp as she did so fueled her passion further.

Slowly she began to suckle him, only the very tip of him fitting in her small mouth. But it was enough for her as she lapped up his milk greedily.

The taste of him was ambrosia to her. Tangy, salty, wondrous. Vaguely it occurred to her that all others before and after him paled in comparison. She would go on to have many more Consorts over the ages, but there would be no other such as he.

She moved one of her hands to the heavy sacs beneath his penis and squeezed ever so lightly. On command, the flow of his Nourishment became stronger, filling her mouth with a thin stream of cream.

It was not nearly enough.

She knew she was already taking this trial too far, even farther than the trial of pain and endurance. But she was addicted. One taste of him and she could not stop.

Just a little longer, she thought as she continued to suckle him hungrily. She'd been starved for far too long.

Valerius' body strained for release. The pressure within him was so intense every cell ached. Even the roots of his hair hurt. Instinct had taken over, and all he wanted was to get inside of her, fill her to the brim with his blood, his seed.

He'd never, ever, felt this way, not even in his dreams. For the first time in his long, stoic existence, he yearned for something more. Not for his people, not for the world he protected, but for himself. He wanted to matter.

To her.

On a shuddering breath, Rain withdrew from him all too soon, her hands and lips reluctantly releasing his still swollen cock. It bobbed in protest when she took her touch away and jutted toward her as if begging her to suckle some more.

Shakily, she stood up but kept her head bowed, her hands held demurely in front of her as if she were suddenly embarrassed.

He could see that her face was flushed from passion, and her body all but hummed for more of him.

But before he could offer himself once more, she said quietly, "I choose you."

With a flick of her hand, his restraints came undone. He rubbed his wrists absent-mindedly, barely registering that they were raw and chafed from his struggles as his body conformed to her needs.

Her head still bowed, she said in the same soft voice, "I choose you, but on one condition."

Slowly, she raised her eyes to meet his.

"You must never fall in love with me, for I will never fall in love with you. Over the course of the Phoenix Cycle you will Serve me as a Mate serves his female. But I will not return the same to you. You will feel ever unfulfilled, even when you find sexual release. You will always hover painfully between want and completion. You will grow weaker with each passing day, as if you are dying, but at the end of the thirty days, you will gradually recover."

She moved away from him to take a long white robe from a side table and handed it to him to cover himself. The soft terry cloth of the robe felt oddly abrasive against his still sensitized skin as he shrugged into it and tied the belt at his waist.

"With your healing abilities, I imagine you will recover far more quickly than others." But even as she said so, Rain sounded hesitant and worried.

"As long as you don't fall in love," she added so quietly he almost didn't hear.

Abruptly, she squared her shoulders and met his eyes again. Her next words stunned him even as he felt soothed by them.

"I'm sorry for pushing you too far," she said, though he didn't know precisely to what she referred, the second trial or the third just now.

"I'm sorry for being cruel. I-I don't know what came over me. But I have been harsh and unfair with you and I am neither."

She bowed her head again and whispered, "I know you are doing this out of some misguided sense of duty, I know you don't want to be here, that you despise being touched."

He tried to reach out to her, but she moved away.

"I want you anyway. I have no pride where you're concerned. And apparently, after two thousand five hundred years, no self-control either."

He began to shake his head.

She was not at fault. He was the one with the demons to overcome. And when he was with Rain, he felt he could finally have a hope, a chance, of putting them behind him.

"I will try not to make this more difficult for you than it has to be," she continued, not seeing his expression.

"Perhaps we don't need to..." she waved her hand around as if expecting the air to fill in the words.

Finally she said, "perhaps we can avoid intercourse unless..."

She darted a glance at his impassive face and couldn't finish her thought.

"Well," she finally said. "You should rest as much as you can over the next day. For the thirty days after, we will share the inner chamber adjoining this Enclosure. We will both go about our days as usual with our mutual responsibilities, but... you will avail yourself to me when I need your Service."

Valerius gave a nod of assent.

Tentatively, he reached out to her again, but she'd already turned away, leaving him alone in a flurry of silk.

Valerius closed his eyes and fell to the nearest seat. He would do his damnest to meet her every desire. He would conquer his demons, his doubts, his fears. But there was one thing he couldn't give her.

The promise not to fall in love.

*** *** *** ***

Sophia startled from her doze when the chair next to her scraped against the floor as it got pulled back.

Drowsily, she rubbed her eyes and blinked at the guy who took the seat beside her.

And blinked some more.

He was truly beautiful.

Sophia didn't use that term lightly. She was surrounded by supernatural beings who were also supernaturally good looking, but this guy took the cake.

Sophia liked to think of herself as a connoisseur of attractive people, men in particular. She appreciated their beauty rather like a devoted art lover appreciated the works of Renaissance masters, or like a lowly imperfect human prized the unattainable perfection.

She had an adjective for every type of beauty: Tristan was gruffly handsome, in an affable golden retriever sort of way. Leonidas was striking. Valerius would be devastatingly gorgeous if not for his infallibly stoic demeanor. Alexandros was rather magnificent, and Dalair...

Well, she hadn't quite decided what he was. The word hadn't been invented yet for what he was.

But the guy beside her was definitely beautiful.

Almost pretty, with his long dark curling lashes framing rich chocolate eyes so dark they were almost black, pale flawless skin and full French-kiss type of mouth. She could see that his hair was long, for it was pulled back in some sort of pony tail at the nape of his neck. Better to show off his fallen-angel visage, she supposed.

His angular features, however, saved him from being too pretty. Those sharp cheekbones that could cut glass, the hard V of his jaw, the long muscles of his neck and the prominent Adam's apple, even the slight widow's peak at his hairline.

"Hello," the dark beauty greeted her, an enchanting lopsided smile gracing his Expensive-Men's-Cologne-model face.

Sophia was not impressed by her own incoherent grunt of a response. It was not her brightest moment.

His bewitching smile grew slightly wider and he leaned forward on his elbow on the table they shared in the school canteen, regarding her with warm amusement.

"Are you a first year?" he asked in that lilting, slightly accented voice.

"Uhn," Sophia grunted again in response.

Really, her verbal prowess was mind boggling.

"Where are you from?"

"Why are you talking to me?" Sophia didn't mean to blurt out the question, but she couldn't help herself.

Beautiful dark strangers didn't usually seek her out for tête à têtes.

He chuckled softly, baring perfect white teeth.

"Can I not have a conversation with a lovely girl?" he teased her with a smile. "You are very lovely, you know."

Was he actually *flirting*? With *her*?

Sophia looked to her left, then to her right. Nope. He didn't seem to be talking to someone else.

"What is your name?" he asked.

"S-Sophia," she managed to stutter her reply.

"My name is Ere," he returned, spelling out the letters in the air with one long, elegant finger.

"Eh-ray," Sophia repeated slowly, trying to roll the *r* slightly like he had.

"Pe*rrr*fect," he praised in encouragement, drawing out the rolling *r* like a feline purring.

Sophia ducked her head as a blush suffused her face. This guy was really too much. She got hot all over just looking at him.

He chuckled again as if amused by her embarrassment, then reached out to touch the stack of books on the table.

"Ancient Chinese History, Ancient Egyptian Civilization, and Greek Mythology. What interesting course choices."

"Yeah," Sophia muttered a bit defensively, "I like that sort of stuff."

"I like it too," Ere responded quickly. "In fact, if you are taking Professor McGowen's class, I am his teaching assistant."

"No way," Sophia breathed with happy surprise.

What were the chances that such an inhumanly beautiful creature would share a class with her? Well, and the forty other students.

"Does that please you?" Ere asked, seeing how her expression brightened considerably.

"Yeah," she blurted out honestly, then added, "I mean, why wouldn't it."

"I am glad," Ere said in his angelic voice.

Catching something out of the corner of his eye, he stood to leave.

"It has been a pleasure meeting you, lovely Sophia. I shall look forward to seeing you in class."

As he departed, striding away in a long, loose, devil-may-care gait, he passed Dalair who was making his way toward Sophia's table. The Paladin paused briefly in passing and turned to assess Ere with a scrutinizing look.

Ere nodded in greeting and smiled a flippant smile, then walked out of the canteen and out of Sophia's view, even as she craned her neck to watch after him.

Dalair approached Sophia and sat in the chair Ere had used, asking without preamble, "What was that all about? Who is he?"

Sophia lost the puppy-love look and turned away from her Elite guard.

"None of your business," she sniffed. "Do I have to report all my friends to you?"

Dalair's eyes narrowed.

"Is he a friend?"

Sophia shrugged.

"Maybe. But not if you keep hovering so close you suck out all the oxygen in the room," she groused.

"I only came to take you to your next class," Dalair explained with patience. He wondered whether she was this antagonistic to all her guards.

"If it pleases you, I will ask no more about him. But tell me this, what is his name?"

"Why? So you can Google him and do a background check?"

At Dalair's impassive expression, Sophia rolled her eyes.

"Fine. His name is Ere. E-R-E. Don't know his last name, but I'll find out soon enough since he's going to be my Ancient Egyptian Civilization class's teaching assistant."

Dalair nodded, letting it go at that. Speaking more about this *Ere* would only incite her temper further.

He tried to help her rise, but she brushed him off, getting to her feet on her own, shoving her books into her book bag and slinging it over her shoulder.

"Don't stand so close," Sophia ordered. "People might think we're together."

"And that is a problem why?" Dalair inquired, sincerely curious.

She rolled her eyes again.

Dalair was really disenchanted with this teenage American habit.

"How am I supposed to get a boyfriend if you're always underfoot?" she asked acidly.

Dalair's eyebrows lifted a notch. "You wish for a boyfriend?"

"Hypothetically speaking," Sophia ground out. "Just because I can't throw away my virginity at the closest dick on hand doesn't mean I can't date."

Dalair frowned with concern, more at her desire to date than at her language.

"You know that is unwise," he said quietly.

"I know," she replied in a small voice, the anger seeping out of her like air out of a balloon. "But sometimes I just want to be a normal girl. This Queen of the Pure Ones business isn't a cake walk. Sometimes I wish…"

He waited patiently for her to finish her train of thought.

Finally she said, "I wish people weren't around me because they had to be, but because they wanted to be. I wish people treated me like a normal human girl rather than some long-awaited ruler who's going to save the universe."

As he digested that, she pushed passed him and threw behind her back, "Don't follow too closely. And stay out of sight."

Dalair hesitated, then obeyed her wishes.

Duty or desire, it didn't matter. He would always be around her, to comfort her, protect her, even though she didn't want it.

Even though he sometimes couldn't bear it.

Chapter Five

The formal bonding ritual between the Healer and her chosen Consort took place on the eve of the third day, concluding the Rite of the Phoenix.

The Royal Zodiac gathered above ground, in the starlit glass dome of the Christian Science cathedral to attend as witnesses to the ceremony, just as they would for any Mating ritual between two of their kind, as they were so rare and special.

They formed a broad ring around Valerius, Rain, and the master of ceremony, Ayelet, each member holding a large, brightly blazing candle.

Valerius, naked but for the ceremonial cloth around his loins, knelt on one knee before the Healer, who stood wreathed in flowing white robes, bowed his head in reverence, both his hands grasping both of hers as Ayelet recited the ancient vows:

In Darkness and Light, in Life and Death
Two souls will join to share One Path
With heart and mind, and every breath
You become each other's present and past
What the future holds only the Goddess can see
Paved by the choices you both shall make
Step by step toward your Destiny
In Bond Eternal that none shall break

Valerius raised his gaze to his Phoenix Mate and solemnly gave his pledge, "My body, my blood, my life are yours. I live to Serve none other but you. Rain. Take from me the Nourishment you crave. Let me become your strength, your protection, and fulfill your every need. I offer you all that I am, all that I was, all that I ever shall be."

A few startled gasps broke the silence of the room, and Rain's eyes filled with tears as she heard her Consort's heart-wrenching words.

He had spoken the pledge for a true Mating ritual, not the Phoenix Bonding Ritual that promised no future beyond the next thirty days.

Though words were just words and imparted no magical bond, she knew the Protector never spoke lightly. Surely he could not mean what he said. Surely he knew that their union would be but a fleeting moment in the long existence they had led and would continue to lead.

Taking a deep breath to brace herself, Rain responded quietly, "I accept you as my Consort, Valerius Marcus Ambrosius. For the next thirty days, I will take your Nourishment. For the next ten years, I shall have no other. I accept you with everything that I have been and everything that I am."

With those words, she pushed a ring of Tiger's Eye onto Valerius' left ring finger. The band automatically adjusted to fit his width.

Valerius' jaw clenched at the pain that obliterated him as she withheld any promise of her future.

Though he knew he was merely her Consort and not her Mate, in his heart he made no distinction. He knew as surely as he breathed that there would be no other for him but Rain, though she'd taken many Consorts in the past and would take many more males in the years to come. It was her fate as the Healer of their race. And it was his to yearn for her, but never receive.

Ayelet placed her hands on theirs and gave a reassuring squeeze.

"Cherish each other for the time you have. May the Goddess be with you both."

Valerius rose to his full height, head and shoulders above the reed-thin Healer. Though the customary seal of the bond was with a kiss, he could not bring himself to do so.

He didn't think his heart could withstand it.

Instead, he pulled his female into the warm strength of his embrace and cradled her silvery white head against his chest.

Rain inhaled deeply the Protector's intoxicating scent and sighed. Her arms wound around his lean waist and she held on with everything she had.

For the first time in all the centuries of her existence, she felt like she was finally home.

*** *** *** ***

"What do you make of the Phoenix Bonding Ritual?" Orion asked Eveline as they wound their way down the spiral staircase to the underground library.

"It was most unusual, the pledge that the Protector gave," Eveline replied with deep concern. "He was not supposed to have promised her his future."

Orion nodded. "I agree. I wonder at the cause of it. I've seen no indication over the last ten years that Valerius even wanted to be Consort to the Healer. In fact, he'd seemed most resistant up until the ceremony."

Eveline sighed, shaking her head.

"True, but sometimes, resistance only leads to the inevitable. Perhaps he always knew he would take the role."

"You know," Orion said, suddenly pausing on the second to last step, "this ritual and the attack on Valerius a few days ago echo something eerily familiar in my mind. In the Fourth Cycle of our Goddess, a century or so before the Great War began, one of our kind's greatest warriors was almost lost to us in an assassination attempt. Shortly thereafter, he became the then Healer's Consort. About twenty years before the first battle of the War was waged, he disappeared. That was the last mention of him in the history tomes, though every Consort the previous Healer had since was accounted for, their bravery in the war described in full."

"Yes, I recall you mentioning this when we went through the scrolls a few days ago," Eveline responded, hurrying to her Orb of Prophesies, a large crystal globe levitating in the middle of the library above a step dais with twelve raised spikes, like metallic claws that held the orb in place.

As the Seer approached, the globe swirled darkly, as if stormy clouds gathered beneath its surface. She placed both hands gently on the translucent shell and closed her eyes.

Orion reached for the large, leather bound book on a stand beside the orb and held it ready to take down her words. The words therein would become part of the Pure Ones' Zodiac Prophesies.

Slowly, the clouds within the orb eased apart as if spread by the heat of her fingertips, revealing two bright balls of green and red flame. The marble-sized spheres circled each other in a hypnotic dance, around and around, spiraling together brightly, almost joyfully.

Then, without warning, they slammed together and melded into one, half red, half green, with the flames forming a pattern like the Classic Taoist Taijitu symbol for yin and yang. But their harmony only lasted a brief moment before the green consumed the red and burst apart in a flash of blinding light. Thus, the globe descended into black opacity once more.

"Upon her choice, the future rests. To welcome the Darkness or create a New Light, only her heart can show the rest," Eveline intoned with her eyes still closed.

Orion scribbled the words down rapidly as she spoke and frowned over them trying to decipher their meaning.

Releasing a deep breath, Eveline disengaged from the globe and moved to stand beside Orion, looking over his shoulder at the words she herself did not recall, even though she'd uttered them only moments before.

She read the words in silence and tapped her chin.

"We should look at these phrases with the ones from the other day," she suggested, turning the page back to find the recordings of her previous glimpse into the possible future.

"With his surrender, the sacrifice is made. Death is near and Darkness surrounds, as the race's Adversary raises its blade," the Seer and the Scribe read aloud together, then flashed hot and cold as the haunting words washed over them.

"Surely this pertains to Valerius and Rain," Orion said slowly, almost in a whisper, as if speaking too loudly would awaken some calamity.

"But what choice must she make?" asked Eveline. "Has she already made it by choosing him as her Consort?"

"If so," Orion followed her train of thought, "then the future is already written."

"And what is this Adversary the prophesies warn us of?" Eveline continued, starting to wear a path down the thick sheepskin rug covering the library floor.

"Whatever it is, we must regard it with the same foreboding and significance as the Great War," Orion determined grimly. "History is repeating itself, I am sure of it."

"But will it lead to a bleaker or better tomorrow?" the Seer asked softly, looking into the fire that blazed in the hearth before them.

That he could not answer, Orion thought, brows drawn together.

No one could.

*** *** *** ***

That night Rain entered the inner chamber of the Phoenix Enclosure to find her Consort already waiting, standing before a massive floor-to-ceiling landscape mural that looked so real and vibrant it seemed to be the window to a living, magical world beyond.

He seemed freshly washed, and he stood naked from head to toe, beads of moisture still clinging to his golden-brown skin.

Rain paused in the doorway just to watch him for a while, unobserved.

She would never tire of gazing upon his long, lean body. She wanted to memorize every line and contour, every muscle and sinew.

Unconsciously, her fangs elongated as her eyes hungrily drank him in. He was everything she had ever dreamed, everything she had ever wanted.

As always, Valerius sensed the Healer's presence before he saw her. He could feel her hot gaze on his back, could feel it slide over his naked skin like a lover's hands, from his shoulder blades to his buttocks, to the back of his thighs, his calves, and ankles.

He grew long and hard in response, his manhood jutting to his navel and throbbing achingly for her attention.

Heat suffused his neck and face at his own helpless reaction. He clenched his fists against the urge to cup himself, to squeeze so hard, the pain would temporarily relieve this tortuous, hollow ache within.

It was always thus when she was near. He never understood why he only felt this way around Rain, but it seemed as if he were made for her.

Made to Serve her every need.

Softly, she approached to stand beside him, shifting her gaze to the silken mural that formed an entire wall of the Enclosure.

"It changes with the cycle of the sun and moon," she said conversationally, referring to the landscape before them.

"When daylight arrives, you will see songbirds flitting across a blue sky filled with wisps of white clouds instead of the pair of swans gliding across the cool darkness of the nighttime lake."

Thankful for the distraction of words, Valerius cleared his throat and asked, "How does it do that?"

Without looking at him, the Healer smiled a mysterious smile, reminding him of the first time he'd met her. He'd seen far too few smiles since then and knew deep down that he was the cause.

The knowledge shamed him.

"It is woven from my hair," Rain replied with a whimsical tone.

"I cut my hair at the end of the Phoenix Cycle, when black roots begin to emerge. By then the strands will have become entirely clear, reflecting only the colors of my imagination. Each tendril has a life of its own, and even when they are cut, they somehow remain part of my conscience, still obeying my will. And I weave them, with Wan'er's assistance, into the scenes of my childhood, the four *Zhou*s as you would call them now. Hangzhou, Suzhou, Guangzhou, and Liuzhou."

Valerius recalled the scrolls he'd seen in her sanctuary, as well as the handkerchief she'd given him when they first met, and nodded in amazement.

"Your homeland must have been very beautiful."

The Healer sighed.

"Indeed, it was. It still is, as you caught a glimpse of it yourself ten years ago, but much has changed. Human advancement and the ever-growing need for housing and industry have bulldozed over much of China's original beauty. I can only hope to preserve it in my memories."

Her lips quirked up at one corner, and he could hear the smile in her voice as she said, "Do you know the Chinese saying? *Heaven Above, Suzhou, and Hangzhou below.* That's how enchanting my homeland was, as wonderful as humans imagined their Heaven on earth could ever be."

Valerius tilted his head to look down on the Healer's silvery crown. His very own Heaven was within reach in the form of one small woman.

And so was his Hell.

Suddenly she grew very still, her shoulders tensing under his gaze.

After a long silence, she said, "Are you ready for me, warrior?"

"Aye," came his deep, abiding answer.

She turned to face him and he did the same, his cheeks turning crimson once more beneath his bronzed skin as her gaze immediately locked upon his raging erection.

Hesitantly, she reached up to flatten her palms against his ribcage, and his muscles jumped in reaction.

He didn't know whether he would ever get used to being touched. Never mind being touched so intimately. But he vowed he would not reveal his inner battle to her, not let his demons tarnish the bond they shared.

"You body is ready but your mind is not," she said quietly, spearing him with her insight. "I can see the aura of anguish and pain around you, every time I am near, every time I touch you. Will you ever tell me why?"

She raised her eyes to his as she asked.

Mutely, he shook his head. It would horrify her to know his past, the filth that he'd lived with, the monster that he'd been.

And in some ways, still was. He was good at only one thing: killing.

She bent forward and pressed the softest kiss to his sternum, like the flutter of butterfly wings, so soft he barely felt the touch. Involuntarily, he leaned slightly into her, his swollen, aching manhood grazing the middle of her stomach. For the first time, he yearned for more. This was Rain, after all.

His Rain.

She sighed deeply and breathed him in, her hands moving to clasp behind his back. She buried her face in his chest and muffled out, "Don't tempt me please. Just knowing that you are mine for the next thirty days is temptation enough. But I will resist for now. We cannot Mate until you are ready."

I am ready, he wanted to respond. Or at least, as ready as he would ever be.

As if hearing his unspoken words, she retorted, "You will not be ready until you let go of your pain. When you trust me enough to share your burden, that is when you will truly be ready."

"But the Nourishment," Valerius protested, feeling panicked and hurt that she was effectively rejecting him.

She smiled a soothing smile. "Your blood I will gladly take, my Consort. As for your body..."

She took her arms away and stepped back until they were no longer touching.

"We will ease into the intimacy slowly," she stated in a firm tone, offering no room for argument. "I want you to enjoy our union as much as I will."

Before he could protest further, she took his hand in a gentle clasp and led him to the gigantic, canopied, Asian style bed in the center of the chamber. She pulled back the silk coverlet and crawled beneath, white robes and all, almost getting lost in the fluffy mattress and mountainous pillows.

She pulled on his hand and tugged him into the bed with her, his much larger and heavier body making a dent that made her roll into him like a magnet attracted to its mate.

She curved her clothed body along his naked one, fitting against his side seamlessly, and draped a slender pale arm over his belly as he lay on his back, stiff and unmoving.

"Does it pain you much when I touch you like this?" she asked as she reached over his torso for his hand on the other side.

It seemed the most natural thing in the world for her to entwine their fingers and settle their clasped hands back on his belly.

"No," Valerius replied gruffly, and surprised himself to realize that it was the truth. It felt right to have her beside him, holding him. For the first time in his long life he felt cared for, even cherished.

"When you were human, did many women hold you thus?" She asked on a whisper, sounding shy.

"No," he answered, his jaw clenching against the memories. He squeezed his eyes tightly shut as if to blot them out.

Unaware of the battle he waged within himself, Rain pursued her curiosity.

"And have you had many lovers?"

At his silence, she expounded, "Was there someone special in your human life? Is that why you can't bear to be touched by another now?"

It was so far from reality Valerius almost laughed. But then the laughter would turn to sobs, and she would look upon him as one would pity the unhinged.

"No," he replied finally, getting control of himself, "there was no one."

At least, not in the tender capacity to which she referred.

Distracted by his own thoughts, he barely noticed when she pulled his hand closer, feeling only the slightest sting when her fangs sank into the vein in his wrist.

But when she began to draw from him, his body came fully awake, jarring his mind back to the present.

His heavy cock bobbed insistently against the silk coverlet, and the air was again infused with his fragrance, stronger and spicier than before.

A burning sensation filled him and drove his hips off the bed. Involuntarily he began to rotate and nudge, his buttocks tightening in time with her methodical pulls on his vein.

He felt as if he were dangling over the edge of a precipice, afraid to take the final leap yet inevitably drawn to the yawning unknown. His penis throbbed and shuddered as if milked by an invisible hand. His pre-cum seeped out of the slit at the head and trailed down the hot rigid length in continuous flow as if his cock were weeping.

"Please," he begged, though he knew not for what.

He'd never asked anything of anyone. Never put himself in such a vulnerable position. But he had no pride in this moment. He was utterly slain by her gentleness.

Answering his plea, she let go of his wrist and licked the wound closed, then shifted downwards so that she lay across his lower body like a sleepy kitten. Her soft hands took hold of his penis and she diligently licked at the fluids that had seeped out, adding her saliva to the tantalizing wetness engulfing the most private part of him.

When her lips finally closed over the swollen head, his back arched high off the bed and a low groan vibrated through his system.

She was suckling him more gently than the night of the Rite, almost reverently. His entire body strained under her ministrations, the muscles in his neck popping in stark relief as he threw his head back into the pillows.

It was not enough, he wanted to shout.

Do it harder, faster. Milk him dry.

But the words wouldn't form, and his power of speech degenerated into animalistic sounds, deep moans and low growls.

The sounds of someone desperate.

The sounds of someone in pain.

Still she softly drew upon him, pausing once in a while to swipe her tongue meticulously around the fat, engorged head. She cradled him like a babe with her bottle, teasing his most sensitive flesh with tiny sucks interspersed with fleeting kisses. Then she would alter the rhythm with deep, soulful pulls and attend to the sacs below.

Valerius writhed helplessly in the bed, his sweat dampening the sheets, all twisted from his struggles.

"Rain!" he managed to call out through a long, deep groan, his voice breaking.

But instead of giving him what he needed, she sighed and pulled away, gathering herself up to a sitting position astride his lower stomach just above his groin.

"I cannot give you the release you crave before you are ready for it yourself, warrior," she explained, licking her lips as if to savor every last drop of him.

Her hands enfolded the sides of his face, and to his utter self-contempt, her thumbs rubbed away the moisture that had leaked from the corners of his eyes.

"Don't be ashamed," she admonished gently, again seeming to read his thoughts. "This experience is not easily endured. Your body is torn between two extremes. On the one hand, it is triggered to Serve me."

She demonstrated by sweeping her hand lightly along the length of his now intensely painful erection.

"On the other hand, we are not truly mated, and your body knows I cannot reciprocate what it gives me. To some Consorts, orgasm is beyond their reach though there are many ways to satisfy me."

She lay her head down on his still shuddering chest, over his rapidly beating heart and sighed, "just the scent of you can make me wet. The taste of you can make me come."

She guided his hand to the place between her thighs and he was stunned at the drenched heat he encountered there, wetting through her robes and the skin of her inner thighs.

"Some?" he barely managed to say, distracted by the exquisite softness beneath his palm.

She nodded slightly and murmured, "Some other Consorts find the balance within themselves and can achieve release. I think it's a sort of guilt they overcome because they feel as if they are betraying their future Mates by having intimacies with the Healer, though these relations are sanctioned by the Goddess as Pure and Good."

Valerius did not have that particular guilt. His inner battle was far more gruesome.

Determinedly putting aside his own needs, he focused his attention on Rain, concentrating on the softness that rested trustingly in his palm.

"How do I please you," he whispered, embarrassed by his own deplorable lack of knowledge and skill.

Rain smiled her Cheshire smile, keeping her face pressed against the warmth of his chest.

"Two thousand years made you a born-again virgin, warrior?"

A wave of pain washed over him as Valerius recalled the day he'd lost his virginity. Two thousand years was not long enough.

"That's perfectly fine by me," Rain continued, urging her hips against his hand in a voluptuous undulation.

"I like feeling as if I were your first."

You are my first, Valerius thought. *And my last.*

He slowly pulled her robes up until he could feel her naked skin and cupped his palm over her drenched core.

She sighed deeply and moaned a little, the sound tickling his senses like kitten fur. He shifted his hand to hold her more fully, instinctively positioning his thumb at the apex of her sex. She made a little mewling sound and used her hand to teach him how to please her. As he rubbed his thumb gently across her pleasure spot just the way she wanted, she moved her hand away.

Her breath quickened against his chest, and he could feel her heart beat in sync. Her small hands reached for his erection again and held him covetously, squeezing up and down the thick, velvet covered shaft of steel in time to the rhythm his thumb made over her clitoris.

His own breathing became increasingly labored once more, and he desperately wanted to get closer. He wrapped his other arm around her body and held her more tightly against his chest. When that wasn't enough, he inserted one long finger, then two, into her wet core and was momentarily satisfied by the long moan of pleasure his action elicited.

She was so swollen and tight inside, even the width of two fingers seemed too much, but slowly he felt her body accommodate the intrusion, relax and accept him. His thumb stroked gently on her nub while the pads of his fingers found the swollen hardness inside of her. As he rubbed with more pressure, both inside and out, she undulated her hips with encouragement.

His body tensed abruptly in anticipation just before hers tightened and spasmed around his hand. She gasped softly as her release washed over them both, the scent of her passion filling the air around them, mingling with his own.

His breath strangled on a groan in response, his cock jerking powerfully within her grasp, though his own release yet eluded him. He ground his teeth together to prevent from shouting at the excruciating pain as his entire body locked and tensed through her orgasm, becoming one giant muscle cramp.

Slowly, they let go of each other, but she remained curled against his chest.

"Thank you," she said when her heartbeat calmed, and placed a tender kiss on his throat.

As the pain gradually subsided, Valerius felt he should be the one thanking her. For no one had ever shared such an intimacy with him.

Not like this. Never like this.

When her pleasure became his own. When her radiant goodness overcame his nightmares, fears, and centuries-old pain.

She was his miracle, he thought as her breathing evened out in slumber.

She was his savior...

Sometime before 200 B.C. Outskirts of Rome.

Valerius yanked with all his might on the chains that secured him against the prison wall.

Though his entire body was one large, gaping wound from the rigors of battle a few hours before, he willed his strength not to leave him, not until he got free and slit the throats of the fuckers who did this to him.

Only a few hours ago, his father was still among the living, badly injured but breathing. He'd half dragged, half carried the aged gladiator from the bloody arena down to the pits below, the crowds' cheers still ringing loudly above ground.

Valerius could have cared less about his victory. All he wanted was to get his father to the healers. With every step, every trickle of blood, he felt his father's life bleed slowly away.

But when he returned to the pits he was waylaid by their master, a bald, ruddy man with beady eyes and double chins.

"You ingrate!" the odious little man erupted, striking Valerius with his brass-knuckled fist.

Taken aback by the unprovoked assault, Valerius staggered off balance and almost dropped his father hard onto the dirt ground.

"Take him!" the master ordered, pointing to Valerius' burden.

Four armed soldiers came forth and pried the fallen gladiator from Valerius' grasp, knocking him back with the blunt hilt of their swords.

"He needs a healer, my lord," Valerius urged, thinking that perhaps their master's displeasure, though he had no clue as to its cause, extended only to him, that his father would be spared.

"He needs to fulfill his bargain," the enraged slave owner hissed, then gestured to the two soldiers holding the unconscious gladiator.

Before Valerius could comprehend what was happening, one of the soldiers held his father upright while the other bared his blade and slit it in one clean strike across the gladiator's throat.

"Nooo!"

Valerius rammed forward with enough force to escape the clutches of the two guards restraining him, but the soldier with the unsheathed blade turned quickly and swiped it in a horizontal arc to block Valerius' momentum.

The blade cut a long gash across the boy's stomach and he lost his footing, giving the two guards behind him the opportunity to catch him around the shoulders and twist his arms behind his back, restraining him once again.

Valerius watched horrified as the soldier holding his father dragged him by the feet deeper into the pits, presumably to be dumped in the bin with all the other dead bodies.

"Why?" he cried, staring after his sire and falling to his knees.

"Why?" the nasty little man echoed. "Why?! Because he is supposed to be dead! Because we made a deal! It was supposed to be his final battle, a glorious battle like no other, and he was supposed to die a glorious death!"

The master rounded on Valerius and grabbed his chin, forcing the boy to face him.

"But you, you little maggot, you ruined all my well-laid plans with that heroic rescue of yours. Do you know how much gold I lost because of you? I'd bet the entire enterprise on this battle!"

"But the crowd cheered," Valerius whispered, tears of bewilderment and frustration and anguish filling his eyes, "they approved."

"To what end!" the master thundered. "It is all a game! And. You. Sabotaged. My. Hand!"

The master punctuated each screech with a swinging fist against Valerius' head.

Then he bent down to the slave boy's level until his bloated visage was not one inch from Valerius' face.

"You stupid, stupid little shit," the master spat, practically foaming at the mouth like a mad dog.

"If you let your pater die like we planned, the profits would have been enough to free you both, and your pathetic womenfolk. But now, oh no, now you're going to PAY!" the master shouted with quivering vengeance.

"I'm going to sell your ass to the highest bidder, and I don't care if they use you for a potty urn. I'm going to whore your mother and sister out. They can kiss their peaceful little farm life goodbye."

Valerius struggled anew and tried to break free, but the pressure on his arms behind his back was unrelenting, forcing him to stay on the ground.

The master inhaled deeply and straightened, appearing to find some small semblance of calm, his rage somewhat subsiding.

"Take him to the dungeons," he ordered the guards, "and see that he's in too much pain to even think of getting free."

The guards dragged Valerius away, chained him to the wall of a square, corner cell and proceeded to rain pain upon his weakened body, with their fists, their boots, their daggers. They knew what they were doing, for they left him no mortal wounds, just enough to put him out of commission for a time.

Now, Valerius leaned his head back and closed his eyes. He knew his father would never have agreed to his own death. He had too much fight left in him, too much life yet to live. And he loved his wife too much to leave her. Loved his daughter.

His son.

Valerius blocked out his anguish and tried to focus on the immediate future. He must break free before the master acted upon his threats against Valerius' family.

He must protect them at all cost.

A sennight, perhaps more, passed while Valerius bided his time and rebuilt his strength in his windowless cell.

His keepers kept him alive on broth, stale bread, and occasionally, moldy cheese and half rotted fruit, the rubbish that the servants threw out at the end of the day. But he ate everything they tossed at him and worked to store up a reserve, forcing his body to absorb every last morsel.

During this time, the master brought various people to look him over, staying true to his words to sell Valerius to the highest bidder.

There were slave traders who poked and prodded him, but deemed him too scrawny to get much hard labor out of. He was still a boy growing into his own body, his lanky frame and long limbs dangling awkwardly from the chains.

There were more polished versions of the traders who procured personal slaves for wealthy patrician households. But they reared back in aversion when he bared his teeth and emitted threatening animalistic growls. Too unrefined and feral to be a personal slave, they decided.

With every failed showing, Valerius received a vicious beating for denying the master the payment he felt due.

And so Valerius bided his time, plotting his escape, teaching the bones of his hands and feet through repeated, painful exercise to bend and contort in ways they never had before.

Then one day, just as he was almost able to wriggle loose of one manacle, the heavy wooden door to his cell opened with a bang. In marched the master with a team of four heavily muscled and armed guards.

This was new, Valerius thought with a tilt of his head. Usually the entourage of brutes and the shower of meaty fists followed visits from prospective buyers, not before.

And then the guards parted to reveal a man and a woman, both expensively dressed in the finest patrician robes.

Valerius could see in the dim light afforded by the torches in the prison hall that the woman was tall and blonde, the man of an equal height, but dark and stocky. They seemed to glide above the bloodstained dirt ground as they stepped lightly forward, their calculating eyes riveted on his person.

"So this is the boy," the master all but spat out in disgust, "you can try him out before you pay if that'll seal the deal."

Valerius raised his head, alerted to the malicious tone in the master's voice.

The woman stepped closer to her quarry and gestured for one of the guards to bring forth a torch.

When the firelight illuminated Valerius' face, she gasped with delight, "Oh my, but I do believe this one has promise beneath all that grime, my husband."

The man moved closer as well and gazed upon Valerius with the same avaricious gleam in his eyes, "You may be quite right, my dear, you have a discerning eye indeed."

Valerius bared his teeth and growled his most ferocious growl, but the woman only laughed behind her hand.

"Oh he has spirit, this young one, how fun he'll be to break."

The man nodded in agreement and smiled slyly at his partner.

"Shall we give him a trial run and see if he lives up to his promise?"

The woman seemed to enjoy that idea immensely, for she gave the man a wet, smacking kiss on the mouth.

A bead of sweat trailed down Valerius' spine as deadly foreboding descended upon him. But he had little time to dwell on that sharp stab of fear before a wide belt wrapped around his throat and cut off all the air.

When he came to, he found himself laid flat on his back on a wooden bench, his legs spread apart on either side, bent at the knees, his feet flat upon the ground. He was held down by a guard at each shoulder and a third at his head, holding it to the bench with the belt that was still clenched around his neck.

And he was naked.

Completely and utterly vulnerable.

Valerius began to struggle with everything he had, but the guards held fast and the cinch around his neck weakened him the more he fought. Breathing heavily, he could only watch, helpless, from the corner of his eye as the woman approached him with a jar of something pungent in her hands.

She sat upon the bench just below the juncture of his thighs and proceeded to spread the slimy stuff she spooned from the jar over his genitals.

Valerius was mortified.

What was she doing?! Why was she touching him there?

He'd only discovered what his penis was capable of at the age of twelve when it stood straight up from his groin one hot morning. He'd tended to it shyly and furtively since then, but his small pleasures were painfully private, though he suspected his father knew what he was doing when he stayed too long in the bath hall.

This woman had no right to touch him there. He'd rather be gutted with a spatha than bear her hands on him.

Valerius struggled anew and tried to kick out at her, but the choke hold on his throat grew tighter and his efforts quickly faded with exhaustion.

She held his penis with both hands and began to stroke and squeeze its entire length, harder and faster until the thing grew enormous and swollen and painfully erect.

Valerius could barely countenance what was happening. He didn't want this!

But his body betrayed him. The ointment she'd rubbed over his genitals was stinging like a fiery rash, but it made his penis elongate and swell despite the horror that froze his mind.

"Look at that," he heard the man say as the patrician stepped closer to view his wife's progress. "Praise the gods but he's a fine young stallion. Have you ever seen the like?"

"Happily, I have not, my love," the woman tittered in response, "I can't wait to try him out."

Valerius heard a throat clearing just beyond his personal hell.

"Just remember, you break him, you pay double," the master put in, then abruptly silenced when the man threw him a pouch of coins.

"For the trial use," the patrician said, then turned back to his wife, now gathering up the folds of her stola and positioning herself above Valerius, "this one is worth it."

As she grabbed his penis and rubbed it against her nether region, Valerius felt sick at the fluids that seeped from her body onto his. Before he could brace himself, she came down fully astride him, taking his length deep within her body.

"Aaaahhh," she cried, then awkwardly rammed her hips against his as if to get a better seat.

"He's so large he barely fits. Just... Just a little more. Oh gods, I can't even take all of him inside!" she laughed hysterically, overjoyed.

After a few more bungling attempts, she seemed to find her stride, though Valerius could feel the tip of his penis bending at an agonizing angle within her. Every movement she made hurt him terribly.

She groaned in ecstasy and began to ride upon him, squeezing his flesh and slapping her moist thighs jarringly against his hips, moving up and down, forward and back.

Valerius felt his throat close around the tears that threatened and struggled to breathe even as he wished for death to blot out the misery and humiliation.

After a long, bruising ride, she stiffened suddenly and let out a keening wail, her inner muscles clenching painfully around his erection.

Was it over? Valerius dared to hope. He breathed more easily as she clambered inelegantly off of him, straightening her robes in the process.

"Well," she said shakily, "that was certainly worth every last dinar in that pouch."

She smoothed her hair away from her face, the knot at her nape having come loose from her jaunty ride.

"My turn, then, my love," her partner said in a covetous voice, as he threw a second bag of coins to the master's awaiting hands.

Valerius was pulled up by his hair and shoved roughly to face the wall where he had been chained for the duration of his imprisonment. He could barely hold himself upright much less try to fight off the guards' restraining hands. His knees buckled and he would have fallen if not for the manacles they secured once again around his wrists, holding him up in a half stance.

Again, heavy hands held him in place flush against the dungeon wall. His legs were kicked apart and his ankles secured, until he stood spread like a virgin sacrifice before the gates of Tartarus. There was some rustling and jangling and what sounded like a coin belt falling to the ground.

And then Valerius felt the man's hands clamp upon his hips a moment before something blunt and hard stabbed into his body.

Valerius bit down hard on his tongue to keep the whimper of pain from escaping. He would not let them see him break, he vowed.

He would never give them the satisfaction of knowing his pain!

The stabbing continued at a steady pace, harder, deeper, faster. The man's rutting hips pushed Valerius into the wall, the force of his movements scraping Valerius' naked torso against the rough, jagged bricks, leaving scratches, cuts and bruises on the boy's chest, stomach, thighs, and even his still swollen erection.

After what seemed like an interminable period of time, when Valerius had grown numb and disoriented from the abuse, the man heaved one final push and bellowed his release.

Stomach acid gurgled up Valerius' esophagus as he felt the man's filthy cum jettison into him.

Amidst the heavy panting and the woman's fervent whispers, the master threw down his demand, "Five hundred gold pieces, and you can use him to your little black hearts' content. He's young, just over fourteen. He's got a long useful life ahead of him."

"Done," the man said without hesitation. "Shall we retire to your receiving chambers to sort out the details of the transaction?"

"Come right this way. And while you're here, I'd like to show you a few other morsels..." The master's voice faded away, along with the footsteps of the guards and the Roman nobles.

Valerius dangled lifelessly from his chains, his head bowed, his breathing coming and going in broken gasps. Blood and fluids trickled down his inner thighs, as the tears he'd held back so bravely leaked out of the corners of his eyes.

Silently he sobbed out his pain and degradation. Though he tried to be the man his father taught him to be, though he fought against their breaking of him, right this moment he wanted to curl into a small ball and hug his brutalized body to himself.

Just for this moment, he allowed himself to mourn.

For his murdered father. For his unprotected mother and sister. And for the innocence he would never reclaim.

Chapter Six

New York City, NY.

Seth Tremaine followed two strikingly attractive females in form-fitting white tuxedos through a hidden corridor leading to a high-security elevator that could have blended completely into the interior walls of the Chrysler Building had one not known it was there.

Entering the narrow space with his two accompaniments, Seth looked neither to his left nor to his right, keeping his gaze straight ahead.

He did notice, however, that there were no buttons and no floor signals on the inside of the elevator, just shiny, unmarked steel casing surrounding the passengers on all sides with three overhead halogen lights. And no one had made any movement or sound, yet the elevator began climbing up as soon as the single sliding door closed before its three occupants.

As the reinforced steel box rose upwards, Seth did not need floor indicators to tell him they were rising from the sixty-sixth floor towards the no-public-access Chrysler Crown.

Back in the mid nineteen hundreds, there used to be a snazzy Cloud Club that occupied three floors from the sixty-sixth to the sixty-eighth, but it closed down in nineteen seventy-nine due to various reasons, not the least of which was that the upper-most floors of the building had never been designed architecturally for luxury and entertainment. There were some half-hearted attempts to revive the establishment or something like it, but all met failure mysteriously. There also used to be a viewing gallery on the seventy-first floor, but that too closed to the public in nineteen forty-five.

Seth had a feeling that the destination of this elevator was going to exceed all expectations.

Soon enough, the polished metal door slid open soundlessly and revealed a breathtaking view. A magnificently opulent, gigantic Great Hall rose thirty feet from the floor to meet at the intricately decorated point of a vaulted dome, surrounded on all sides by floor to ceiling triangular windows, alternating with ribbed and riveted stainless-steel cladding, radiating outwards in the world-famous sunburst pattern.

Someone, Seth suspected his host, had managed to combine the vertical space of three floors into one and spruced the place up with an ingenious interior decorator without anyone the wiser. That someone, he also suspected, was the true owner of the Chrysler Building, though public records assigned that honor to the Abu Dhabi Investment Council—ninety percent of the ownership, anyway.

The two female adornments at his side closely escorted him into the massive, brightly lit hall, and he noticed that the floor beneath his feet was made of Italian marble. There was no clutter of ostentatious statues, fountains or paintings to distract from the elegant beauty of the architecture itself, but what embellishments were there were of the highest quality and taste.

As they approached the far end of the hall, he could see his host sitting on a well-appointed throne, Chinese in style, but not in construction. Pure gold furniture would surely clash with the rest of the cool, modern décor. Around the throne sat a wide circle of lounges and deep-seated sofas, all black and white with splashes of red in the silk pillows or detailing. Lying, sitting on, loosely standing by and reclining on the floor before those luxurious pieces of furniture were a dozen or so scantily clad, highly sexualized, outrageously good-looking young men and women.

His host was holding court, apparently.

Or perhaps it was just another day in the life of a one-thousand-eight-hundred-year-old Vampire Queen.

His escorts brought him into the circle of dissolute blood-suckers, stopping a few feet before their queen.

Seth could feel a dozen pairs of curious black eyes roaming up and down his body, as if to strip him bare to their voracious view. He could also sense the heightened state of their sexual arousal, as well as hear it, when a couple of females and even a male, began to touch themselves and moan loudly.

"Silence," the regal Vampire Queen commanded in a soft voice that instantly muted all sounds from her court.

Then she regarded her visitor without words, casually sitting back in her throne, a wine glass dangling precariously from her fingertips. Red wine, of course.

But Seth wouldn't bet it was actually of the grape variety.

The Consul returned the vampire's steady gaze and conducted a thorough assessment of his own.

No one would argue that Jade Cicada, as she was known since her rebirth, was not a sublimely beautiful woman. To every race, to every breed, human and non-humans alike, she was spell-binding.

Her large, almond-shaped eyes tilted slightly at the corners in that mysterious Asian way, long, straight lashes fringing both upper and lower lids, delicate frames for the startling deep blue irises and large black pupils within.

She had a classic oval face, with high cheekbones and a pointy little chin. Wisps of reddish-black hair caressed her temples and beside her small ears while the rest of the thick, silky mass was gathered intricately into braids on top of her head, most of the length falling freely down her shoulders and back.

If his knowledge of Chinese history served him well, Seth guessed that her coiffure dated back to third century China, late Eastern Han or Three Kingdoms period.

Like Seth's twin escorts, Jade was also dressed in a body-hugging ensemble, though the slightly transparent silk flowed over her skin in caressing folds. She was covered from head to toe by the simple long black dress, yet Seth felt his breath quicken as if she were lounging before him entirely naked.

The semi-transparent silk slid teasingly over her curves, and though she was slender in her limbs and waist, her breasts, hips and buttocks were generously round. She wore nothing beneath the delicate black sheath.

He could see the pointed tips of her high breasts, the aureoles large and dark. He could see the tantalizing groove that bisected her taut, but infinitely flexible torso as she sat with her upper body curved to one side, her lower body curved to the other in a voluptuous S.

And then she shifted her thighs as if opening herself further to his perusal, encouraging him to continue. When he gazed upon the neat dark triangle there and just a hint of pink at the juncture, his eyes flew back to hers.

She smiled enticingly, knowingly at him, and he fought to break the spell.

For Goddess sake, he was known broadly as the Pure One's "Monk."

Not that he was any more self-controlled than the rest of them, for they all had to be by the Sacred Laws. But he'd known the love and passion of a good woman when he was human. And he'd given all of himself to her in return. When he died, and was reborn, he had always loved her still.

He'd watched his human wife grow old from afar, watched his small daughter grow into a lovely young lady, marry a kind, diligent man, and raise a family of her own. He'd watched their progeny come into this world and leave it as the ages went by, and he'd protected and guided them from the shadows as much as he could.

He was simply not interested in finding a Mate. And he loved his wife too much to even look, much less stir, at the charms of another woman.

But today, as he beheld the Vampire Queen, he felt himself stir.

More than just stir.

He was veritably roasting in the flames of desire.

*** *** *** ***

Valerius awakened to find his body curled closely against Rain's like a living, heat radiating cocoon.

Sometime in the night, after he relaxed to the sound of her even breathing, after exhaustion from her feeding had finally overcome him, he'd drifted into a dreamless sleep and unconsciously tucked her body closer to his, wrapping himself around her as if he wanted to absorb her into himself.

Also during the night, her filmy white robes had shifted and her bare backside was now pressing firmly and tantalizingly into his groin, giving him a clue for the source of his raging erection.

And then there were the invisible hands that caressed him all over, the culprits, in fact, that teased him painfully awake this early morning.

He blinked hard, trying to dispel the last vestiges of slumber, and looked down at himself, trying to ascertain whether he'd dreamed the silken caresses that set him aflame.

Her hair.

Flowing white tendrils curved this way and that all over his naked body, meandering like languid serpents seeking the comfort of heat in the cool, autumn dawn. Some tresses pooled over his chest and biceps, tickling his nipples and throat. Other tresses slid impishly over his stomach and thighs, trailing along his hips bones lovingly to wrap around his swollen manhood in a satiny glove.

There they tended him with gentle pressure, punctuated with voluptuous twists that milked him slowly. He could see the transparent strands surge with the milky glow of his Nourishment as it flowed through the silken needles to vitalize the Healer's body.

"They have a mind of their own sometimes," the warm female in his arms sighed sleepily. "Sorry about that."

Slowly, the silvery white tresses left his body, lingering over his crotch as if sad to depart, obediently wove themselves into a fishtail braid and curled like a chastised child against the Healer's breast.

"I-" Valerius swallowed hard and cleared his throat.

Goddess above, would he ever get used to these intimacies?

"I would Serve you before you start the day, if it pleases you," he finally said in a low, husky rumble.

Haltingly, painstakingly, he guided one of her hands to his swollen flesh and wrapped her fingers around him. Even though he'd brought her touch himself, his body still shuddered involuntarily from head to toe as a wave of inner pain washed over him.

She gave him a long, lazy squeeze, but then took her hand away, taking his hand instead and bringing their entwined fingers to her lips, kissing his knuckles lightly.

Curling her backside deeper into his groin, she sighed in contentment and said, "There will be no Service this morning, warrior, you need to recover your strength. And besides, my misbehaving tresses have already stolen shamelessly from you and I feel better than I've felt in ages."

Valerius could feel her smile against the back of his hand, and his entire being tingled with something akin to pleasure in response. To have fulfilled her, even for a brief period of time, made him feel a hundred times the man he had ever been.

"When must you begin your hunt, Protector?" she asked, a worried note in her voice.

"I am not to hunt today," Valerius replied, a slow flush heating up his face. "The Circlet advised that I should attend to your needs until you are able to build a sufficient reserve."

Her smile spread wider and he blushed harder.

"The Royal Council is most considerate," Rain demurred. "Far be it for me to gainsay them."

She twisted around in his arms until they were facing each other, one of her hands holding his stubbly cheek and the other still in an affectionate clasp with his.

"But I am satisfied for now, *airen*," she smiled a dazzling smile at him. "You have been everything I ever needed. I am humbled by your sacrifice."

Valerius started to shake his head, but she stopped him with a kiss to his nose.

"Don't deny how difficult this whole ordeal is to you. We both know the truth. I don't care anymore why you decided to apply to Serve me. Whether because you felt indebted or because you're just plain heroic. I'm so happy you're here."

She scooched closer and threw a slender leg possessively over his hips.

"You can't know how delighted I am to have you as mine own for this brief period of time."

She rubbed her thumb tenderly over his sharp cheekbone.

"I've wanted you since the first time we met, you know."

Valerius blinked at her confession. His heart pounded faster as her words flowed forth.

"You are the most beautiful man I've ever beheld. Beauty is in the eye of the beholder, and wow, you more than meet all my aesthetic requirements. But the Healer in me wanted you for another reason."

She softly nuzzled his face with hers, the kittenish touch startlingly as arousing to him as her lips around his cock.

She met his gaze again and said in a saddened whisper, "You are one large, open wound. I can practically feel the pain and torment radiating from your body. How can I possibly resist wanting to heal that wound. It is the purpose of my very existence."

Valerius dropped his gaze and felt himself withdraw, even as his body stayed still.

"Don't hide from me, Valerius."

At her use of his name his eyes flew to hers once more.

She smiled her Mona Lisa smile and said, "I can't make promises, but I truly feel that this union will help heal us both. You provide me Nourishment. Let me take care of you in return. Let me love you for a little while."

Valerius' breath hitched and his heart stuttered.

How could he possibly deny her? But it wasn't enough. Her kindness and generosity wasn't nearly enough. He wanted...

Goddess above, he wanted Eternity.

"So," she said, oblivious to his inner turmoil, "this morning I shall serve you. You must be hungry. It will only take me a little while to prepare some traditional Chinese dim sum."

Before he could tighten his embrace to keep her with him, she bounced off the bed in a flurry of silk and skipped lightly to the adjoining chamber like a spritely water nymph.

Soon thereafter, he heard the water run and pots and pans clanging, the sounds strangely soothing in their domesticity.

No woman, since his human age of fourteen-years-old, had ever made him a meal.

Then he heard Rain's voice humming a bright, cheerful melody, and he gazed at the living mural.

Just as she'd promised, the scenery had shifted from night to dawn, with a vibrant pinkish-orange disk rising behind green mountains, playing hide and seek with curls of clouds that drifted past. The songbirds seemed to chirp along with their enchantress as they flitted across the pale blue skies reflecting over a glistening lake.

And slowly, surely, Valerius felt his soul begin to heal.

*** *** *** ***

Leonidas entered the abandoned railroad tunnel with arm raised over his shoulder, ready to unsheathe his *makhaira*, one of the cross swords secured against his back, at the slightest scent of danger.

The General Alexandros followed closely behind, his extra long *sagaris* axe at the ready.

They were some fifty miles north of Boston city, in a remote suburb that met in the middle of three different counties.

In the early nineteen hundreds, there used to be a thriving town built around the rails which transported manufactured goods to the south, but presently the town center consisted of one main street the length of two stop lights. There wasn't even a McDonalds nearby.

But the body count in the surrounding towns was taking a sharp rise.

Their tracking of the Horde had led them here, and if their sources were right, deep in the tunnel they would discover a secret labyrinth that would take them to an underground cavern where as many as a dozen vampires slept during the day.

A Horde of this size was unusual. When vampires became well-organized, they formed Hives, or structured societies led by one vampire queen. Rogue vampires seldom traveled in large packs as the position of *alpha* was highly contested in the absence of a natural leader, but they could still form groups for the convenience of hunting.

In the Elite's experience, Hordes were typically no larger than six to eight vampires, and even then they tended to split off into smaller factions of two to four. A dozen rogue vampires resting in one place was extremely rare. Unheard of.

As Leonidas and Alexandros found the entrance to the labyrinth and made their way down the narrow passage that took them deeper and deeper underground, their senses were intensely alert, for both males felt that something was not quite right.

At the end of the maze, they entered a large cavern, just as the source had described. Dim disks of halogen lights placed in nooks of stalagmites provided some illumination, while dragon-teeth stalactites descended sharply from the ceiling, the combination casting eerie shadows on the cavern walls. The air was devoid of wind and sound, save a methodical dripping of water.

And there they were, twelve large sarcophaguses, scattered at different angles across the damp floor.

The two Pure males exchanged a silent look and each took position beside one sarcophagus, weapons raised. As they slowly and as quietly as possible tipped the lids, what they found sent shivers of shock and wariness down their spines.

Both beds were empty, but for two piles of dead vampire ashes. Someone had taken care of business before them.

But before they could check the remaining beds, the trap they'd walked into became all too clear.

*** *** *** ***

Thank the Goddess Aella was her Elite guard today, Sophia thought as she hustled to her second class.

Aella she didn't need to hide for fear the folks on campus would look at her askance. The Amazon looked as young as a college student herself, and she even signed up to audit the classes Sophia was taking so she could sit in class with her on her days to guard the young queen.

Aella was the closest thing to a girlfriend Sophia had.

Sophia had always been too in awe of Rain and Eveline, both because of their ethereal beauty and because of their mind-blowing Gifts. And Ayelet was too much like a parent.

Aella, however, looked, and mostly acted, as if they were of an age. Aella was the coolest friend—funny, trendy, loved to talk about boys—except when she performed her role as one of the Elite in formal Royal Zodiac gatherings. Then she got all solemn and Xena-Warrior-Princess-like.

To see her with Sophia, one would never guess she was almost two thousand five hundred years old. Sophia also liked to show her friend off, like small kids did with shiny new toys to gain popularity and attention.

Though it didn't do Sophia any favors walking beside a guy's wet-dream-cross between Rosie Huntington and Candice Swanepoel.

They were chatting and laughing as they entered the classroom, and Sophia didn't notice a pair of chocolate brown eyes tracing her every move.

They found a seat towards the back of the lecture hall, large enough to seat fifty or sixty students. But before they even sat their butts down, three upperclassmen, by the looks of them, already formed a tight circle around Aella, shutting Sophia completely out.

"Hey gorgeous," the tallest of the three greeted, hitching a hip against the edge of their table.

Sophia rolled her eyes at the asinine opening.

"Are you one of those Victoria Secret supermodels?"

"Hey ass-wipe," Aella responded in the same tone, "Did anyone ever tell you the quickest way to piss off a girl is to pretend her best friend doesn't exist? Now get out of my personal space and go harass a female in your own orbit, because I'm so far out of your league I'm in a different universe."

To complete the shutdown, Aella glared until all three boys paled at her lethal gaze and moved away with a lot less swagger than their approach.

Sophia grinned and sighed reverently, "I love you, Aella."

"Back at you babe," the Amazon returned with a cheeky smile.

"But you know," Sophia said quietly, more seriously, "you don't have to dismiss guys just because they ignore me. I'm used to it, I'm OK."

"Sophia," Aella said in that tone that warned Sophia of an impending lecture, "how many times do I have to tell you that you're a beautiful girl? No, don't shake your head at me, missy. I'm not being biased because I'm your friend."

Aella leaned in to whisper, "Or because you're my queen."

"You have all the makings of a stunning beauty, but you just have to grow into it first. I hate it when you put yourself down."

Sophia shrugged, knowing argument was futile.

Instead she said, "Well, there was this one guy who did pay attention to me."

Aella leaned forward on her fist in conspiracy.

"Do tell."

"You're not going to lecture me about no dating and no boyfriends on pain of death, et cetera?" Sophia mumbled warily.

Aella did a slow blink, her more refined version of rolling of the eyes.

"I don't need to lecture you on things you already know well. I trust that you know what you're doing and you're level-headed enough to not take it too far. And I'm hardly one to tell you to eschew having a little fun with boys you like. I've had countless 'boyfriends' over the years, and believe me, I've figured out every way there is to toe the One Sacred Law without actually breaking it. Hell, I've invented some new ways myself."

Aella grinned broadly at that little boast.

She flicked a finger against Sophia's arm. "So tell me about this brilliant guy with exquisite taste."

"Well," Sophia started, squirming a little in her seat.

"He's hot."

"Promising," Aella encouraged.

"And... and... he's totally hot hot."

Aella gave her a half-pitying look.

"Honey, you didn't get too far beyond that, huh?"

Sophia twirled her hands in the air as if frustrated she couldn't find the words.

"I mean, he's so hot I want to go buy a book on kama sutra and—"

"Hello, Sophia."

At the sound of the velvety male voice, Sophia turned the shade of a boiled lobster.

Without turning around to face the owner of that voice, she made a pained face at Aella and wished the floor would just open up and suck her into a black abyss.

Aella smiled lopsidedly at her teenage queen before raising her eyes to the male who had approached them, standing just behind Sophia's seat.

Giving him a thorough and appreciative once over, Aella said warmly, "Hello."

She then elbowed Sophia none too gently and urged, "Shouldn't you introduce me to your new friend?"

Sophia fantasized for a few more seconds that she was an ostrich and her head was in the sand, then took a deep breath to bolster her confidence and turned to face the "hot hot guy."

"Hullo," she greeted in a small voice and gestured with her hand to her companion. "This is Aella, my best friend since forever. Aella, this is Ere. He's the teaching assistant for this class."

Aella batted her eyes flirtatiously and Sophia could have kicked her, except what would be the point? It wasn't like she had dibs on Ere or anything.

"Nice to meet you, Sophia's friend," Ere said with an affable smile, though his words made clear whom he was focused on.

"May I sit beside you?" he asked Sophia, "you have the best view of the class from here."

Sophia shrugged ungraciously, but Ere didn't seem to take offense and sat down beside her.

Aella widened her eyes like an owl and mouthed to Sophia, "Wow, he's really hot!"

Sophia gave her a look that said "told you so."

Then Aella frowned and poked Sophia with a finger, again mouthing, "Be nice to him."

Sophia decided to ignore that last broadcast and looked straight ahead, trying to focus on the professor as he started the lecture.

Things got a little tamer after that, and Sophia's stiff posture finally began to relax half way into the fifty minute class.

Until she felt Ere's knee brush hers under the table.

Sophia let out a tiny squeak and bumped her knee on the underside of the table in reaction. She darted a glance at Aella and saw her friend shaking her head in disgust.

"Amateur," the Amazon formed with her lips.

Yeah, Sophia thought dejectedly, that about covered it. Right next to "wimp" and "loser."

And then she saw a slip of paper slide a few inches from Ere to her. She picked it up and read, "How do you like the class so far?"

Strangely gladdened by the grade-school note passing, she quickly wrote back, "I love it! I wish Professor McGowan taught a course on ancient Persian history too. But no one in the faculty seems to think it deserves its own full class."

Ere replied, "My Ph.D. thesis is on ancient Persian history, the rise and fall of an empire. Maybe I can share the progress with you sometime if you're interested?"

Sophia was so delighted by the offer she broke her mechanical pencil lead twice before she managed to scribble, "That would be so awesome! Do you need help with research? Cuz I'm pretty good at that."

"I would really appreciate your help," came the reply that gave Sophia the warm fuzzies.

But then she almost fell out of her chair at the next line, "So you think I'm hot, huh?"

The boiled lobster impression was back. If he heard that much, then he would have heard the rest...

Oh, she was so dead. She could probably fry an egg on her face.

She darted a look at her tormenter and saw that he was looking right back at her with a grin so radiant, she felt momentarily blinded.

Carefully averting her eyes again, she spent the next few moments, while the buzzing and echo in her ears from the sonic boom of his beauty subsided, painstakingly folding the notes into halves and fourths and eights and tucking them away into her laptop bag.

And just when she thought her equilibrium had been restored, he wrote her one final note.

"I think you're hot too, Sophia."

It was quite possibly the best day of Sophia's life.

Chapter Seven

Rain brought Valerius with her to work this day, since his agenda was free. She was eager to share the "normal" aspects of her life with him, apart from being the Healer of the Pure Ones.

They decided to walk to her clinic in Chinatown together despite Valerius' protests that she was too weak. Rain loved to walk, and it was too gorgeous an autumn day in Boston not to take every advantage.

Wan'er had already left and would be there to set up ahead of them. As in ages past, it was understood that Rain would see less of her handmaiden during the Phoenix Cycle as Healer and Consort formed their own bond.

Valerius couldn't stop looking at Rain in her civilian clothes.

Because she was so thin and weakened, she needed extra layers to keep her temperature up. This day she chose to wear a white over-sized cashmere and rabbit hair sweater over black skinny jeans and white calf-high gigantic furry boots. Completing her look was a thick, luxurious red scarf, bright blue wool coat, furry white gloves and a matching knitted cap to hide her startling white mane.

She brought to mind a long-haired kitten, and she looked all of twelve years old.

"Let's take Boylston Street and go through the Garden and the Commons," Rain said as they rounded Prudential. "It's my favorite walk in Boston."

"Why?" Valerius asked.

He never took notice of scenery or sights. He had a duty, and everything else was irrelevant. But seeing Rain's obvious enthusiasm, he became curious about the cityscape for the first time.

"Because I love the different architecture you get to see," Rain answered, her face all but hidden by the fuzzy scarf, "the wide sidewalks and the shops, the people in such different sizes, shapes and colors who come and go, the Swan Boats in the little lake, the dogs running around in the park... I just love it. Makes me feel good to be alive."

Listening to her talk, Valerius felt her joy vicariously and couldn't help a smile that dimpled his cheek.

Rain paused in her jaunty steps and stuck a furry gloved finger down the groove in his cheek.

"My, but your smile is breathtaking, "she exclaimed, "you should do it more often."

And before Valerius could feel self-conscious, she grabbed his hand in hers and took off again.

Holding hands with Rain, strolling down a bustling city street, like any number of couples who passed them along the way, was an experience Valerius would never forget. He felt so good right now he feared it was only a dream and he'd wake up back on the estate of the patrician couple who had purchased him from the gladiator arena.

"I used to walk every morning for three miles around the West Lake in Hangzhou," Rain's words brought Valerius back to the present. "Somehow there's always something new to see, a new treasure to find."

She sighed longingly for her homeland.

"Would you..." Valerius didn't know how or whether he could ask her about her past.

But he had a burning desire to know more about her, so he decided to just say it, "Would you tell me about your human life? You seem to remember it fondly."

"Oh, that wasn't during my human life," Rain replied, "but if you wish to know, then I will tell you my story."

She looked up at him, and he nodded in confirmation.

"Very well," she said, looking ahead again as they walked leisurely, side by side.

"I was born the daughter of a tea trader from Ningluo Mountain village in the Zhuji county of what is now Zhejiang Province in the southeast region of China. Back then, it was part of the ancient state of Yue. My given name was Xishi."

Valerius listened to her intently, mesmerized by her soft, lilting voice. He forgot about their surroundings, forgot about the throngs of people who rushed passed them on their way to work. He was so drawn to her tale, he felt transported back in time to her ancient homeland.

"As a child, I followed my father in his travels whenever I could. My mother was very ill, and I am ashamed to say I did not want to be around the sickness; it felt suffocating. Ever loving, she encouraged me to go with my father—to keep him company, she said. But as I grew older, I came to realize that she did not want me to see her waste away day after day."

"We lived a simple life in the mountains, barely aware of the war that was waging between our state and the state of Wu. All I knew was that I loved my father and mother, my pet rabbit Momo and my village friends."

She smiled fleetingly in memory. It was a sad, haunting smile.

"My mother succumbed to her illness when I was ten. And from that day I vowed to face disease head on, not cowardly hiding in the sidelines. I apprenticed with a local medicine man and learned how to make poultices for all kinds of wounds, brew medicines from rare mountain flowers and roots. I began studying the *qi* system with him, learning about the energy cycles that create balance within our bodies. I was so passionate about healing I could barely sleep at night for the ideas and theories running through my head."

Rain took a deep breath before continuing, and Valerius instinctively braced himself for what she was about to tell him next.

"Then one day when I was nineteen, a man came to visit our little cottage. He was a minister of our King Gou Jian, and his name was Fan Li. I was by the river washing sheets when he first arrived. And when I got home, I saw him deep in discussion with my father."

Rain recalled hiding behind the back door to eavesdrop on their conversation. She'd spied the back of the seated minister, looking extravagant in their humble abode, but balancing gracefully on a wobbly wooden chair as he spoke in low tones with her father.

Sir, at the behest of our King Gou Jian, I have come to request your aid. What's more, to beg your daughter's aid.

My daughter? But she is a simple country girl.

Let me start at the beginning, kind sir. As you know, our state has become a tributary to our conquerors, and our King has been bound to serve Prince Fuchai of Wu. The people of Yue and our King are outraged by the loss of our independence and would do anything to reclaim it. And we have a plan.

You see the Prince is enamored of feminine beauty. He... spends an inordinate amount of time in his harem, and depending on who his favorite mistress is at any given moment, so his mood sways. We, that is, our King and the high court, have a plan to control the source of his influence.

We plan to send our own beauty into the palace of Wu to... charm the prince and divert his attention. This agent of Yue will be trained in political intrigue and royal court etiquette. Besides the requisite beauty, she must have cleverness, strength, and most of all, courage.

Are you asking for my daughter? How can this be? How can I possibly agree?

Sir, your daughter's beauty has become a legend throughout all of Yue. Second only to her compassion and wit. If you—if she—would agree to be our agent in the Wu palace, we could finally have a chance at redeeming our freedom from Wu.

I cannot imagine sending my daughter so far and for such a purpose. She is a simple, innocent girl. Will I be able to see her again?

When the mission is complete we will bring her home to you, but... you must know that there is also the danger of failure.

I cannot ask her to make that sacrifice. I will not. She is all I have left in this world...

"But I went inside then and faced the minister, and I agreed to his plan," Rain smiled her sad smile again.

"You see, the Prince of Wu cared not about our people. He raised taxes and sent soldiers to collect them when villagers could not pay. I had treated many patients dying of hunger because they had to send away their own food stocks as tax payment, men old and young who were beaten by the soldiers when they resisted payment. In medicine you have to find the root cause of an illness or injury and address it; soothing the symptoms was not a cure."

Rain's gaze hardened with remembered determination. "I had a chance to vanquish the root of our state's illness, and I had to take it."

"So I traveled with Fan Li to the capital, where they dressed me in fine robes and taught me courtly manners. I spent one year learning history, how to write poetry, play the *konghou*, a Chinese harp, play games that only men were supposed to play, like *weiqi*—in short I was trained to be the perfect consort, an entertainer, a confidante, a friend and—lover."

Rain's steps slowed as she spoke until she came to a complete stop in the middle of the bridge crossing over the swan lake. She looked up at Valerius and searched his eyes for long silent moments.

Finally she asked, "Shall I go on?"

Mutely he nodded. He must know the rest of her story. He ached for the sacrifice she'd made at such an innocent age, even as he swelled with pride at her courage.

She gave him a small smile, as if *she* were reassuring *him*, as if she knew that hearing the rest of her tale would not be easy to bear.

"When I was ready, Fan Li took me before Prince Fucai as a tribute gift from Yue. During our journey there, I fell in love with the wise minister, who had been my teacher, my friend, my inspiration. It was an innocent love, I now know, but I did dream about a life together, back in my village, where we'd grow vegetables, fruits and herbs and have a couple of goats and chickens to keep my Momo company. To my joy, and more importantly, hope, Fan Li returned my affections and pledged to me his undying love before we parted ways."

Involuntarily, Valerius felt a stab of envy, but he tamped it down. He had no right to feel possessiveness toward her.

He was nothing, and she, she was everything.

"I was welcomed into the capital of Wu with enthusiasm that exceeded our wildest expectations. Prince Fucai dismissed Fan Li immediately and took me to his inner court. Very quickly he came to dote on me, I suspect at least partly because I withheld that which he wanted most. But I accommodated him in every other way."

Valerius did not need clarification.

"Gradually, he began to neglect his sovereign duties, preferring to play games with me instead. He would take me out on carriage rides throughout the city and boast about having me in his treasure trove."

Her lips twisted slightly in a bitter smile.

"Ever the businessman, he would charge people gold coins to look at me. But the added income from those fees did not lead him to reduce any taxes on the villagers."

"Over four years, I wove my spell around him. And though I succeeded in eluding his advances for the first year..." she laughed shortly, "he finally managed to catch me."

The slight emphasis on the word "catch" shot through Valerius like a javelin.

He looked sharply at her and was about to pull her to a stop, when she wrapped both arms around one of his and leaned into him, determinedly dragging him forward.

"Finally, his subjects grew restless with his distractions, and his friends began to desert him. My killing move was to convince him to execute his shrewdest advisor, the great general Wu Zixu. Political chaos ensued and our King invaded the state of Wu, defeated our oppressors and liberated our kingdom."

"True to his word, Fan Li brought me back home, but my father was no longer among the living. Fan Li asked me to marry him, but I…"

She stopped again and breathed deeply, a little brokenly.

Without looking at Valerius she said in a small voice, "Please don't think me a coward."

Valerius pulled her roughly against him and enveloped her in his heat.

"Never," he said fervently.

As if his answer gave her the strength to continue, she said, "I was too ashamed by what I had done, what had to be done to ensure Fucai's favor. I couldn't marry a good man and live with him and share his bed, not when I knew how unfaithful I'd been."

She shuddered and sniffed against Valerius' chest, her voice beginning to shake.

"So on the day of our betrothal, I took a walk along the river that ran through my village. The currents were fast and the rocks were sharp. I-I went in to cool my skin from the summer heat, and fell. I-I fell."

Valerius squeezed her tightly against him, wanting to absorb her pain. So small a woman, so enormous her burden.

After a long silence, Rain breathed more evenly.

"When I woke up, I was surrounded by a bright light, and a woman's voice asked me, 'If you could be anything in the world, if you were given a new beginning, what would you be?' And I answered that I wanted to be a healer, I wanted to devote my life to healing others. So now here I am."

"Here you are," Valerius agreed quietly. "My heart is glad that you are here."

At those brief words, Rain's spirit eased. She hugged the warrior to her tightly, wanting to extend this moment for as long as she could.

Once again, he had healed her.

*** *** *** ***

Upon Valerius and Rain's return to the Shield that evening, the entire complex was on high alert.

Without pausing to explain, Ayelet pulled Rain by the arm, as soon as she entered the underground passage, toward the Pure One's military clinic at a dead run. Valerius followed behind and didn't ask questions.

Whatever was happening was a Code Red emergency.

They rushed down to the wing where they housed wounded chevaliers and trainees recovering from particularly strenuous mock combat sessions and threw the doors open to find Alexandros lying crippled, ashen and unconscious amidst bloody sheets on one of the beds.

Rain flew to his side and immediately began to work.

Valerius stood back against the far wall adjacent to patient and Healer and crossed his arms, gritting his teeth.

He knew how weak Rain was, he knew what it took from her to heal him, and his comrade was in a much worse condition than he'd been in. This healing process would cost her dearly. It was all he could do to resist pulling her away. But he knew he could not interfere.

This was her power. This was her deepest desire.

To heal others, especially those she cherished.

Tristan came to stand beside him, fists clenched, gaze grim.

"We've lost Leonidas," he said roughly.

"Dead or taken?" came Valerius' stoic response.

"Xandros saw him fall, then he disappeared. We have to assume he's taken until proven otherwise."

Valerius nodded grimly. "Ambush?"

"Aye," the Champion responded, "ten or more assassins. Same breed as the ones who attacked you. Same tricks too, it seems, for their weapons were tipped with poison. The Horde had been destroyed before Leo and Xandros even arrived, by these assassins or someone else, we can't know for sure. That was all Xandros revealed before he blacked out."

"We must recover Leonidas when Alexandros revives. Perhaps he will remember more," Valerius stated with resolve.

Tristan put a hand on his comrade's shoulder despite knowing how Valerius eschewed physical contact. This time, the warrior didn't seem to mind.

"We will get him back," Tristan agreed, his tone not leaving room for any other possibility.

Valerius scanned the room and found the rest of the Dozen present and accounted for. Sophia was chewing on her fingers and watching silently with wet eyes in Ayelet's arms. Aella and Eveline sat beside Alexandros and held his hands as if trying to give him their strength. Wan'er gave her lady room to do her magic, but stood close enough to assist if need be. Dalair and Orion leaned against the opposite wall, masks of stoicism on their faces to hide their fury and grief.

Seth, however, sat with his head bowed on a bed beside Alexandros', seemingly deep in thought. And if the muscle ticking in his jaw were any indication, he was wrestling with some grim decisions.

As if feeling himself watched, Seth raised his eyes to meet Valerius', and the Protector saw that his friend was deeply shaken. Somehow, Valerius knew that it wasn't just the ambush and the aftermath, it was more.

The Consul appeared permanently changed after his trip to see the vampire queen.

Rain's collapse, like a paper doll folding over Xandros' considerably healthier looking form, brought Valerius' focus back to the Healer.

Without a word, he reached her in two long strides, gathered her up in his arms and took her from the clinic, not once looking back.

When he reached the inner chamber of their Enclosure, he locked the double-doors and laid her carefully on the bed. With some frantic rips and tears, he doffed his clothes and joined her under the coverlets, bringing her pale, fragile body into his naked heat.

He rolled onto his back and draped her on top of him, holding her head against his throat, urging her lips to his vein.

"Sweetheart," he entreated huskily, desperately, "time to feed."

He began to panic when she held still for long moments; he could barely feel her breath against his skin. Just when he tensed to leave the bed and find his dagger to cut open a vein to feed her himself, she stirred ever so slightly against him, her lips moving before the soft words reached him.

"Let me rest a while," she murmured groggily, "I am well. Though the General sustained many wounds, the poison was yet freshly in his system. It was not so difficult to neutralize and take out."

She pressed closer to him and inhaled deeply his scent at his throat and sighed as if it comforted her.

"I just need a little nap. I'll be hungry when I wake up."

He could feel her smile against his skin.

"I promise to indulge myself fully with you then."

Reassured for the time being, Valerius held her close while she slept and felt himself drift into dreamless slumber as her even breathing allayed his fears.

*** *** *** ***

The vampire gazed into the crackling fire and popped a piece of French chocolate truffle between its full red lips, colored by the aged red wine in the glass beside its chessboard.

On one side, the diamond white pieces sparkled brilliantly in the firelight. On the other side, black obsidian pieces reflected a red glow within them, like red flags in the eyes of an enraged bull.

But there was something peculiar about this particular chessboard: the white side had no pawns in the front line. Instead, those eight positions were taken by two more knights, three more bishops and three empty seats. And in the position of the king, there was a pawn in its place. The white side had no king.

The black side, however, was assembled in the traditional array.

It seemed like a spectacularly ill-matched display. Surely the white had too much advantage.

But then the vampire smiled a knowing smile.

Pawns had their uses. And when they reached the last line of the other side, they could become as powerful as queens.

Besides, a knight and a bishop had already been sidelined, and two more white knights had fallen.

The vampire carefully took those pieces off the board and arranged them perfectly on the edge of the table between the white and black sides. It surveyed its handiwork with satisfaction.

It was indeed an ill-matched set. The advantage was entirely with the black.

Echoes of pain reached the vampire from a distance, and it perked its ears to listen. The sounds of torment resonated in undulating waves off the underground walls.

Hmm, it purred with a devious smile, the new addition to its company of pawns must be enjoying his induction. Becoming a vampire assassin was a messy business, and not particularly pleasant for the inductee. The vampire almost rubbed its hands together with glee.

A new toy to play with! And such a large and handsome piece.

There was so much to look forward to, its delighted laughter drowned out the distant shouts of pain.

*** *** *** ***

Valerius' body erupted in flames as Rain took his vein while he still slept.

Unconsciously, he raised his hips and arched his back to offer more of himself, his arms tightening around the Healer.

Not wanting to disturb his much needed rest, Rain kept him in slumber by triggering calming energy throughout his system with selective insertions of strands of *zhen* into his pores. She lay on his chest and fed languorously from his throat, still half asleep herself.

Although Valerius did not awaken, the intense, painful need within his body ignited by her feeding blossomed darkly into haunting dreams of the past...

Sometime before 200 B.C. City of Rome.

The stately Roman manor that rose in the heart of Rome, amidst a circular border of olive trees with stone paved roads that led to a grand fountain outside its entrance, boasted serenity, charm and elegance.

But the depravities that carried on within put the trials of Tartarus to shame.

Valerius' days and nights folded into each other with predictable monotony that blurred the passage of time.

Wake up. Eat. Get cleaned.

Get dragged to the "entertainment" chamber. Fight the guards with fist, feet, nails, teeth, and any movable object that could be used as a weapon.

Get beaten and subdued. Get restrained to whatever instrument of torture that was the special of the day.

Get raped for the next few hours by the patrician and his wife, their friends, random strangers who paid to be entertained, even the guards if their masters felt particularly generous.

Get dragged back to his isolated cell. Wait for the pain to become somewhat manageable.

Eat. Sleep.

And start all over again.

One month crawled into a year. One year stretched into several.

Valerius became intimately familiar with every kind of debasement, every sort of pain. As his body grew into manhood, so did his masters' fascination with it. They were endlessly inventive with their games. And if Valerius became more difficult to subdue with his increasing size, muscle and life-and-death fighting techniques, his masters happily accommodated these changes with cruel creativity.

Body parts, poles, sword hits, even broken shards of pottery—Valerius had been brutalized with more objects than he could count.

He learned to disengage his mind from his body early on. Learned to distance the pain and the unholy acts of violence. He only focused on getting stronger, fighting tougher and plotting his escape.

One day when Valerius was in his twenty-fifth year, there was some commotion in the slaves' compound towards the back of the manor.

Two female bodies were dragged across the canopied garden walkways linking the slaves' quarters to the main residence. They were obviously dead, for the grayness to their skin and the fact that they made no sound as the guards dragged them over rocks, steps and debris.

Valerius watched the guards' progression through the masters' bedroom window with stoic eyes. He was too concerned with his own upcoming struggle to have any curiosity about the female victims.

Today the masters decided to change their routine.

Instead of shackling their favorite toy in the entertainment center below stairs, they had him brought to their own chambers for a group orgy. They were having guests after all, and Valerius was the main attraction. But to make sure they had nothing to fear from their feral, troublesome slave, they doubled the guards and kept the stud in tight chains that wound from his neck to his wrists to his ankles.

Valerius kept his gaze on the back gardens and stared sightlessly while two of the guests came forth to admire and grope his body. In his head he calculated the probability of success if he tried to fight off the six guards, four guests and his patrician masters. He also weighed the consequences in the event of failure, which was by far the most likely outcome.

Not that he cared.

A surreptitious sweep of his surroundings told Valerius that two of the guards were new and young, bulky but bumbling. Their weapons weren't even strapped properly, and by some miracle, they were the two that held Valerius' chains.

The guests would offer no resistance, for they appeared to be inbred patricians from the noblest Roman families; none of them had an ounce of muscle or nerve. His masters had been imbibing heavily before his arrival, for their breaths reeked and their movements were clumsy. And because it was the master's bedroom, he had easy access to the grounds outside.

Valerius almost smiled. His chances of success had increased considerably.

As he planned his maneuvers, a knock came on the chamber door.

"I ordered not to be disturbed!" the master thundered from the bed.

"My lord, what do you want us to do with the females?" came a muffled reply from the hall.

"Just get rid of them over the cliff by the river out back," the mistress responded, then groused to herself, "such tiresome creatures."

There was an obedient response from outside and the sounds of departing feet with dragging bodies.

"I hope they were worth your pleasure," the mistress shot a venomous look toward her husband, as if she were jealous. "It's not fair you had fun without me."

"Didn't you enjoy watching, my love?" the master responded with a sly leer, "and didn't I let you keep the trophies?"

The mistress fingered a simple gold chain around her neck with a small pendant in the shape of a bird, carved out of some sort of stone. Around her wrist sparkled a bracelet made out of beads, circling around a bird that matched the one on the necklace.

Valerius' gaze suddenly sharpened, and when he realized what he was looking at, the ground beneath him seemed to shift.

The trophies the master alluded to were as familiar to Valerius as the back of his hands. For he'd made the simple jewelry for his mother and sister with those very hands when he'd been a boy. They were parting gifts to the two women in his life before he and his father left for the arenas after a brief visit home.

It was the last time he'd seen them.

Unbridled rage and grief flooded Valerius in tidal waves, infusing him with a superhuman strength and clarity.

Before anyone knew what had happened, he leaned forward on one knee, yanked on the chains that held him with such force, the ends escaped the two guards' grasps. Winding the sections near him around his wrists, he swung the free ends like whips across the guards and guests who were closest, striking them unerringly on soft, exposed flesh and vulnerable eyes, nose and groins.

By the time two guards and two guests had been beaten down, Valerius was already ramming his shoulder into one of the new guards, pushing him hard into the wall and knocking his head back against it. He then deftly unsheathed the dagger and short sword and wielded them with deadly accuracy with the chains wound loosely across his shoulder, chest and around one arm, out of his way.

The shouts from his masters, grunts of pain from the guards and squeals of distress from the guests faded like background noise as Valerius honed in on his next targets with lethal precision and skill.

Four more bodies crumpled to the ground as he cut a path to the bedroom window. But he was in no hurry to make his escape.

No, he was going to kill each and every one of them, and he'd leave the masters for dessert.

The rest of the guards on retainer in the manor had gotten wind of the massacre and arrived just outside the chamber door.

At the first pound, Valerius squeezed the life out of the guard whose neck was in a chokehold between his bicep and forearm while taking the guard's long staff and inserting it into the hollow handles of the door, keeping the reinforcements at bay.

Within minutes, all six guards and four guests littered the floor in pools of blood and tangles of limbs.

Valerius wiped his bloodied lip on his forearm and regarded the quarries left for last.

The master and mistress clung to one another on their bed, looking almost mad with fright. By now their screams and crying had faded into whimpers, like two cornered animals awaiting slaughter.

Valerius advanced slowly and purposely upon them, a spatha at the ready. Wordlessly, he dragged his tormenters to the floor and urged them to their knees.

As he poised to strike with sword raised, he was oblivious to their groveling and blubbering. The accumulated pain and grief for his family rose within him, blotting out all else. Death was too good for these two demons from hell. And their death would not give him any comfort, any absolution.

But death would have to do.

As Valerius' blade met its targets, dealing killing blows, the chamber door burst open and guards and Roman soldiers flooded the room.

Valerius neither struggled nor spoke when they dragged him away. He would be executed for his deeds, he knew. A slave doing mortal harm to his masters was a capital crime. It mattered not all the cruelties they'd inflicted upon him.

A slave had no rights, after all. Not even to his own humanity...

Three days later, Valerius considered his short and violent existence as he breathed shallowly upon the crucifix he'd been hammered to the night of his revenge.

Three days and nights he'd rotted up here beneath the blistering sun and the chilling night winds. Strangers had pelted him with stones for amusement. Vultures had picked at his wounds and sun-burnt skin. He felt his strength ebb out of his body, felt the last breaths of life deserting him.

Any moment now, he would finally be able to rest. But he would have no peace, for his deepest regret was failing to protect his family.

With a soft breath, his eyes eased shut and his world went black even as he felt the first drops of soothing rain.

Sometime later, when he stopped before the River Styxx that carried the dead across the underworld, a glowing mass of energy floated towards him and blocked out the darkness.

"Before you go, warrior, consider this choice: what would you do if you had a second life? What one regret would you abolish?" a haunting female voice penetrated his consciousness.

Valerius automatically replied, "I would protect the ones I love. I would protect the weak who cannot protect themselves."

"Then rise again, my Pure One," the voice grew stronger and the light grew brighter until Valerius was blinded by the glare.

"Rise again, Protector."

Chapter Eight

When Valerius awoke the next day, he found Rain already gone, not only from their bed, but also from the Shield.

She and Ayelet had started off early to the clinic as a peculiarly high incidence of patients complaining of symptoms that sounded like anemia had called to book appointments the day before.

Ayelet wanted to have a look for herself and assess the situation for signs of vampire tampering. Usually, when vampires took blood, they also took souls, for blood alone was not enough to sustain them. But the Dozen feared that something sinister was in the air, something that changed vampire biology, and by extension, the fragile Balance that had been maintained since the last Great War.

Glancing at the oriental clock against the opposite wall, Valerius grimaced in self-disgust. He'd slept most of the day away, and yet he still felt exhausted.

And haunted.

The dreams had been so vivid in the night that he felt as if he'd relived the worst part of his past all over again.

It happened frequently, as often as every other night, being overwhelmed by demons from his human life, and he'd spend his waking hours struggling to distinguish reality from memories. It was an involuntary reflex to want to cut off any body part of any person who touched him. For the last ten years of his human life, touch equaled humiliation and pain.

His body tingling with sensitivity from the remnants of the dream and Rain's feeding, Valerius moved cautiously to get dressed. Just when he shrugged into a light black jersey, a soft knock sounded at the Enclosure's door.

It was Wan'er. She seemed hesitant, almost nervous, as she gained entrance to the chamber.

She stood just a few feet inside the threshold and clasped her hands in front of her.

"Protector, I need to speak with you about a private matter," she began without preamble, some of her no-nonsense straightforwardness coming to the fore despite her nerves.

Valerius gestured for her to come further inside and take a seat on any of the comfortable silk chaises, but she shook her head no. In order to not tower over her, he took a seat instead on a bench nearby and gave her a nod to continue.

Wan'er took a deep breath as if to bolster her courage, and blurted, "My lady Rain is not recovering fast enough."

Valerius sat up straighter and gave the handmaiden his fullest attention.

Wan'er plunged on in a rush of words, "You do not realize what it cost her to heal you, and now the General too, so soon after. And she would never complain of it. She always over-stretches herself to ensure the health and well-being of others."

"You see, by the time of this Phoenix Cycle she was weaker than she'd ever been in the twelve hundred years that I have been her handmaiden. The last ten years had taken too much of a toll, and the last Consort had not been the strongest."

At this, Wan'er gave Valerius a pointed glare.

A muscle ticked in the Protector's jaw as he silently berated himself for his cowardice ten years ago. He'd give anything to do it over, but he also knew that back then, *nothing* could have made him apply for the Service of a woman he'd only just met, no matter how moved by her he'd felt upon first sight.

"What must I do to revive her strength?" Valerius tried to focus on what he could control, for the past could never be changed.

"Intercourse," Wan'er stated matter-of-factly.

Valerius felt the blood drain from his face. It was not something he wanted to think about, much less talk to the Healer's handmaiden about.

"You must release within her as often as possible, as vigorously as possible," Wan'er continued without batting an eyelash.

"Didn't she explain to you the Consort's role? You are essentially her Mate for this duration. Blood is not enough. And it is obvious to me by looking at her state of health that you have not yet bedded her."

Valerius abruptly got to his feet and paced away from the handmaiden to get some air in his lungs. He felt like the walls were closing in, and his pulse was leaping in panic.

"I do not know why you have not done the deed, but it appears my lady is accommodating your timeline and disregarding her own. But if you don't do your duty by the Healer, she will not survive another week."

Valerius remained silent and squeezed his eyes shut, as if to shut out Rain's reality and his own consuming fears. He nodded once in comprehension, sensed the handmaiden bowing to him and heard her parting words.

"I leave my lady Rain in your hands. Please care for her well. I—*we* cannot bear to lose her."

And neither could he.

*** *** *** ***

The evening found Seth disappeared with only a briefly scrawled note: "I will be away indefinitely. Do not try to find me."

As the remaining members of the Dozen gathered around to regroup and strategize, the gloom and sadness in the throne room was thick enough to cut.

Orion and Eveline would share Seth's duties until his return—no one would even imagine that he wouldn't. Aella would take over training of the recruits, whose numbers included the three Pure males that had applied, and failed, to Serve the Healer.

Part of the time, she would benefit from Valerius' assistance, but his primary duty was to strengthen the Healer and ensure her safety. Tristan and Dalair would rotate between guarding Sophia and hunting rogues, as well as tracking down the whereabouts of Leonidas. Aella would partner whichever one was on duty during the night.

Ayelet, meanwhile, continued her duties as Guardian and took up the search for potential replacements for the missing Consul and Elite warrior, as per protocol when one or more of the Zodiac went missing in action. It was not a responsibility she enjoyed, for she was essentially hedging against the safe return of her friends.

Sophia wanted to take a leave from school to help, but none of her Council would hear of it.

One, there was not an obvious place for her to add value. Two, everyone wanted to shield her from the unhappy immediacy of their situation. Her normality seemed to give the Zodiac something positive to focus on.

Sophia, however, felt helpless and angry at their protectiveness. She was young, but she was resourceful. There were many things she could do to ease their burdens, even if it meant deciphering and stamping official papers that often took hours of Seth's day.

She stomped to her bedroom in a fit of temper and despair, Dalair following a few paces behind.

Slamming into her room, she stormed without looking behind, "Why do you have to follow me everywhere? We're in the Shield, I'm safe as can be, for crying out loud!"

Dalair took small favors where he could—at least she hadn't slammed the door in his face.

"You know that it's protocol when we're in Code Red. You know that one of the Elite must be with you at all times," he reminded her gently, his voice quiet and low.

"But why does it have to be you!" Sophia practically whined, throwing up her hands in disgust. "Why can't it be Aella or Tristan?"

Dalair did not understand her displeasure with him, which had been increasing lately at an alarming pace. He knew why she *should* detest him, but Sophia didn't know herself. And he would do everything in his power to keep it that way.

He calmly answered her question, "Tristan and Aella are hunting tonight."

"I know that," Sophia muttered, "it was a rhetorical question."

She grabbed her pajamas and headed into her bathroom, leaving the door open so he wouldn't have to come over and beat it down in case she were to drown in the bathtub.

Geez! How stupid could this situation get?

Dalair stood against the outside wall beside the bathroom door with folded arms. He listened to her brushing her teeth, turning on the shower and removing her clothes. He closed his eyes to magnify his other senses so that he could tune out the background noise.

"You're sleeping on the floor," Sophia called out in a raised voice to be heard over the strong spray of the water.

Unfortunately, she often forgot that Dalair's Gift was his hyper-developed senses, so her loud voice was like fingernails against the chalkboard of his eardrums.

"I have a sleeping bag and an extra comforter you can use," she continued in the same pitch, causing Dalair to cringe ever so slightly. He concentrated for a moment and dialed his hearing down, while still blocking out the background noise.

He wouldn't need the comforter, Dalair thought, but he remained silent.

"And I don't want to get any argument from you about my leaving the lights on when I sleep," Sophia groused some more, "that's the way I like it so you can just deal."

Again, Dalair didn't feel he needed to comment. Of course he would adhere to her preferences. She was his queen. He would never gainsay her.

Unless it was for her own protection.

Some minutes of silence passed and then he heard, "You better keep your clothes on when you sleep. I don't ever want to see you naked."

A pause. Then, "Not that I give that a lot of thought, I mean, I don't think about you naked at all. But just in case you do that sort of thing—you know—sleep naked. You just better not do it near me."

Dalair frowned slightly.

Verily, he didn't understand her at all. It seemed like she was an entirely different person from the queen he once served. But sometimes... sometimes he felt a recognition for her deep within his soul.

Another few minutes, and Sophia emerged from the bathroom in a fluffy white robe, the baby animals on her light blue PJs on full display beneath its hem. Over-stuffed pink piggy slippers warmed her feet and made her waddle rather than walk.

She was toweling off her shoulder-length chestnut hair as she came around the enormous four-poster, king-sized bed to pull back the covers and stack her pillows for bed-time reading.

Looking at her comfortable bed and the hard floor beside the bed covered only by a colorful thin wool rug, Sophia felt a pang of conscience. If it were Aella, or any other of the Elite for that matter, she wouldn't hesitate to invite them to share her comforts. She'd been raised by the Zodiac, after all. They were family to her—parents, aunts and uncles, elder brothers and sisters.

In the beginning, she'd felt the same familial affection and love for everyone, including Dalair.

In fact, when she'd been a child, he was always her favorite companion. He spent more time guarding her and taking care of her than any other Elite member, despite Valerius' role as Protector. And up until Sophia was seven, she'd often slept in his bed, seeking him out in the middle of the night when nightmares plagued her. In many ways, he'd been her security blanket.

And then she'd discovered that she liked boys.

She had crushes on various boys from her schools and was quite inspired by a couple to compose exceedingly bad love letters. But somehow, when she came home to the Shield, one look at Dalair and she felt dissatisfied, frustrated, and downright angry.

Her attitude towards him changed very gradually.

First there was the separation, until the Elite resumed their normal rotational schedule for taking care of her, and she saw Dalair more and more infrequently compared to the earlier years of her childhood. Then there was the distancing, when she purposefully forced herself to take a more active and consistent interest in boys her own age—human boys. She made herself look upon Dalair with the same indifference as one would gaze at scenery and art.

Incredibly amazing scenery and art. On the same relative scale as the Taj Mahal or Michelangelo's David, but scenery and art nevertheless.

And finally, there was resentment. For some reason, very recently in fact, Sophia felt inexplicably irritated, annoyed and all out frustrated whenever Dalair was near. It was as if PMS hit her hard and fast only in his presence. He could do and say nothing right.

Sometimes, she even hated him.

"Um, look," Sophia muttered grudgingly, as if speaking the words left a bitter taste in her mouth, "you don't have to sleep on the floor. You can take the other side of the bed and we can roll the comforter and sleeping bag into a barrier between us so you don't get slapped and kicked when I spread out during the night. I tend to move around a lot."

"No need," he replied in an even tone, always that blasted even tone, "the floor is fine."

"Suit yourself," Sophia said rather haughtily with a toss of her hair. "Don't blame me if you catch cold or get back pains."

Without responding, Dalair spread the sleeping bag and comforter on the floor right beside Sophia's side of the bed and lay down on his side facing away from her, using his bicep as a pillow.

He would not sleep this night, he knew, not when the danger was ever increasing, but he didn't want to sit or stand looking wide awake and making his presence seem more intrusive.

Sophia got settled in her bed, leaned back against her tall stack of pillows and pretended to read. The room was brightly lit with an overhead chandelier and her bedside lamp.

She used this opportunity to assess the Paladin unobserved.

He was the leanest and shortest Elite warrior, though he still stood over six feet tall. His build reminded Sophia of Middle Eastern or Latin American men, leaner in the chest and especially at the waist than Europeans. But proportionally, at least in Sophia's opinion, his type of figure was the most beautiful.

Broad shoulders tapered to a narrow waist and hips with long, lean limbs, his torso making a perfect upside down trapezoid. The only curve on his unyielding body was his taut, muscular buttocks, and that only made him even more appealing in his overwhelming masculinity.

Sophia was an ass woman and his ass was probably the finest she'd ever seen. Her fingers itched to test it for resilience, her teeth tingled to sink into the tantalizing flesh. No doubt about it, the Paladin had a world-class backside.

Rather like a wild Arabian stallion.

Dalair did nothing to emphasize his "charms," though that didn't stop Sophia from ogling him every chance she got. It was an involuntary reaction. She often didn't even know she was doing it until someone or something alerted her that she hadn't blinked in a long period of time.

When she caught herself in the act, she was always very annoyed.

What was the point of lusting after the Paladin? Like they would ever end up dating.

She kept reminding herself to save her hormones for the human boys. The risk/ reward ratio was much more attractive in that case.

Sophia watched his deep, even breathing lift and depress his ribcage with utter fascination. It was hypnotic, really, and strangely soothing. If she could just see Dalair breathe like this, then everything was all right with the world. And if it wasn't, then it would be. Because he was here, and she had absolute faith he would make it so.

Reminding herself to keep up the pretense of reading, she flipped over a page of her romance novel but kept her gaze glued to Dalair's back. And then it roved covetously down his spine to his perfectly developed backside.

Sophia licked her lips as the room began to grow warmer and her mouth grow drier.

Abruptly, she wondered how he compared to Ere.

Both were dark-haired, of similar height. If she put them side by side, Dalair was by far more masculine with his bronzed skin, lean muscles and ever-serious weight-of-the-world expression.

Ere, on the other hand, while intensely masculine when Sophia didn't have Dalair to compare him to, seemed more refined, elegant, definitely more of a scholar type than a warrior type, which made sense. He was hauntingly beautiful, whereas Dalair was...

Well, Sophia still didn't know what Dalair was.

Both men exuded a powerful undercurrent of sexual magnetism. Sophia had an idea Ere was well attuned to his own powers of attraction and knew how to use them. Dalair, on the other hand, didn't have a clue.

But Goddess above, he sure poured out that sexual energy in wave after rolling wave, somehow made more potent by the fact that he wasn't even trying, wasn't even aware he was doing it.

Like now.

She felt the pull from him like the moon felt enslaved to the sun. It made her want to *do things*. Even raunchier things than biting his ass.

Made her want to spread herself like a second layer of skin over his naked body and crawl into him. Made her wish she had Pure-female fangs to sink into this throat, his biceps, his lower abdomen just above his pubic bone, his inner thighs, his—

"Go to sleep, Sophia," Dalair ordered gruffly in a surprisingly unsettled tone, startling her enough to drop her book to the floor.

He didn't help her pick it up, but remained in his long held position, lying on his side.

Sophia shot daggers at his back as she dangled half off the bed, almost losing her balance, trying to fetch her novel.

She slapped the novel onto her bedside table and made a production of getting settled into her cocoon of thick comforters and pillows, moving around and flipping about.

"Good night," she called out in a muffled voice, sounding peeved and pouting.

Dalair did not respond in kind, focusing all of his energy into making his body calm down.

It wasn't going to be a good night for him, not by a long shot. Not when his body ached so badly to get inside of hers, it was all he could do not to cup himself in agony.

He'd felt her gaze upon him ever since he'd lain down. He'd sensed her increasing arousal by listening to her breathing quicken, her heart pound, by inhaling her heady scent, blossoming thickly with her excitement. He could almost see in his mind's eye what she saw in hers as she scrutinized his body with sexual interest.

But he would never be the one for her, Dalair thought as his heart clenched in pain. He'd never had that right and he knew he never would.

*** *** *** ***

Tristan came behind his Mate and wrapped his arms around her waist, kissing her neck in small light grazes, nuzzling against her and inhaling deeply her familiar scent.

"You're home early tonight," Ayelet greeted, tilting her head to one side to give him better access.

But she kept her gaze fixed on the giant dual-screen display in front of her, her fingers busy tapping keys as she continued her search for Seth and Leonidas' potential replacements.

"We have some leads," Tristan responded, hugging her back to his front and settling his chin lightly on top of her head as was their habit.

"We ran into a rogue vampire who used to belong to the faction that was annihilated in the train tunnel. They used to have dealings with another group, much older, much more powerful in its members, to divide territories and agree on ground rules for hunting humans. The older group wanted to absorb this faction into its midst, but not to build a Hive—instead it seemed like they were recruiting for an army. The faction refused."

"Who is the other vampire Horde's leader?" Ayelet asked, her key strokes stilling.

"The vampire didn't know. He's never seen or heard the person, but the older vampire faction was definitely acting under orders. They were also remarkably organized and well-behaved, as if they were trained soldiers. Yet their general never made an appearance."

Ayelet absorbed that with a nod. "And how did you manage to get so much information out of a rogue vampire?"

She felt her Mate smile against her head. "Aella can be very persuasive. Between his attraction to her and the business end of her dagger, the Rogue couldn't deny us what he knew."

"How much of what he divulged can we trust?"

"Some more digging will tell," the Champion answered.

"But I am inclined to follow the leads he gave us. He seemed to be trying to reform—he was gaunt with starvation and he professed that he would continue to avoid harming humans while trying to find another way to survive. He says he's in love with a human woman, if you can imagine that."

"I can," Ayelet sighed. "We often view the vampires as blood-sucking monsters, our nemesis and the nemesis of human kind. But we must not forget that they were once just like us, Pure Ones devoted to protecting this world and the humans within it. It is tragic that they became what they are simply because they lost their hearts to the wrong partners. The yearning to love and be loved in return should not warrant such cruel punishment."

"Your words can be considered blasphemous," Tristan commented without heat, "I didn't know you were a vampire sympathizer."

Ayelet turned in her Mate's arms to regard him.

"I sympathize with them as living, feeling creatures of this earth. If the Goddess saw fit to allow them this path of life, surely they cannot all be evil. Since their creation, they seem to be as much a part of the Universal Balance as we are."

"And people change, souls transform. It is a cycle we all serve. Perhaps the vampires are changing too. Just look at the increasing number of Hives around the world. They are becoming much more organized, even civilized. They even have their own Queens."

She rested her head against her lover's chest and was immediately gratified by the strong beat of his heart.

"Besides, I sympathize because I have you. I know how rare and special our bond is. This is what a Pure One reached out for when they broke the One Sacred Law. How can I begrudge them that desire when I myself have felt the same?"

Tristan hugged her tightly to him and stroked her long tawny mane soothingly.

"I remember the first time I saw you," Ayelet murmured dreamily.

"You had just been revived. You looked so bewildered and in so much pain from the transformation. And all I could think was 'I want him for my own. I would do anything to have him, even if it cost me everything.'"

"I took that risk with you knowing full well the consequences if you didn't return my love, but I never hesitated even for a moment. If my death was a consequence, I wouldn't have regretted making that choice. My existence would have been meaningless without you to share it."

Ayelet put her hands on her Mate's hips, then smoothed them covetously over his taut backside, massaging and squeezing leisurely, stoking the fire within him.

"I do not know if I would have taken death or life as a vampire, and I'm eternally grateful I didn't have to face that impossible choice. So I can't righteously judge those who have walked a similar path, get their heart broken, and then be confronted with such a brutal reality. I suppose my own happiness has made me more in tune with the sadness of others."

"It is one of the many reasons I love you," Tristan responded warmly and pushed his arousal into the softness of her belly.

"Come, my dearest one, let me show you the depth of my devotion."

*** *** *** ***

Valerius held Rain tightly as she slept, her back to his front as he curved around her in their customary cocoon.

It was almost dawn, but he'd been wide awake all night with embattled thoughts, struggling between his body's imperative to Serve her and his mind's terror at the true mating act. Added to this was Wan'er's warning from earlier in the day.

No matter what it cost him, he had to try.

Involuntarily he shuddered as his heart clenched painfully.

What if he could not overcome his demons? What if his body was too tainted with the horrors and filth of his past to fulfill her needs? What if his mind denied the release she needed from him?

What if he failed to please her?

He'd never been kissed.

Never kissed a female in a non-filial way. The tormenters in his human life had always avoided his mouth after the first time they ventured near and almost went away with a missing body part.

He'd never had to control his body, having always had it controlled for him, used as his abusers saw fit.

And he was too big. If he couldn't fit into the mistress despite her countless and cruelly inventive efforts, how could he possibly fit inside the tiny, utterly fragile Healer?

She'd shown him a small insight on how to bring her pleasure the other night. But that was all he knew. He didn't know where to begin or how to end. He feared down to his bones that she might have been right—he didn't know the first thing about being her Consort.

Didn't know how to be a Pure male.

There were times he fell into deep despair, feeling trapped again inside the fourteen year-old boy who'd been brutalized and traumatized. Wanting to claw his way out of his own skin, yet feeling as if he would just get dragged back down, further and further into the abyss. Into a black void of pain and hopelessness.

When they'd retired to their chamber earlier in the night, he'd awkwardly offered to Service her. She gently declined, saying she wished to sleep and that all she wanted was for him to hold her.

But he could see the strain of exhaustion and weakness in her eyes, in the small white lines around her mouth, the way she barely held herself upright, the translucent paleness of her skin.

If there was one good thing he accomplished in his long existence, Valerius wanted to ensure the Healer's strength and vitality.

Rain's strength and vitality.

There was only ever Rain. He dared not think of her as his, but he knew from the first time they met that he was unequivocally hers. He'd only been delaying the inevitable. Denying the very reason for his being.

Tentatively, he trailed a hand down her side, over her slim hip and along her thigh to the edge of her filmy silk nightgown. He eased the material upwards and over her sleeping form, moving her limbs easily to pull the gown over her head, leaving her body naked against his own.

She stirred a little, but remained in slumber, curling more tightly into a ball, her arms crossed over her small, pink-tipped breasts as if she were cold or shy.

Valerius fitted himself closer to her huddled form and smoothed a large hand over her body, soothing her enough to relax gradually and reveal more of her front to his delicate touch.

As she'd taught him, he covered her pubic area with one hand, cupping her gently between her thighs. With his thumb he began a fluttering rub, back and forth across her special spot, encouraging it into a hard little button.

Rain sighed deeply and instinctively widened her legs a fraction to give him better access. He took it as a welcome and delved one finger slowly into her damp heat.

Her hand came over his but she exerted no pressure, merely holding onto his wrist in anticipation. As her arousal and readiness increased, giving off a heady fragrance, his own body tautened incredibly in reaction, his mating scent joining hers.

Before long, her body shuddered in delight, the walls of her tight canal spasming around his finger, making his engorged cock jerk in jealousy and torment against her backside.

When her shivers slowly subsided, she turned around in his arms without opening her eyes.

"You're making it impossible to resist you," she complained in a teasing tone. "Don't say I didn't warn you when you're sore and bruised in the aftermath."

"No," he agreed, "just let me make love to you. Let me give you what you need."

Vaguely, it occurred to Rain's still sleepy subconscious that he'd said "make love," not "Service." Somehow she recognized the significance in the distinction, but immediately forgot all about it when she felt his erection probe between her thighs.

"Hmmm," she purred, wriggling against him until the satiny lips of her vagina rubbed teasingly over the swollen head of his penis, wetting it in an intimate kiss.

Valerius shuddered at the sensation, but kept himself still, letting her slowly gyrate against him, pleasuring herself with the pressure of his cock.

With a shaking hand, he raised her chin and leaned his face closer to hers. When their lips were but a whisper away, he inhaled her scent deeply as if to brace himself, harnessing inner strength.

And then his lips met hers in a graze so light, Rain felt tickled. She edged her mouth closer and wound a hand behind his neck, barricading a potential retreat.

One slight graze became two brushes. Two brushes blossomed into arduous strokes. And still his lips remained closed against her slightly open ones.

He was driving her slowly mad.

But she wanted him to take his time, like waiting patiently for a wounded tiger to approach. Wherever he led, she would follow. She wanted to be blessed with the gift of him rather than take him as if she had every right.

Which she had. As the rules of the Phoenix Cycle dictated.

But she never viewed her Consorts as possessions, or even as her servants, though technically they were for the duration of the Cycle. She always viewed their Service as a privilege to be honored, even cherished. Each one deserved her affection, admiration and respect.

Rain was so caught up in Valerius' generous mouth that she forgot for a moment everything else. Her hips stilled in their undulation against his. With all her being she concentrated on his tentative, excruciatingly gentle kiss.

Finally his mouth opened slightly and he began to pull at her lips more strongly with his own, sucking and releasing, nibbling and rubbing. She'd never felt so aroused because of a simple kiss.

Maybe it was his tenderness. Maybe it was his shyness. Or maybe it was the anticipation of more to come that built urgently within her, igniting every cell and nerve. For she'd never been kissed with so much...

Love.

There was no other word for it. It was as if he was pouring his heart and soul into this one act, his body literally vibrating with the intensity of it.

Again, Rain felt a sting of alarm. But Goddess above, this felt so good. So right. She never wanted him to stop.

And then she felt his tongue lightly lick her upper lip.

Oh please please please come closer, said the spider to the fly. Unconsciously, she squeezed the back of his neck with urgency. *Please please please come inside*.

All at once, he did, inserting his tongue into her mouth with a voluptuous sweep. They both moaned at the sensation and struggled to get even closer, though they were already glued together, front to front.

Thoroughly, methodically, he explored her mouth with his tongue and lips, surging inside and retreating over and over and over. Both their hips mimicked their mouths, pushing against each other, undulating, arching.

It seemed to go on forever. She wanted it to go on forever. But still she needed more.

Craved him at her core.

Suddenly Valerius broke away with a shuddering breath, chest heaving and heart pounding.

"I want to be inside you," he whispered, his voice so deep and husky and carnal she broke out in goose bumps in response.

"Yes," she answered with exalted relief.

"*Please.*"

"I-I don't..." Valerius' body tightened into a bowstring as he struggled for words.

"Show me how," he finally said, a wave of embarrassment and pain washing over him.

She didn't hesitate, the hand at the back of his neck gliding down to his shoulders, over his chest and abdomen, roamed possessively over his hip and around to his buttocks, squeezing and kneading gently as if to prepare him, but also to delay a few moments to give him time to change his mind.

Valerius brought his mouth urgently back to Rain's, plumping her lips with small desperate bites even as he grasped her hand firmly in his and brought it to his groin, cupping her fingers around him. Wordlessly, he urged her on with his mouth, his body.

Please, Goddess, don't let him fail her.

Still entwined with him, both on their sides facing each other, Rain gripped his thick length as firmly as she could, her fingers only able to meet around his girth halfway, and brought him to her entrance.

She moved him back and forth against her nether lips, wetting him with her excitement, wetting herself with his dew. She did this for endless moments, torturing both of them, until Valerius couldn't bear it any more.

"Do it," he gasped into her mouth, "now."

She shifted her hips, and with a slow undulation, took the plump head of his penis inside.

His body racked with shivers, and he made a low sound of pain.

Rain immediately stilled, opening her eyes, and saw that his eyes were tightly shut, his face contorted with anguish.

As if sensing that she looked upon him, he turned his face inward toward the pillows, hiding from her penetrating gaze.

Without warning, he pushed his hips into her, gaining another inch.

Even as Rain moaned in pleasure at the fullness of him, her body stretching to accommodate and to take more of him, she was distinctly aware that his shivers had become jerks, as if someone was hurting him so severely he couldn't control his reaction. She saw the tendons in his neck strain against his skin and his jaw clench repeatedly, saw his Adam's apple bob once, twice, as he swallowed, as he struggled to breathe.

And she saw one tear leak out of the corner of his eye.

Her heart broke.

Nothing was worth the pain he suffered. Not her Nourishment, not her vitality, and right this moment, not even the Pure Ones' survival.

She tried to pull back, tried to let go of him, but he held her tightly to him, a steely arm around her back.

"No!" he pleaded, his voice breaking with emotion, "you need this, I want to—"

"Look at me, *airen*," she ordered softly, but powerfully.

She reached up to hold his cheek, her thumb rubbing the moisture there away.

He refused to give her his eyes, pushing again with his hips. But she'd anticipated him and eased back at the same time he pushed, thwarting his efforts.

"Look at me, Valerius," she urged again, her voice deep with heartache. "Don't do this to yourself. To us. Talk to me."

His eyes suddenly opened wide, staring bleakly, heart-wrenchingly into hers. Shining with his barely checked tears, he bared his soul to her scrutiny for one brief moment.

What Rain saw there devastated her.

And then the glimpse was gone.

He removed himself from her body, scrambled awkwardly off the bed and shut himself in the bathroom in two long strides.

Rain lay still on the bed, bereft without his warmth, and listened to the sounds from the bathroom.

The shower had come on. But there was nothing else. She was torn between going to him and staying put.

What if he didn't want her comfort? What if he rejected her?

It didn't matter, she thought with conviction. She couldn't let him be alone.

Not now.

Carefully, she got up from the bed and padded silently to the bathroom, stopping just outside. The bathroom door remained open a crack, and she gingerly pressed it open some more, revealing the tortured warrior inside.

Valerius was hunched over the sink counter, his head bowed in defeat, his body bunched in agony. Suddenly he looked up at his reflection and unleashed a powerful fist against the mirror, shattering it and breaking through to the wall behind, cracking the mortar with his knuckles.

He exploded again and again, hitting the same spot over and over until the entire wall length mirror shattered to pieces, the wall behind it flaking apart, the exposed bricks stained with his blood.

He would have continued with the destruction and self-abuse had Rain not rushed forward to wrap her arms around his waist, holding his back to her front.

But he was heedless of his surroundings, too caught up in his own nightmares, and at the feel of someone behind him, their skin touching his skin, Valerius went berserk.

He twisted his back to buck her off and swiped an arm under hers to break her hold on him.

The force of the action sent her flying backwards against the wall and she hit it with a loud thud and a startled gasp of pain.

Valerius whirled immediately around at Rain's sound of distress. The sight of her crumpled naked body curled against the wall broke through the red haze of pain that blinded his vision.

"No!" he choked out, kneeling before her on the floor, bringing her body into his with wildly shaking hands.

"No no no no no no," he chanted despondently, cradling her close and rocking back and forth.

She stirred in his embrace and put a slim hand on his cheek.

"Don't worry so, my warrior," she whispered weakly against his chest. "I'm all right, I'll be all right. Come back to bed with me. Talk to me."

Valerius obeyed after checking her thoroughly for the extent of damage. Finding no broken bones or twisted ligaments, he turned off the water and carried her to their bed. But he hesitated to join her, and she saw in his face self-hatred and despair.

There would be no more of that, Rain determined once and for all. She would not let him fall back into the abyss. She opened her arms to him and waited.

For long moments, he stood there, frozen with fear and self-doubt.

And she waited.

With a shuddering sigh, he joined her in bed and pulled her tightly against him, hugging her like a frightened child clutching his security blanket on a dark, stormy night.

"Talk to me," she repeated on a whisper.

An eternity passed by, but he remained silent.

Still she waited, stroking softly the arms that wrapped around her protectively, reverently, regretfully.

And finally, she heard his voice, raw and broken beside her ear. She could even hear the child within, crying, hurting, but trying desperately to stay strong.

Rain wept silently for that child and for the incredible, vulnerable, beautiful warrior he'd become despite the tragedies of his past.

Against all odds, he'd conquered his demons. For Valerius Marcus Ambrosius was first and foremost a *good* man.

He was the very best male she knew.

Chapter Nine

10 years ago...Hangzhou, China.

Valerius did not want to stay one more day than necessary.

For thirty days he'd loitered around, presumably doing surveillance and making sure the Sanctuary was secure.

But really he was waiting.

Waiting for Rain to take her Nourishment from her chosen Consort. Waiting for her to take another male's body into hers over and over and over again.

No matter where he was in the Sanctuary, Valerius could smell the scent of her passion. His body trembled in sympathy whenever hers found release.

He knew it was all in his sick, twisted imagination. In reality, he could hear nothing coming from her Enclosure. The walls were too thick and too well sealed for scents to escape.

And yet he somehow felt it all, as if she were taking her Nourishment at *his* vein, fulfilling her needs with *his* body. He was painfully swollen most of the time, reduced to nothing but a walking erection. So yeah, he'd really like to leave as soon as possible.

As in today. As in *now*.

But his preference was overruled when the child Queen lit up like fireworks at the invitation from the Healer to stay for the beginning of the Mid-Autumn or Moon Festival where she would get to sample countless varieties of moon cakes and view the dazzling display of multi-colored floating sky lanterns at the night market.

Just what he needed, Valerius thought with a scowl, protecting three females in throngs of strangers amidst a loud and chaotic celebration and through meandering streets and alleys. What's more, the festival occurred on the night of the harvest moon, a full moon closest to the autumnal equinox—one of vampires' favorite hunting periods.

Fantastic.

Sophia was out of bed before dawn that morning, too excited with anticipation to sleep. Ayelet rose as well to help the little girl dress in traditional Chinese silk robes, a red and gold vest with a matching skirt, elaborately decorated with flower and phoenix embroidery.

Wan'er also came to help the visitors start their day, bringing with her a large tray of food and *longjing* tea, a delicacy of the area. She laughed with pleasure when she saw the child queen's exuberance and adorable costume, bringing Sophia to stand between her knees as she sat in front of the antique Chinese vanity to comb through Sophia's long chestnut hair and proceeded to braid it into coils on each side of her head.

While the females chatted cheerfully and readied themselves for the day, Valerius partook of the sumptuous breakfast, but was too concentrated on studying maps of city streets and terrain to savor the taste.

And then the Healer, Rain, entered after a soft knock at their chamber door.

Valerius abruptly choked on his red bean bun and hastily swallowed it down with gulps of tea.

The Healer looked radiant in her light blue dress, a simple style somewhere between traditional and modern, but every inch of feminine appeal. The conclusion of the Phoenix Cycle had left her with glowing milky skin, youthful pink-tinged cheeks, luminous large phoenix-tail eyes that tilted alluringly at the corners, and plump red lips.

Valerius took in the transformation with a wildly thumping heart. He had never seen anything more beautiful. And then he noticed the last detail:

She'd shaven all of her hair.

He could see the shadow of black roots that were already starting to grow. Without the curtain of hair shielding her face, her ethereal beauty was all the more stunning.

She glanced in his direction and caught him staring like a lummox. Self-consciously, she smoothed a hand over her shaven head and looked down with a blush.

It occurred to Valerius that she mistook his scrutiny for something other than utter fascination and enthrallment. Instead of correcting her misconception, he remained silent, letting her think what she would.

Rain looked up at the warrior again and saw that his gaze had become stoic once more, as if he were looking through her rather than at her. As if he didn't wish to see her at all.

Squaring her shoulders, she decided to approach him despite his impassive expression, a veritable mask of unwelcome.

"Did you have a good night's rest, Protector?" she greeted when she stood not two feet before him.

He appeared startled that she spoke to him. Wasn't he used to being greeted in the morning?

"Aye," he answered in that deep, husky voice.

Rain involuntarily shivered at the sound.

She'd just spent thirty days and nights in feeding and orgy with a robust Pure male. Normally, she wouldn't feel even a hint of attraction to another male until closer to the time of the next Phoenix Cycle.

But this time was different.

Over the course of the thirty days, she'd taken the Nourishment of one male but dreamed of another. When she closed her eyes, all she saw was *his* face in her mind, *his* naked body next to hers, inside of hers, filling hers.

She'd tried and tried to concentrate on the Consort she'd chosen, tried to give that honorable male all her attention, affection and devotion during the time they spent together, but deep down she wished he was someone else.

She wanted Valerius. Only Valerius.

But that wasn't likely to happen, Rain chided herself for having false hopes. The Protector made it clear from the moment they'd met that he was off limits. He didn't want to speak to her, have contact with her, be in her presence, much less sign up as her Consort.

Rain had never met anyone she repelled so strongly. People usually gravitated towards her. She gave them a sense of comfort and calm.

But, apparently, not this warrior. His body language practically shouted that he felt her nearness disturbing.

Invading.

"Are there any sights you'd like to see today?" Rain doggedly continued, trying to draw the reticent warrior into conversation.

His blank stare was response enough. Clearly, he would rather they'd already been on their way back to the Shield this morning, rather than preparing to attend the Mid-Autumn Festival.

"No?" she responded, as if he'd spoken, "well, we'll take you around a few places nevertheless so you get a feel for my homeland. It's especially beautiful this time of year—autumn and spring are my favorite seasons."

Valerius merely continued to stare.

He knew he was being unforgivably rude, but he couldn't find his tongue if his life depended upon it.

She was smiling at him.

Invitingly.

He felt his cock begin to swell, and he struggled for mastery over his own body, turning half away from the Healer to hide the evidence of his inexplicable arousal. Self-disgust blackened his countenance and his stare grew into a scowl of discomfort.

Rain blinked rapidly at the sudden ominous change in his expression and awkwardly looked away, turning to join Wan'er, Ayelet and Sophia for breakfast.

"I am eager to learn of your homeland," Valerius said through a clenched jaw, not wanting the delicate Healer to think he was some uncivilized cretin.

She turned her head back briefly like a graceful swan.

For a moment, she looked confused and uncertain, as if she'd expected him to say something off-putting but heard the opposite.

And then she smiled.

A beaming, radiant, glowing smile.

She dipped her head slightly in acknowledgement, hesitated briefly, then stepped closer so that the fabric of her dress skimmed fleetingly against his thigh.

Valerius sucked his breath in sharply, electrified by the slight graze.

Only when he regulated his lungs once more did he notice that she was holding something out to him in her small pale hand.

"I made this for you," she said shyly, in a low voice only he could hear.

It was what appeared to be a silk handkerchief. But it wasn't quite silk, Valerius realized as he solemnly received the gift she placed gently in his hand, careful not to touch his skin. It was made of something finer, more luminescent, more delicate.

And it changed with the light, like the scrolls on the walls of the corridors. It depicted a traditional Chinese scene, with a glistening lake and Chinese elms.

What drew his gaze in the center of the scene was a lone black rock in the middle of the lake, appearing both opaque and translucent, like obsidian under different light. Somehow, it displayed both characteristics in the handkerchief, for the drizzling summer rain that descended upon the landscape like fine needles illuminated the rock's shining core despite the seemingly impenetrable exterior.

A tingling warmth spread within Valerius' chest as he continued to gaze upon the exquisite handkerchief. He could almost feel the healing rain dance upon his own body, cleansing him, washing away his past, his pain, polishing away the filth and shame.

"It's old-fashioned, I know," Rain spoke hesitantly, feeling awkward. "No one uses handkerchiefs any more, but I thought..." she abruptly stopped herself.

"Well. It's a small reminder of your time here in China."

And a tiny reminder of me, she added silently.

Speechless at her generosity, Valerius could only nod his gratitude. Swallowing the lump in his throat, he turned away until she was faced with his broad back.

Except for his mother and sister, it was the first gift a female had ever given him.

Bluntly dismissed by the warrior once more, Rain stepped back with concern creasing her brow.

Had she offended him somehow? His body was radiating strong emotional energy, but she could not discern what it was. Shaking her head slightly, as if to dispel the confusion, she squared her shoulders and joined the other females on the bed, breaking her fast and engaging in lively conversation.

Once he got hold of himself, Valerius took a seat on the far side of the chamber and proceeded to sharpen his scythe and dagger. Just to be safe, he secured a *chakram* Aella lent him for the trip to his waist as backup.

Every so often, he would touch the area where his heart resided to make sure that the handkerchief was safe inside the inner chest pocket of his shirt.

Once in a while, female laughter drifted to his ears, and he could have sworn they were talking about him at times, for they would turn to him in unison during parts of the chatter and immediately break into giggles.

What they found so amusing about his person, Valerius couldn't begin to guess, but he didn't mind being the butt of their jokes, if that was what he was, because he got to see Rain's laughter light up the entire room.

Not once, however, did he think to join them. He did not have the diplomatic charm of Seth, nor the easy affability of Tristan. He was not cheerfully outgoing like Aella, and he had not the confident gravitas of Alexandros. He was uncomfortable around people and hated to be touched.

Verily, he would not have any friends to call his own if not for the position he was recruited to.

In the beginning it was a duty—his chosen duty to protect the weak. The Elite and Circlet members were his comrades who shared the same purpose and belief. But gradually they became more.

They became friends. And then family. Valerius would not hesitate to give his life for any one of them.

Most of all for their newest member—the Healer.

Rain.

By the time they headed above ground, it was only an hour after dawn. They took a lift to rise to the grassy grounds of one of the islands in the middle of West Lake.

The sun was still low in the sky, hiding behind a blanket of clouds, slowly stretching its warm rays outward in tendrils of orange and pink. A slight mist covered the landscape like a dewy curtain of dragon's smoke. The beauty around him was so unreal, Valerius could only gape in wonderment and awe.

Two little girls no more than twelve with braided coils on either side of their heads skipped forth to take them to the awaiting boats. One girl shyly ventured up to Valerius and held out a small hand to him in invitation.

Wordlessly, he took it and was rewarded with a gamine smile, exposing a rather enchanting gap between her two front teeth.

She tugged him to the boat and gestured for him to sit at the very back, while Ayelet, Rain, Wan'er and Sophia sat on two padded benches in the middle.

"They are distributing our weight," Rain explained to him. "You likely weigh more than those two girls combined, but if we sit closer to the front of the boat, we should be relatively balanced."

The two girls stood at the front of the boat with long paddles twice their height. They smoothly pushed the pretty, canopied boat off shore and began to stroke the paddles leisurely in sync, harnessing the strength of the breeze that pushed them toward the mainland.

Valerius felt embarrassed that he was sitting idly on his ass while two little girls did all the hard work. But he took note of their experienced technique and realized he'd probably be more embarrassed if he tried a hand at paddling. Maybe even sink them all in the middle of the lake.

After a few moments of silent enjoyment, each passenger absorbing the graceful sunrise over a glistening West Lake, the girls began to sing with a crystal resonance that nightingales would envy.

"They like you," Rain whispered to Valerius with a warm twinkle in her eye.

She sat closest to him toward the back, her front facing his, her back against Ayelet's, who was facing the front of the boat.

Startled, Valerius only blinked at her without comprehension.

Rain smiled her Mona Lisa smile and nodded to their ferry-girls.

"They want to impress you with their lilting song because they've never seen such a handsome man as you."

Valerius' face went up in flames, and he struggled for composure though he knew she was only teasing him.

People—females—simply didn't tease him. He tried to respond with practiced nonchalance, but he feared he sounded just plain stupid.

"Why do you say that?" he asked, then grimaced. He sounded like he was fishing for compliments.

The Healer chuckled behind her hand.

She quoted to him, " 'Oh my heart, my heart be still, is that my lover o'er yon green hill? Ah, my heart, my heart does sing, what joyous occasion this day brings. For ne'er have I beheld such a fine bodied lad, and ne'er have I seen such beauty he has—oh my heart, my heart be still, let it be my lover o'er yon green hill.' "

Valerius could no longer meet the Healer's twinkling eyes by the time she'd finished translating the song. He turned away to view the scenery around the lake, but he knew that her gaze was still riveted upon him, for he felt the weight of its languorous heat in the cool autumn morning.

They spent the better part of the morning strolling around the lake, Wan'er acting as tour guide and introducing them to the inhabitants of the Sanctuary, the history behind the various landmarks and architecture, and the myths about the West Lake itself.

In one such legend, the lake was said to be a reincarnation of a famous Chinese beauty from ancient times. Gazing surreptitiously at Rain, Valerius thought the story might have been about her, for no other beauty could match the enchantment and serenity of the West Lake.

For lunch, they had a picnic beneath the Leifeng Pagoda. Midway through the meal, however, the Healer rose to greet a long line of children who approached, strung together with some sort of silk rope around each of their waists.

At the end of the snake-like procession was an elderly woman in a Buddhist nun habit who smiled in greeting. She and Rain conversed quietly in Chinese while Wan'er also finished up her *baozi* and went to join them.

"It is the day for the children's annual check-up," Ayelet explained to Sophia and Valerius, who watched the proceedings curiously.

"Wan'er told me that every year on this day, the orphans in the surrounding villages travel here to see Rain so that she can give their health a boost and rid them of any ailments. They cannot afford to go to the clinics in town, nor do they have time to wait for days to be seen by a physician. So they come to the Sanctuary to see Lady Rain who doles out magical kisses that make them all better."

Valerius looked at her disbelievingly at the "magical kisses" remark, but Ayelet only smiled.

"To children, a mother's kiss is imbued with magical powers. To these orphans, Rain is like their fairytale mother for the kindness and affection she brings into their lives. And coincidentally, her kisses do indeed heal, if she harnesses her Gift to transfer energy through them."

Valerius could relate to that. He could use a billion, trillion magical kisses himself.

While the children lined up in an orderly fashion before the pagoda, Rain and Wan'er set up their "clinic" within. Valerius watched the Healer do her duty with loving care, as generous with her time and patience as she was with the magical kisses she smothered the children with, making many giggle with delight.

And for the first time since his human boyhood, the warrior found his heart clench with yearning.

What he'd give to be smothered in Rain's tender kisses. Hell, what he *wouldn't* give just to get one kiss.

Tiny, sticky fingers pulling at the fabric of his trousers pulled his attention away from the beautiful Healer.

Sitting on the grass beside the pagoda, long legs stretched before him, elbows on his slightly bent knees, he was eye level with a thumb-sucking little girl with what looked to be a disproportionately large head atop a bone-thin body. She popped her thumb out of her mouth with a wet noise and held both arms toward him expectantly.

Valerius stared at her motionlessly, uncertain what he should do.

She tilted her head sideways as if in thought, then seemed to make a decision.

If the mountain wouldn't come to her, she was going to take herself to the mountain.

She waddled bravely between the warrior's spread legs and crawled unceremoniously into his lap. She grabbed one of his forearms with both little hands, surprisingly strong in their sticky grip, yanking a few of his hairs in the process, and pulled his arm around to hold her securely in his lap, where she wriggled around to find a comfortable position and promptly stuck her thumb back into her mouth.

Once in a while she would look up at him to see if he paid attention to her, briefly meeting his consternated eyes. Satisfied that he was focused on her, she would pat his forearm with wet little smacks as if petting a well-behaved dog.

Before Valerius knew it, two more pint-sized kids joined her in his lap, and then two more, sitting by his booted feet, seemingly fascinated with his utilitarian footwear. Pretty soon, he was crawling with children, like a hill conquered by an army of ants.

"I see the children, too, have fallen under your spell," came the teasingly warm voice of the Healer.

Valerius avoided her gaze to hide his embarrassment. Some mighty warrior Pure male he must have looked.

"You must like them too," she said, her voice growing softer, "for you let them touch you freely."

Valerius flicked his eyes to her in surprise and was nearly bowled over by her next words—

"How I envy them."

Without waiting to see his response, she went back to the makeshift clinic within the pagoda.

Yes, Valerius thought with some amazement at himself, he liked children very much.

He'd always liked children, and they seemed to be naturally drawn to him in return. Perhaps they viewed him as just another child, albeit a hell of a lot bigger. They represented to him the innocence he'd lost. They represented all the good and pure things in life.

The laughter of children was what he fought to protect.

And protect them he did, literally later that evening, when his group of four Pure Ones chaperoned Sophia and the twenty odd orphans along with the elderly nun to the street festival in an old part of Hangzhou city.

The festivities were in full swing by the time they arrived, thousands of lanterns lighting up the approaching night. Lanterns on towers, outside every window of every house, strung up on telephone poles and wires so that they appeared to be floating in the darkening sky. Every man, woman and child carried a lantern of their own, Valerius' entourage carrying lanterns shaped like animals.

As they strolled down the crowded night market streets, all that could be seen was a meandering parade of happy turtles, rabbits, birds, pandas, and other more mythical creatures of old.

Valerius felt particularly proud that he'd helped Rain and Wan'er make these lanterns by hand for most of the afternoon. He ended up gluing more of his thick fingers than the delicate rice paper the lanterns were made out of, but the children didn't seem to mind if the animals he made were missing an ear or tail. They accepted his awkward creations with effervescent joy, hugging him and kissing him in eagerness and gratitude.

It was by far the best day of his existence.

As the children ran around to browse the multitude of shops and stands, and sample the treats that were cooked right before their eyes, Valerius lagged behind to gain a better view of their surroundings and position.

He took in each and every face and form with practiced skill, gauging potential threats and danger with unparalleled experience.

As if the human residents and visitors sensed the powerful and lethal energy around the warrior, they inadvertently gave him wider berth so that despite the rush and the throngs of people, Valerius stood almost alone, untouched, unbothered, against the side wall of a candy shop.

Until the Healer decided to join him.

"Have you a celebration like this where you hail from?" Rain asked him as she came to stand beside him, forcing him to take a step back to keep at least three feet of distance between them.

"No," he replied with some awe, "I've never seen anything like this."

"Wait until you see the fire dragon dance," she told him, sounding as if the display was more than worth the wait.

"What is the festival about?" he asked, more to distract himself from her nearness than out of sincere curiosity.

"Oh, many things," she answered. "It's a celebration of a fruitful harvest, a time to be with one's family and thank the gods for our fortunes. A time of reunion and love-making."

"What?" Valerius startled at her last words and almost lost his footing.

She kept her gaze on the children and smiled.

"There's a legend behind the Moon Festival, as it is sometimes called, hence all the *yuebing* you see, the moon-shaped cakes with red bean filling and a salted duck egg yolk inside."

She gestured to the very shop they stood beside, and Valerius saw what she meant by the rows of golden moon cakes on tantalizing display.

"Legend has it that over four thousand years ago, there was a young couple who served the Emperor of Heaven. The husband, Houyi, was an archer of unrivaled skill, and his wife, Chang'e, was a lady of surpassing beauty. The earth at the time thrived on the heat from ten suns in the form of three-legged birds that resided in a mulberry tree in the eastern sea. Each day, one bird would run across the sky, bathing the earth with its warmth and light."

"But one day, all ten birds ran across the sky, surrounding the earth in a ring of fire. To end the devastating drought that ensued, the Emperor of Heaven commanded Houyi to shoot down all of the birds save one, and the archer carried out his task successfully."

No longer listening just to distract himself, Valerius found that he was entranced by her story, by her soft lilting voice. Unconsciously, he moved a step closer, until she could feel the heat of his body in the chilly night.

Rain leaned ever so slightly toward him, though careful not to touch. She didn't want to scare away this lonely, lost child in the guise of a mighty warrior.

She'd seen him play joyfully with the children in the afternoon, seen the mesmerizing light of his rare smiles and even heard the sound of a rarer laugh. If she could have, she would have been content to watch him all day long.

"As a reward for his service, the Emperor granted him a palace on the sun and a magical pill," Rain continued with the story, "which he hid beneath his rafters that night. But when he was on duty the next day, the light from the magical pill beckoned to his wife, who swallowed it by mistake."

"The pill made her spread wings and fly, and to her fright and panic, the wings took her to the distant moon. Houyi returned that night to find her gone. He tried to go after her, but strong winds knocked him down. And thus, Chang'e remained on the moon, longing every day and night for her beloved mate."

Valerius vaguely wondered that Houyi wasn't angry with his wife for devouring the magical pill that he had won, but he thought he understood the archer's perspective. For if he had been the husband, and Rain the wife, he would have given every gift, every reward, everything he had to his mate.

And he wouldn't have been stupid enough to let her fly away from him.

"There was a hare that lived on the moon," Rain continued, "a hare who could make magical potions from the herbs that thrived there. Chang'e bid the hare to pound the herbs into a pill for her husband so that he could fly too and visit her. The hare succeeded in making such a potion, but the magical powers only lasted for one night out of each year."

"So, on the Moon Festival every year, Houyi flies from his palace on the Sun to visit his wife's tower on the Moon, and in anticipation of her husband's arrival, the moon puts on her most beguiling dress, shimmering in fullness and light."

At that, Valerius raised his eyes to the night sky and gazed upon the low-hanging, bright full moon. Indeed it seemed to shimmer with unusual brilliance, like a beautiful woman glowing with love.

He then glanced down at the woman beside him, the exquisite profile of her face etched forever in his mind.

The story of Chang'e reminded him of the Healer, who glowed resplendently this night with renewed strength and vitality. Her Houyi was her Consort, who visited her for thirty days during the Phoenix Cycle once every decade.

He suddenly wished he could break her free of this never ending chain, somehow ensure that strength and vitality resided within her always, that her beauty ever shone like it did tonight, never waning, never dim.

He'd do anything to be her strength.

Almost.

He didn't dare show her his true self, didn't dare expose his demons.

They stood in silence for a while, watching the beginning of the fire dragon dance together as a parade of men wearing brightly colored trousers painted to look like dragon scales wound their way through the crowd, their bodies and heads covered in a long, flowing canopy made to resemble the body of a Chinese dragon.

The men dipped and rose, twisted and turned in sync, following the beat of an ancient drum, mesmerizing in their meandering dance, like a giant fire-breathing dragon floating leisurely through a sea of people, looking this way and that, the giant, elaborately decorated head with its wide-eyed stare taking in its surroundings like a deity descended from the heavens.

The children, escorted by Ayelet, Wan'er and the nun, followed Sophia's lead and skipped merrily alongside the dancing dragon with their animal lanterns in one hand and long sticks of incense in the other. The incense was for the Moon Goddess, Chang'e, wishing her a happy reunion with her husband, Houyi, so that they would bless the earth with continued bounty and good fortune.

Rain grasped the sleeve of Valerius' shirt and tugged him along as they followed the children's progress through the crowds, keeping them within view.

Along the way she procured two sticks of candied cranberries and gave one to Valerius, gesturing for him to take a bite.

He did so, and savored the distinctive combination of crunchy sugary coating and tangy sour fruit within. He looked at her small hand gripping his sleeve and had the inexplicable urge to take her hand in his own, to weave their fingers together.

They wound their way through the crowded streets, passing houses, shops and stands with strings of colorful lanterns hanging from bamboo poles at their highest points, from roofs and terraces, rafters and antennas. The lanterns waved and floated like giant fireflies in the breeze, illuminating the night with multi-colored radiance.

They stopped beneath a makeshift tower, constructed with long, heavy wooden beams and bamboo stilts for the explicit purpose of hanging lanterns. The fire dragon had started its ceremonial dance, circling its tail and twitching its long, curly whiskers in the middle of the crowd that had formed a wide ring around the performers.

Sophia and the children were in the front lines of the crowd, getting an up-close and personal view of the spectacular display.

Though they were now standing still, Rain kept her loose grip on Valerius' sleeve, not wanting their connection to break.

She tried to focus on the festivities before her, instead of the warrior standing beside her, but she had very little success. She wanted to scoot closer to the heat his large body radiated in comforting waves, wanted to wrap an arm about his lean waist and lay her head on his chest.

Despite having had hundreds of Consorts over her existence as a Pure One, she had never been so drawn to one particular male.

Not for the first time she wished he was hers. She wished she could keep him with her beyond just one Phoenix Cycle.

It was pure madness, that particular wish. She knew full well she couldn't afford to risk attachment.

On that thought, she slowly let go of Valerius' sleeve, letting her hand dangle empty by her side.

This warrior should never be hers. It would be too dangerous, especially for him. She knew herself and her own desires and limits. She would quickly become addicted to his Nourishment and strength and crave him like a female starved. And she'd be tempted to break her own cardinal rule—to never take the same Consort twice.

Once upon a time, she'd made that mistake. She'd grown fond of a male during her first Phoenix Cycle as the Healer. The intimacies they shared deceived her into feeling something more than just sexual attraction, basic need and affection. She thought perhaps they could become like Mates, though they would only come together for thirty days every ten years. She thought she loved him enough to make it work.

He fell in love with her in earnest, pining for her and waiting impatiently for the second Phoenix Cycle when they could be together again. Over the years, they lived separately, for fear of the temptation of being too close.

Finally, the time approached again for the Healer to choose a Consort, and as they'd promised each other, Rain again chose him.

But the second cycle was different from the first. Instead of feeling fulfilled when they came together, the more Rain fed, the hungrier she felt. Yet, her Consort only became weaker, his strength rapidly depleting.

Towards the end of the thirty days, they realized that the Consort was in fact dying, for he had offered everything to her—his body, blood, heart and soul, but she was not able to reciprocate. Despite the deep affection and caring she felt for him, despite the grief and guilt his Decline incited, she could not give him equal measure even as she used her powers to try to heal him.

At the end of the Cycle, he died peacefully in her arms, giving her the last of his strength and power so that she finally felt her vitality return. She'd wept until there were no tears, until only dry heaves racked her body.

It was a lesson she would never forget: the Healer could not fall in love.

No matter how much she craved and cared for a male, she was not capable of giving; she only took. Her energy and power she gave only to her patients as the Pure Ones' designated Healer. She had nothing left to give to a male of her choice.

She could never take a Mate.

To Serve her for one Phoenix Cycle was manageable if a male was strong. Eventually, he would heal and recover his strength. But to Serve her more than once was incredible risk, one that deluded both Healer and Consort into thinking their bond might be more permanent, more true.

She knew now that she could never form the Mating bond with a Pure male, no matter his strength and devotion, no matter the depth of her feeling and determination. She would never love him enough.

Perhaps because she loved healing more.

She could not prioritize personal love over a Gift that benefited her entire race.

Valerius sensed more than felt the Healer's withdrawal. He could almost feel her pain and regret and had the inexplicable urge to comfort her.

But before he could act on that whim, he stiffened as he sensed danger a split moment before the tower they leaned against began to creak and shift.

Looking up, he saw that a fallen lantern had started a fire, but the breeze had carried the burning scent away and masked the impending danger. As the heavy wood beams swayed toward them, Valerius threw himself upon the Healer, knocking her to the hard ground, just before one of the beams collapsed on top of Valerius.

Rain's breath was knocked out of her in a whoosh, and she braced herself for more impact but realized belatedly that none came.

Valerius' body served as a protective barrier over hers, his torso a hair's breadth away from hers, his arms and legs like godly columns that kept the heavens from toppling.

His face was turned away from hers, her lips lightly grazing the muscles of his throat.

Before she could collect her wits, he ground out in low urgent tones, "Get out from underneath me. Hurry."

She pulled herself together enough to pedal backwards with her hands and feet, slowly easing out of the crevice he made with his body. She was helped the rest of the way by Ayelet and Wan'er who pulled her out by her arms.

When she was safely pulled aside, Valerius tensed his muscles in one great heave, pushing the collapsed beams a fraction upwards before executing a drive and a roll to extract himself from the deadly lock. As he rolled away, the tower collapsed fully, the debris of lanterns and bamboo and broken beams barely missing him on their way down.

He stayed lying on the ground in the aftermath and tilted his head back to check for the safety of the children, spectators and Rain. Seeing that they were a good distance away by now, the adrenaline flowed out of his body, leaving bone-deep agony in its wake.

Getting squashed by a thirty-foot tower weighing a ton tended to leave one feeling like a roach that just got flattened by a particularly heavy rock.

And then Rain was by his side, her hands flying across his throbbing body.

A different kind of pain immediately triggered, and Valerius gritted his teeth against the onslaught.

"Don't touch me," he hissed out, making a monumental effort to roll away.

"But I have to—" she tried to follow him, her hands skimming across his chest and biceps.

"Don't touch me!" he almost shouted, desperately trying to get away.

He staggered to a half stance, holding his left shoulder with one hand, and limped as rapidly as he could to the nearest brick establishment.

She watched him go but did not follow, her eyes round with hurt and worry.

Before she knew what he was about, he slammed his left side against the wall, and the noise his bone and flesh made as his shoulder popped back into its socket made her cringe in vicarious pain.

Valerius did not make a sound, however. He simply slid down the wall in an exhausted heap and sat with his legs sprawled haphazardly before him.

Rain felt Ayelet's gentle hands on her shoulder.

"Leave him be," the Guardian said. "His body will heal within the night. He may be one large sore when we depart for the Shield tomorrow, but he'll be fine very soon."

Then she added, after hesitating a beat, "Don't be offended by his rejection of your aid. That's just the way he is. Don't take it personally."

Rain nodded, even though she didn't understand.

For the first time, her Gift as a Healer was staunchly rejected. For the first time, she felt uncertain and lost. For, if there was one living creature in all the world, across all eternity that she yearned to heal, it was this man.

The Protector.

Chapter Ten

"Goddess above, those new recruits are *killing* me," Aella griped as she threw herself down on a deep seated chaise in the antechamber adjoining the throne room.

"I don't know how Alexandros put up with it."

Ayelet smiled slightly at Aella's complaining and asked, without looking up from her research, "I take it the training of Chevaliers is not going as smoothly as you hoped?"

"To put it mildly," Aella quickly responded. "Those boys barely know the business end of a *spatha* much less how to defend themselves when vampires attack in Hordes. A couple of human males are showing far more promise than their Pure counterparts, despite being physically weaker and slower."

"I am not surprised," Ayelet said. "Our Pure recruits are mostly peace-loving civilians not accustomed to combat. Fighting is something against the grain for them. Causing injury unto others must not be stomached well."

"But the humans we've recruited are chosen largely because of their warrior leanings. I take it one of the two humans you spoke of is the ex-Navy SEAL and the other is the mixed martial arts champion?"

"Yep," Aella agreed, "I'm having a blast throwing those two around."

She grinned beatifically, then abruptly sobered and sighed.

"But I'm nowhere near as natural at this as the General. I have a whole new appreciation for his patience and innate ability to be a leader of men. I am praying fervently for Xandros' speedy recovery."

At that, Ayelet turned to face the Amazon.

"How is he by the way? When I looked in last night, he was still deep in slumber, his body exhausted from both the blood loss and the healing process."

Aella grew serious.

"We almost lost him, that's how bad his wounds were. He's a tough bugger to take down too. Hell, he's the one who trained me and whipped my ass more times than I care to recount."

"I know," Ayelet agreed, knowing where Aella's thoughts were headed. "If whoever is orchestrating these ambushes can take down two of our fiercest and most experienced—and don't forget they almost succeeded with Val as well—it doesn't bear thinking what they could be up to next."

"I think these past events are skirmishes," Aella mused contemplatively. "It's as if she's testing us, trying our strength, searching for our weaknesses and waiting for the right time to exploit them."

"We don't know that it's a she," Ayelet reminded her.

"True enough," Aella agreed, "but I've never met a male vampire who is so well organized, so methodical and devious. The males are more prone to letting their instincts rule them, the need to eat, fuck, claim territory. Females are a lot more manipulative. I feel like whoever it is likes to toy with her prey before she goes in for the kill."

"How weak are our defenses?" Ayelet dreaded the question but she must know. "How prepared are the Chevaliers?"

Aella took a deep breath and let it out in a frustrated gush as she combed one hand through her wild golden mane.

"First, we are short on numbers. There are only a dozen fully-trained Chevaliers on site after we lost some good soldiers in the battle with the Hordes last year. New recruits are few and far between. Pure males of warrior class are more and more difficult to find. Dalair and I are having to consider more humans to fill in the gap, and I don't want to expose our race to others any more than absolutely necessary."

"Second, of the Chevaliers we have, few are experienced warriors. They may be battle-ready, but they haven't learned the hard way through thousands of years of warfare how to be cunning, how to survive. The oldest one is only a few hundred years old, and he is not of warrior class."

Ayelet grimaced. They were yet babes compared to the ancient vampire assassins who threatened them.

"Third, we must stop hobbling along with less than the full Dozen," Aella continued, referring to the Royal Zodiac. "Either we find and bring back Leonidas and Seth or we move on without them."

Though she hated to say the words, and Ayelet hated hearing them, they both knew it was the truth.

"Already, the guard rotation around Sophia and our hunting patterns are less than ideal. And with Val for the most part out of the rounds due to his Service, we are even more exposed to our enemies whenever we go out. Not only does this new opponent have the upper hand, so does every vampire Horde out there who wants to take a shot at us."

Ayelet nodded and added worriedly, "Meanwhile, the Healer is not recovering her strength as she should."

"What?" Aella didn't think she could stomach more bad news.

Ayelet sighed heavily and looked back to her computer screens.

"It's been almost a fortnight since the Phoenix Cycle began. She should be starting to recover her color and vitality, but I only see her continue to weaken. It's true that healing Val and Xandros took a lot out of her, especially in her weakened state, but the Nourishment should have reinvigorated her, or at least stem the decline."

"Unless Val isn't providing the full Nourishment," Aella said quietly.

"To tell you the truth, I was surprised when I found out he applied to Serve her. I never thought he would volunteer to put himself in that situation. In any situation where he has to be intimate with someone."

"I am less surprised," Ayelet admitted. "Since the first time they met, I've noticed a certain push and pull between them. That he becomes her Consort is inevitable. It was just a question of when. And whether he can fulfill her or not depends on whether he can conquer his inner demons."

"You know of his past then?" Aella asked, feeling as if she was the only one left out of a well-known secret.

Ayelet shook her head. "I don't know the specifics. I don't think any of us do. The eleven of us have lived together, fought alongside one another for centuries, for some of us, millennia. Besides Xandros, I might say I know Valerius the best. And even then I can't own to knowing him very well. All I can say is that he is deeply troubled by his past. And sometimes..."

Ayelet closed her eyes as if her heart ached.

"Sometimes I see shadows of anguish and torment in his eyes."

"Why did he put himself in such a position?" Aella asked, sounding rather frustrated at Valerius for pushing himself too hard.

"I'd guess because he found something more important to focus on than his own substantial pain," Ayelet answered.

"Though the Healer can only cure our bodily wounds, perhaps in this instance she can work her magic on the Protector's soul as well."

*** *** *** ***

Valerius gunned his Hayabusa around a sharp corner, then swerved at the last second to avoid an oncoming truck, barely missing the sixteen wheeler as it blared its horn at him in passing.

Tristan struggled to keep up in his Lamborghini Murciélago, the twists and turns of the mountainous roads lending advantage to the adroit Hayabusa.

The Champion cursed beneath his breath as Valerius took another sharp turn without any regard for safety, riding the edge of the single lane, a foot away from opposite traffic, to pass the slower car in front of him.

If Tristan got into an accident or got stopped by cops because of *Tron Legacy* wannabe over there, he was going to drag the Roman off his bike and pound him into mincemeat for making Ayelet worry.

If Tristan could catch the suicidal maniac that was.

They were on their way back to the Shield from a full day's hunt and search for Leonidas. Tristan was surprised at first that Valerius was accompanying him instead of Dalair or Aella, as the Consort seldom left the Healer's side. His first priority was to Service her needs.

At least, that was what Tristan understood from past Consorts—which included each of the male Elite except himself since he'd been Mated to Ayelet shortly after his revival.

Duty and Service aside, Tristan assumed any full-blooded warrior male would prefer to stay with the female who required his Nourishment just for the sex and release this small loophole in the Sacred Laws provided.

Having had more than his fair share of women in his human life, and then having his days and nights full with Ayelet, Tristan considered himself extremely fortunate, ridiculously fortunate, to not have had to live out even a year of celibacy.

He'd like to think he wasn't a weak man, a man without some semblance of self-control. But where sex was concerned, well, he was a male of voracious appetites. The Goddess, in her infinite wisdom, blessed him with Ayelet, who was every bit his match, and then some.

So having the Protector partner him on this day was deeply perplexing to the medieval knight. It was as if Valerius was purposely avoiding his duty as Consort, which just didn't make a lick of sense to Tristan.

Tristan flashed his fog lights at the crazy bastard when Valerius pulled another kamikaze maneuver that made Tristan struggle to prevent his Murciélago from heading into a tail spin as he spun the wheels away from a Tahoe that had swerved into his lane to avoid the Haybusa.

In response, he saw Valerius hold up a middle finger, then gun the Hayabusa into a roar that left Tristan to eat up his dust.

Oh yeah, there was going to be some serious throw down in the training room tonight.

Tristan cracked his knuckles with anticipation.

*** *** *** ***

Ayelet stood before two giant digital monitors with the Scribe and Seer on either side.

She pulled up the first image from her final search compilation and recited, "Name, Cloud Drako. Current residence, Lushui County, Nujiang Lisu Autonomous Prefecture in the Southwestern border of China, Yunnan Province. Current occupation, local artist and calligrapher. Probably around two thousand years old. Took some digging and calling on favors to find him. He certainly doesn't seem like he wants to be found."

"By any chance is he related to Rain?" Orion asked with a straight face.

Ayelet shot him a quick glance and realized that he wasn't jesting. She suspected he wouldn't know sarcasm if it bit him in the ass.

The Scribe was as serious and as dry as they came.

She answered him with a similar expression of solemnity.

"Not that I am aware. Cloud is just his chosen name as a Pure One. I haven't been able to determine his real name."

"Then how can you be sure he's of warrior class?" Eveline inquired.

Ayelet often wondered why the Scribe and Seer didn't get together. They seemed so well suited for each other.

On the other hand, their personalities were so similar they could also pass for twins.

"My sources tell me there are legends about him throughout China, or at least, about the human warrior he used to be. In fact, those legends have spread widely around the world, though how much is truth and how much fiction I can't say."

Ayelet clicked the mouse to open a video showing the warrior in question concentrating on forming a particular work of Chinese calligraphy art.

"This was shot a few days ago by one of my human sources posing as a tourist in Kunming. Apparently, there was an annual art fair and Cloud's work was one of the main attractions. Rarely does he venture out of his village in the mountains, but for this fair, he decided to make an exception. You see the way he holds the brush?"

Orion and Eveline peered at the display closely, noticing the leanly muscular forearm that strained gracefully beneath the thin fabric of the warrior's sleeve as he held a long, large calligraphy brush whose head was as big as a fist.

The way he stroked the brush down the floor-length scroll was deceptive in its power, graceful and fluid in well-practiced technique, and somehow militaristic in style.

Ayelet clicked on another video that opened beside the previous one.

"This was taken by the same tourist early the next morning. Drako apparently rode to Kunming on horseback, eschewing modern modes of transportation. They say his horse, a distinctive white stallion, is also immortal and is his constant companion."

She zoomed in on the video image. "You see how he sits astride the horse? As if he was born atop it? As if their bodies were one? That is not something a calligraphy artist hidden in the remote hills of Lushui County should know how to do. That posture and power can only be achieved from years of riding, and from the alertness of his body language, years of riding into war."

As they watched, the warrior turned towards the hidden camera and looked straight at them. They could almost feel the intensity of his gaze from within the display monitor.

"Does he know we're searching for him?" Eveline whispered, mesmerized by the startling laser blue eyes, a shock to see in an Asian face.

The image was taken too far away for them to see his face clearly, but she could still *feel* his spell-binding eyes.

'I'm sure he does," Ayelet replied.

"Don't stare too long."

She abruptly closed the videos, and Orion and Eveline had to blink rapidly as if to clear the descending fog in their heads.

"Even though it's only a video capture, his power is so great the intent behind his gaze can still be felt," Ayelet explained.

"I believe his Gift is one of telepathy. When I first watched the video and came to this frame, I stared blankly at the screen for several minutes before Tristan shook me awake. Then I felt like I wanted to erase the images and the file entirely and almost did except for Tristan's help. He pulled me away from the monitor and traced back with me what I was doing and thinking before I watched the video, and I realized that this warrior had been trying to convince me to stop searching for him with his gaze."

"I felt it too," Orion said, still shaking the cobwebs from his head.

"He is incredibly strong if he can force his will upon us from just a video that was taken days ago. This will make our efforts to recruit him far more difficult than we expected."

"Indeed," Ayelet agreed. "But he is my first choice to..." she hesitated with a pang of sadness, but plunged on resolutely, "to replace the Sentinel."

She read the expressions on the Scribe and Seer's faces.

"Looks like you both would agree with me?"

Orion and Eveline nodded in chorus.

"This warrior definitely fits the description from the Zodiac Scrolls and Prophesies," Orion said. "But show us the others you have discovered. We must ensure we consider all possibilities."

Ayelet proceeded to show them the files on a Viking warrior residing in Sweden as a university professor on Norse mythology and history, and a Russian living in St. Petersburg as the CEO of a local oil and gas company.

They agreed in the end that they needed to hasten the recruitment process, with not a moment to delay. The Seer and Scribe would depart immediately for Europe while Ayelet would take Rain and Valerius to China, given Rain's familiarity with the landscape and people.

It was a risky move since the Shield would only be left with four Elite guards, one still recovering from his extensive injuries, one handmaiden on whose small shoulders rested the health of an entire encampment. Moreover, the Seer and Scribe would travel without protective escort.

But Orion and Eveline insisted that their skills were not simply limited to the cerebral. The Scribe had the power of telekinesis and the Seer had the ability to see events five minutes before they happened. Though untrained in combat, they had strong survival instincts and could take care of themselves and each other.

And so it was decided. On the morrow they would embark on their journey.

*** *** *** ***

Valerius rammed his left shoulder into Tristan's taut belly and ground his right fist into the Champion's ribs, pushing him into the wall with bone-jarring force.

Tristan took the impact with a grunt but didn't lose a beat. He jack-knifed his knee into Valerius' sternum and stabbed the warrior's neck where it joined his shoulder with a well-aimed elbow, making him step back half a pace to twist out of range.

They carried on in a blur of sharp fists, elbows, knees and feet. Tristan's brute strength was staggering when he landed a blow, while Valerius' more agile maneuvers delivered hits where it counted the most.

Finally, both males paused in their no-holds-barred fight to regard each other warily, chest heaving and sweat running in rivers down their faces and bodies.

"Fuck," Tristan ground out, shaking his head like a wet dog, sending bullets of sweat in all directions.

"Who taught you to fight like that? I'm pretty sure those moves aren't legal. At least Xandros and Leo never pulled any like that when we sparred."

"Necessity," Valerius answered grimly. "There are no rules in the gladiator arena."

Or when you were trying to escape over a decade's worth of brutality and imprisonment.

Tristan nodded with respect.

"More power to you, my brother. You gotta teach me some of those moves."

He then promptly descended onto his ass, sprawling against the wall in sheer exhaustion.

Valerius eyed him for a moment, decided they'd worked out their frustrations enough for one day, and joined the Champion against the wall, keeping a foot of distance between them.

"So you wanna tell me why you're hell-bent on suicide?" Tristan asked without preamble.

"I know how far I can push myself," Valerius replied in a low voice that vibrated with the message "back the fuck off."

"Yeah, okay," Tristan said, "but it's not just yourself you have to worry about now, it's the Healer too. What would become of her if something should happen to you?"

Right now, in the middle of the Phoenix Cycle, it didn't bear thinking, but Valerius knew that after she survived him, there would be other Consorts. It wasn't as if her longevity depended solely on him.

The thought of future Consorts Nourishing the Healer made his heart shrivel and his soul recoil, so he focused back on the present. As much as he hated to admit it, the knight had a point. But with things as they were, he was hardly of use to the Healer. He was a sorry excuse as a Consort.

For the past few days, Rain had barely fed from him. And then, only from his wrist when she was obviously starving and couldn't help herself any more. She went about her days as if they had never been bonded, as if she were perfectly well and Nourishment was a luxury rather than a sheer necessity.

He'd tried to tempt her into more than just taking his blood, but she resisted gently, always with a ready excuse, always with a tender smile as if he were a fragile, wounded animal who couldn't withstand further injury.

And he was so useless he constantly flagellated himself with derision and hatred. He knew any Pure male worth his salt would be able to drum up a seduction to break through her reticence, but he didn't know the first thing about seduction.

He was overwhelmed with uncertainty and mortification every time he tried to offer himself to her, and then he wallowed in hurt and self-disgust so acute from her gentle rejection that his blood turned to ice in his veins and tears of acid corroded his throat.

He didn't delude himself of the truth: she no longer wanted him.

After he'd told her the horrors of his past, sparing the details but still revealing the sordid reality, she'd let him hold her tight, let him find redemption and comfort in the heat and softness of her body, like a lost little boy hugging his security blanket.

But everything changed after that night.

She no longer looked upon him with covetous, desirous eyes. She barely looked at him at all.

He felt the distance between them stretch into a veritable chasm, and an excruciating hollowness grew within him in equal proportion.

He disgusted her now, he knew. She was too kind to give it expression. He felt her pity in the gentle tone of her voice. He saw her recoil whenever he tried to get closer.

It was killing him by slow degrees.

All the pain and torment of his past paled in comparison to how much it hurt to be rejected by her, to know that she would never want him again.

For the first time in his existence he wished he'd never been born. He'd always fought the demons in his private hell without complaint, his only regret that he couldn't protect his family. With his Gift and his power to defend the weak, he'd accepted his past as payment towards a greater good.

But now his skin felt too tight for his flesh, blood and bones. Every breath he took in her presence felt like he was sucking sulfuric acid into his lungs rather than air.

He felt defeated. Destroyed.

Like his soul had splintered into a million shards and he was an empty shell going through the motions of a well-practiced routine.

And the worst of it was that he knew she was steadily weakening. At this rate, his insanity to apply to be her Consort would lead to her death.

She'd been right from the very beginning. He could never fulfill her needs.

"Snap out of it." Tristan smacked Valerius' head against the wall with enough force to make stars flash before the Protector's eyes.

"I don't know where your mind just went, but I don't like that look on your face."

Valerius decided not to respond to the head banging with equal violence, but instead started to rise. Tristan pulled him back down with a hard yank.

"I'm not finished lecturing you," the Champion said, keeping a restraining hand on Valerius' arm.

Valerius resisted breaking the hand off for Ayelet's sake but he speared the knight with a glare of warning.

"Yeah yeah, you're going to shove my own fist up my ass if I don't let go, I get it," Tristan said without much concern, though he did loosen his hold on Valerius' arm.

"Just sit down for a minute and hear me out. Then you can wallow in self-pity to your heart's content."

Valerius scowled ferociously at the Champion's words, but sat back down again, the determination and—strangely— understanding in the other male's gaze making his body obey despite his mind's rebellion.

"Look, I haven't known you as long as Leo or Xandros. One might say I barely know you at all," Tristan began in a low serious tone.

"You're not exactly the chummy sort. We're probably polar opposites where our personalities and preferences are concerned. But I trust you as a comrade. I care for you as a brother. I know you're uncomfortable hearing it, but you have to know that."

Tristan waited for Valerius' reluctant nod.

"And as a brother, even when I don't understand it, I can feel your pain. It's my pain too," Tristan continued, his gaze focused on the wall of weapons in the far end of the training room.

"I can even recognize the source of it, the real source of it," he added when he felt Valerius' dubious gaze.

"There's only one source for such depth of feeling, my man, and its name is woman."

Valerius looked straight ahead again, realizing Tristan saw more than he let on.

"You have that same glassy eyed hypnotized look on your face that I used to have, and still have on many occasions, when I first found Ayelet, or rather when she found me. It's called love."

Valerius was well familiar with that particular beast. He'd wrestled with it every day for ten years.

"And when a Pure male falls in love, hell, when any male falls in love, you're a slave to age-old instincts to win her, protect her, provide for her, Nourish her," Tristan said with passion.

"It has nothing to do with being her Consort, my brother, and everything to do with being her Mate."

Tristan looked over at his silent comrade and sighed.

"I see you've come to terms with the obvious. Now the question is what you're going to do about it. In love, there's no holding back," Tristan told him with sudden, uncharacteristic insight.

"You have to lay yourself bare, everything you are, at her feet, and pray that she'll put you out of your misery and accept you."

"And if she doesn't," Tristan went on, "it has no bearing on what you have to do. You're hers regardless of her choice. It is your duty, your very purpose for existing, to ensure her strength and vitality. You have what she needs, Val."

When Valerius' eyes became shuttered with self-doubt, Tristan laid a reassuring hand on his shoulder.

"You have what she needs," he said again. "And you're capable of giving her more than she'd ever bargained for because you love her. Whether she wants it or not, it's your gift to give her. True love requires no reciprocation. True love is unconditional."

Valerius could barely feel the male's hand on his shoulder as he absorbed the words and realized the truth of them. Vaguely, he felt Tristan rise to his feet, but he didn't look up.

"Go to her, Valerius," he heard the Champion say.

"Before it's too late."

*** *** *** ***

"No fair! You cheated!" Sophia exclaimed, shoving Aella aside with one hand, the other still madly squeezing the buttons of the remote.

At the rate she was going, her new game console wasn't going to last a week.

Aella calmly glided her thumbs across the action buttons and pulled a double spin kick and lethal overhead slam on Sophia's character, knocking him flat into the ground with a loud echoing groan of death.

Game over.

Sophia threw the remote down with more force than necessary and kicked it to the wall for good measure.

"It's just *wrong* to have an ancient Amazon kicking my ass on Dynasty Warrior," she pouted.

"Hey, watch who you're calling ancient," Aella retorted, stretching her arms above her head with feline grace.

She remained sitting cross-legged on the floor, almost Buddha like, zen master of fighting games that she was.

"Can't you at least pick a different character to play with?" Sophia whined. "You always play with Zhao Yun. I, at least, try everyone else and get well-rounded in my combat tactics, but you just excel with one character."

It sounded like sour grapes, but Aella didn't point that out.

Instead she said, "Why mess with perfection? Zhao Yun is my favorite fighting character. I'm not about to trust a military campaign upon enemy forces with an untested general. And as it happens, he's also one of the most powerful characters. In my hands, at least, he's invincible."

"You can at least teach me the tricks," Sophia insisted. She was never going to beat Aella at the game at this rate.

"It's not like I hoard secrets," Aella replied. "I showed you the combo moves and the power moves, but your fingers aren't agile enough. Not my fault."

Sophia narrowed her eyes. "You rigged the console, didn't you?"

Aella chortled at the outrageous accusation.

"Come on, babe, have the grace to admit defeat. I can't help it if Yun and I are like this," she said, crossing her fingers to indicate the tightness of their virtual bond.

"I barely have to stroke the buttons and he kicks ass like nobody's business. We make an unbeatable team. What can I say?"

Giving up on her tirade with a huff, Sophia sat back down beside the Amazon, switching the display to a new game, a single-player racing game that Aella couldn't beat her at.

"So what's eating at you, chica?" Aella asked quietly, noting the lines of frustration around the young queen's mouth.

"I don't know what you're talking about," came the rote denial.

Aella did her elegant non-eye-rolling move.

"Oh, just that you seem a little stressed lately. A little more prone to throw tantrums. PMS?"

"I do not throw tantrums!" Sophia retorted at a near shout, then lowered her voice and said, "I'm just a little pissed off."

"Hmm. Boy trouble?"

"Is there any other kind?"

Aella shrugged. She wouldn't know. She didn't ever have boy troubles. Whatever male she wanted, she got. Not all the way of course, but close enough.

Intercourse was overrated.

Sophia's slim shoulders drooped an inch.

"I'm kinda confused," she admitted.

Then she asked without turning toward Aella, "Have you ever liked two guys at once?"

Aella gave that a minute or two of thought.

Finally she said, "I'm a one-man woman. At least, I'm only interested in one man at a time. Now, the attraction might not last past a day or two, or sometimes even an hour or two, but while I'm with a man, I'm completely focused on him. I see no others."

"Huh," Sophia absorbed that as her shoulders slumped a little more. "I guess I'm more of a two-timer."

She sounded very upset at herself at the revelation.

Aella smiled at Sophia's disgruntled look. "Ere got competition, does he?"

The queen sighed dramatically. "I don't know. Maybe it's because I haven't seen him in a while. The professor says he went on a short research trip and would be back in a few more days. I probably just miss him."

Suddenly Sophia squared her shoulders.

"Not that I have any right to miss him. I mean, he's just my teaching assistant, and he's very nice and all. It's not like we have any relationship beyond class."

Aella did not argue. What would be the point? Rather, she focused the topic on the mysterious male Sophia confessed to two timing Ere with.

"So who's behind door number two?" she asked casually, making sure she didn't sound too curious.

Sophia hunched again, hiding the side of her face with her shoulder and arm. "Nobody you know."

Aella smelled the big fat lie from a mile away.

"I won't point out that it's my business to know everyone you know," she reminded the girl. "I'll just say that this guy must be pretty incredible to have you compare him against Ere. That male was one fine piece of—"

"Yeah, thanks," Sophia cut her off before she got too graphic.

She never felt threatened by Aella's beauty and sexuality before, but right this moment she felt inexplicably possessive and protective of both her men. Not that they were hers, she added to herself.

"And I'm not really comparing them. They're just... different. Polar opposites, almost. They're not comparable."

"But you like both of them," Aella said, her tone not a question.

"I don't know if I like either of them," Sophia replied. "I just feel... confused when I'm with them. It's no big deal."

As the young queen concentrated on increasing her racing score, Aella knew that the conversation had ended. Sophia wasn't about to reveal more tonight.

Ah, young love, Aella thought. There was nothing like the headiness of a first crush. Or first crushes, rather. It was all good.

She narrowed her eyes at Sophia's profile.

It was all good as long as the queen didn't fall in love in earnest.

Chapter Eleven

Rain wearily dragged herself into the Phoenix Enclosure around midnight.

Her legs felt like they weighed a ton, and she was so dizzy, her head felt like it was about to roll off her shoulders.

Despite her resolve to spare Valerius as much as possible from her needs, she must avail herself to his Nourishment tonight. The how, she'd have to be creative about. Perhaps while he slept, perhaps she would simply use her *zhen*…

Abruptly, Rain stopped just as she stepped beyond the threshold of the inner chamber of the Enclosure. Just like the night of their bonding, Valerius stood before the wall tapestry, gazing silently at the landscape of her homeland.

Entirely nude.

Waiting for her.

Every time she beheld him, her heart threatened to pound its way out of her chest. Just the sight of him invigorated her.

At the sound of the chamber door closing, Valerius turned toward the Healer, revealing the state of his arousal and readiness to Serve her.

"I will Nourish you this night," he said in his low, husky voice.

Rain started to protest. He could see her grasping at excuses, but he interrupted her before she could speak, "You *will* take me," he said resolutely.

"You will accept me into your body."

Rain was speechless, his words making her flash hot and cold.

He sounded commanding, and Valerius was never commanding. Not with her. Not like this. He always relented to her wishes, even when she was just torturing herself with denial.

As she watched him agape, he closed the distance between them in three long strides, and before she could blink, his mouth was hot and insistent upon hers.

Oh the male could kiss!

Rain reflexively arched her body upwards and stood on tiptoe to better match his passionate assault. She wrapped her arms around his waist and stretched her hands possessively over his muscular backside, her nails digging into the unyielding flesh as she tried to get better purchase.

He slanted his hot mouth over and over against hers, his tongue sweeping in voluptuous strokes, mating with her own. He sucked at her plump lips with a single-minded focus, as if every action was calculated to deliver the maximum impact, to arouse her beyond control.

Rain rejoiced in the feel of his massive erection prodding demandingly at her belly, refusing to be ignored.

Not tonight.

Oh Goddess she'd waited so long for this. Too long to feel him against her like this. She barely dared to imagine that soon his blood would be flowing through her veins, his body joined intimately with hers, filling her, Nourishing her, bringing her untold pleasure.

She squeezed his buttocks with surprising force, and he groaned deeply at the wordless urging to mate.

At the guttural sound, the haze of mindless passion lifted enough for Rain to realize what she was doing.

What she was pushing him to do.

Abruptly she pulled out of his embrace and took a couple of hasty steps back, then one more for good measure, until she was out of arm's reach.

Chest heaving, ears ringing, she stared at him aghast, furious with herself for losing control.

"I-I don't think this is a good night for me," she lied through her teeth.

"And besides, we have to set out early tomorrow for China," she stuttered, desperately searching her frazzled brain for a plausible excuse.

"I had a long day and I-I just need a bit of blood. But it doesn't have to be right now," she added. "I can take it tomorrow morning before you're awake."

Like she'd been doing for the past few days.

Valerius forced himself to stay still, even though his heart and soul staggered back like the fatally wounded at the cruelty of her rejection.

Yet again.

He forced his expression to remain stoic, though the muscle in his jaw ticked involuntarily as the only outward sign of his distress, and stated quietly, "We *will* mate tonight. You *will* take me into your body."

"Valerius, please," she started to say, shaking her head, "you don't have to do this. You don't have to—"

"Isn't this the duty of the Consort?" he broke in. "Isn't this what you shared with every other Consort you've chosen? There must have been hundreds. You said you admired and respected each one. I am not asking that of you. I don't expect that much."

In a voice so low she almost couldn't hear, he added, "I know I am worthless."

And in that moment, Rain understood the source of his pain.

She'd been entirely mistaken all this time. She'd intended to give him space and not demand his Service of her when she knew the way in which he'd been brutalized in the past, the memories that must still haunt him whenever he felt another's touch. She thought she was being kind, she thought staying away would atone for the selfishness and greed that had led her to choose him as her Consort.

But she saw now that her refusal to take his Nourishment only hurt him more.

And her heart broke at the sight of this brave, strong, beautiful warrior bowing his head in shame.

Without a word she threw herself at him, wrapping her arms tightly around his back, pressing her tear-streaked face to his chest, shaking her head to refute his self-condemnation.

She was sobbing so hard she couldn't get enough air to speak, so she just hugged him to her tighter, willing him to feel her apology, her empathy, her unfettered desire for him.

His arms full of weeping woman, Valerius knew not what to do.

Had he gone too far to demand her acceptance of him?

"I-" he forced down the lump in his throat and tried again, "I would Serve you any way you want, just tell me how. I would do anything you want."

He swallowed and forced out, "Anything."

Rain continued to shake her head, the power of speech beyond her.

The raw words that tore from him only made it worse. She could feel how much it cost him to say these things, to surrender so much of himself, in essence laying himself entirely vulnerable before her, to do with as she pleased.

But Valerius could not read her as clearly as she was able to read him.

Besieged by self-doubt, he couldn't even begin to guess how she felt. Was she afraid of his size? Maybe he'd hurt her the last time, he feared, a wave of nausea overwhelming him. Maybe he'd pushed her too hard.

"You can tie me down if it eases your mind," he offered with a note of desperation, the very idea almost killing him.

"There are chains that—" he squeezed his eyes shut as horrific memories assailed him, making his body quake with torment, but he made himself go on.

"You can keep me restrained. You can have all control. Just... *please*... take my Nourishment. Take me."

Unable to stand it anymore, Rain grabbed the back of his neck and tugged his head down to hers, silencing him with a soul-searing kiss. She told him with her body and mouth how much she wanted him, how endlessly she craved him, how beautiful and pure he was to her.

"There will be no restraint," she finally uttered against his mouth. "Not for either one of us. I want to lose myself in your body. I want to fill myself to overflowing with your Nourishment."

Valerius released a long shuddering breath he didn't realize he'd been holding.

She would accept him. She *wanted* him.

He swept her into his arms and carried her to the bed in two ground-eating strides. When he bent over to lay her down upon the silken sheets, she yanked her thin white slip off, wrapped her arms and legs around his neck and hips and brought him down on top of her.

As he pushed to his elbows to keep some weight off her, she sank her fangs voraciously into the vein along his throat.

Valerius hissed at the sensation of her first deep draw and the transformation that blind-sighted him, elongating and infusing his muscles with the irresistible urge to Mate.

The scent of his essence blossomed in the air, surrounding them both with its intoxicating headiness.

He struggled to keep his weight off of her, tried to keep his body from overwhelming her. And he almost succeeded but for the persistent push of his penis as it burrowed unerringly at the lips to her core.

Rain opened herself immediately to his possession. She let go of his throat and arched her back like a bow, thrusting her hips forward in one fluid motion to take the head of him inside.

They both gasped at the incredible pleasure, but for Valerius, it was also pain, for the pressure building inside of him made him feel like he was going to explode out of his own skin.

Rain's hands moved down to clutch his shoulders, her nails digging into his trapezius as she widened her legs and flexed her hips to take more of him inside. Again she pushed in a voluptuous undulation and gained two more hot, steely inches.

Valerius couldn't control his body's trembling, but he willed himself with everything he had to stay still, to let her set the pace, let her take control. Every instinct told him to ram the rest of the way into her, but he held back.

He'd die before he hurt her.

As if her bones had melted and her flesh turned to liquid, Rain continued to stretch and open herself, taking more of him inside by slow, rapturous degrees. The process itself of taking him fully within her body had ignited so much pleasure, her inner muscles contracted repeatedly in small bursts of orgasms.

Valerius gritted his teeth through the feeling of her vaginal walls milking him, stoking the pressure and fire within to unbearable heights.

After what seemed like an eternity, he was seated within her to the hilt. Rain splayed beneath him like a butterfly pinned to a wall, and then she slowly tightened her limbs around him, linking her hands around his lower back, locking her ankles around his buttocks.

That action in itself, enfolding him fully in her embrace, rubbed the head of him deliciously against her pleasure center deep inside. And while she'd stretched to accommodate his size, her pleasure spot had elongated along with her internal walls until it felt like her entire vaginal canal was one giant clitoris turned inside out.

Even the smallest friction, the slightest rub of his satiny staff within her sparked torrents of pleasure throughout her body.

On a long, broken moan, she crested upon an orgasm so intense her entire body squeezed him like a steel vise.

Valerius couldn't help his answering groan, vibrating throughout his tortured, sweat-dampened body.

He raised his head to look down upon her.

The sight of her head thrown back in ecstasy, her cheeks glowing with heat and arousal, her soft, pliant body trembling at the intensity of the pleasure he brought her almost sent him over the edge.

But he couldn't let go.

His body wouldn't release. And he hurt so badly he could barely breathe.

Fighting back the incredible pain, Valerius squeezed his eyes shut, clenching his jaw against cowardly cries that threatened to escape.

As the long, euphoric crest of her orgasm subsided, Rain looked upon the Protector and felt her heart stutter.

Knowing the depth of his anguish, the source of his torment, Rain reached up with both hands to cup his face.

"Come with me, *airen*," she entreated him, "look at me."

Slowly, Valerius relaxed his tightly shut eyes and gazed into the Healer's shimmering orbs. In them he saw understanding, acceptance, admiration and gratitude.

And then she smiled. That slow, Mona Lisa smile that set every cell in his body ablaze.

She pulled his face down to hers and nibbled gently on his earlobe. At the same time, her lower body squeezed him languorously, wetly, silkily drawing him deeper into her, then releasing slightly, only to draw him back.

Valerius gasped at the inexorable pulls of her core upon his sex. All of his energy and power coalesced in the place where they were intimately joined. All he wanted to do was to release his life force into her.

It was the Nourishment she needed. It was the release that would heal him.

Her lips beside his ear, Rain began to whisper softly in her native tongue. Her hands roamed down his back to clutch his buttocks possessively, urgently.

He didn't know what she said to him, but he caught the one word that she repeated over and over again.

Airen.

Lover. Beloved.

Valerius let loose his deepest desires and let himself imagine, for one moment, that she truly loved him. As his mind and heart opened, he felt his heavy testicles contract sharply a split second before his orgasm exploded throughout his body, filling her with his seed, the Nourishment she craved, in great undulating waves.

He groaned deeply at the indescribable sensation of being set free.

Finally, after an eternity of Hell, after millennia of restraint, his body, mind, and spirit soared. For the first time in his too-long existence, he felt undiluted pleasure.

In Rain's embrace, he tasted his first slice of happiness and peace.

Rain sobbed with relief and joy at the feeling of being filled by Valerius' Nourishment. Her body drank him thirstily in shuddering gulps. Immediately, she was infused with strength and vitality. Her blood practically sang at the return of her power.

In his body, she found Heaven. Never had she known such bliss.

It seemed to go on forever, the shockwaves that racked him, the intense pleasure-pain that blazed through him, and she seemed to absorb it all into herself, her core sucking and pulling at him even more hungrily. He could no longer keep his weight balanced off her. Every muscle seemed to flash fire, then numbness, then fire again.

And then she whispered, "I'm sorry" as she wrapped her limbs more tightly around him, needles of her hair penetrating his pores.

Just as his orgasm started to ebb, a blast of breathtaking pain followed so close on its heels, Valerius reeled from the impact.

It was the same splintering pain he'd felt during the second day of the Rite when she'd tested him for endurance. She was releasing the accumulation of pain from the wounds she'd healed over the past ten years into him. Even dissipated and diffused, the onslaught brought him to his knees.

Valerius gulped for breath, his chest hurting with his wildly pounding heart, his entire body reduced to one giant wound.

But before he could even remotely prepare himself, she moaned huskily:

"Again."

On command, Valerius' body tightened from head to toe as another orgasmic onslaught overwhelmed him, jetting hot pulses of Nourishment into her.

The rapture of the release was quickly followed by the mind-blowing pain she funneled into him, making his veins stand out against his too-tight skin.

The warrior's broken gasps gusting against her ear, Rain waited for the tremors to subside and rolled until she was draped like a rag doll on top of Valerius' magnificent torso. She knew she was a glutton, she knew she was pushing him dangerously to the edge. She knew she should pace herself, but Goddess above, it felt so *gooood*.

His Nourishment was like no other she'd ever had. It was her very own ambrosia, her incurable addiction. And the way his body fit hers, stretched hers, filled hers—there was no pleasure greater in her entire existence.

The feel of him, the scent of him, the taste of him... her fangs ached so badly to sink into him, she gave into the compulsion and latched onto his throat once more.

"Again."

On a groan so guttural and deep he physically vibrated with the primal sound, Valerius's body erupted once more into the Healer's.

Continuously, he gave and gave and gave.

He felt wrung out, yet so full he was bursting at the seams. He felt depleted, yet powerful and invigorated at the same time. He felt such wondrous pleasure it brought tears to his eyes, yet never had he endured pain so acute, so devastating.

For hours, she fed.

Endless hours, she milked him.

Until the bed was sticky and wet from their fluids, his blood and sweat. And still she feasted on him, brought them both to climax over and over and over.

As the mural changed from night to dawn, Valerius could no longer move, his body so sore and heavy it was all he could do to draw breath.

Because he'd given so much of himself, even his enhanced healing ability couldn't erase the evidence of her feeding.

Bluish purple bruises covered his entire frame—his neck, wrists, chest, lower stomach just above his pubic bone, the inside of his thighs... wherever there was a vein that caught her attention, she nursed at it with insatiable appetite.

Rain was now sprawled around his legs, her face level with his still throbbing, engorged manhood as Valerius lay wasted on his back.

Like a starving woman savoring the last morsel of cake, she meticulously bathed his cock with her tongue, drew strongly on the plump, aching head, and ran her fangs along the dark vein that pulsed against the satiny skin.

Valerius was so drained and hurt so badly from both the Mating and the persistent urge to keep Mating that a soul-deep moan of surrender broke from his lips.

The sound seemed to spike her arousal even higher, and she closed her mouth around the weeping head of him at the same time as her fangs sank into the thickest vein in his cock.

Valerius shouted hoarsely in agony and ecstasy, his body arching high off the bed as his blood and semen shot into her mouth.

To keep him trapped within her web, Rain's hair wrapped their silken tendrils around his body, a few needles inserting into the areas where she'd already bitten him.

Valerius gasped soundlessly at the invasion, at the bottomless depth of her penetration into his helpless body.

She was everywhere. She took everything.

Her fangs, her hands, her *zhen*, her mouth.

Rain drank him greedily, sucking harder, drawing faster. One of her hands closed around the base of his penis and squeezed in time with her pulls upon his cock, the other tending masterfully to his scrotum, making his orgasm go on and on.

Valerius ground his teeth against the plea for her to stop.

It was too much. He felt shattered, broken, reduced to raw flesh and bones.

Despite all the Nourishment he gave her, he received no Sustenance, no equal exchange of spiritual fulfillment, in return. At the same time, his hand cradled the back of her head, urging her to continue taking from him. Even if there was nothing left of him, even if she took everything, he would give into her without complaint.

She owned him, body, blood and soul.

A lifetime passed before she finally disengaged from him, crawling up his prone body to nestle against his chest.

Using the last ounce of strength, he turned his face toward hers, his lips brushing her temple with exquisite tenderness.

She sighed long and deep and murmured two little words that filled Valerius with reverence and peace.

"Thank you," she whispered before slumber finally took her.

Valerius lay awake despite his mind-numbing exhaustion. Everything had changed.

He knew there was no turning back. Just as surely as he loved her with all his being, he faced and accepted a second irrefutable truth:

With this joining, with the surrender of his life force into the female he loved, he had entered his Decline.

Valerius had begun to die.

*** *** *** ***

Sophia found an unaddressed manila envelope in her on-campus mailbox.

Curious, she quickly broke the seal and peeked inside. There was a pinky drive and a folded piece of notebook paper. Without taking either item out, she spied the masculine signature at the bottom of the sheet.

Ere.

Startled, she closed the envelope and darted a glance at Dalair, who was on duty this day to chaperone her around school.

Though he was a good fifteen feet away and completely inconspicuous, she hissed, "Do you mind? A little privacy please?"

A small frown drew the warrior's dark brows together, but he didn't argue, turning away until he faced Harvard Yard instead of the inner classroom corridors.

An involuntary smile of delight brightening her face, Sophia carefully took the folded note out and read:

Sophia,

My sincerest apologies for abandoning you to the disorganization and confusion that is Professor McGowen's constant companion. A researcher's dream find came up at the last moment and I had to depart immediately for the Louvre.

Not that I expect you to think of me when I am away, but I couldn't help but plant the seed. On the USB is a song I hope you'll like. (I noticed that you are never without your iPhone with buds in your ears.)

It is before your time, I suppose, I'm not sure what your generation is listening to these days, but it is one of my favorite songs.

I hope you think of me whenever you hear it. Lyrics enclosed below.

Ere

"Creep"—by Radiohead

When you were here before/ Couldn't look you in the eye
You're just like an angel/ Your skin makes me cry
You float like a feather/ In a beautiful world
I wish I was special/ You're so fucking special...

I don't care if it hurts/ I want to have control
I want a perfect body/ I want a perfect soul
I want you to notice when I'm not around
You're so fucking special/ I wish I was special...

Whatever makes you happy/ Whatever you want
You're so fucking special/ I wish I was special

But I'm a creep/ I'm a weirdo
What the hell am I doing here?
I don't belong here/ I don't belong here

Sophia gripped the note until her palms began to sweat. Shivers of hot and cold made her break out in goose bumps.

Oh Goddess above, what did this mean?!

She'd never gotten a personal letter from a boy before, much less a present.

He gave her a song! He wrote her a letter with his own hand!

Not an email or text or Facebook post or Tweet. He wrote actual English words on paper with what looked like a fountain pen if the little curly cues and elegant slashes were any indication.

Sophia was so giddy she could barely contain the squeal that threatened to spill forth in an undignified manner from her lips.

She held the paper to her nose and inhaled deeply to see if she could still catch a whiff of his scent—she did! There was a faint fragrance of dark spices, chocolate, and… pure decadence.

She was going to faint with euphoria!

She read and re-read the note with the abbreviated song lyrics three more times, barely noticing that students had begun filing into the lecture hall around her, like schools of fish diverting around an obtrusive rock.

What could he mean by sharing this song with her? Was it some sort of message to her? Some representation of himself and how he viewed her?

But that couldn't be, she thought with confusion. Who in their right mind would describe him as a "creep" and Sophia as an "angel"? It made more sense if they flipped the descriptors. But then she should be giving this song to him, not the other way around, right?

What did it all mean???

"Sophia, your class is starting."

She jumped at Dalair's voice close beside her and hastily hid the note and envelope behind her back.

"Why are you spying on me?" she accused with a scowl.

His expression remained bland. "I am merely reminding you that the lecture hall door is about to close."

Sophia stuck her foot in the threshold before it did and regarded him with her nose haughtily in the air.

"Fine. I'm going in. You stay out here and out of view. And keep your distance when I come out. I might actually make a friend or two today and I don't want them to get freaked out with you lurking around."

The statement was so ridiculous Sophia almost winced as she said it. If anything, Dalair's presence would attract "friends" to her like bees to honey, rather than repel them away. But she wasn't about to admit that to him.

"As you wish," he replied with a slight nod and watched her slip into the classroom.

Dalair narrowed his eyes when the queen was inside the lecture hall.

He'd glanced at the note when she first unfolded it. Even from fifteen feet away, his enhanced eyesight took in one word as if it were flashing on a giant billboard in neon lights.

Ere.

*** *** *** ***

Ayelet, Rain and Valerius sank back in their First Class seats on American Airlines three hours into their trans-Atlantic flight from Boston to Kunming, China.

They'd make a transfer in Beijing onto Air China, take a connecting flight from Kunming to Shangri-La, then a train to just outside Lushui County, then rent a local tour van to drive them up the mountainous paths, and finally trek the rest of the way on foot to the remote village where Cloud Drako secluded himself.

If they were lucky, they could probably hitch a ride on a donkey cart.

Ayelet snuck a glance at her two companions across the aisle.

The transformation in both Protector and Healer boggled the mind. After more than six hours in their presence, from the time they chugged down breakfast to getting to the airport and settling into their designated seats, Ayelet still couldn't get used to their changed appearances.

Rain looked more refreshed and vital than Ayelet had ever seen her, and they were only half way into the Phoenix Cycle. Her complexion had taken on a rosy hue, her eyes bright and shining, no bluish shadows to be found beneath them. Overnight her face seemed slightly rounder, her cheeks filled out rather than gaunt, and there was actually flesh beneath her skin, which looked more resilient and healthy instead of their previous paper-thin fragility. Even her hair glistened like diamonds rather than semi-transparent glass.

And then there was her expression.

Ayelet had never beheld such a look of utter bliss and contentment on the Healer's face. Truly she seemed like a completely different female.

Valerius, on the other hand, looked like he'd been flattened by a freight train, backed over by a mac truck, and thrown over a ravine just for the hell of it.

He was covered from head to toe in a form-fitting long-sleeve black turtleneck and loose black trousers, so it wasn't as if the countless bruises Ayelet knew he bore were visible to the public eye.

But she knew his body was wasted. Whatever could make the stoic warrior grimace in pain every time he moved—hell—every time he breathed was beyond Ayelet's ken. She wouldn't have caught his fleeting expressions of pain had she not been watching him closely, or had she not known what to watch for.

But Ayelet was very familiar with the Phoenix Cycle and the effects it had on Consorts. Leonidas, Alexandros, and Dalair, among other Pure males of warrior class, had all Served the Healer before, over the two thousand five hundred years she'd been in her role. While they had looked exhausted and drained over the thirty days, they also looked strangely relaxed, loose-boned, probably due to the release of sexual tension.

Well, maybe not Dalair.

Valerius, however, looked tenser than ever, as if his entire body was a tightly coiled spring. His shaven head magnified the sharpness of his cheekbones, the hollows beneath them, the acute angle of his jaw. Veins stood out on the back of his large, lean hands, and his chest rose and depressed as if he were struggling to breathe. As if it hurt to breathe.

But the expression on his face was at odds with the obvious pain radiating from his body. His usual focus and determination seemed doubled. But along with that, there was an underlying peace and even pride.

And when the Protector looked upon Rain, his eyes shimmered with reverence, yearning, possessiveness and most of all—

Love.

It was so private, carnal and heart-wrenching that Ayelet blushed to witness it. She felt compelled to look away as if she'd seen something she shouldn't have seen, as if she were glimpsing into the deepest, most hidden corners of the warrior's soul.

The interaction between the Healer and her Consort had also metamorphosed from a distant and reluctant regard to a closeness that surpassed most mated bonds.

Their bodies seemed so in tune to each other, it was as if they were one and the same. When she shifted to her left to better access her overhead light, he followed as if pulled by an invisible string. When they lay back in their seats, the armrest folded back so that there was no barrier between them, their bodies and faces unconsciously leaned into each other, until both her arms tightly hugged one of his, her face turned into his chest, his lips brushing the top of her head.

Ayelet possessed the Gift of empathy. It was more than simply putting herself in someone else's shoes; it was the ability to truly feel the emotions herself that someone else felt, as if the emotions were her own.

Ayelet rarely used it, for the repercussions to herself were unpredictable, and she always felt as if she were prying into someone else's private world without their permission. But even without it, she could see how Rain's body hummed with desire whenever Valerius was near, and how his body vibrated to fulfill hers in return.

It was as if where the two of them were concerned, no one else existed. They were only aware of each other. All they wanted and needed was each other.

With a pang, Ayelet thought of her Mate.

She would not see Tristan for the next few days, hopefully no longer than a week. But it seemed like an eternity when the bond Rain and Valerius shared were a constant reminder of the absence of her knight. She prayed for Tristan's safety along with everyone else remaining at the Shield, as well as for the success of hers, Orion's and Eveline's mission.

Ayelet glanced once more, a lot enviously and a little worriedly, at the couple entwined in the middle row of seats across the narrow aisle. She did not know what to make of the exponentially growing bond between Healer and Protector, but even if she did have that knowledge, it wouldn't be her place to interfere.

Loathe to disturb their exclusive connection, Ayelet put on her headset and turned on her TV screen, browsing through the videos on demand AA stored in their system to distract herself on this long, long flight.

She chose *Red Cliff*, a movie about the War of the Three Kingdoms in ancient China. Perhaps it would set the mood for the journey ahead. For, if her research was any indication, they were about to enter into one of the remotest corners of China, where the landscape remained largely unchanged, where industry and modernization had yet to make its mark.

And where they would hopefully find the destined Elite warrior.

Chapter Twelve

Alexandros swung his leaden legs over the side of the bed and sat still for long moments, orienting himself as the dizziness from being upright for the first time in days gradually faded away.

Thanks to the Healer's touch, his broken bones had knitted properly, his internal organs regenerated and his flesh wounds closed with nary a scar. He was still weak as a babe, however, his muscles enervated and sore.

What he wouldn't give for Valerius' enhanced healing ability right now. It killed him to lie around useless, a liability to the Dozen, when he should be out there searching for Leonidas and bringing the vampire Hordes to their knees.

Focusing his eyes, he scanned the orderliness and disinfected whiteness of the clinic. He was alone but for a small, light blue bundle on the bed beside his own. The figure was so tightly curled, no sign of her face was visible from behind her coltishly folded arms and legs. All Leonidas could make out was long black hair and slim ankles and feet, one ankle adorned by a simple gold chain with tiny bells.

He'd recognize that anklet anywhere. It belonged to the Healer's handmaiden, Wan'er.

The General tried to rise to his feet with a shaky push from both arms on the bed, but he severely overestimated the strength of his muscles, and fell in an undignified heap to the floor beside the bed.

Before he could even grunt in pain, a blur of blue silk appeared at his side, strong little hands grabbing him around one of his biceps.

"You should not be out of bed, General," Wan'er said in a chiding but worried tone.

Alexandros shook his head as if to clear it and leaned on the handmaiden slightly as he staggered to his feet.

"I can't stay one more hour as an invalid. The faster I get back in action, the quicker I'll get my strength back."

The handmaiden frowned but chose not to argue. It was her experience with warriors that one had to carefully choose one's battles: these Pure males did not take direction well.

Once he steadied himself and felt relatively certain he wouldn't fall over without Wan'er's support, Alexandros casually removed her hands from his arm and leaned against the clinic wall.

"How long have I been out? Where are the others? Where's Leonidas?" he asked in a rapid torrent.

Despite his obvious desire to avoid her touch, Wan'er calmly stepped close to him and smoothed her hands over his torso and limbs, checking methodically for the condition of his wounds.

To distract him from her feather light touch, she answered, "You have been unconscious for over a week. It was a minor miracle that you'd made it back to the Shield with the extent of damage to your body. You were an inch away from death, and despite Rain's infusion of healing energy, it took every ounce of strength for your body to regenerate. I'm surprised you are able to get up so soon, to be honest."

Unsuccessfully dodging the handmaiden's persistent hands, Alexandros finally relented and stood still beneath her perusal. He hoped he was too weak to get aroused, but with Wan'er, he didn't have much confidence in his otherwise unbreakable self-control.

Her thumb suddenly pressed down on one of his ribs and Alexandros almost doubled over in pain.

"Hmm," she mused, "right lung not completely regenerated, rib fracture still tender. While I cannot keep you from action, I do strongly advise you restrict yourself to a sedate walk and don't move too suddenly."

She speared him with a gimlet glare. "In the interest of a speedy recovery, you had better heed my words, else I'll make sure you regret it."

Alexandros found himself unable to hold the intensity of her stare and looked away uncomfortably.

"And the others?"

Wan'er continued with her gentle probing and replied, "Ayelet, Rain and Valerius are headed to China; Orion and Eveline to Europe to recruit. I believe Tristan and Aella found a lead to the Sentinel's location, but they are awaiting your recovery to confer."

When he would have moved outside the silken cage of her arms and body, she stayed him with one hand around his ankle, as she balanced on the balls of her feet in a stoop before him, examining his lower body.

"I am not finished," she stated authoritatively, leaving Alexandros to wonder who here was the General and who the handmaiden.

At her prodding, he lifted one foot, balancing his weight against the wall. She rotated his ankle this way and that, nodding at the healing progress made, then slid her hand up his calf, squeezing systematically around to his knee and upwards along his thigh.

"Enough," Alexandros stopped her when she would have filled her hand with his swollen staff.

Wan'er easily wrestled her hand out of the warrior's grip and rose to face him.

"Rather prudish for a Macedonian, aren't you?" she eyed him curiously.

"I'm just trying to preserve your maidenhood," the General retorted.

She gave him a sideways smirk.

"I've seen and held it all, warrior," she replied without even a hint of embarrassment, even as heat inched up his neck and filled his cheeks.

Switching topics easily, she said, "Come, I shall take you to Aella and Tristan. They are conferring in the throne room."

It occurred to Alexandros that if she had indeed examined him while unconscious, she must have known already that as far as his manhood was concerned, he was entirely intact. Then the wandering hand was for…

Startled, he jerked his gaze to her back just as she looked over her shoulder and threw him another lopsided, mischievous smile. She turned back around and led the way out of the clinic to the throne room with a sassy sway of her hips.

Vixen, the General thought, even as an answering smile curved his own lips.

In the throne room, he found Aella and Tristan already fully armed and ready to head out. At the sight of him, Aella rushed forth to embrace him heartily and Tristan pounded his back a bit too gladly, making Alexandros' shoulders creak in protest.

"Welcome back to the living, General," Tristan greeted with a bark of laughter.

"You look good," Aella added, looking him up and down, "like raw meat warmed over under the noon sun."

Alexandros grimaced at the graphic picture that came to mind. Unfortunately, he felt rather like the Amazon's description as well.

"Just give me five minutes and I'll be ready to join you," Alexandros said, but even before he finished speaking, all three were shaking their heads.

"No sudden movements," Wan'er reminded him, "that includes vampire hunting."

"I'm sorry, General, but it's too dangerous to take you with us," Aella said.

Implicit in her statement was that as long as he was not fully healed, he would be a liability on the hunt.

Alexandros was loathe to face the truth, but he knew she was right.

"Besides," Tristan commented, "we need you here."

He handed Alexandros a thumb drive.

"This contains images we took from the past few hunts around Greater Boston, including a revisit to the tunnel in which you and Leonidas were ambushed. Look through them and tell us if anything triggers a memory or a feeling. We will plan our next course of action upon our return tonight."

Alexandros did not argue with this assignment of responsibilities. His Gift was the ability to track any prey, under any circumstances.

He could view, touch, listen, smell anything his target had come in contact with, and even if he'd never encountered it himself, he would be able to pinpoint at which time the target had passed it, used it, worn it, as well as ascertain the direction in which the target was headed afterwards. As long as there were three such objects for him to react to, he would be able to triangulate the exact location of the target with laser precision.

If the USB contained three relevant images, by nightfall he would be able to locate where Leonidas had been taken. Dead or alive, he would bring his comrade home.

For his enemies' sake, the Sentinel had better be alive.

*** *** *** ***

Forty-eight hours after they took off from Boston Logan Airport, Ayelet and Valerius waited in front of a beaten down train station for Rain to purchase their tickets from Shangri-La to the outskirts of Lushui County.

"I feel a bit like a circus sideshow," Ayelet muttered as various Chinese travelers passed by them with undisguised interest, and sometimes, with outright consternation in their expressions.

With her long curly dark hair, voluptuous proportions and form fitting leathers, Ayelet looked like an ancient Byzantine goddess come down to earth. Valerius, hard as he tried, simply could not blend into any background in Yunnan, China. Well over head and shoulders, and more often chest, above the average Chinese, his biceps larger than most men's thighs, his shoulders wider than twice their breadth, he was a veritable Goliath.

Northern Chinese were known to be taller—after all, they produced the likes of Yaoming, the NBA legend. But Ayelet and company were traveling through Southwest China, where people were generally smaller, darker, more prone to gawk at the foreigners, for the living monoliths they appeared to be.

"But you are a very beautiful attraction," Rain said, smiling as she walked back to her awaiting friends with their train tickets.

"I am sure the men are wondering how best to approach such a goddess. It's not everyday people around here get to see the likes of you and Valerius."

"They look more terrified than titillated," Ayelet responded wryly. "My arms are bigger than those men's legs."

She nodded to a group of what looked to be construction workers sitting on the steps of the train, staring unabashedly at her.

"Oh but they are much stronger than they look," Rain assured her. "You have to be to live in these mountains. Both men and women have to carry more than twice their weight sometimes to transport goods and necessities from the closest town to their homes in the mountains. You'll see soon enough."

She moved to stand beside Valerius and wrapped both her arms around one of his, leaning into him.

"Are you tired, Healer?" the warrior asked with concern, wondering whether Rain was strong enough to undertake the journey ahead of them.

She shook her head and beamed up at him, momentarily blinding him with her dazzling smile.

"I just want to stake my claim so those girls know that you are mine," she said cheerfully, making Valerius look around them, spotting a few giggling young women leaning out of windows on the train, staring and gesturing at him.

Valerius quickly looked away, uncomfortable with the attention, only to hear Rain's amused chuckle.

"And I like to be close to you," she added, making him blush harder. "If I could, I'd wrap around your body like a second layer of skin."

Though the whispered words were for his ears only, Valerius face burned as if she'd shouted them for all the world to hear.

Despite his embarrassment, however, he felt ridiculously pleased. It was incredible to him that this ravishing, ethereal, angelic creature wanted him, even coveted him.

"I also bought sustenance for our four hour train ride," Rain said more loudly to include Ayelet in the conversation.

She raised one fist that held a large bag, weighed down with food.

Ayelet came forth to examine its contents and raised her head with a dubious expression.

"What's in there?"

"Tea eggs," Rain answered, pointing to six large eggs swimming in what looked like soy sauce and tea leaves in a clear plastic bag, the shells colored darkly and cracked to bits. The better to let the juices absorb into the eggs, Rain explained.

"Pork buns, plain *mantou*, and tangerines. All for twenty yuan," the Healer announced proudly. There was enough food there to feed half a dozen people, and it was less than four U.S. dollars.

"And I got you this," Rain said, holding up a shallow paper carton to Valerius with something that jiggled on the inside.

"It's blood jelly. Lots of iron. Good for you to keep up your strength."

Ayelet made a face even as Valerius accepted the food with a gracious nod of thanks. She liked Chinese food just fine, but anything to do with congealed pig's blood she'd just as soon pass on.

After they boarded the train and settled into their seats, no more than two long hard benches separated by a wooden table, Ayelet asked of the Healer, "Have you ever been to this part of China before? Do you happen to know Cloud Drako?"

Rain nodded in answer to the first question.

"Yes, I've been to these parts a few times. After two thousand five hundred years, I've been to just about every place in China more than once. When I want to get away for a while from modern civilization, I come down here or go up to Tibet, Inner Mongolia, places still relatively unsettled, secluded from all but the most adventurous tourists. But I do not believe I have met Cloud."

She thought back to the pictures Ayelet had shown her on the flight.

"He must really not want to be found. It is rare that Pure Ones residing in the same country, even on the same continent, would not know of all the other Pure Ones around. And as he is of warrior class, if your sources are true, it is doubly rare that I would not have known him through the Rites of the Phoenix."

Valerius stiffened imperceptibly beside the Healer when she mentioned the Rites.

He needed to find a way to overcome the blood boiling territoriality where Rain was concerned. The Rites were a part of her life, written into her destiny. He knew from the start that he wasn't her first Consort and he wouldn't be her last, but it was a bitter pill to swallow nonetheless.

Unaware of the Protector's troubles, Rain continued, "Perhaps I would have heard of his human name. Do you know it?"

Ayelet shook her head. "It's hard to trace his original human name. His soul is almost two thousand years old, but I believe this current incarnation is not his original body."

"That would explain why I don't recognize him," Rain said. "Perhaps I knew his soul from a previous or even the original incarnation, but I don't know this current face and form. He looks only partially Han."

Ayelet knew that Rain referred to the race that made up the majority of the Chinese population and gave the people the traditional "oriental" looks.

Indeed, Cloud Drako, with his lightning blue eyes, height of six feet four inches, broad shoulders and leanly muscular build, appeared to be a mix between Asian and possibly Russian ancestry, which was not uncommon around the borderlands of western China.

"Is he still human then?" Rain asked.

Only Pure Ones directly resurrected in their original human form were guaranteed to be immortal. Reincarnated Pure Ones would have to have an Awakening before they could embrace their immortality. Until that time, they would age and live like any other human.

Sophia was one such example.

Ayelet narrowed her eyes in thought. "I am not sure. It is possible he has already passed his Awakening. His Gift is tremendously powerful. I cannot imagine that he is able to wield it with such strength as a human."

"A Gift of telepathy?" Valerius queried, his protective instincts heightening.

Ayelet nodded. "I believe he has the ability to mesmerize others. He can push his will into people who meet his gaze. I almost gave up the search before it began, suddenly feeling as if there was nothing to be found even though I held the evidence of his existence in my hands."

"How can we get around his Gift when we find him?" Rain worried. "If he does not want to come with us, how can we possibly convince him?"

"I've considered this ad nauseum," Ayelet replied, her brows drawn in concentration.

"First, we must avoid his gaze at all costs. We must make use of all our other senses and not rely on our sight."

Briefly, she wished Dalair was here, but during the Phoenix Cycle, the Healer could not be far away from her Consort, and they could not afford to take two Elite guards from the Shield.

"Second..." she hesitated, darting a glance at Rain, and then at Valerius.

Valerius braced himself, knowing that he wouldn't like the next words to come from the Guardian.

Ayelet addressed the Healer, "Second, if you get close enough to Drako, Rain, you can calm his defenses with your *zhen*," referring to the needles of Rain's hair.

"Perhaps if he feels your positive energy, he will let down his guard and allow us some time to at least make our case. He can always reject our offer later, but we need him to let us in long enough to be heard."

Rain was nodding even as Valerius stated, "It's too dangerous. We don't know whether we can trust him."

Rain took one of his hands in both of hers and entwined their fingers to reassure him.

"Valerius, the same can be said of us, can it not? Why should he trust us? We are seeking him out in his own home, which he has taken great pains to hide. We are planning to take him out of a peaceful, simple existence into a world of violence and danger. He has every reason to try to thwart us in our mission."

Valerius opened his mouth to object, but she silenced him with a finger against his lips.

"Ayelet is right. Among the three of us, I have the greatest chance of reaching through his barriers. He is a Pure One, don't forget. He's using his powers to protect himself, not to harm us. Don't worry so for me. I am powerful in my own right. You have witnessed it personally, have you not?"

Her smile took some of the sting out of her admonishment, but Valerius was not ready to relent.

"There must be another way," he insisted. "You could also throw a few *zhen* to force his eyes closed, and we can convince him at a distance."

"Hardly a way to build trust," Rain rejected the idea right away. "And if he is as superior a warrior as we expect, he would have intercepted my needles before they reached him. He would then interpret the action as aggression and there's no telling how he'd respond. We could be escalating the encounter to a full out battle."

"I agree," Ayelet interjected, trying to ignore the piercing glare that the Protector threw her way.

"We cannot afford inciting mistrust even before the conversation begins, and Rain is the only one of us he'd let near, if for no other reason than their shared ancestry, language and the fact that she appears the least threatening of us three."

Rain smiled wryly. "My smallness has its uses."

Valerius knew defeat when he met it. He would not be able to change the Healer's mind. As one of the Dozen, he respected her decision as well as her ability to take care of herself. But as her Consort... no, he admitted to himself, it was more than that.

As the male who loved her.

His entire being rebelled at the idea that his female was putting herself at risk. Every nerve, every cell shouted to protect her.

But he did not have that right, he knew. He was merely her Consort for the remainder of the Phoenix Cycle. He was far from her Eternal Mate. He dared not even imagine that his wishes mattered to her.

Valerius was not aware that the Guardian watched him closely as he systematically tried to shut down his Mated male urges to protect his female. But Ayelet saw the truth.

The Protector had Fallen.

Suddenly, it all made sense. The starkness of his countenance. The shadows beneath his eyes. The tremendous pain that weighed him down, so pervasive, she could almost see it eating away at his flesh and bones.

This was not the appearance of a Consort, no matter how much strength the Healer drew from him into her own body. This was the appearance of the Fallen—a Pure One who loved, but who did not receive in kind.

This was the visage of the dying.

Ayelet averted her face and looked out the train's window at the scenery outside.

Tears filled her eyes at the sight of her friend wasting away. She knew that he must be in constant, unimaginable pain. She knew what it cost him to cover the signs of his Decline from the Healer, from her.

If she hadn't watched him so closely, if she didn't know what to look for... If she hadn't seen the soul-deep anguish in his eyes when he looked upon the female he loved with such longing and hopelessness...

Tristan must have known, it occurred to her. Before they departed on their journey, her Mate had warned her not to interfere, referring to the Healer and the relationship with her Consort. Ayelet had been puzzled that she would have any cause to interfere in the first place. But Tristan had not enlightened her further. He just pulled her into a tight embrace and told her to have faith in the ways of the Goddess.

Now she knew what Tristan had meant. And no, she would not, *could* not, interfere, even if she wanted to.

The Protector had made his choice.

He'd Fallen for the one Pure female who could never fall in love. To do so, she would have to give up everything she was— her Gift as the Healer, her very identity as a Pure One.

Ayelet prayed to the Goddess for a miracle even as she prepared herself for the inevitable.

*** *** *** ***

Alexandros pushed his body to the limit in the training room after hours.

Aella had already dismissed the last of the Chevaliers, and he'd sat uselessly on the benches against the wall and watched her while she trained the recruits with a mastery he was impressed by even as he involuntarily resented her for taking over his job.

She'd given him a warning look before heading to the showers, wordlessly advising him not to overextend himself with the training weapons in her absence.

He'd raised an eyebrow at her in reply, effectively telling her to shove her concern where the sun didn't shine. She'd quirked a corner of her mouth in response and shrugged.

There was no holding back a warrior if he was bent on self-destruction.

Now Alexandros ached from head to toe, barely able to catch his breath, sweat pouring off him in rivulets. He was reacquainting his body with fighting moves, but he was also exorcising his frustration.

A whole day of concentration and he was not able to pinpoint where the vampire assassins had taken Leonidas. He'd only been able to hone in on two points from the images Aella and Tristan had taken on their hunts. But the points were several days, if not weeks, old. He needed at least a third point to give him some confidence in the coordinates.

As it was, he'd be sending the team out to find a needle in a haystack if he took wild guesses on the two old tracks.

Sitting against the wall with his legs spread before him, his head leaned back, eyes closed as he concentrated on getting his breath back, Alexandros didn't notice that the handmaiden had entered the training room with a basket of balms.

His hand jerked out reflexively when he sensed someone near. Opening his eyes, he realized he was gripping Wan'er's wrist with almost enough force to break her bones. Immediately, he released her, but frowned instead of apologize for the hard clasp that must have hurt her.

"What are you doing here? I don't need a babysitter," he groused.

Wan'er resisted rubbing her wrist to ease the soreness from the warrior's grip.

Instead she answered calmly, "You were not in your quarters when I sought you out earlier. Do recall that you still have a few days of treatment left. And since you ignored my advice not to strain yourself physically, I have to make sure I give your body a chance to recover from the wringer you put it through."

She handed him a towel and gestured for him to wipe himself off before she could administer the balms.

Alexandros roughly did as she bid, taking a second hot damp towel from her hands after wiping off his sweat with the first. The second towel had some sort of mint or menthol in it for it opened up his pores as he rubbed it over his skin. Immediately, he breathed easier and his muscles began to relax.

"Now the balms," the handmaiden said as she opened a large jar and scooped a portion out with her fingers.

"I'll do it."

Alexandros quickly took the hunk of jelly from her hand and rubbed it between both of his, then began to slather it over his arms and chest. He relished a little too much the idea of her rubbing her hands all over his body. It was safer for both of them that he took care of business himself.

Wan'er watched the warrior methodically rub the balm into his skin as rapidly as he could, as if he was racing to get done so he could depart from her presence. She couldn't help the smile that curved her lips.

"Are you afraid of me, General?" she asked teasingly.

Abruptly, Alexandros jerked his eyes to meet hers, but quickly looked away from the amusement and attraction he saw there. He grunted in response, hoping she would let the absurd subject drop.

Wan'er chuckled softly at his discomfiture, and didn't needle him more.

Wordlessly, she took the balm from him when he'd finished with all of his body except his back, which she began to work on herself. He didn't fight her on it, she was glad to note. Perhaps he realized she was not so dangerous after all.

"You are adept at this," the General said gruffly after a few moments.

Then cleared his throat and added, "Healing, I mean. Have you always been handmaiden to the Healer?"

He sensed, rather than saw her nodding.

"I met Rain shortly after I was revived as a Pure One. She'd already established the Jade Lotus Society by then. I heard of her good deeds and her sanctuary and decided to join. My wish, you see, when the Goddess offered me a second chance was to be able to save lives, especially the lives of persecuted women during my time."

She paused at that and Alexandros waited patiently for her to continue. After a while, her hands began roving across his back again.

"Apparently, I had a knack for the healing arts, though I always thought I was destined to be a woman of literature or perhaps a royal scribe."

She gave a delicate shrug.

"As it were, I was one of Rain's best students."

"One of?" Alexandros inquired, noticing the slight emphasis in the handmaiden's words.

"Yes, I excelled in Chinese medicine and natural remedies. I was proficient in acupuncture and other physical cures, but I was by no means expert."

Wan'er paused again as if struggling with a disturbing memory.

Hesitantly, she said, "There was one other student who mastered the technique of harnessing the energy within living creatures, though it was before my time at the sanctuary. Some say she manipulated the energy for her own gains, that she misused her powers. Had she not disappeared the year before I joined the Society, undoubtedly she would have been the favorite as Rain's handmaiden."

"You are the best candidate for the role," the General reassured her quietly, "I have never met such dedication to a craft as you are to healing."

Wan'er gave the warrior's shoulders an extra squeeze, and he felt the tension there dissipate like fog in a strong warm breeze.

"You are likely biased. I do not tend to all my patients with the same dedication as I tend to you, General," she said in her lilting voice, the teasing tone back in full force.

Alexandros was prepared for her verbal spurs this time and grasped one of her hands over his shoulder.

"I am glad to hear it," he murmured in a rumbling baritone, sending shivers of delight dancing down the handmaiden's spine.

Oh she knew she was playing with fire, but how delicious the burn.

Chapter Thirteen

Aella silently gestured to Dalair to advance from the left while she took the right path.

They were on the trail of three vampire assassins in the suburbs of Worcester, almost fifty miles outside of Boston city.

They'd noticed the vampires following them when they were conducting surveillance close to South End, the location of Valerius' previous attack. As dawn approached, they decided not to engage their foes but rather play a game of cat and mouse. They hoped to keep their prey engaged in the chase until the night eroded with the first rays of sun, when the vampires would need to retreat to their lair.

Then the hunted would become the hunters.

The vampires did not bring their own mode of transportation. Instead, they traveled on foot and hitched rides on top of trucks and buses, making it extremely difficult to keep track of their movements.

Aella suspected that was their goal, to confuse and disorient any tail they might have, so that they couldn't be traced back to their Horde. But the two Elite warriors kept up with their targets, leaping from vehicle to vehicle at a distance enough not to be detected.

The vampires went back on foot within the city limits of Worcester, disappearing like shadows into an underground tunnel.

As Aella and Dalair followed, they came upon a forked passage that led in two directions. There was no other choice but to split up, even though they sensed a trap. Two of the vampires went down the left tunnel and one went down the right.

Dalair gestured earlier that the tunnels would eventually meet, since he traced the sound of dripping water and echoes through the passageways ahead. If they split up, at least they wouldn't lose each other in the underground maze.

If they stayed alive of course.

Aella pulled out two chakrams and locked them together to form a short saw. She held a third in her other hand to let fly at the first scent of danger.

Her senses were nowhere near as sharp as Dalair's, so she moved more slowly, not wanting to rush into an ambush. As she felt along the almost pitch black passageway, she encountered slime, rats, debris and water that dripped from the ceiling and ran along the bricks. There was also the pungent odor of decay and refuse, confirming her earlier suspicion that they were in a sewer system.

There was a dim light ahead, filtered from above ground through a drain gutter. Aella approached more carefully, knowing that she would expose her position, however briefly, when she went past the point of illumination.

Then she heard the clanging of metal not too far ahead, followed by a grunt and thumps that sounded like a body getting slammed into the passage wall and ground.

Dalair must have engaged the two vampires he'd been tracking, and if she could hear the sounds of their battle so clearly, the two passageways must have merged ahead.

Aella broke into a silent sprint.

Goddess forbid the three vampires had rounded upon Dalair all at once.

Under normal circumstances, she would not be in such a rush to offer assistance, but these were not average vampires and they did not fight fair.

Sure enough, as she pulled around the corner where ghostly tentacles of light shot through the gutter bars, she caught glimpses of the vampires circling Dalair like sharks drawn by the scent of blood.

The Paladin tried to keep his enemies at bay with his two giant crescent blades, one in each hand. His hyper-developed senses helped him to anticipate the vampires' moves, keeping him always one step ahead of them.

Aella assessed the situation with one fleeting glance.

Soon, the vampires would figure out the best way to attack. They could swarm Dalair all at once, and two would probably sacrifice themselves against his blades in the process, but the third would surely be able to execute a lethal blow. From what she knew about these assassins after studying the tactics they used with Valerius, then Leonidas and Alexandros, she knew that such a kamikaze move would be right up their alley.

They had no fear of death. They were concentrated on one goal and one goal only.

To exterminate the Pure Ones.

Aella leapt into the fray with two bounding strides while letting fly her chakram with deadly force.

At the screeching whirl of the steel, the vampire nearest to her looked up and narrowed his eyes, which was exactly what she wanted him to do, for the chakram zinged against the wall to his left, bounced off at a seventy degree angle with a flare of metallic sparks and sliced clean through the vampire's neck from the side.

And not a moment too soon, for Dalair had his hands full fighting back the two other vampires who redoubled their efforts in concert. It was all he could do to parry and deflect their varied blows, as they advanced upon him with increasing speed.

"Jump!" Aella shouted a split second before she left fly her other two chakrams in opposite directions at a one hundred twenty degree angle from a deep one-kneed crouch.

Dalair obeyed without hesitation and so did one of the vampires, but the other vampire was not quick enough and suffered the consequences as one of the chakram sliced through his shin, taking him down to one leg instantly.

As he fell with a shout of pain, he released twin daggers on the way down in Aella's direction. She deflected one with her wrist cuffs crossed together in front of her and would not have been able to dodge the other if not for her Gift— superhuman speed.

Dalair pushed back the remaining vampire by spinning the crescent blades so fast, they became the lethal wheels of death in his hands. Despite how the vampire jabbed and swung at the warrior with his long axe, Dalair's saws did not falter, until finally, the vampire could move no further, his back against the tunnel wall.

With a twist of his wrist, Dalair severed the bloodsucker's axe arm from his shoulder and pressed forward with the other crescent blade, now stationary once more, against the vampire's throat. Behind him, he heard Aella make short work of the fallen vampire and collect her chakrams within seconds.

As Aella came up beside her partner, she could see that the vampire still struggled despite the edge of Dalair's blade against his throat. He was cutting himself in the process, but he didn't relent.

"He's not talking," the Paladin said grimly, trying to keep the vampire alive long enough to question. Perhaps Aella would have better luck.

Aella tilted her head to get a better look at the vampire's face, streaked with blood and hidden by straggles of sweat-soaked hair.

An icy tingling began at the base of her neck, sending shivers down her spine.

"I know him," she uttered with shock and horror.

"Tolya," she whispered the vampire's name.

Involuntarily, the bloodsucker turned toward her, revealing more of his face, and Aella gasped in full recognition.

He was once her lover, hundreds of years ago. She'd spent more time with him than any other beau. They'd been so decadent and carnal in their creativity around the Sacred Law that intercourse was but an overrated indulgence.

Of all her lovers, Tolya was the only one she considered taking the leap with. And if she didn't truly love him, she certainly cared deeply for him.

But the bloodshot vampire eyes that stared back at her did not hold the same recognition. Instead, Tolya bared his fangs and hissed, reaching behind his back.

Before he could take out whatever it was he reached for, Dalair ended his life by pressing the crescent blade all the way through his neck in one forceful punch.

"No!" Aella cried, rushing forth to push Dalair away only to see Tolya's torso slide against the wall to the ground while his head rolled forward and fell separately with a wet thud.

Within seconds, he disintegrated into gray nothingness.

"I'm sorry, but I could not take the chance," Dalair said from behind her, regret in his voice.

Aella nodded even as tears of sorrow slid down her cheeks. She crouched before the ashes of the fallen vampire and examined the object he'd left behind—a small throwing knife, its tip blackened with poison.

Dalair had saved her life. She'd been immobilized with shock. She doubted she would have noticed if someone had thumped her over the head with a two by four.

"You knew him," Dalair stated, knowing from the way that Aella remained on her knees beside the vampire's remains that there was no mistake.

Again she nodded.

"He was a friend," she whispered, "more than a friend. He was a good male, a Pure male. I used to live in what is now Ukraine for a period of time in the sixteen hundreds. For a while, he was my family."

Dalair lowered himself to a crouch beside her, laying a comforting hand on her shoulder.

"He was of warrior class, I gather."

"Yes," Aella responded. "When Ayelet recruited me to join the Elite, I wanted him to join with me. He-he refused."

She swiped an arm across her eyes and refocused.

"He said that we could not remain in the same place together for he would not be able to maintain distance."

She laughed briefly, despondently. "He fancied himself in love with me."

"He is no longer Pure," Dalair observed, frowning at the fact.

Aella frowned as well, unable to make sense of it. Could it be that Tolya Fell for a Pure female in the time they'd lost touch with one another? And the female did not return his feelings?

Briefly, Aella felt a pang of loss. There was a time she'd wanted to be that female. Ultimately, she could not take the leap of faith. She did not love him with all her heart and soul.

She was saddened that Tolya might have devoted himself to a female only to have his love unreturned. He had been a male of worth. He deserved happiness with his Eternal Mate. Yet he'd died as a vampire. One who did not recognize Aella.

She could not understand why he would have no memory of her if he'd Fallen and failed. In the instant when their eyes had met, he'd seemed mindless, an empty shell of his former self.

Soul-less.

He did not recognize her, and in that moment, as she gazed into his bloodshot vampire eyes, she did not recognize him either.

"He was changed."

Dalair regarded Aella closely at that pronouncement.

He knew that the words were not chosen at random. She didn't say "he changed," or "he Fell." What she said implied that the change was forced upon him, likely against his will.

They'd always suspected there was a new way to create vampires. Now they had irrefutable evidence that it was true.

Goddess help them.

*** *** *** ***

The vampire eyed the chess set before it with a smile of amusement. Things were starting to get interesting.

It moved the black queen diagonally to challenge the white queen, then sat back in its cushy chaise lounge and steepled its fingers contemplatively.

Your move.

The only sound to break the heavy silence in the catacombs was a small, blue flamed fire crackling in the hearth, providing ghostly illumination for the battlefield that stretched before the beautiful vampire.

What would the white troops do? Sacrifice a knight? A bishop? A rook?

The possibilities left the vampire breathless with anticipation.

They must make a sacrifice, of that it was certain. The white side would do anything to protect their precious queen.

Which exquisite piece would it be? *Who* would it be?

The vampire was so giddy it wriggled a bit in its seat as a giggle of delight gurgled forth.

And then a pale hand extended from the robed figure sitting across from the vampire, its guest's body all but swallowed in the luxuriously deep cushions of the velvet red and gold armchair.

With elegant fingers, the one and only white pawn was picked up and deposited in between the white and black queen.

The vampire's eyes widened a fraction as its glee turned to fascination.

To anyone observing the game, it looked as if the pawn was sacrificing itself to protect the queen.

But the vampire knew better.

If the black queen took the pawn, she would be immediately taken in turn by the white queen. Instead, the most logical move would be to remain stationery and maintain the challenge while a black pawn continued to advance.

So decided and acted upon, the vampire leaned forward to await its opponent's next move.

While it waited, it said silkily with a flash of shiny white fangs, "You must be over-warm, my darling. Those robes must be stifling."

Wordlessly, the figure in the armchair shrugged, and the robe fell away to reveal pale, naked skin to the vampire's avaricious gaze.

"How lovely," it murmured as it rose from the chaise and floated to the figure's side.

A graceful hand reached up to lie flat upon the vampire's smooth belly, revealed by the opening of its satin kimono. The hand slid steadily down, brushing the inside of the vampire's thighs, finally curving around its sex.

What a delicious game, the vampire thought as it bent forward at the waist, its lips seeking the guest's long, pale throat.

A few sips of Pure blood would make the evening complete.

*** *** *** ***

At dusk, after another day of hiking up a mountain whose barely-there roads were too steep and narrow for vehicles to pass, Ayelet, Rain and Valerius came to a yawning ravine that they needed to cross to get to Cloud Drako's village on the other side.

"You've got to be kidding me," the Guardian muttered when they came to the edge of the ravine.

Looking down, *way* down, she saw the rushing rapids of Nujiang (translated directly as Furious Ford, how appropriate) below, crashing against sharp rocks.

They were so high up on the mountain, mists of clouds whirled at their feet. The wind was so strong, if she didn't brace herself she'd be pushed off the slippery ledge. There was no safety railing, no ropes, nothing to prevent a deadly fall.

And they were going to cross the quarter of a mile ravine by dangling at the end of a chain that hooked around a person's backside to form a makeshift seat. With momentum gained by the passenger pushing off the ledge with their feet, the chain would slide along a thick rope that hung between the two sides of the ravine to a lower point on the opposite mountain ledge, transporting its passenger across.

The three travelers watched as local folk stepped fearlessly up to the rope, rubbed their hands with the juices from plant leaves that grew nearby to prevent slippage and slid effortlessly down the hanging rope to the other side as if it were just a breezy walk in the park.

"How much weight can the rope support?" Valerius asked, and Rain translated the question to one of the villagers.

"Up to one hundred and twenty kilos or so, about two hundred sixty pounds" the Healer replied.

Just enough for his weight, Valerius thought. He hoped the "or so" didn't mean ten kilos less than the estimate, because then things would get a bit precarious.

"Let's get this over with," Ayelet said, a few minutes after the last villager had gone, the autumn sun having just set, volunteering to be the first one to cross.

Never a fan of heights, she was not looking forward to this particular roller coaster, but she had a mission to accomplish and she'd never yet let fear get the better of her.

Breath held, she made it to the opposite side more smoothly than she expected. Using a makeshift pulley, she reeled the chain back towards her companions across the ravine.

Valerius secured the chain around Rain's hips and the back of her thighs to make a seat. As he lingered on the fastenings, she reached a hand to his cheek and brought his face to hers.

Lightly, she brushed a kiss across his lips and murmured, "I'll be fine. I've done this before."

Valerius hesitated for a moment before cupping the back of her head and kissing her full and hard. He said nothing as he pulled away from her, but his eyes conveyed his worry for her safety.

Rain smiled her dazzling smile and pushed off from the ledge with her feet before he could change his mind and keep her with him. Effortlessly, she glided to the other side like a white dove floating with the wind beneath her wings.

The relief that washed over Valerius when she safely stepped onto solid ground with Ayelet's help almost buckled his knees.

Immediately, he felt compelled to make short work of his own harness and join the Healer as fast as possible. The separation of the ravine between them beset him with unease.

The rope creaked ominously with Valerius' weight, signaling that it had reached its limit. Testing it with a small bounce, Valerius felt assured that the rope could hold him without incident. He pushed off from the ledge and slid with dizzying speed toward the opposite side.

And then he heard the zing of an arrow as it broke through a piece of rope a few feet ahead of him. A second arrow followed closely behind, piercing through another section of rope.

It all happened so fast, the strands of rope breaking apart, unraveling with rapid twists, Valerius only had a second to react before the rope broke completely away three quarters of the way across the ravine.

He grasped the chain above him, swung his legs over his head, curled and rolled with the momentum of the downward slide and the force of his swing, then stretched into an arc in midair, and shot the chained scythe from his hands toward the broken piece of rope attached to the other side just as it was starting to swing backwards.

The chain of his scythe wrapped around the thick rope, the blade itself providing the anchoring weight, and Valerius braced his arms as the rope snapped taut with his weight.

He increased the momentum of the swing by kicking out his legs and released the scythe's grip on the rope at the last possible second. Rolling twice in the air to break his velocity, he landed hard on all fours on the opposite ledge a few feet away from Ayelet and Rain.

As the females rushed to him, he pushed them back with arm extended.

"Get back!" he ordered, then covered their bodies with his own against the rocky mountain side just before a slew of arrows whizzed their way.

Expecting the arrows to pierce his back, Valerius was stunned to find them whipped off course at the moment before impact by a steel object that boomeranged back to its invisible owner.

A piercing whistle immediately followed, and a white stallion galloped toward them with amazing agility and speed.

The gigantic horse swung its head up, then down, as if gesturing for them to get on. Acting on instinct, Valerius took action and boosted Ayelet and Rain on the steed's unsaddled back, then swung behind Rain, at the same time lifting her to sit on his thighs so all three of them could fit.

Without his urging, the stallion turned quickly around and galloped up the mountain path as more arrows zipped past, missing them by a hair.

They soon reached a plateau, and the stallion sped into the awaiting woods. By now, no more arrows dogged them, though their steed maintained its incredible speed until the trees around them became green blurs in the rapidly darkening night.

Valerius bent forward to shield the females with his broad back in case they were pursued from behind. A quick check told him that both Ayelet and Rain were unharmed. Winded, but whole.

Finally, the stallion pulled to a halt before a wooden hut with a straw roof. Shaking its head, it nickered for its passengers to alight.

Valerius swung off first and helped the two women down.

He pushed them behind him and surveyed their surroundings with a three-sixty view. Dense woods barricaded one side, a ravine another side, and a steep rocky slope extended behind the unassuming hut. There was only one way to get to the hut and it was through the woods. Whoever lived here would be alerted to approach far in advance.

Valerius assumed the owner of the hut had ready escape routes on hand, but looking at the mountain side and the sharp ravine, none came quickly to mind.

Feeling confident that no danger lurked in the surrounding area, Valerius cautiously approached the secluded hut, keeping Ayelet and Rain within reach behind him.

The wooden door to the hut, apparently the only entrance and exit, was unlocked. With a slight push, the door eased open with a creak of hinges.

A quick scan of the inside told Valerius that there were three small rooms, with the largest just before him, a sort of living room. Sleeping quarters to the left, exposed by a cloth drape that was tied back, and a small kitchen to the right, also exposed by a pulled back drape. Earlier, he'd spied a small shack slightly separate from the hut toward the back corner, and he assumed that was the outhouse.

Behind him, he heard the stallion snort and shake its head, then canter off to the west side of the hut where a makeshift stall stood with a similar straw roof.

Valerius quickly checked all three interior rooms and, finding no sign of occupants, gave the signal for Ayelet and Rain to follow him inside.

"Well that was more than enough adventure for one day," Ayelet commented drily when she stepped over the threshold.

"Are you all right?" Rain gently tugged on Valerius' sleeve, noticing that the fabric on the upper arm was slashed.

"I am unharmed," the Protector answered, showing her that his skin wasn't scratched from the arrow that pierced through his shirt.

Rain's hair automatically reached out to ascertain the situation for herself, but Valerius stepped away.

"There is no need, Healer," he said gruffly, avoiding the seeking tendrils.

He could not afford to let her probe him with her *zhen*. There was the risk that she would discover his Decline.

Taken slightly aback by the warrior's abrupt refusal, Rain's hair slowly eased back down. Although the Healer did not argue, her eyes roamed his body worriedly.

"Look at this place," Ayelet said in awe, gaining their attention. "It's filled with Chinese calligraphy scrolls. I've never seen such beautiful writing."

All three surveyed the room from top to bottom. Covering most of the walls were scrolls of calligraphy art. Stacked on tables and benches and above the ledge of the small fireplace were ink wells and calligraphy brushes of all shapes and sizes, held upright by various stands made out of metal and bamboo.

All three rooms were well illuminated by oil lamps, lanterns and candles. In a corner of the living room was a mat along a long, blank, rolled out scroll. It must be where the artist did his work.

Though Ayelet and Valerius could not distinguish the writing styles, they could appreciate the artistic mastery and flair, the power and elegance of the strokes, the sentiment of the artist when he put characters to paper.

"This must be Drako's abode," Ayelet observed out loud what all three had concluded. "The stallion must be his as well, I recognize it from the surveillance videos. I suppose we should thank him for our rescue."

"Unless he staged the attack," Valerius voiced one possibility.

"There are easier ways to hasten your departure," came a smooth voice behind them from the bedroom.

Valerius shot out his arms to prevent Ayelet and Rain from turning around, remembering to avoid the hypnotic gaze of their host.

"There were two vampires," the voice explained, moving slowly out of the room, circling around Valerius' back. "Rare for these remote parts. You three attract an entourage."

"Our apologies for the inconvenience," Ayelet said without turning to face the voice despite the instinct to do so. "And our gratitude for the rescue."

There was a soft sigh of resignation.

"Your determination to find me is as much a nuisance as it is admirable."

Their host shifted so that Valerius could see him out of the corner of his right eye. He knew that Drako was purposely positioning himself within view. He was establishing an unspoken truce, so that Valerius would lower his guard.

"You can rest assured I will not try to force my will upon you," Drako said aloud. "There's only so long I can avoid this encounter. I have the right to refuse your invitation in the end, have I not?"

Despite Valerius' restraining arm, Rain turned fully toward their host. She greeted him in Chinese and bowed formally.

Drako returned the gesture, then bowed in turn to Ayelet and Valerius.

Bound by politeness and protocol, the Guardian and Protector turned to face him and bowed as well.

Straightening, Valerius gazed directly into the warrior's eyes.

Curious, slightly amused twin ice blue lights flashed back at him. Though Valerius could not feel any imposition upon his will, he still felt the unnerving impact of the glittering aquamarine gaze.

"Your moves crossing the ravine were impressive, Protector," Drako acknowledged with a nod of respect.

Valerius inclined his head briefly in return. "Your steed is courageous as he is steadfast, warrior. I thank you for loaning us his aid."

Drako smiled slightly and agreed, "Yes, he is my lifelong friend and companion. He's pulled me out of many a sticky situation. He's been waiting centuries for my present incarnation, I suppose. Without him, I might not have survived my Awakening."

Drako looked to Ayelet and Rain.

"Allow me to show you to your quarters. I suspect you will remain for three days at least. A day to make your proposal. A day for me to consider—for I cannot reject out of hand, correct?"

Ayelet quirked her lips in an almost apologetic smile.

Drako smiled back in good humor. "And a day to give you my answer and help prepare for the return journey."

"*Our* return journey," Ayelet stated with emphasis.

"That remains to be seen, Guardian," Drako replied blithely, then gestured for all three guests to follow him.

"Come, you must be tired from your travels. A hot bath, cooked meal and long rest, in whichever order you prefer, will relieve all ailments."

Curious as to where exactly they would procure such accommodations given the size of the hut, Valerius followed his host into the bedroom.

As they stepped over the threshold, Drako pulled on an invisible string and one of the ceiling-to-floor scrolls raised like a rolling window blind. Drako approached the wall of rock behind the scroll and pressed the tips of three fingers against it at shoulder level. With a groan and a click, the rock began to shift.

The mountain behind the hut was hollow.

Valerius followed directly behind Drako but kept Ayelet and Rain close at hand. As the rock shifted back behind them, torches on the jagged walls lit automatically with bright orange flames.

The passageway Drako led them through was surprisingly wide and tall, enough for Valerius to stand upright with still a few inches to spare. After a few twists and turns, they arrived at the opening to a gigantic underground cavern.

A circular ring of torches around a dark pool more than thirty feet in diameter lit a large waterfall from below. Other strategically placed torches in the nooks and crannies of the cavern walls illuminated their surroundings with a warm, soft glow.

To their left and right were four brightly lit corridors symmetrically positioned on either side of the waterfall. In this central area, along the banks, tent-like structures shrouded with heavy, transparent cloth beckoned with their plush cushioned seats and tables piled with fruits and dried meats on large platters.

Quite a luxurious encampment for a humble calligraphy artist in the middle of nowhere in Lushui County, Yunnan.

"Shall we dine first or do you prefer the bath and rest?" Drako inquired politely.

All three voted for food.

Their host quickly got to work on fixing their supper, with Rain volunteering her help, while Valerius and Ayelet relaxed under a tent and snacked on the victuals provided.

Ayelet was chatting amicably beside him, but Valerius paid only enough attention to what she was saying to nod and murmur at the appropriate times. Most of his focus rested on Cloud Drako and Rain, moving in harmony around a stone fire pit in the center of the cavern, preparing the vegetables and meats for their evening meal.

They chatted easily like two long-lost friends in their mother tongue. Throughout the conversation, Rain smiled her dazzling, whole-hearted smile, and often Valerius caught echoes of her laughter as the bell-like sounds drifted toward him despite the splashing of the waterfall.

Cloud Drako was slightly shorter than Valerius, but still well over six feet. Standing beside the petite Healer, he seemed a veritable giant.

Valerius wondered how he himself and Rain looked together, for the difference in their heights was even more dramatic. The top of her head barely reached his sternum.

Rain and Drako were standing together at a chopping table, apparently sorted as to who would dice which ingredient. She laughed at something he said and elbowed him playfully in the ribs, while he smiled warmly down at her and nudged her back. They looked as if they'd known each other for ages.

They looked comfortable, familiar and domestic standing hip to hip, cutting the food and teasing each other in a language Valerius did not understand.

They looked... Mated.

The thought speared through Valerius with a blinding flash of pain. Involuntarily, his entire body drew taut and his hands gripped the bench he sat upon until his knuckles turned white.

"Are you all right?" he heard Ayelet ask beside him, as if in a distant echo, her voice muffled by the roaring in his ears, a haze of possessiveness and fury descending upon his mind.

He made himself nod, remotely aware that the motion was stiff and jerky.

She fell silent, however, so he didn't bother to maintain the pretense of being all right.

He was not all right. Not anywhere close to all right.

Was Rain ever so light-hearted and joyful with him? He'd seen her smile and laugh more in the quarter of an hour with Drako than he'd witnessed in the ten years he'd known her.

Had she ever looked upon him with such carefree delight? Such comfort and ease?

The answer was a resounding and gut-wrenching *no*.

Valerius realized that he'd never beheld this side of the Healer. The female for whom he'd Fallen. Even ten years ago at the Mid-Autumn festival, he hadn't seen her so relaxed and happy. Where he was concerned, she always seemed to hide behind a barrier, her emotions muted, her expressions controlled.

This was the side of her she shared freely with others, even near strangers, but very rarely, if ever truly, with him.

And yet Valerius had never shared more of himself with anyone else. He'd exposed the demons of his past, opened his heart, his mind.

Bared his soul to her.

For him there was never, and never would be, another. But for her, there ever was and would be one Consort after another.

Perhaps Drako would be the next.

Unable to bear the pain of seeing them together one moment longer, Valerius abruptly rose to his feet and blindly made his way to the chamber that Drako had earlier gestured to be his and Rain's.

Rain watched the Protector's departure with concern. She saw the aura of torment spike in waves around his body, but she could not diagnose the source. She was fairly certain, despite his rebuff of her probing earlier, that he did not suffer physical wounds. At least, none that was apparent.

Did he think of something disturbing? Every fiber of her being yearned to go after him and give him comfort.

"Let's finish cooking first," Drako said beside her, as if reading her mind, "perhaps the hot meal you bring him will help meet his needs."

Rain nodded numbly, slowly chopping the vegetables before her without looking at her actions, her gaze trained on the corridor through which Valerius had disappeared.

"He means a lot to you, your Consort," Drako observed quietly, drawing Rain's startled gaze back to him.

She looked down at the vegetables on the cutting board and quickened her motions with practiced ease.

"As do all my Consorts, in one way or another. But Valerius is more than a Consort," she amended.

"Ah," the warrior acknowledged and said nothing further.

"He is everything," Rain whispered fiercely to herself, trying to concentrate on completing her tasks quickly so that she could go to Valerius.

She didn't know why, but she knew that he needed her now.

Needed her desperately.

Chapter Fourteen

Late for her afternoon class, Sophia yanked open her locker in haste and almost didn't notice the manila envelope that fell to the floor.

Tristan picked it up for her and said, "This yours?"

Seeing the familiar, unaddressed envelope, Sophia's heart began to race. She snatched it from her Elite guard and hustled inside the classroom as the door swung shut behind her.

Once at her desk, she opened her text book and pulled out the photocopied articles she was supposed to have read for today's lecture and laid it beside her book. In her lap, she surreptitiously opened the manila envelope while keeping her gaze on Professor McGowen at the head of the class.

She inched the note within above the opening of the envelope by slow degrees and looked down to read the elegantly scrawled lines one by one.

Sophia,

Have you missed me?

Allow me the pleasure of imagining that you have. Tomorrow I shall be back in Boston. I cannot wait.

I write this from a brasserie opposite the Notre Dame Cathedral. The sun is just beginning to set, torching the sky afire with splashes of gold, purples and reds.

I wish you could see this with me. I have ordered a hot chocolate with my expresso on your behalf. It tastes sweet, rich and comforting.

Much like you, I fancy?

Sophia blushed furiously as she read and reread the last line. Her heart was beating so hard, she thought the whole class would hear.

I would like to invite you to my place this Saturday to celebrate the spoils of my trip with me. There is also some assistance I was hoping you could provide with the research ahead. I believe you will enjoy it.

Please say you will come.

310 Marlborough Street, Back Bay. 5pm.

Ere.

P.S. Enclosed is another song for you. Roughly translated lyrics from original Korean language attached below.

"That Man"—by Hyun Bin
One man loves you
That man loves you with all his heart
Everyday like a shadow he follows you around
When that man smiles he is crying on the inside
How much longer
Do I have to just look at you alone
This love like the wind
This worthless love
If I keep trying will it make you fall in love with me
Come a little bit closer
Just a little bit
I'm the one who loves you
Right now by your side
That man is crying
That man is very shy
So he learned how to laugh
There is so much that can't be said even amongst close friends
That man's heart is full of scars
So that man
Loved you because you were the same
Just another fool
Just another fool
Is it wrong to ask you to hold me once before you leave
I want to be loved... it's true
Everyday inside...inside his heart...he shouted and
That man is by your side again today

Do you know that I'm that man?
You wouldn't act this way if you knew
You wouldn't know because you're a fool
How much longer
Do I have to look at you like this alone?
This stupid love
This worthless love
If I keep trying will it make you fall in love with me
Come a little bit closer
Just a little bit
If I take one step forward you take two steps back
I'm the one who loves you
Right now by your side
That man is crying

With shaking hands, Sophia unzipped her iPad from its sleeve and booted it up. Without looking down, she navigated to iTunes, plugged in the pinky drive and uploaded the song to her music library. She synced her iPhone with the device and stealthily inserted her ear pieces.

For the rest of the class, she heard nothing of Pharohs, tombs and gods of the Underworld. All she heard was the haunting melody and voice of the singer. Though she didn't understand a whit of Korean, she followed along with the lines of lyrics in her lap, jotted down for her in Ere's elegant handwriting.

By the end of class, she'd memorized the tune and every translated word.

Saturday. The day after tomorrow. 5pm.

An army of vampires couldn't stop her from going.

*** *** *** ***

Valerius opened his eyes as the scent of the Healer preceded her into their chamber.

"I brought roasted rabbit and sautéed wild spinach with green onions and straw mushrooms," she said as she approached, balancing a large tray of food, water and heated rice wine.

Not turning around to face her, Valerius took a few moments to ensure that his countenance was a mask of stoicism before springing up and out of the steaming, waist-deep hot-spring pool with his arms pushing off the ledge.

His broad back facing her, he turned his head to the side to acknowledge her approach as her soft footsteps drew closer. He drew his knees up and casually draped an arm over his lap to hide his nakedness and arousal at her nearness when she laid the tray on the stone floor and sat cross-legged beside him.

"You must be famished," Rain observed, "Please eat it all. Ayelet, Cloud and I have already dined. We decided not to call for you in case you were resting."

Without responding, Valerius picked up a bowl of rice, deftly used the chopsticks to portion a leg of rabbit and a large heap of spinach on top and began to shovel his food, barely chewing before swallowing.

Either he was starving or he didn't want to talk, Rain thought as she watched him eat. Since she entered, he hadn't looked at her. The aura of pain was still glowing intensely around him, and she didn't know what to do, what to say.

Did he wish to be alone or was he content with her company? All she knew was that she wanted to be close to him. So close, she wanted to crawl beneath his skin.

"I hope you like it," she tried for idle conversation, "I used a dash of star anise to flavor the meat."

Pausing to swallow and take a gulp of rice wine to wash down the food, Valerius said, still not meeting her gaze, "I thank you for the meal. It is fulfilling."

And then he dug into another rabbit thigh and what remained of the vegetables, too occupied with polishing off his meal to speak further.

Rain felt unease at the Protector's distant, formal tone. Had she done something to upset him? Did he suffer from a physical wound that he hid from her? She decided simply to ask.

"Are you... displeased with me?" she inquired tentatively, her voice hitching a little.

Valerius slowed in his chewing and swallowed the last mouthful.

He raised his gaze to hers briefly and replied, "You worry for naught, Healer. I was merely lost in thought."

Her woman's intuition told her that he lied, but Rain did not dare press him further. Instead, she reached out a hand toward him, wanting a physical connection to reassure herself, but just as her fingertips brushed his knee, he flinched away like the first time she'd touched him ten years ago.

"I'm s-sorry," she stuttered, trying to disguise her hurt at his rejection, and when she would have continued making excuses, he interrupted with:

"You seem to know Cloud Drako well."

Startled, Rain blinked in confusion at the sudden introduction of the topic.

Gathering her wits, she folded her hands once more in her lap and said, "I know of him. We share common friends, it turns out, and he enjoyed our stroll down memory lane for he'd only recently regained consciousness of his past lives. His eternal soul has barely Awakened. He was—*is*—a very good man."

"He would make a superior Consort as well," Valerius stated, and tasted acid as the words tumbled recklessly out of his mouth.

Unconsciously, he worried the Tiger's Eye ring on his left hand with his thumb, turning it round and round. Perhaps Drako would be the next male to wear it.

Rain's prolonged silence at his pronouncement made him grudgingly look at her.

She was staring at him with wide, pained eyes.

"Have I spoken an untruth?" Valerius persisted, though part of his soul screamed for him to cease and desist.

Even the thought of Rain taking another Consort, sharing her body, her life, however briefly with another male, shredded Valerius' heart to bloody bits.

Rain held his unreadable gaze for long moments, then turned to face the pool.

"Why are you mentioning this?" she asked, her voice a little too controlled, a little too calm. "Have you already tired of your Service? Have I made too many demands?"

Valerius fell silent for a spell as well, struggling to rein in his emotions, fighting for his pride.

Finally, resignedly, he responded in his deep, husky baritone, "There is nothing you can ask of me that I would not give you readily, were it in my power to do so."

He paused, and then, "Please forgive my impertinence. I had no right to question you."

He moved to rise, but her hand on his forearm halted him.

Her voice quiet yet powerful, Rain said, still looking towards the water, "You are all I see, Valerius. I do not notice anyone else whenever you are near. Right now, you are my entire world. I have no past, no future, only the present. With you. Only with you."

She turned to look at him directly, her heart in her eyes.

"Do not speak to me again of Consorts," she whispered. "You are my *airen*. I only need you. *Want* you."

Want. Not love.

Yet in his moment of weakness, Valerius did not distinguish between the two. Overwhelmed by the power of her words, by the depth of his feelings, he rose and pulled Rain to her feet as well. With a shuddering breath, he enveloped her in his embrace, pressing her face into his chest.

Desperately he entreated, "Show me."

Rain took one step back and lifted her arms. Valerius followed her lead and pulled her light blouse over her head. She unhooked her simple white bra and stripped it from her shoulders, revealing her small, pale breasts and their large pink aureoles to his hungry gaze.

As he reverently cupped one breast, Rain drew her flowing trousers down her slim hips and let it fall with her panties around her feet. As naked as he, she leaned into him once more and mirrored his caress, laying one hand upon his steely pectoral, making the muscle jump beneath her palm.

"You are the most beautiful vision I have ever beheld," Valerius spoke in a hushed tone, as if afraid to wake up from a sweet, elusive dream.

"I was about to say the same to you," Rain said in return, a shy smile glowing on her face. "You are everything I have ever dared to dream. And so much more."

Valerius pulled her against him until their fronts were flush and his manhood jutted insistently against her stomach, begging for her attention.

"Take me," he offered himself to her, wishing to give her everything he had, everything he was. "Take my Nourishment. Release your store of pain."

Resolutely, she shook her head, moving to hold her hand over his against her breast. "Not tonight, *airen*. There will be no pain. Only release and fulfillment."

When he would have protested, she took his other hand and held it to her cheek, turning into it and pressing a tender kiss against his palm.

"And pleasure," she promised huskily. "All I want is to make love with you. All I want is you."

Shaking with the effort to hold himself in check lest he overwhelm her with his size and terrifying need, Valerius slowly dipped his head down to trace his lips along her temple, her brow, her cheek and nose.

With one hand he tilted her face up to give him better access; with the other, he ever so gently massaged her breast, rubbing his thumb over her nipple, sending sparks of pleasure through the hard bud.

As if knowing that he restrained himself, Rain trailed one hand along his arm and down his back to spread over his gluteus and urged his hips further into hers.

"Valerius, don't hold back," she encouraged, catching his full lower lip between her teeth. "Let go, my warrior. I want to know all of you."

On a sharp intake of breath, Valerius turned his mouth full upon hers, devouring her with his lips and tongue. As he surged into her wet, welcoming mouth again and again, he grabbed the back of her thighs and lifted her off the ground until her legs wound tightly around his waist and the hot core of her opened against his painful arousal.

Rain held onto him with both arms around his neck and pulled herself higher up his unyielding body, sliding her nether lips, damp with the juices of her excitement, along the entire length of his penis from bottom to top in one long, luxurious lick.

Once positioned above the plump, delicious head of him, she gyrated downwards in a graceful twist and took him half way inside her body.

Unprepared for the incredible pleasure that fired his nerves in a volcanic rush, Valerius staggered on a deep groan, the back of his calves meeting the edge of the large, tented platform bed set up a few paces from the heated pool.

With another twist of her hips, Rain took in more of his length, the action buckling his knees so that he fell backwards to sit upon the thick mattress. The sudden descent effectively pushed the rest of him fully inside her body, and the electrifying friction triggered Rain's first explosive orgasm.

Her sex squeezed with incredible strength around his in long, deep pulls as she arched her body back and keened in ecstasy.

Valerius bent forward over her arched torso and latched his mouth onto one of her breasts, suckling strongly upon the soft mound and plump nipple in time with her vaginal convulsions, drawing her orgasm out endlessly.

Without breaking their locked bodies, he smoothly shifted to his knees, keeping her splayed before him on the bed, her legs still wound tightly around his waist. His penis pulsed so deep and thick within her, the angle so perfect that he rubbed along her entire inner erogenous zone, she came again on a broken wail, her body desperately trying to milk from him the release that would magnify her rapture tenfold while Nourishing her with his life force at the same time.

Perspiration dampened Valerius' skin as he struggled to contain his own release. Though he knew the fulfillment it would bring both the Healer and himself, he also knew the limits of his own body.

The more he gave of himself, the faster his Decline would be.

With danger intensifying, the number of vampire attacks ever increasing, he needed to reserve enough strength to see them all safely home.

On the other hand, despite the constant pain of his Decline, his body yearned to Nourish her.

She had not fed from him since the night before their trip, and though their joining had vitalized her considerably, her strength was only half restored. With less than a fortnight left in the Phoenix Cycle, Valerius must ensure she took from him all that she needed, all that he had to give, while balancing his duty to protect, his ability to defend his loved ones effectively.

So he held back, gritting his teeth, as his body clenched tightly on the precipice of orgasm but was forcibly denied gratification.

Valerius focused on Rain's pleasure instead, spreading his large, calloused hands on either side of her ribcage, smoothing his thumbs over the satiny skin of her stomach, moving slowly lower until he spanned her hips and reached the folds of her vagina, stretched open around his turgid length.

Lightly, he rubbed the pads of this thumbs along the dewy lips of her sex, drawing a guttural moan from her throat. He inched one thumb upwards to cover her clit and moved the other hand to grip her hip so that he had full control of her body, still helplessly bowed backwards.

And then he began to flex his hips. Slowly. Inexorably. Devastatingly.

In this position, he felt the least friction from his movements, but she felt every infinitesimal fraction acutely against her pleasure center. The unrelenting pressure from his thumb pressing against her clitoris intensified the feeling of the mouth of his penis kissing her G-spot, rubbing it, massaging it, loving it.

It was too much. The pleasure was so mind-numbing, so overwhelming, Rain could no longer breathe. Her hands gripped his forearms desperately, her fingers digging into the corded muscles. Every nerve, every cell, every fiber of her being focused completely on the methodical contraction and release of his powerful hips.

An orgasm the likes of which she'd never dreamed much less experienced spread like molten lava throughout her body.

Her breath hitched as she began to come. But it was not yet the climax: it was still building, the pleasure was steadily, mind-blowingly growing.

Valerius clenched his jaw when Rain began to orgasm, the walls of her vagina squeezing his tortured sex until the pain was so intense sweat ran in rivulets down the sides of his face, the deep groove of his back. Still, he maintained the precise flexing of his hips, the perfect pressure of his thumb against her clit.

When she began to flail and buck, when she was reduced to helpless sobs of rapture, he gradually increased his speed until he too became enslaved to the breathtaking friction, to the hungry pulls of her sex, and his own bone-deep need to fulfill her.

They reached nirvana at the same moment and each half cried the other's name as they splintered with ecstasy, only to come back together as one, and explode in bliss once more.

His seed washed over her womb in Nourishing milky waves, filling her to the brim. But her body drank him greedily, absorbing all he had to give and ever striving for more.

After an interminable period of time, the quakes that racked their bodies reduced to small, sensitized shivers, and their breath returned to deep inhales and exhales instead of broken gasps of passion.

Valerius pulled Rain's boneless body up and forward against him and buried his face in the crook of her neck.

I love you.

He silently poured out his heart and soul to her, even as his body tightened with excruciating pain when he did not receive the exchange of spiritual energy from her as a sign of her answering love.

He did not expect it.

Her love.

It was enough that she cared for him, needed him, wanted him. It was enough that in her arms, he was just a male. The demons from his past had no place here.

He was simply hers.

They slept together for a few hours, their bodies remaining intimately joined. She drank from his throat for a bit in the middle of the night, and they woke twice before dawn to make love again.

Each time, he did everything in his power to prolong her pleasure, sacrificing his own. Each time, he gave into her in the end, Nourishing her with his release.

And invariably, each time, ravaging pain followed the orgasmic bliss as his strength depleted and his life force diminished.

As she had promised, not once during the entire night did she release her stored pain into him. Had it not been for his unrequited love, he would have only felt the heady pleasure of their joining.

It was enough, he chanted over and over in his mind.

Even as his heart bled at the irrefutable, annihilating truth that she did not love him in return.

*** *** *** ***

"Where are you going?" Dalair asked as he followed Sophia to her bedroom, but remained on the other side of the threshold.

"None of your business," came the ungracious reply.

She grabbed a change of clothes from her closet and disappeared into the bathroom.

Dalair noticed that she'd chosen a bright blue sweater dress and black stockings dotted with little pink hearts. A dramatic departure from her usual sweatshirt and pants. Dalair was slightly shocked that she even owned a dress.

"It is my duty to know your every move, my queen," Dalair responded, adding in the formal address because he knew how it irked her.

She hated to be reminded of her position and rank, hated to recall that she was not the average teenager.

"Fine," she called with annoyance from the bathroom, her raised voice grating on his hyper-sensitive hearing.

"I'm going to a friend's place to help with research. It's for school. Boring stuff. You don't have to come with me."

"You know that I do," he stated patiently. "You are under my protection today."

Before she could argue, and he knew that she was gearing up for it, he continued, "We are on high alert, as you are well aware. The vampire assassins we are dealing with are far more powerful and organized than we initially assessed. More than ever, you must maintain the highest level of protection."

"That means you, I suppose," Sophia groused from the bathroom.

She was putting on makeup, Dalair could hear from the clicks of cases and popping of mascara brush from its tube. Another first.

"After all, aren't you ranked number two in body count after Val?" the young queen all but growled.

"I do not keep score," Dalair evenly replied, "but I do agree with you that I am the best protection you can have in Valerius' absence."

Sophia emerged from the bathroom half dressed, the back zipper of her dress still down around her tailbone, to face him with a scowl, her wavy chestnut hair in a lioness halo around her head.

"That was not my point and you know it! I don't want you to come with me today and that's that. Being queen has to mean for something beyond just having a title and having my life turned inside out by vampires and strict rules! I need a social life and you're a pain in my ass!"

Unruffled by her outburst, the Paladin continued to regard her steadily, though he chose not to respond.

Sophia viciously yanked a brush through her tangled mane, so upset with her situation that she didn't even wince at the pain of pulling hairs out as she forcefully tugged through the snarls.

"Well?" she demanded when he continued his silence.

"My duty to protect you outweighs your wishes in this instance, my queen," Dalair finally said. "And it is too late to change guards as Tristan and Aella are on a mission. You know that Xandros is not at full capacity yet. I am your only option today, and you must have protective escort."

When Sophia inhaled deeply, whether to prepare for screaming in frustration or to shout further arguments at him, Dalair quickly broke in before she could fully charge her lungs.

"Perhaps a compromise can be reached between us. I will escort you to the meeting place and stay outside and out of sight. I promise you your friend will not see or hear me, will not know I escorted you there. I also promise to tune out my hearing on spoken words so that I cannot understand your conversation, but I will magnify my hearing on all other sounds as well as the rest of my senses to detect and anticipate any danger."

Sophia exhaled without blasting his ears, but her rebellious scowl remained.

Dalair pushed for closure, "Do we have a deal? Will you now tell me where you are going?"

Sophia wanted to accuse him of false promises just to be a bitch, but she knew that would be unwise. With a warrior like Dalair, you never ever hinted, much less outright questioned, that his honor might not be upheld, that he would fail to deliver on his promises once he gave them. So she swallowed back the caustic remarks burning on the tip of her tongue and admitted defeat.

She was stuck with him today and there was nothing she could do about it.

It wasn't just that his presence put a crimp in her normal teenage social life, or at least her best imitation of it, it was more that she simply didn't want *him* of all people to escort her to Ere's apartment.

It just felt wrong.

It made Sophia feel inordinately guilty. As if she were cheating on her boyfriend with someone else.

But that was ridiculous! Dalair wasn't anywhere near boyfriend material.

Not for Sophia anyway.

If anything, she should be feeling guilty toward Ere for showing up at his place with another hot, hot guy. She still hadn't put her finger on the perfect descriptor for Dalair, but he was definitely double hot.

Hotness squared.

Hotness times infinity.

Ugh! She was so disgusted with herself. How lame to be lusting after your bodyguard who saw you as his bratty kid sister at best, bothersome, incompetent baggage at worst. How could she crush on someone who had changed her diapers?

She had to suck it up and be responsible. At least he was willing to give her some leeway.

"Back Bay," she finally answered him, while turning around to present him with her back. "Can you please zip me up?"

Dalair was faced with a tantalizing view of Sophia's smooth, slender back, the curve of her spine gracefully leading to the lacy edge of low-rise panties.

It was pink.

Clenching his jaw, Dalair complied with efficiency, careful not to brush her skin.

Sophia flipped her hair out over the neck of the dress, sending a cloud of her personal fragrance to besiege Dalair's senses. He immediately tried to block his sense of smell, but he was an instant too late and inhaled her unique combination of orchid and innocence.

After all these millennia, even in a different form, she still smelled the same.

Would she also taste the same?

Dalair unconsciously backed up two steps as his body hardened in recognition.

Oblivious to the Elite guard's potent reaction to her nearness, Sophia stomped back into the bathroom to finish her preparations. In the end, she opted to pull her rebellious mane into a plump ponytail, leaving tendrils of hair framing her face prettily, despite their haphazardness.

She completed her outfit will furry UGG booties that Aella had given her last Christmas in an attempt to bring her into more fashionable territory. Not quite a match for her ensemble, but they were the most stylish footwear she owned. All the rest of her shoes were sneakers, with the exception of one pair of bright red rain boots.

She slung her book bag over her shoulder and cast a narrow-eyed look at Dalair, warning him silently to fulfill his promises.

"Let's go."

Chapter Fifteen

"We need to head back a day early," Ayelet said grimly as she deciphered the encrypted messages from the Shield.

"What has happened?" Rain raised her head to ask, startled and concerned.

She was starting preparations for midday meal while Valerius and Cloud were out on surveillance. Cloud had foiled two vampires during their attack yesterday but there could well be more.

"Dalair and Aella believe that someone is forcefully turning Pure Ones into vampires," Ayelet replied, exhaling deeply in worry and frustration.

"And not just any Pure One, but highly trained, ancient warriors. Meanwhile, Orion and Eveline are already on their way back to the Shield. Their search for the two warriors in Russia and Sweden has turned up empty, and they barely escaped a trap. If Aella is not mistaken, the vampire assassin she recently fought was the Russian warrior we were trying to recruit. We must consider the possibility that the Viking warrior has been turned as well."

"Goddess above," Rain whispered, laying down the dicing knife. "We need Cloud to return with us more than ever."

"Agreed," Ayelet nodded, closing her tablet.

She met Rain's eyes and hesitated, unsure how best to approach the question.

Finally, she asked, "What is your level of confidence that Cloud will consent to join our ranks?"

Rain blinked and frowned a little. Why would Ayelet assume she'd have a better read on the warrior's intentions when Ayelet was the one with the Gift of empathy?

"I'm not sure," she responded slowly. "He clearly prefers his seclusion and this peaceful way of life. Yet, I also know that he is extremely honorable and would struggle to deny our request for aid. If we put our case before him, update him on the recent events, surely he would lend his strength."

"And there would be no other incentive besides an appeal on his honor?" Ayelet pressed softly.

Rain's frown deepened. "What are you implying?"

Ayelet sighed and went to stand opposite Rain across the stone table where she worked on the ingredients for their luncheon.

"I apologize for being roundabout," Ayelet said. "I just thought that there was a more intimate connection between you and Cloud from your interactions yesterday. Perhaps an old friendship, perhaps a cultural bond. And maybe some... mutual attraction as well?"

The Healer's cheeks pinkened, whether from embarrassment or anger, Ayelet could not tell.

Rain cast her eyes downward and said, "You are mistaken. Cloud and I do not have a prior relationship, nor do I imagine we will be more intimate than comrades in the future. Valerius asked me much the same yesterday."

At that realization, Rain looked back at Ayelet.

"Why are you both asking me these things? There is nothing out of the ordinary between me and Cloud."

Ayelet held Rain's gaze and, despite her Mate's warning, she couldn't resist interfering just a little.

"Drako seems like a prime candidate for your next Consort, Rain. Anyone can see that. He is more than qualified to Serve you, and you seem to genuinely like each other. If Cloud thought along the same lines, perhaps it would be added incentive for him to return with us."

Before Rain could object, as she was clearly getting ready to do, her frown darkening into a scowl, her head already shaking, Ayelet put up a hand to delay her.

"But clearly, you are preoccupied with the current Phoenix Cycle, and very much invested in your current Consort."

"Rain."

The heavy emphasis Ayelet put on her name made Rain grow still and listen closely to what the Guardian had to say.

"Exactly what does Valerius mean to you?"

Ayelet paused several moments to let the question sink in.

When the combativeness deflated from the Healer as she considered her feelings, Ayelet continued softly, "It seems to me that he is more than just your Consort. Even when you first met, you seemed inordinately drawn to each other. Although at first I thought it was negative tension, it did not escape me how he drew your attention whenever he was near, despite that at the time, you had a different Consort."

Ayelet leaned in and clasped one of Rain's hands in both of hers.

"I've known you for centuries, my friend. I've never seen you so involved in a male."

Rain looked away, unable to deny the truth of Ayelet's words. The Guardian knew her past. Knew the calamity she caused with her first Consort. Knew why she always held herself back, guarding her emotions closely, with every other Consort and male thereafter.

But Valerius was different. And she was different when she was with him.

"Do you love him?"

Rain gasped at the sudden pain that exploded in her heart when she heard her friend's question. Involuntarily, her chin began to quiver and tears flooded her eyes.

Yes! She wanted to shout, to declare to the world. She loved Valerius more than her own life. More than anyone she'd ever known.

But she didn't dare utter a sound. She didn't know if it was enough. When she thought she'd loved her first Consort, as well as Fan Li during her human life, neither of those loves was great enough to change her destiny.

True, her feelings for Valerius was far deeper, far more encompassing. But was it because he was the one true Mate for her, or because she'd been starving for decades and he was the strongest Consort she'd ever had? Had she become addicted to his Nourishment? Did addiction equal love?

She'd never known anyone like the Protector. Full of pain, restraint, ever plagued by demons from his past, knowing little joy in his long existence. Yet so strong, so selfless and brave to win his battles against darkness and despair.

A male less worthy would not have survived the suffering he'd endured. And not only survive, but remain *good* and pure of soul.

Rain was in awe of him. In lust with him. Enraptured by him.

Of course she *loved* him.

But there were many forms of love. She knew what Ayelet asked, and no matter how Rain searched within herself, the answer would not come.

The Guardian sighed and squeezed Rain's hand.

"Forgive my intrusion. Forget I said anything. It is not my place to ask. It is between you and Val. I just…"

She tilted her head to the side to gain Rain's attention and met the Healer's eyes.

"I just want the best for both of you. And I'll say just one last thing. Trust yourself, Rain. Don't let the past confuse your feelings. Don't second-guess yourself. And trust Valerius. He is a male of few words and fewer expressions. But you *know* him. Deep down, you know him."

As Rain held her friend's compassionate gaze, the tears streaked silently down her cheeks. Enforcing discipline upon herself, she blinked them away and straightened her spine.

Resolutely she nodded. Whatever it cost, she would not repeat the mistakes of her past.

"They have returned," Ayelet said, turning toward the cavern entrance at the sound of the secret gateway sliding open.

"We must ready for departure."

*** *** *** ***

Sophia climbed the few brick steps to the front entrance of the Back Bay brownstone with some trepidation.

She was meeting with a *man*.

A man to whom she was attracted. And he was so out of her league he might as well be from an alternate universe.

She surreptitiously looked around before buzzing Ere's apartment.

As he'd promised, Dalair made himself invisible. By all appearances, Sophia had walked to Marlborough Street from the Christian Science Center by herself.

But all along the way she knew he was there, her designated protector.

Her nemesis.

Sophia took a deep breath and pushed the buzzer a tad more forcefully than she intended as she tried to block Dalair from her thoughts. She was here to see Ere. She was here to help him with research. And to ogle him when he wasn't paying attention.

She wouldn't let Dalair distract or detract from her treat.

The door unlocked. Sophia squared her shoulders and went inside.

Ere's apartment was in the basement of the three story townhouse. He shared the residence with two other families, Sophia deduced, glancing quickly at the mailboxes on the first floor. As she braced herself to knock on his door, it swung open before she had a chance.

And there stood the beautiful fallen angel himself, beaming blindingly down at her.

"Welcome, Sophia," Ere said in his melodious voice. "Please come in and make yourself at home."

He ushered Sophia inside with a hand on the small of her back, sending tingles of delight through her torso from the warm, gentle pressure.

"May I take your coat?" he asked solicitously.

Sophia readily handed it over, for the apartment was surprisingly warm, almost overly so, from a fire that blazed in the hearth and the bright lights that made her feel they were bathed in daylight rather than in an almost windowless basement.

"Would you like something to drink? Water, juice, tea?"

"Uhn."

That was the first sound to come from her lips. She was off to a fantastic start.

Ere tilted his head slightly at her mastery of the English language and etiquette.

But he seemed more amused than disappointed, for he said with a smile, "Juice it is. I hope mango will do."

Sophia nodded sheepishly and changed her weight from foot to foot. She watched him pour her juice in the small but modern kitchen and was too hypnotized by his lithe form and graceful movements to take in her surroundings. Her eyes were riveted on his person.

He came back to her shortly with her juice, brushing her fingers casually when handing her the glass.

Sophia didn't think her heart could handle too much more of this touchy feely stuff, not when every slight brush of skin against skin sent shocks of electricity through her.

She clumsily stepped away from him and almost tripped over an ornate velvet-cushioned chair behind her. Thankfully, her knees buckled in a timely manner and her backside managed to find the chair rather than the wooden floor.

The juice sloshed dangerously in her glass, but by sheer force of will, she stared it into submission and managed to keep from spilling.

"If you don't mind, I will partake of some wine," Ere said, his lips quirking at one corner as he witnessed her near tumble.

Sophia gestured for him to do as he pleased, and he returned to the kitchen.

That was when Sophia's surroundings finally hit her: Ere's apartment was a veritable treasure trove.

In awe, she glanced around the walls full of antique sconces, paintings, murals, silk scrolls. There were shelves upon shelves of books, sculptures and what looked to be genuine artifacts from various places around the world and times across history.

The furniture was comfortable and lived in, but beautiful in design, an eclectic collection of vintage pieces. Before the fireplace was a large, fluffy, well-worn sheepskin rug. In the center was a small stone table just large enough to support an exquisite chess set. Sophia could almost hear the invitation to come sit beside the fire and indulge in an intimate game.

There was background music playing, the soothing melodies reaching her ears from the room on the other side of a short, narrow hallway. She leaned back in her chair slightly to see better, but it was too dark to make anything out.

It must be his bedroom, she thought with a nervous swallow of juice. Better to focus the rest of her perusal on her immediate quarters.

Ere emerged from the kitchen once more with a glass of red wine and a tray of cheeses and fruit. He set the tray on a small coffee table within Sophia's reach.

Casually folding his long, lean limbs onto a mahogany Victorian chaise lounge with gold and red striped cushions and pillows, Ere looked like an exotic bird of prey in his very own paradise.

Sophia, by contrast, felt like a drab, out-of-place, inferior creature, potentially of the rodent variety.

Ere took a slow sip of wine and hypnotized the unfortunate little gray mouse with his glittering gaze.

Smiling a little, he said, "Did you miss me?"

Sophia just stared back unblinkingly in response, tried to take another swallow of her juice, only to find she'd already drank it all.

She set the glass down on the table and, with no small effort, dragged her eyes away from his.

"You have a really nice place," she uttered her first coherent sentence, ignoring his question. "Is everything genuine or are they replicas?"

"Do you think I can afford the genuine articles on a teaching assistant's salary?" Ere asked in return.

"I guess not," Sophia murmured, "but they sure look like the real thing."

Vaguely, it occurred to her that he had not answered her question directly.

"Were you able to find this address easily?" Ere leaned forward to pick a couple of luscious green grapes from the tea tray.

Sophia nodded. "I live pretty close by."

"Really? You do not live on campus as do most Freshmen?"

Tempted by the way Ere seemed to enjoy his grapes, Sophia plucked a few for herself.

"No, I live in Boston city with friends."

"Ah," he said, twirling the wine in his glass before taking another small sip. "Did one of your friends escort you here?"

Sophia startled at the question. Strangely, she felt almost as if she were being interrogated.

But then Ere smiled and added with an endearing expression of embarrassment, "It's just that you never seem to be alone. On the first day of class you were with your friend Aella, and the first time we met, there was a man coming to your table to join you just as I was leaving. The times I've seen you walking around campus you were always with someone. I must admit it took me a bit of courage to approach you that day in the cafeteria."

Sophia blushed and looked down at her lap.

"I don't understand why you'd have trouble approaching anyone," she said honestly.

Ere leaned forward with elbows on knees and waited until Sophia looked at him again.

"Perhaps I am shy," he told her, "especially around a girl as lovely as you."

Sophia turned beet red. Uncomfortably, she dropped her gaze and changed the subject.

"So, what treasures did you bring from the Louvre?"

Ere sighed and sat back. Apparently it was too early for more intimate conversations with his little mouse. Somehow, Sophia's reticence only made her more attractive to him.

"Come, I will show you the etchings I made."

Sophia was in her element after that, poring through notes from Ere's research and the etchings of millennia-old symbols and drawings. They spent hours brainstorming, searching through the considerable library of research Ere had in the apartment on ancient Persia, chatting, snacking, even joking and laughing.

Sophia got past her awe of Ere's physical beauty and focused more on the meeting of minds.

He was exceptionally knowledgeable and sharp, quick to raise alternative possibilities to established theories and written records. She was enthralled by the way he brought the ancient world to life with his sketches and descriptions. They felt so real, it was as if he had actually been to the places and times he studied.

It was almost midnight before Sophia could no longer ignore the vibration against her wrist on the underside of her turquoise bracelet, which served as both jewelry and a hidden communication channel between her, her guard and the Shield. Over the last hour, it vibrated every ten minutes, then every five.

Dalair must be getting impatient.

Slowly, Sophia stretched to a sitting position from her lazy sprawl on the sheepskin rug, then stood and hugged her arms around her torso.

"I better go home," she said regretfully. "It's really late and my friends are waiting for me."

Ere stood as well. There was barely half a foot separating them, and whereas the Sophia who entered the apartment would have automatically stepped back to distance herself, after spending the past few hours with Ere, the present Sophia kept her footing firm.

She met his eyes and said sincerely, "I had a really great time. You're a brilliant researcher and teacher."

Ere smiled a little at her compliment. "Is that all I am to you?"

She blinked a few times and felt a flush working its way up her neck, but she refused to let the acceleration in her heartbeat fluster her like it did before.

"I'd like to think you're my friend," she responded, holding his penetrating gaze. "I like you very much."

Astonishingly, it was Ere who took a slight step back. He looked away briefly, then returned to her with a different smile.

A darker, almost ironic smile.

"I like you too, Sophia. Very much."

He started to say something else, but then seemed to change his mind, shaking his head a little.

"Come, I'll retrieve your coat and walk you out. May I see you home?"

"No thanks," she quickly replied. "A friend is coming to pick me up and, really, it's just a few blocks away."

"Ah," he murmured in the same tone he did before.

She tried not to read too much into that one little word, but she could have sworn he sounded disappointed.

They parted ways at the bottom of the front steps to the brownstone.

Before she left, he surprised her by pulling her into a warm hug and brushing his lips lingeringly against her forehead.

"'Til we meet again," he said softly.

"I'll see you in class next Thursday, right?" Sophia couldn't keep the eagerness out of her voice. Four whole days seemed like an eternity before she saw him again.

"Of course, my lovely Sophia."

He released her reluctantly from his embrace and sent her on her way, standing in place and watching her round the corner of the block until she was completely out of sight.

*** *** *** ***

"Whoa, girlfriend, where are you storming off to in such a rage?" Aella asked, jerking Sophia to a stop with a restraining hand on the young queen's arm.

"He's impossible!" Sophia practically yelled, snatching her arm back with a furious tug.

Looking beyond her to the Paladin, who followed Sophia into the Shield a few steps behind, Aella could only assume that he was the target of the queen's anger.

"Care to explain, Dalair?" Aella asked with a cocked eyebrow and faintly amused expression.

It had become an increasingly frequent occurrence over the last couple of years that Sophia was in one snit or another with this particular Elite guard.

"I am merely taking precautions," the Paladin said grimly, stopping in his approach a few feet away from them, as if purposely keeping himself out of Sophia's kicking and spitting range.

"How many times do I have to tell you that there's nothing wrong with Ere!" Sophia thundered, throwing up her hands.

"He's human, not vampire. You saw yourself that he was perfectly normal during the day. Yeah he's a little pale, but give the guy a break! He lives in a basement! *And*, I felt no ill intentions from him. I'm not so taken in by his pretty face to forsake my own safety for Goddess sake. In fact, I think he might have a Pure soul. I definitely sense something special in him."

"Are you sure you are not influenced by hormonal imbalances?" Dalair responded calmly. "I can smell the onset of your monthly cycle."

"Oh, you did not just say that," Aella muttered under her breath, then extended an arm reflexively to hold Sophia back as the queen launched herself toward Dalair with a snarl.

Dalair watched Sophia struggle against the Amazon's hold energetically but futilely with the same calm expression.

Finally, Sophia wore herself out and shoved Aella's restraining arm away.

Huffing with her efforts, she speared Dalair with a ferocious glare and ground out, "I really hate you."

With that, she spun on her heel and marched away, presumably to her quarters.

Aella shook her head at the Paladin and tsked, "You have such a smooth way with the ladies, Dalair."

His determined expression did not change.

"Every instinct tells me that something about this *Ere* is off. If he's innocent and legitimate, a thorough background check can't hurt him. I don't see why the queen takes umbrage to mere precautions."

"Are you serious?" Aella snorted. "You didn't strike me as slow-witted before, my friend."

Finally, a small frown creased the warrior's brows. Aella didn't know whether he frowned at her insult or because he still didn't realize what he'd done or said wrong.

With a sigh, she threw an arm around his shoulder.

"Come on, old friend, you need some rest. Everything will become clearer in the morning. I'll stay with Sophia tonight— there's no hunt, as we're expecting Ayelet and cohort to return from China early tomorrow and we'll have a group get together after breakfast."

Together, they began to walk to the private quarters.

"You do what you need to do, Dalair," Aella continued, "but don't throw it in Sophia's face. And if I were you, I'd keep my distance from our vigorous little queen for a while, at least until she's no longer shooting daggers and spitting nails at you."

When Dalair was about to object, Aella squeezed his shoulder and silenced him.

"Xandros will be fully recovered in a couple more days and Valerius will be back as well. If they were successful in China, we'll be welcoming a new Elite warrior into our midst. So you can rotate out of Sophia's protection for a while. I think it will do both of you good."

Some fight went out of Dalair at that.

Aella was right. Somehow, he couldn't help rubbing Sophia the wrong way no matter how hard he tried not to. He sensed a certain irrationality in his own actions when he spent too much time with her, as if her nearness caused his reason and sense to take flight. He felt irritable, angry, and scared when she was with Ere.

Dalair knew that feeling well, though he'd not encountered it since his human life. He cringed to put a name to the emotion, but he knew full well what it was:

Jealousy.

Chapter Sixteen

"Well, fuck me."

The whispered explicative from the tall, golden-haired, voluptuous beauty drew Cloud's gaze directly to hers.

Within minutes of their arrival to the Shield, he was formally introduced to the Royal Zodiac by Ayelet as they gathered together in the throne room.

Cloud did not know any of the new faces, nor did he recognize their souls. Perhaps even in his past lives he had not ever encountered them.

But as he stared into the bright sapphire eyes of the female warrior before him, he felt a pang of...

Unease was not the right word. Recognition was too strong.

Awareness.

It was awareness. As if every nerve in his body sprang to attention. Disorientingly so, Cloud realized.

Beside the blonde, the young Pure Queen, Sophia, put her shared consternation and excitement into more coherent words.

"You look just like one of the characters from Dynasty Warrior, my favorite video game," she said breathlessly. "Except you're *waaay* cooler."

And *waaay* yummier, Aella thought to herself.

Goddess help her, but she wouldn't be surprised if she was actually drooling onto the expensive Italian marble floor.

Maybe it was the glorious contrast of the male's Asian and Western features. The shape of his eyes was distinctly oriental, long and tilted down at the inner corners, tilted up at the outer corners, reminding her of wolf's eyes.

The slash of his black brows and long black hair, pulled back with a wide metallic band at his nape with a matching band around his forehead to keep the shorter tufts from his face, looked thick and silky, and she itched to run her fingers through the waist-length mane. His jaw and chin, too, were more Asian than Western, acutely angular, smooth and stubble-less.

But then there were the piercing, mesmerizing ice blue eyes, framed by spiky, thick black lashes, which again reminded Aella of the Montana Gray Wolf.

His nose was long and narrow, his cheekbones sharp and high. His lower lip was fuller than the upper and the way he held his mouth made her want to take a bite out of him. His bone structure and musculature reminded her more of the Italian, Spanish or Greek, with broad shoulders and narrow hips.

And from what she could tell without circling him like a lioness around her prey, he was in possession of a very fine backside.

She wondered if his golden skin was smooth and stubble-less all over.

Aella roused from her X-rated mental exploration of the warrior's body at the sound of throat clearing beside her.

"Aella," Sophia whispered loudly, elbowing her in the ribs, "you're ogling our new recruit and you've ignored the introduction."

Blinking rapidly to clear the unclothed fantasy version of the warrior from her mind's eye, she snapped to attention and quickly replaced her dumbstruck expression with a self-confident, inviting smile.

"An honor," she said and returned the warrior's formal bow, albeit a few beats delayed. Her eyes fairly sparkled with amusement and pleasure as she raised her eyes again to meet his.

Cloud was stunned by the sudden transformation in Aella's countenance. He didn't know which of her expressions made him feel more uncomfortable, the one where she looked at him like he was a succulent meal after years of starvation, or the one she was giving him now, as if she had already tasted every inch of him and was insatiable for more.

He should have remained in the remote mountain villages of Yunnan, he thought belatedly, where the only creature who saw him on a regular basis was his devoted steed.

Unfortunately, he had to leave his peace and tranquility behind to take his place as one of the Elite. At least his equestrian companion would follow him to the Shield at a later date—when Tristan completed the underground stables to accommodate their four-legged member.

He didn't mean to do it, but as if Cloud's mind was erecting protective barriers, he tried to push blankness into Aella's consciousness, or at least tone down whatever emotion or fantasy that was making her look at him as if he stood naked and vulnerable before her.

He was stunned, however, by the backlash that resulted from his reflexive action. His head jerked slightly back as if he'd received a physical blow. For the first time since he'd come into his Gift, he could not push his will onto another person.

Aella frowned a little and absently rubbed her temple as she felt a sharp but brief sting. It had come and gone so quickly it was as though she'd imagined it.

Mentally shrugging, she focused back on the warrior as he turned to greet Orion and Eveline. Remotely, she heard that they had bestowed upon him the formal Elite title of "the Valiant."

It intrigued her, for every title, besides being indicative of an inner circle member's role, had a history behind it, as well as an omen for the future. Cloud Drako must have been spectacularly courageous in his past lives to earn such a moniker.

"Now to business," Alexandros announced when the introductions were complete.

"We called you back because the situation has grown dire. As you all know, we have reason to believe that there is a new way of making vampires, and that whoever is behind it is targeting warrior-class Pure Ones to turn. Moreover, he or she is old and powerful enough to control these newly created vampire assassins, who are targeting the Royal Zodiac purposefully. To what end, we have yet to determine. Regardless, we must stop them before they progress further."

He looked to Tristan, who nodded and stepped forth, drawing everyone's attention.

"What you don't know is that we recently received a projection from Seth."

This news drew a few gasps from the Dozen. That they received word from Seth meant that he was still alive; that he sent a projection meant that he was strong enough to use his Gift, part of which entailed the ability to project his image and voice across time and space to any person or location of his choosing.

"He assured us that he was safe and strong, though he did not reveal his mission or location. He warned us about the vampire assassins and confirmed, at the very least, that Jade is not behind the plot against us. Based on Seth's knowledge, we must assume that Leonidas is lost to us. If he is not dead, then he has been turned assassin."

Tristan let the group absorb the implications of his words.

Alexandros looked away, clenching his fists in fury and frustration.

Though he'd already witnessed Seth's projection, and he'd privately feared that the worst had happened to his comrade, he felt the pain of loss most acutely for he saw it as his own failure that Leonidas had been taken from them.

"To prepare for the battles to come," Tristan continued grimly, "Alexandros will train each of us, including the Circlet, in the best ways to combat the Sentinel. If he has indeed been turned, the threat to all of us has increased tenfold. He knows our fighting styles, our strengths and weaknesses. He could be training vampire assassins as we speak."

"Except Cloud," Ayelet interjected. "He does not know Cloud."

"Exactly," Aella responded. "Drako is our edge."

She locked eyes with the warrior in question and felt strangely reassured in the calm, quiet strength of the new recruit. In his presence, she felt as if everything would turn out as the Goddess willed, and that her will would include their triumph.

When Aella looked back to the rest of the group, the sense of peace abruptly lifted, and she narrowed her eyes.

"However, I wouldn't be surprised if they've studied him thoroughly as they've undoubtedly studied all the others. We have a lot to catch up on. We've started to compile all the profiles of known warrior-class Pure Ones across the world, based on Ayelet's work. We need to familiarize ourselves with their history, training, weapons and techniques. There's no telling which ones have been turned and we need to prepare ourselves for all possibilities."

"My queen," Dalair said, addressing Sophia, who caught the force of his solemn gaze like a startled rabbit before a feline predator, "we need you to harness the full power of your Gift to start identifying and narrowing down Pure souls among the humans, especially those on the cusp of their Awakening. This is another advantage we have over our unseen foes. They can only target the known existing Pure Ones, but we can double our efforts to educate, recruit and train new members. In so doing, we can stay one step ahead of our enemy."

Sophia almost clicked her heels together and saluted the Paladin, feeling like a stripling soldier receiving a crucial responsibility from her CO, but she settled for a swallow and a nod.

She just hoped she wouldn't let him, *all of them*, down.

"Trouble is brewing at an accelerated pace," Aella said and looked at the Scribe and Seer each in turn.

"Not only do we have Seth's warning, the Zodiac Scrolls and Prophesies have also confirmed an imminent battle that will be critical in deciding our future course. All of us need to undergo intensive combat training, especially Sophia and the Circlet. We need to quickly determine your natural abilities and match you with appropriate weapons."

She regarded the Protector. "Valerius, you are best suited to train the Elite. You are the strongest among us."

Next she turned to the General. "Alexandros, you will train and educate everyone on Leonidas' fighting style and how he thinks strategically so that we can anticipate his moves."

Finally, she looked to the Paladin.

"Dalair, you will train the Circlet and Sophia on basic attack maneuvers and self-defense, leveraging each person's Gift to the extent possible. Though our non-combat members are not easy prey by any means, as Orion and Eveline have demonstrated on their recent trip, we need to up the ante several notches. If there is an all-out battle, no one will be a liability; no one will be left behind."

"Should I take leave from school?" Sophia asked.

Given the urgency of the situation, she thought that might be the best course of action.

"No," Aella responded firmly. "We must not signal to our enemies that we've caught their scent. Thus far, they've been bringing the fight to us, and now it's our turn to turn defense into offense. But we must maintain the element of surprise."

"My sense is that they are getting too sure of themselves, too cocky, despite their failed assassination attempts. It's almost as if they're toying with us, testing our strengths and weaknesses. We should keep up all appearances that we are none the wiser."

"Besides," the Amazon said after a thoughtful pause, "your classes are during the day, when vampires are not active. The risk is relatively low."

Dalair shot the Strategist a skeptical look, silently disagreeing with her assessment of the level of threat to Sophia.

Aella looked calmly and meaningfully back at him.

It was then that he realized that Aella had lied. The risk to Sophia's safety was not low. In fact, Aella was counting on a move against the Queen.

She was to be bait.

When Dalair shifted his body aggressively, on the verge of calling Aella out for his suspicions, the Amazon slowly shook her head at him. She promised with her eyes that she would explain her reasons.

Offline. In private.

Thus agreed, the Dozen separated into smaller groups to hash out details, schedules and strategies.

Before Dalair could corner her, Aella grabbed hold of Valerius and pulled him to a side corridor.

"How are you feeling?" she asked the Protector with some concern. "I named you as the intensive combat trainer for the Elite because you're the best candidate for the job, but I can easily sign up one of the others for it, maybe even Cloud if he's as good as he's reputed to be."

Valerius frowned. "You doubt my abilities?"

Aella did her non-rolling-eyes maneuver and speared him with a "don't be obtuse" look.

"I just said you're the best candidate, didn't I? But let's be honest with each other, Val. A, you're not looking your best right now—I expected you to exhibit signs of decreasing strength as the Phoenix Cycle progressed, but you're looking worse for wear. And B, you have a more important duty to fulfill to the Healer until the Cycle is complete. She needs to be one hundred percent as soon as possible. Before this battle is over, there will be many casualties, and it's only the beginning, I feel. There will be many more battles to come before we win the war."

Valerius clenched his jaw and looked away.

Aella spoke the truth, and he was well aware of his body's limitations. Training the Elite would take a heavy toll on his already depleted strength. Meanwhile, he still had his duties as Consort to fulfill. Both roles were crucial to their survival, but he knew without deliberating which responsibility he needed to prioritize.

"Cloud and I can share the task of training the Elite," he finally responded. "And yes, from what little I have seen, the Valiant is deserving of his reputation."

Aella nodded with an assessing gleam in her eyes.

"You two bonded over the journey, have you? Interesting."

Valerius narrowed his eyes. "What is your meaning?"

The Amazon shrugged in answer. "Can't wait to see for myself whether he's all he's cracked up to be."

Valerius knew that she didn't say what was really on her mind, but he had no interest in pursuing the topic further. Instead, he took his leave and went in search of Rain.

Since their night in the cavern, he could not escape the notion that she was purposely avoiding him. Though she stayed close to him physically, often taking his arm or curling her body against his during their return journey, she seemed distant emotionally.

She seldom met his gaze and often stared into the distance as if lost in thought. It took over two days for them to make all the arrangements and return to the Shield, and during that time, they'd barely exchanged two sentences.

His heart ached.

He knew what it meant to give himself fully to her without expectation of anything in return. He'd anticipated the pain and torment of love unrequited, but he'd underestimated the intensity of his agony and the speed of his Decline.

If he sparred with any member of the Elite as he was now, it would only be a matter of time before they knew his condition as well. His distance combat techniques might be able to help conceal his waning strength. But how would he keep his Decline from Rain herself?

As the Cycle progressed, she became more insistent on probing him with her *zhen* to assess his condition. He knew that she worried constantly about overtaxing him, taking too much Nourishment. He had been able to distract her from a thorough health and energy assessment up to this point, but she was growing increasingly concerned. And the more she attuned herself to his body, the more difficult it became to hide the truth from her.

The good news was that her vitality had returned at a much faster rate than previous Cycles by all accounts. Most of her hair had already turned a rich black at the roots. Only a few streaks of white remained. He needed her to take the rest of his Nourishment and build up a deep reserve for the future.

He needed her to take all of him.

Valerius found the Healer waiting for him before the wall mural in the inner chamber of the Enclosure they shared.

He knew that she was purposefully waiting because she met his eyes with solemnity and determination the moment he walked inside and closed the door behind him.

"I release you from your duties as Consort," she announced without preamble, hands clasped before her, back straight, head high.

The words were like a physical blow.

Valerius barely managed to hold his ground, though his soul staggered from the impact of what she said.

"Why?" he forced out, though he couldn't hear his own voice for the ringing in his ears.

"You have a more important and urgent duty now, and it will take all of your strength to fulfill," she answered placidly, as if she'd rehearsed her words beforehand.

"I feel better than I have in centuries. There's no need to complete the Cycle. I can more than accommodate my responsibilities as the Healer with the store of energy you have already given me."

When Valerius made to object, she put up one hand to still him.

"Besides, I find myself in need of solitude."

282

Her eyes flickered ever so slightly, but her voice did not waiver.

"I no longer desire your Service."

This time, Valerius did falter.

Overwhelming pain engulfed him in black, merciless waves. He felt the blood drain from his face, from his limbs. He couldn't breathe, and his vision began to blur.

Surely she did not mean what she just said! Surely he could change her mind. If he could just take her in his arms, if he could—

"Please leave the Enclosure."

She turned around to face the mural once more.

Valerius swallowed thickly. "Rain—"

"Please leave now. I grow weary."

Valerius could no longer see for the thick red wall before his eyes. Absently, he rubbed at one eye and realized that the slippery, viscous liquid on his fingers was blood, not tears. He felt twin trails slowly leak out the corners of his eyes down his cheeks.

But before they could drip from the edge of his jaw, he pivoted on his heel, felt his way around the chamber door and left the Enclosure without a sound.

Rain felt his departure with every fiber of her being. The moment his presence was removed from the room, she crumpled like a paper doll onto the floor.

It was for his own good! she told herself.

Both for his health and for satisfying the current situation. It would be selfish of her to keep him by her side, and it would tear him apart physically to carry out both responsibilities of Elite Trainer and Consort.

She hadn't lied about how she felt physically. She was indeed far stronger than she'd been in many Phoenix Cycles, even though they had not yet reached the full thirty days. She was close enough to full strength that, technically, she no longer needed his Nourishment.

But oh how she wanted him!

And therein lay the danger. The more she wanted him, the higher the risk of taking too much from him. In addition, she could no longer distinguish duty from desire.

Ayelet had asked her if she loved Valerius.

She did!

To the point she was obsessed with him. She craved his body, his blood, his love-making constantly. She couldn't look at him, hear him, smell him without wanting him with an urgency and intensity that shook her to the core. She was becoming so dependent on him, so addicted, being apart from him for even brief moments made her want to cry.

She had never felt this way before, not even remotely close. All the passion she'd felt for her first Consort seemed like mere puppy love, yet she recalled the devastation his death left behind with intense clarity. She still bore the scars on her soul.

But did she love Valerius *enough*? Did he love her in return? Could she risk his life and her sanity to find out?

She couldn't.

Even if he hated her for rejecting him so coldly, even if she had to live with the agony of their damaged relationship forever after this, as long as he was healthy and alive, as long as he was in this world, she could bear it.

Time healed all wounds, did it not?

Perhaps she was too sensitive, perhaps he wasn't hurt by her dismissal at all. For all she knew he was relieved to be freed to do his duty to the Elite to the fullest. He'd never wanted to Serve her. It was an obligation for saving his life.

And she'd get over this addiction. She had to.

Ten years later she would be in someone else's arms, taking Nourishment from another male's body. She would not see Valerius in her mind's eye, she would not dream that it was he who kissed her, filled her, completed her. She could not afford to.

Curling into a small ball, the Healer sobbed herself to sleep.

*** *** *** ***

"Again."

Sweat pouring down her face as though her very own storm cloud enfolded and followed her with its smothering rain, arms and legs quivering from exertion, muscles so sore they virtually screamed in protest, Sophia speared her opponent with a hate-filled glare.

Letting out a hearty roar that belied her bone-deep exhaustion, she charged at Dalair with her training *spatha*, her light leather shield discarded and forgotten somewhere behind her.

Easily, Dalair avoided her thrust by leaning an inch to one side. Without breaking movement, he shifted his body and used the rotation of his torso to reel Sophia in closer while harnessing her momentum to increase the velocity of her forward fall.

Without a body to absorb the force of her lunge, Sophia found herself pitching forward at an alarming speed. Before she could brace for impact, the ground rose up to meet her face.

Splat. Thud. Whimper. Groan.

She was so sick of that particular sequence of sounds.

"Get up," came the unrelenting, unsympathetic voice of her tormenter.

"Go fuck yourself," Sophia muttered against the cold hard floor, her squashed cheek making her words come out in a jumble.

But he got the drift.

Dalair squatted on his haunches in front of her face, his crotch within jabbing distance, Sophia thought perversely. Too bad she didn't have the strength to even attempt unmanning him.

"My queen," the Paladin said in his ever-serious tone, lest Sophia thought she was getting beat up for shits and giggles, "you are the weakest among the Dozen. You have the most to learn in a very short period of time. We can't start at the beginning to teach you technique, we can only drill the responses in you through brute force and repetition."

He paused, then said, "For every bruise and hit you receive, you can revisit that pain upon me twice over, whenever and however you choose to deliver it. I promise you that justice. But right now, you need to get up."

Strengthened by the fantasy of her eventual revenge upon the Paladin, Sophia wobbled to her feet, picked up her sword and shield and took the combat stance he taught her.

Dalair took his position as well and crooked his hand.

"Again."

Two hours later, Sophia flopped flat on her bed like wrung-out rags. She was so exhausted she could barely breathe, but the weariness did not numb her countless aches, some in muscles she never knew she had.

Aella quietly came into her room and shut the door. The Amazon pushed Sophia to one side since the girl couldn't move herself if she tried, and lay down on the massive bed beside her.

"Tough day?"

"Uhn," came the incoherent reply.

"Hate him, huh?"

Growl.

Aella chuckled softly. "He's just doing his job, he's just trying to prepare you thoroughly for battles to come."

"Ewil."

"What?" Aella turned her head towards the young queen.

"He evil. Likes torture."

The Amazon looked back at the ceiling and kept her smile to herself.

"You think he enjoys tossing you around and marking you with blue and black bruises?"

"Uhn."

"But you'll have your revenge, right? Dalair is nothing if not fair-minded. Surely he will allow you your retribution."

Some strange sounds came out of the teenager, half cackle half wheeze.

"Then just think of it this way," Aella reasoned, "the stronger you get, the more potent your revenge."

More cackling and wheezing.

"I can teach you a few cool tricks tomorrow," Aella promised, "stuff that is guaranteed to bring any man to his knees."

"Wuv you."

Aella rolled to her side to face Sophia, reaching out one hand to smooth the unruly brown tresses from her face.

Guilt and worry consumed her as she thought about the danger in which she placed her queen—by design. She was gambling with Sophia's life and she and Dalair both knew it. The Paladin barely resisted tearing off one of her limbs earlier when they'd had their happy confrontation before Dalair's training session with Sophia. He didn't agree with her methods, didn't support her plan, but he understood why she put their queen in such a precarious position.

Aella would die before she let anything happen to Sophia. Dalair knew the depth of her devotion. Only that made him back down in the end.

"Love you too, sweetheart," Aella whispered and comforted herself with the sounds of Sophia's deep, even breathing as restoring sleep claimed the young Queen.

*** *** *** ***

Something in the air had changed.

The vampire grew restless and anxious with anticipation. Could it be that its Pure little playmates were beginning to catch on to the rules of the game?

The thought was exhilarating.

They had been such easy prey thus far, moving to and fro according to its will. Even the most patient cat grew bored with toying with stupid mice who just didn't *get it*, no matter how many clues you threw at them.

Useless little rodents.

But the vampire sensed the shift in its playmates' positioning and energy, as if they were preparing themselves for the fun to come.

Guess sending the Russian finally roused the white knights to action.

It was well worth the sacrifice. After all, how often did three pawns manage to draw out an entire battalion of Elite warriors?

The vampire eyed its chess set avariciously. Which white knights would be eliminated? In what way? There were so many delicious possibilities.

But the vampire must make the first move. As always. They would be waiting for its opening salvo.

The vampire would make sure it was worth their wait.

Chapter Seventeen

Sophia practically limped to class on Thursday afternoon.

Tristan, her designated Elite guard for the day, looked as if he felt twice as bad as she felt. Sophia didn't envy him the pain he must be suffering.

Valerius' training of the Elite over the past three days had been single-minded, relentless, and brutal. Sophia was relieved beyond words not to have him for a trainer. Next to the Protector, Dalair's instruction was cake walk.

Sophia avoided Valerius as much as possible. She had it on good authority that each of the Elite would too, if they could, but the combat training was not something they could opt out on. Alexandros, in particular, seemed to be less than at his full strength. Perhaps he was still recovering from his wounds, but Sophia sensed a deeper issue, though she could not pinpoint exactly what that was.

Only Cloud seemed to walk out of the grueling sessions relatively unscathed, and he even began to train the others beforehand, so that they would be better prepared for the wrath of the Roman. Perhaps it was because Cloud also specialized in distance combat. Thus, he was better able to anticipate his opponent's moves.

Sophia didn't know what to make of the black aura around the Protector. It radiated from his skin like an ominous shadow.

More than a shadow—it appeared to have a life of its own.

It was misery, despair, anger, and loathing all wrapped into one. And at the core of it all, there was pure anguish.

The strange thing was that the tentacles of negative energy seemed inwardly focused, rather than outwardly projected. The obsidian waves consumed his body like a personal black hole, or at least what Sophia imagined black holes might look like.

Bottomless. Fathomless. Light-less.

Lifeless.

She was surprised at first that Valerius spent so much time in training. It seemed to be all he did during the day. At night, he was either with a couple of other Elite warriors hunting or he was conferring with Ayelet, Orion and Eveline.

In fact, Sophia hadn't seen him with the Healer together in one place since their return from China.

Rain, meanwhile, was seldom seen, except with Wan'er in the Shield's clinic to tend to more severe wounds late at night. During the day, she attended to her human patients with her handmaiden in Chinatown. The timings of her comings and goings allowed her to avoid the other Dozen perfectly. When she was at the Shield, she kept to herself in the Enclosure. Only Wan'er attended her.

Wasn't the Phoenix Cycle still ongoing?

Sophia was confused.

For a while, the Healer and her Consort seemed inseparable despite the ten years of tension between them since the first time they met. And now the tension was back.

But it was a thousand times worse.

When Sophia did see Rain, she felt the same bleak aura consuming the Healer that surrounded Valerius. It was not so obvious, but it was nevertheless there.

That the Healer was so unsettled and depressed was something Sophia had never seen and never expected. Rain was equanimity and soothing calm personified. Though her Gift only allowed her to heal physical wounds, her compassion, sweetness and inner joy magnified her impact on the spiritual as well.

Only one person was ever able to fluster her, just by being in the same room. Valerius.

But wasn't that all over? Didn't they forge a deep and abiding bond through the Phoenix Rite and Cycle?

Sophia chalked it up to a "lover's spat."

Not that she knew personally what that meant, but it seemed somehow appropriate. She wished Valerius and Rain would just kiss and make up and have some mind-blowing orgies and get over whatever misunderstanding it was that caused them to behave like melodramatic teenagers. Especially since their "get out of jail free" card was about to expire in a little over a week's time.

But what did she know? Maybe adults (especially the thousands years old ones) experienced deeper, more profound emotions that were beyond Sophia's ability to grasp.

With Tristan waiting for her in Harvard yard, Sophia swung into her Ancient Egyptian Civ class and took her habitual spot in the back of the room.

Ere was already there waiting for her.

"Hello Sophia," he smiled at her in greeting.

Sophia resisted sighing out loud in pleasure at the sound of his voice. She loved hearing him say those two little words.

Secretly, she thought about recording his voice whenever they were together so she could play it back at night to lull herself to sleep. But that was a little creepy, even for melodramatic teenagers.

"Hi Ere," she greeted in return.

After the hours she spent helping him with research at his apartment, she was now comfortable enough in his presence to form coherent sentences. Not very elaborate, articulate ones, but at least she rose above grunting and gibberish.

"Did you miss me?" he asked with a teasing quirk of his lips.

"It's only been four days," she replied with a slight roll of her eyes, but inwardly she delighted in this almost ritualistic inquiry.

He was flirting with her. She loved it when he flirted with her.

Now that she didn't turn lobster red every time he did it, she enjoyed the teasing so much more.

"One day," he predicted in a delicious whisper that made Sophia shiver with anticipation, "you will tell me what I want to hear."

And then he turned toward the front of the class where Professor McGowan launched into his monologue about the Valley of Kings.

Sophia heard the professor's words, but her sight and thoughts were focused upon the beautiful creature sitting beside her, his knee casually touching hers underneath the table.

He reminded her of ice. With the indefinable, ever-varying beauty of snowflakes. The perfect, smooth, glossy exterior of glass.

There was a cool tranquility about him that both intimidated and comforted. No doubt he could freeze anyone over with one arctic glare. But when his chocolate eyes melted, they sparkled with liquid heat, so compelling, anyone would fall under his spell.

Sophia was suddenly reminded of the fire blazing in his living room, making the chamber almost overly hot. What a strange idea that a man of ice would adore the heat.

Similarly, Sophia observed a muted white aura around him, as if he kept his true emotions frozen. But underneath the pale white glow there was an incandescent orange flame, its sparks licking the edges of the ghostly shell, as if it was trying to melt away his icy armor.

More alert than ever to her responsibility of discovering and helping to recruit Pure souls, Sophia assessed Ere with new concentration. He had a Pure soul, she was almost certain of it.

But something was off.

There were times, so rarely she thought she might have imagined it, that he seemed resentful, antagonistic, lost.

She caught only a flash of darkness in his aura when he'd walked past Dalair the first day they met in the school cafeteria. But it made a strong enough impression that Sophia remembered it.

If she didn't know better, she would have read danger and harm in his intentions at the time toward the Paladin. Toward herself, she'd never felt a single negative emotion from him.

In the beginning there was curiosity. Then there was attraction and amusement. And now, sincere friendship.

She liked Ere. A lot. And she knew without a doubt that he liked her too.

Maybe she would bring up the possibility that he could be recruited with Ayelet and Aella. Definitely not Dalair though. The animosity Ere projected toward the warrior seemed entirely mutual.

"Come to my apartment after school," Ere leaned in to whisper, startling Sophia out of her musings.

Blinking rapidly, Sophia struggled to formulate a reply. Half of her really, really wanted to go, but the other half was weighed down by duties. She had daily training with Dalair and Aella in the evenings, and she'd feel bad for enjoying herself with a gorgeous guy at his cozy abode, even if all they did was study, when everyone at the Shield was on edge, preparing for Armageddon.

"I can't," she said after a while. "I'm kind of busy with stuff right now, but maybe things will get better after a couple of weeks."

Sophia almost fell backwards in her chair when she felt Ere take her right hand in his left and settle both their hands on his hard thigh.

"Just for an hour or two," Ere coaxed with his sinful voice, his thumb rubbing sensuously over her palm.

For an iceman, he certainly knew how to melt others, Sophia thought, trying to pull her hand away from the tantalizing heat and friction of his touch.

"I really can't," she repeated desperately, not sure how long she could stick to her refusal if he kept up his seduction.

Miraculously, he stilled. But instead of releasing her hand, he brought it to his lips and placed a hot, open-mouthed kiss upon her sensitive palm.

Sophia was so enchanted by his action and the feelings he evoked that she didn't care if they were in the middle of class. She wouldn't have noticed if everyone were staring agape at them.

Right now, she felt as if she and Ere were entirely alone, in their own invisible world.

"I will miss you," he said with resignation and disappointment, even a hint of sadness.

But then, as if he pulled a façade back in place, his lips quirked in a small, amused smile.

"Until next time, lovely Sophia."

Before Sophia could react, Ere had risen from his seat and left the classroom in a few long strides. She didn't even notice that the class had ended.

Suddenly, she was craning her neck to watch after him as his figure became obscured by the throng of students pushing out of the room.

She missed him already.

*** *** *** ***

"Your hair is so healthy now," Wan'er said as she stroked through the long, silky black mass with Rain's favorite comb that night.

"It fairly glows with blue highlights."

"Hmm," the Healer murmured, not really paying attention.

She wondered whether Valerius had finished the day's training and was back in his chamber or out again on a hunt.

Every morning before the first rays of dawn, she would stand for long minutes outside his room, her hand poised to knock on his door.

She only wanted to know whether he was feeling all right, she told herself. Whether he was beginning to gain his strength back. From what she'd seen and heard from the Elite, he'd been pushing everyone to their limits. She just hoped that he was not overextending himself. Her demands upon him had drained him considerably, she knew.

And she wanted to see him. Preferably when he couldn't see her. She could not bear what she felt for sure would be in his eyes.

Confusion. Resentment. Hurt.

She knew she should have explained her heart more clearly. She knew that there was the risk he misunderstood her letting him go as rejection, but she could not find the words. She did not have the composure nor the courage to pour out her feelings for him.

What if telling him how she felt instigated his own feelings? What if he Fell for her because of her own selfish desires and cravings?

What if he laughed at her, or worse, pitied her for loving her Consort when she'd made him promise not to love her?

"I still say you should have stayed with the Protector for the full course of the Phoenix Cycle," her handmaiden chided her.

It was an oft repeated refrain, and Rain no longer bothered to explain herself.

"You are not yet fully recovered, and it's obvious Valerius is capable of providing more Nourishment. If even half the energy he expends on training were to go to you—"

"You may retire," Rain abruptly cut her off. "I want to be alone."

Wan'er paused in the middle of the seventy-seventh stroke.

"But I am not finished with your hair," she protested.

"I shall do the rest," Rain replied, gently taking the comb from her handmaiden.

"Go to bed. You are exhausted from tending the human and Pure clinics from dawn to dusk. I should not rely so heavily on you."

Wan'er tidied up a few things and folded back Rain's silk coverlet on her bed.

"I only wish I had half your Gift," she said wistfully, "I wish I could more equally share your burden."

The handmaiden bid her goodnight and left the Enclosure quietly.

And sometimes I wish I didn't have this role, Rain thought to herself.

Since meeting Valerius, I wish I were just like any other female, capable of loving a male with my whole heart and spirit.

But in truth, she didn't know whether it was her role as Healer or an innate flaw that she could not love a male completely. Was it her will to hold back or was it her inherent disposition?

She thought she had loved Fan Li in her human life. When the enemy prince finally grew impatient with the sexual chase she led him on, he'd taken her by force.

Brutally. Overpoweringly. Several times a day.

He'd seemed obsessed with her and sensed that she withheld something from him, so he tried to dominate her physically and wring her surrender out of her.

That she never surrendered was probably why he continued to be fascinated by her over the years. But that only made him redouble his efforts to force her into submission.

Through it all, she kept her sanity and maintained her courtesan playfulness and sensuality by thinking of Fan Li. Imagining going back to him when it was all over, getting married like they'd planned and starting a family.

But when that day had finally come, her love for him had not been enough. She'd chosen a cowardly death. She hadn't been strong enough to live with her pain, humiliation and self-derision.

And then there was her first Consort.

To this day she couldn't speak his name, even in her own mind. She hadn't been looking for love; it was the farthest thing from her mind at the time. All she wanted to do was her duty as the Healer. Use the Gift the Goddess had granted her to its fullest. What love she had she wanted to give to her people, and to all the wounded, ailing, and mistreated.

But *he* had tempted her as a woman. She had been both fascinated and frightened by the side of her that he brought out that she never knew she possessed.

A carnal side. Sexual, greedy, covetous.

A whimsical side. Playful, teasing, laughing.

She had thought, surely, this was the male she was destined to be with. He'd helped her grow and heal so much.

And he loved her. He wanted her forever.

But she had failed him.

After he'd given her so much, she'd utterly betrayed him. Though she tried everything to funnel her healing energy into him during his Decline, nothing worked. He was not a patient she could fix. Whatever he needed from her, she couldn't find a way to give him.

Maybe she was broken, Rain thought numbly as she put the comb down. Or maybe she was simply a selfish coward.

Moving as if her body had a mind of its own, she rose from her seat before the vanity and left the chamber, making her way quickly down the twists of corridors to Valerius' room.

It was only midnight, but she couldn't wait, even at the risk of running into him.

Pausing only briefly in front of his door, she did not bother to knock before turning the knob and entering.

He was not there.

She breathed a sigh of relief and slowed her steps, walking around his bedroom more leisurely, taking in the sparse but rich and masculine furnishings, the gigantic bed that dwarfed everything else in the room, the wall of weapons, the closet of entirely black clothes, with the occasional dark gray thrown in.

After a thorough tour of his personal space, she stopped beside his bed. Affectionately, she petted the dark blue coverlet, so dark it was almost back. She extended her fingers, then curled them back into fists, then extended them once more as if finally making up her mind, and snatched a large pillow off the mattress.

It was the pillow he slept upon most often, she knew, based on her experience with his bedside preferences. He always slept on the left side of the bed, while she used the right. But more often than not, when they slept together, they were so entwined it didn't matter which side they were on.

Her heart constricted painfully at the thought and she hugged the pillow tightly to her chest, dipping her head down to bury her nose in the satiny casing. She inhaled deeply his heady scent, and her body immediately responded with blissful delight, sending a rush of hot liquid to her core.

How she missed him!

Would it always be such torture? After their shared experiences, she couldn't imagine ever being so close to him, under the same roof, and not have him. Did time really wear down all edges? Would her emotions become less intense, more controllable?

And then her eyes alighted on what was beneath the pillow.

The handkerchief she'd given him ten years ago.

"Why are you here?"

Rain spun toward Valerius with a startled gasp and hid the handkerchief in her fist behind her back. She'd been so engulfed in her own thoughts and desires, she hadn't noticed when he entered the room and closed the door behind him.

Involuntarily, her face lit with happiness at the sight of him, but just as quickly it fell when she noticed the blood and sweat streaking down his face and arms.

"You're hurt," she blurted, stumbling in her haste to reach him.

"Don't."

With one brusque word, he halted her movement. Shifting his gaze away, he pulled off his ripped shirt, revealing more blood, sweat and bruises, and stalked to the bathroom, completely ignoring her.

Tentatively, she followed him to the bathroom threshold and peeked inside. He'd turned on the shower and was in the process of stripping off his sweats.

Worry overrode desire as his beaten body was fully revealed to her. Why did he insist on taking things too far? Surely the training didn't require him to put in a pound of flesh every day along with his energy and time?

Standing beneath the shower, Valerius closed his eyes and let the full blast of the ice cold spray drench through his hot, too-tight skin. He was fully aroused at the mere scent of her. But seeing her hug his pillow the way she used to hug his body made every one of his nerves scream to be with her.

"Valerius..." her soft voice wrapped around his cock like loving hands, and the swollen bastard jerked eagerly in response.

He couldn't take any more of this!

"If you want blood, come and get it. If you're here to fuck me, name your place and position. Otherwise, get out."

Rain reeled back as if slapped.

Why was he saying such ugly things? Why was he being so cruel?

But before she could formulate a reply, he suddenly twisted to face her, though his gaze was focused upon something beyond the bathroom door.

"Get down!" he growled, one second before he leapt upon her and brought them both crashing to the hard floor.

"Wha—"

Before she could finish her thought, the bathroom wall exploded in a blast of bricks, glass and debris.

She gasped as one small splinter of mirror bit through her forearm, but she knew Valerius bore most of the damage, for he was bent over her like a protective cocoon of solid muscle.

Barely able to take half a breath, Rain abruptly found herself jerked upright and shoved across the room as Valerius pulled on his sweats in the next second.

"We need to get out of here and find the others," he said urgently as he grabbed hold of her arm.

"The Shield is under attack."

Pausing to take a few weapons off his wall, Valerius pulled Rain behind him as he made his way down the pitch black corridor. They were engulfed in a blackout. The main circuits were probably cut, and the central alarm had been disabled.

Only someone from within would know enough to infiltrate the Shield.

Rain struggled to keep up with Valerius' rapid pace, and then she concentrated on the strength and warmth of his grip on her forearm and took a deep breath. She harnessed all her energy so that she could match his speed and determination; she vowed she wouldn't be a liability.

A couple of twists and turns down the hallway, and they'd arrived at the training center, where a few low-burning torches provided enough light to see by. Aella was hunkered down along the wall with Alexandros, each with weapons and shields drawn.

Valerius and Rain joined them along the adjacent corner, and he asked, "Damage?"

"Explosions throughout the West wing and central atrium," Aella reported. "We should expect our exit through the throne room to be cut off, and they've probably destroyed most of our vehicles and sealed the exit through the garage."

His Hayabusa might still be safe, Valerius thought, for he kept it in the East wing where the forge resided, directly above the Vault. That part of the Shield was currently under construction for the stables Tristan was building beside the forge. Their only exit option now was in that direction.

Their enemies knew the Shield's weaknesses well.

Exit through the East wing required going down two levels to the library and into narrow tunnels. They would have little room to maneuver, and Valerius would bet his life there would be a vampire welcoming committee lying in wait for them along the way. Without illumination, vampires had an added advantage, for their night vision was far superior to Pure Ones and humans.

After all, they lived for the night.

"The others?" Valerius bit out.

"Dalair, Cloud and Tristan are rounding up Sophia, Orion and Eveline. Ayelet is already with them," Alexandros replied.

"If the Scribe and Seer are in the library, they should be protected from the blasts. I believe the queen is with them."

He frowned at that. Sophia should never be without an Elite guard. In fact, Aella should have been watching her, but the Amazon was here instead.

"Unless the vampires have infiltrated the library already," Aella stated grimly.

"What about Wan'er and the humans?" Rain asked, a spark of alarm coursing through her.

"The human trainees and servants have already gone home, I'm fairly certain none remain," Aella answered.

"As to the handmaiden..."

"I will find her," Valerius said.

He thrust Rain forward into Aella's awaiting arms.

"Take Rain and head to the Vault. I will meet up with you when I have Wan'er."

"No!" Rain reached out to Valerius, trying to keep him with her, or make him take her with him, but he was already gone, disappearing without a sound into the blackness that surrounded them.

*** *** *** ***

Sophia limped as fast as she could along the narrow passageway leading from the library to the exit three levels above on a side street behind the Prudential Tower.

She tried to blot out the pain from her ankle and leg, shoulder and side. If Orion hadn't pushed her forcefully out of the way of the barrage of throwing stars and daggers, she would probably be dead right now.

She had no time for pain. She had to get out and get help. She didn't know who to call on, but she didn't think that far ahead. She didn't care if she had to scream down the bloody neighborhood, she'd find someone.

Orion and Eveline were still back there, trying to keep the vampires from coming after her. She knew that they would fight to their last breath to keep her safe, though they were no match for trained assassins. She'd wanted to stay behind and fight alongside them, but they kept shoving her back. She would only distract them, they argued, she needed to get out and hide. Do whatever it took to keep herself alive.

Sophia blinked away her tears and refused to give into the despair that welled up within her. She would not let their sacrifice be in vain!

By sheer force of will, she trudged onward, up a long flight of stone stairs and around a tight corner.

And then she hit a brick wall.

But it wasn't a wall, for large hands with the strength of steel manacles locked upon her shoulders, making her wince at the instant pain in her injured side.

"I have been waiting for you, my queen," a familiar deep voice reached her through the darkness.

Sophia gasped in recognition.

Leonidas.

Chapter Eighteen

An oppressive silence descended upon the Shield as the remaining Dozen took in the extent of damage and loss.

They'd eliminated all vampire infiltrators and restored electricity and connectivity to the underground fortress, but not without severe casualties and sacrifices.

Orion was one such sacrifice.

Eveline was the last to see his body upon this earth.

With his final breath, he'd used all his strength and concentration to send a wave of ancient weapons, mere decorations on the library wall, in a deadly barrage against the vampire assassins advancing upon them. Two of the remaining vampire foes lost their heads in the unstoppable onslaught. The remaining vampire was so severely wounded, Eveline marshaled her injured limbs into action, took a nearby discarded axe and ended his miserable existence.

She'd reached Orion just as his eyes began to close. The last thing he saw was her sad, heartfelt smile of goodbye. Holding his head in her lap, she watched as his body loosened, as the weight of him began to lift.

As his soul departed from his corporal form, his physical self began to lose substance, slowly unraveling into stardust that drifted like dandelion puffs into the air surrounding her.

Until finally, there was nothing left to hold.

Eveline had barely a few moments to grieve and regain her composure before the others joined her.

Just before she lost consciousness from her wounds, she informed them:

"The queen is taken."

Without waiting for anyone else to react, Dalair immediately took off down the narrow tunnel that led to the only remaining exit from the Shield.

"I'll go with him," Alexandros said, bounding after the Paladin. "I have enough to trace their exact location. No doubt that is what our enemies want, but there is no other choice. Time is of the essence."

Rain knelt before Eveline's crumpled body and began to assess the damage, initiating the healing process with her *zhen*. Thankfully, the Seer had not been poisoned in addition to her physical wounds. It would take at least a couple of weeks to heal the broken bones and internal bleeding completely, but she would make a full recovery.

Distantly, Rain was aware of Tristan, Ayelet, Aella and Cloud debating their next course of action. Rain's sub-group with Alexandros and Aella alone had encountered and subdued half a dozen vampire assassins on their way to the library. She imagined the others must have dealt with much the same odds.

Such a large-scale invasion with a veritable army of trained vampire assassins was unprecedented and regrettably unexpected. They should have bolstered the security of the Shield the moment they suspected that Leonidas had been turned. Either that, or they should have relocated to a new base, one of which the Spartan had no prior knowledge.

But it had happened so fast. And perhaps part of their error in calculation was due to the fact that none of them wanted to accept that Leonidas was lost to them forever.

They all knew that Alexandros and Dalair were headed into a trap. Goddess knew how large a vampire Horde was awaiting them. Whoever was behind these attacks wanted all of the Royal Zodiac demolished.

Methodically, their enemy was hunting each and every one of them. If they only wanted Sophia, they had many opportunities to obtain the queen without the full-on assault, without losing so many of their own in the process.

Rain had a feeling the evil mastermind did not care how many vampires he or she sent to their deaths. Somehow, she knew that their nemesis wouldn't quit until they were all eliminated, no matter the cost. It was as if the vampire was targeting the entire Pure race, as if they wanted to bring the ancient civilization to its knees.

As her comrades debated their plan of action nearby, a flash of light burst in the middle of the library, just in front of the fallen Orb of Prophesies. The white light rapidly coalesced into a nucleus of energy, then elongated into the shape of a man.

Seth.

"I was afraid this would happen," he spoke to them in his projected, semi-transparent form.

"I am deeply saddened to be two steps too late."

His eyes scanned the damage littering the once regal library and hovered regretfully on Eveline's unconscious form.

"But the critical battle is yet ahead," he continued with intense determination. "Doubtless you know that taking Sophia is a ploy to lure us to their playing ground. For some of us," he looked briefly at Aella, "this was probably expected, even anticipated. With the destruction here, they aim to separate us into smaller groups, the easier to pick us off like stragglers from a herd."

"Nonetheless we must act," Tristan said gravely. "They leave us no choice."

"Perhaps not," the Consul conceded, "but we have a few surprises up our sleeves."

He turned to face the new Elite member. "Though they have experienced a bit of your lethal abilities, Cloud Drako, I wager no vampire left here alive to tell about it."

The warrior blinked once in confirmation.

Seth nodded his admiration. "You shall remain one of our sharpest weapons. But you will not be alone."

The Consul met each pair of eyes in the room one by one.

"We will fight fire with fire. We will have our own vampire Horde to combat our foes."

Shocked gasps and gapes met his bold words.

Aella was the first to recover.

"What do you mean? Why would vampires help us? How is that even possible?"

A flicker of pain crossed the Consul's stoic mask, but it was so quickly gone, it was as if it was never there.

"I cannot answer you at this time," he replied quietly, his expression calm and confident. "I only ask that you trust me in this. When you have located the assassins' base, when you storm their compound and engage their numbers, know that if you see vampires with red satin bands around their necks, they are not your foe, but rather your friend."

"What—"

Tristan and Ayelet both started to speak at the same time, burning questions on the tip of their tongues, but Seth's projection was already dimming as he pulled back his presence from the Shield.

"I will alert Dalair and Alexandros as well," he said as his figure became so airy he was like the shadow of a ghost.

"Remember the red bands around their necks." With that, the Consul disappeared, leaving the Dozen with a ton of unanswered questions but also new hope.

As Aella called the Elite together to regroup and plan for their imminent invasion of enemy ranks, Valerius staggered into the library carrying Wan'er in his arms.

"You're safe!" Rain eased her healing *zhen* away from Eveline and ran toward her warrior as fast as her legs could carry her.

She skidded to a halt a foot away from Valerius as he set Wan'er gently on her feet. The handmaiden hobbled slightly but righted herself against one of the floor-to-ceiling marble columns that supported the entryway to the library.

"Are you all right?" Rain asked her faithful companion with concern.

Wan'er shook her head, "It's just a sprain. Don't waste your healing energy on me. I can tend to it myself."

Nodding with relief, Rain focused back on Valerius and would have thrown herself into his arms had his pained scowl not made her hesitate uncertainly. Beneath rivulets of blood, sweat and grime from countless wounds, his entire body vibrated with tension, throbbing with the silent neon sign to "back off."

"There's no time to waste," he said to his comrades, looking beyond the Healer's small form. "We must take this fight to them. Aella, what is the plan?"

"Alexandros has discovered their hideout. He's sending us his coordinates as we speak. If we hotwire a car, we can be there within fifteen minutes. You may be able to get there in twelve on the Hayabusa, assuming it's still intact."

"It is."

"I'll explain the rest on the way," Aella said as she became a blur of motion.

"Tristan, with me. Valerius, you take Cloud. Ayelet, you know the emergency protocol. Wait in the safe room until we return."

The Guardian gave one firm nod.

As the four Elite warriors assembled their weapons and protective gear, preparing to depart within minutes, Rain hovered near Valerius, struggling to tamp down her selfishness.

But in the end, she couldn't contain her plea:

"Don't go," she begged the Protector. "Please stay with me—with us," she amended after a pause.

"You are severely wounded, both from the earlier explosion protecting me and now from engaging the assassins. I don't need to probe you to know that you are an inch away from collapsing... please ..."

She tried to grab his forearm, but he shrugged out of reach.

"It's nothing," he said brusquely, avoiding her touch and her searching eyes, methodically securing triple the usual amount of weapons to his person.

"Take care of Wan'er and Eveline and stay out of sight." He turned his back to her and took the first step to leave.

Swallowing her pride, her fears, her insecurities, Rain took a gamble on Fate. She threw herself at his back and locked her arms around his waist, hugging him tightly from behind, plastering herself to him like a second layer of skin.

"I was wrong, I'm sorry," she cried against his leather-encased back. "I didn't mean any of the things I said. I want you forever. Only you. Please don't go. Please, please, *please* don't go. I can't bear to lose you. I don't want to live without you!"

Their comrades paused in their movements as if suspended in time, watching the exchange between Rain and Valerius with awe and compassion.

Rain didn't care who witnessed her outburst in this moment. She didn't care if she looked like the world's greatest fool. She knew with every fiber of her being that if he left her now, he would not return to her whole.

She knew she should put her people, her queen, above her own selfish desires, but she couldn't let go of him. Not when it had taken thousands of years to find him.

Valerius turned slowly in her arms until her tear-streaked cheek pressed hotly to his chest. Tenderly, he lifted her chin so that he could look down into her deep brown eyes.

"It's too late," he said quietly so that only she could hear, absorbing more the rumble of his voice rather than the sound of his words.

"You cannot save me even were I to stay."

Taking a gulp of breath, Rain looked upon him more alertly, the needles of her hair skimming millimeters above his skin.

He had been poisoned, she realized as her heart fell to the soles of her feet. And in his already weakened state from his Service, the vile tentacles of death were spreading through his system at an accelerated pace. Even if she were to use all her energy to try to heal him now, she wasn't guaranteed success.

But there was also something else, something that made death inescapable.

Even before a few of her *zhen* inserted into his pores, she came face to face with the truth: Valerius was in the final stages of Decline.

No! The word ricocheted in an echoing scream within her skull.

"Hear me well, my heart," he spoke to her in the deepest, gentlest, calmest voice.

"I love you. I have ever, and ever shall, love only you."

He wrapped his arms around her when she tried to push away, keeping her securely in his warm embrace.

"It is my choice to give myself to you," he continued inexorably, "just as it was his choice in the beginning."

She knew that he meant her first Consort; he was telling her that none of this was her fault. Her breath began to hitch wetly, her hands clawing into the leather at his back.

"It is my deepest regret not to be able to fulfill my Service to the end," he said huskily. "I wanted to give you everything. I let my pride get in the way, I let my demons keep me from you."

He shuddered slightly and bent his lips to her ear.

"I know I am unworthy," he said, holding her so tightly against him she couldn't even shake her head.

"I am honored and grateful to have Served you... my healing Rain."

And then, before she could brace herself, he was gone.

One moment her arms encircled the heat of his body and the next there was only cold emptiness and silence.

The echoing screams in her skull magnified in volume and force until Rain could no longer contain the shattering wail of loss that exploded through her body.

*** *** *** ***

Sophia sat on her haunches with her knees drawn before her, her arms wrapped around them, her chin resting on her linked hands.

As prisons went, her golden cage was rather luxurious, as if she were an exotic bird to pet and pamper.

There was a cozy bed in one corner, covered with fresh-smelling sheets and heaped with thick blankets and goose-down pillows. A small escritoire and chair took up the opposite corner, with pen and paper neatly arranged on top.

Was she supposed to be writing a suicide note? Sophia thought darkly. Yeah, good luck getting that out of her.

If only she knew how to pull a Jason Bourne maneuver and use the pen to gouge out one of the eyeballs of the vampire guard standing beyond the bars of her cage. But alas, she probably wouldn't be able to get very far before Cyclops took off her head in retaliation.

How could Leonidas do this?! She thought futilely for the hundredth time.

Even if he'd been turned into one of the enemy, surely he remembered enough of her, of his friends, to abstain from the fight?

Sophia wasn't given the opportunity to talk some sense into him since he'd gagged her for the entire abduction. And then he'd dumped her unceremoniously into this gilded cage and left her alone without a word.

She saw no remnant of the man who used to bounce her on his knee when she was a child, or tease her mercilessly about her youthful crushes when she started liking boys.

This Leonidas had blood red eyes that seemed to stare through her rather than see her as a person.

And then there were his long, white fangs.

He'd actually looked at her strangely for a few heartbeats when he shoved her in the cage as if he was thirsty and she was a tall glass of lemonade.

Sophia shuddered with revulsion at the memory. Her abductor was no longer the Pure Ones' Sentinel. He had turned into a conscience-less blood-sucker.

Speaking of which, Sophia raised her chin a fraction as the creature she assumed to be her host floated soundlessly into the chamber. The aura around her visitor was so powerful, Sophia lost her breath for a moment, as if the creature had sucked all the air out of the room with its commanding presence.

The vampire was tall and stately, lithe and slender. Sophia could not tell whether it was a female or male, for its figure was hidden in a long, loose robe, its face obscured by a large, attached hood.

She could see the long, wavy hair cascading freely down both sides of the vampire's chest and shoulders, but again, with creatures this ancient, one could not assume a luxurious mane equated to the feminine sex.

"What an honor to have the Pure Queen amongst us," the vampire said in a sing-song voice, both fragile and strong at the same time. There was a masculine undertone with a higher feminine pitch layered on top.

What a confusing creature, Sophia thought to herself. She wouldn't be surprised if it had a split personality disorder.

"Are you settled in and comfortable?" the vampire asked solicitously.

"I don't plan to stay long," Sophia replied.

The vampire laughed with delight, truly amused by its precious guest.

"No," it returned, "I don't imagine you will. Not when your friends are already on their way to come to your rescue."

"I suppose it's too much to ask you to let them take me back without a fight?" Sophia ventured.

The vampire shook its head almost regrettably. "I'm afraid I cannot grant your request, lovely one. But never fear, even if the last one of your rescuers fall, you will remain unharmed."

A tingle of recognition flitted down Sophia's spine. She almost felt like she knew this vampire.

But then her host revealed its face, taking the hood down as it walked closer to Sophia's cage.

It was a beautiful woman, but it was also a stunning man. Truly, Sophia could not tell at all its gender.

Large, heavily lashed black eyes with red centers gazed curiously, avariciously back at her. Elegant black brows, a thin, high-bridged nose, sharp cheekbones and blood-red lips completed the mesmerizing pale visage.

The thick, dark brown, almost black, wavy hair further blurred the boundaries of sex. Even more confusing, it was wearing heavy mascara and eyeliner, reminding Sophia of ancient Egyptian pharaohs and queens.

And then there was the flat chest and Adam's apple that bobbed in the creature's throat, Sophia noticed upon closer inspection.

So it was a male?

"I am whatever and whoever you wish me to be," the vampire said with a sensuous smile, as if reading Sophia's mind. "If I became your deepest desire, would you stay with me?"

Sophia abruptly blinked away her confusion. She'd almost been hypnotized by the vampire's ghostly beauty.

"I don't stay with monsters who hurt my friends," she replied matter-of-factly, without heat, as if she were having a casual conversation across a tea table. "No matter how you portray yourself."

"You judge without knowing," the vampire said, moving ever closer, until it stood almost flush against the bars of Sophia's cage.

"Who is to say what monsters are? Your friends have killed many of my Kind across the millennia. Why do you not call them monsters? Why only me?"

"Vampires started the war," Sophia said with conviction, "*you* sent assassins after one of us first."

The vampire nodded to the latter part of Sophia's proclamation.

"I did indeed put a test to the Roman warrior. You call him the Protector, don't you? But as to who started the war… don't be so certain of what you think you know."

"You invaded and destroyed our home," Sophia accused, ignoring the vampire's last words. "You took my friend and turned him into a monster like you."

"Collateral damage," the vampire responded quickly, dismissing its hand in Leonidas' fate.

"And don't worry, your friends will now have the chance to invade and destroy my home as well, and probably wipe out most of my Horde in the process. So we're soon to be even on that score."

Sophia looked at her host in consternation.

"Don't you care what happens to your own? You act like we are all just toy soldiers to play with and crash together and break at will."

The vampire tilted its head like a curious child.

"More like chess pieces," it corrected Sophia's analogy upon consideration. "I like to play with my pretty chess pieces."

"Life and death is not a game," Sophia said vehemently.

"Oh but it is," came the vampire's hiss. "It's all just one big game. And we're all dispensable toy soldiers in the end. I do not fear my death and neither should you."

"Then why don't you kill yourself right now?" Sophia goaded, "Or give me a sword and I'll be happy to do it for you."

The vampire chuckled behind its hand with delicate amusement, the sounds of its laughter tinkling like chimes.

"What a bloodthirsty child you are," it said after catching its breath, "what an adorable playmate you'll make."

Leaning closer until its haunting face pressed ever so gently upon the gold bars of the cage, the vampire widened its gaze until red flames danced within its bottomless black orbs.

"Let's make a bargain right now," it said on a dark, venomous whisper. "It's no fun to play the game when you have no control of the pieces, so I'll give you a choice. As we speak, six Elite warriors are headed to my humble abode to rescue you. If you had the ability to save four and sacrifice two, which two would it be?"

"I wouldn't sacrifice any," Sophia quickly replied, "they'll kill you all first."

The vampire pressed even closer, until the bars of the cage rubbed against its lips, lifting them until they revealed its sharp white fangs.

"So bloodthirsty," it murmured with delight. "What fun we could have together... but that is not the choice I gave you, lovely Sophia. Choose the two friends that will die, or all of them will perish."

Sophia uncurled from her position and stood immediately before the bars on the inside of the cage, facing her foe almost nose to nose.

Defiantly, fearlessly, in a woman's voice that was not her own, she said, "If there is to be a sacrifice, then take my life in exchange for my friends. Otherwise, there is no bargain. If we must, we will all die together and see you in Hell."

The vampire hissed and darted its long tongue out at her through the bars, but Sophia did not retreat. She held her ground and stared the creature down, awaiting for its next move, whatever blow might come.

"Magnificent," the vampire said on an almost reverent sigh. "You are indeed a worthy playmate."

With that, it quickly withdrew, leaving Sophia once again alone in her cage with her sole vampire guard in the dimly-lit underground catacomb.

*** *** *** ***

Four piles of ashes behind them, Dalair and Alexandros advanced stealthily through the maze of tunnels, the rest of the Elite only minutes on their heels.

Thus far, the enemy base seemed almost unguarded. The vampires they'd just disposed of were merely civilian brutes, not the trained assassins they'd faced before. But they knew better than to take their situation for granted.

They were undoubtedly walking into a trap.

At a locus where several tunnels met like the center of a spider web, the trap finally revealed itself.

Standing in front of each tunnel entrance were three to four fully armed vampire warriors. At the mouth of the largest tunnel that Dalair instinctively knew led to Sophia's captivity stood the Spartan himself, a *makhaira* at the ready in each hand.

"You go no further, Pure Ones," the former Sentinel said with grim determination.

"I will be the judge of my own destiny," Alexandros answered as he stood back to back with Dalair, facing the throngs of vampires that surrounded them without the slightest hint of fear.

Leonidas inclined his head in acknowledgement a moment before he leapt high into the air for a full-frontal attack.

And thus the bloodbath began.

Two minutes into the carnage, just when Dalair and Alexandros' defenses were weakening, Aella, Tristan, Valerius and Cloud arrived at the scene through two separate tunnels, obliterating the vampires that stood in their way. With the odds improved from twenty to one to a little under seven to one, the weary pair was invigorated with renewed confidence and strength.

"Dalair," Alexandros shouted above the fray, "leave Leonidas to me. You find the queen."

Dalair nodded and lowered to a crouch, then leapt into the air like a powerful panther just as Alexandros swiped at Leonidas' shins with his long *sagaris*.

Forced to roll sideways, the Sentinel moved far enough from the entrance of the tunnel he guarded for Dalair to fly over his head and land safely on all fours on the other side. Without a backward glance, Dalair raced down the passageway, the faint scent of Sophia guiding him, urging him on.

"Let us finish this," Alexandros said to his longtime friend, his brother in arms. "It is my fault you were taken. It is my duty to release your soul from this monstrous shell."

Leonidas smirked darkly. "Not if I release you first."

They came together in a mighty clash of swords and axe, each warrior of similar build, height and strength. They'd sparred with each other and fought alongside one another over countless years. They were as familiar with the other's moves and style as their own.

But Alexandros was fighting for a heftier cause: his love for, and his need to save, his comrade fueled him with extra vigor and stamina, despite his recent weakening. With each stroke of his axe he pushed the Sentinel back. With each swing, he chanted to himself that he could not fail his friend again. He could not let a Pure, courageous soul shrivel and die within this vampire form.

But Leonidas was matching him stroke for stroke. Though he gave ground, his strength did not wane. It was almost as if he were testing Alexandros, waiting for the right moment to land the lethal blow.

And then Alexandros realized what he needed to do.

As the Spartan faked to the left, then twisted around to thrust his cross swords into his opponent, Alexandros did not evade the blades. Instead, he pushed forward at the same time Leonidas thrust and took the twin blades inside his flesh, one through the heart, one through the liver.

"See you in the next life, my friend," Alexandros said as he gazed into the Spartan's blood-red eyes, widened in shock and disbelief, and in the next split second, the General's axe swung through Leonidas' neck, cleanly severing head from body.

Falling to his knees, Alexandros watched his old friend disintegrate into gray specks of dust even as he felt his own body shifting to mingle with the air around them.

He heard the other Elite call out his name, was vaguely aware of their rushing footsteps, but soon his vision became blinded by an intense white light.

The General sighed.

It was time to rest at last.

*** *** *** ***

Dalair burst into the chamber at the end of the tunnel without thought to his own safety.

He was ready to face ten assassins, a hundred. He was tired of playing hide and seek. He'd tear down the entire catacomb with his bare hands if that was what it took to find Sophia and bring her home.

Only one guard accosted him on his way to the center of the chamber where a gilded golden cage drew his entire concentration. He disposed of the impediment quickly, not even tossing the vampire a glance as he slashed his way through the bloodsucker.

But when he halted just before the cage, he saw that his senses had deceived him, for on the bed lay a bundle of crumpled clothes, the ones Sophia had been wearing that day.

"Looking for your Mate?" a whispered hiss echoed along the cavern walls.

Dalair stilled himself and turned full circle very slowly, assessing his surroundings with heightened vision, smell and hearing. He could tell that Sophia was very close, but her exact location was difficult to pinpoint, her soft scent masked by the pungent musk of his enemy.

"Return my queen," Dalair demanded with utter confidence and certainty, "before I rip your head from your body."

Delighted laughter bounced off the damp stone bricks in a haunting tinkle of chimes.

"Such vehemence, such passion!" the disembodied voice exclaimed. "And you hide it all so well behind that mask of stoicism and restraint."

Dalair chose to remain silent and concentrated on the information that the air around him carried. He could faintly hear Sophia's breathing. It was deep and even, as if she slept. He moved purposefully to the east side of the chamber, but was confronted with a solid rock wall.

"If you admit your feelings, perhaps I can be persuaded to give her back to you," the voice taunted.

"But you can't do that, can you? Not when you know she'll never forgive you for the sins of the past."

Dalair ignored the fission of alarm at the secret truth of the vampire's words. It wasn't the time now to dwell on how the bastard knew about his past. He had one single-minded goal—to get Sophia out of here alive.

Dalair pressed his palms flat against the wall, feeling for any crack, and breath of air. Suddenly, he heard a click as the rock beneath his palm depressed and the entire wall began to shift to the left. His crescent blades at the ready, Dalair stepped carefully into the secret passage, drawn inexorably toward a pale light at the end of the tunnel.

As he drew closer, he saw the stone table shrouded in a bluish light, and upon that table lay Sophia, dressed head to toe in a long white robe. Standing behind the table was an exquisitely beautiful vampire who beckoned Dalair forth with smiling blood-red lips.

The Paladin's eagle sight confirmed that the lips were not simply crimson, they were glossy with fresh blood.

Sophia's blood.

Involuntarily, Dalair lurched forward in a deadly move, but was stopped mid stride by the glint of steel held against Sophia's throat.

"Wisely done," the vampire said with approval when Dalair drew back slightly and grew still again, a few feet away from the table.

"Another step and my blade might have slipped across her delicate skin as I quivered in fright."

Dalair's gaze shifted to the twin puncture marks on Sophia's neck, already healing but still leaking a few drops of blood. His entire body tensed into a bow as he thought through the ramifications. Had she been turned? Was he too late?

"She is simply resting," the vampire answered his unspoken thoughts. "No need to panic just yet. I merely sampled a bit of her sweetness. No harm done."

A guttural growl echoed against the tunnel walls, and Dalair belatedly realized that it came from within himself.

The vampire giggled behind one pale hand at Dalair's reaction to its words.

And then Dalair held his breath in shock, for the vampire's face and form began to change, shimmering at the edges with an eerie red glow, until it turned into a ghost from Dalair's long-buried past.

"Did you miss me?" the vampire said in a melodious woman's voice, a voice that haunted Dalair's dreams every single night.

His knees buckling, Dalair staggered back a step and shook his head to clear it. Surely this was a trick. *She* could not be here when Sophia lay sleeping right in front of him!

The vampire smiled an achingly familiar smile, a smile that was etched in Dalair's memory for all of eternity. A smile he'd received a hundred times, a thousand times, but that was never meant for him.

It had always belonged to another.

And then the face changed again, the figure growing taller and broader until Dalair felt as if he were looking into a mirror, for his reflection stared back at him.

Except the irises were pitch black with red glowing centers instead of his own pale gray.

"Or perhaps you missed this," his twin said in his voice as it bent toward Sophia, all the while keeping its serpent-like eyes focused on Dalair.

Slowly, the vampire kissed Sophia's lips, all the while keeping the dagger poised at her throat. As it licked at the seam of her mouth and smiled evilly, Dalair heard the rattle of his own blades as his fists shook and his body strained to attack and tear the bloodsucker to pieces.

"Just tell me how you feel," his devilish twin murmured, swiping the entire length of its tongue leisurely along Sophia's cheek.

"Give me your deepest, darkest secret and I will let you have her. For now."

Desperately, Dalair calculated the chances he could take the vampire down without hurting Sophia. Instinctively, he knew that whatever creature stood behind the table was extremely powerful. And old. Millennia older than even Dalair.

It was too risky to attack with Sophia so vulnerable. Dalair could not take the gamble.

"Or do you prefer to confess to him," the vampire said as he transformed once more.

"Tell me the truth," the man said in a clear, crisp tenor. "I will forgive you if you tell me the truth."

As if his voice was not his own, Dalair surrendered the words he'd never dared utter in the two thousand five hundred years of his existence.

He closed his eyes as the confession poured out, as if he expected to be struck down for his sins right there and then.

But when he opened his eyes again, the vampire had disappeared, leaving him alone with Sophia, who continued to sleep soundly upon the illuminated stone table.

Brushing aside the tears that escaped his lids, Dalair scooped her into his arms and strode back through the tunnel, holding her soft warmth a tad too tightly.

This would be the last time, he told himself.

He would indulge in the feel and weight of her in his embrace this one last time.

Chapter Nineteen

"If you no longer have need of us, we shall return to the Cove," the striking leader of the sextet of vampire warriors wearing red satin bands around their necks declared with stately formality.

Aella nodded and bowed in gratitude.

The six Chosen warriors that formed the Vampire Queen Jade Cicada's personal guard had more than evened the odds in the final battle. Their timing and skills had been impeccable. However Seth managed to convince the Dark Queen to send her finest in aid of her sometime enemies was beyond Aella's ken.

The leader returned the bow with all due respect, but instead of placing right hand flat over heart as was the Pure Ones' custom, he tapped his chest instead with his right fist twice.

Without further words, he led the two other male and three female vampires away. Moments after their graceful departure, as the dust settled in the catacombs, it was as if they were never there.

Aella surveyed her team and assessed the damage. Though they were wounded and worse for wear, none of them had been poisoned, thank the Goddess; it would only be a matter of time before the flesh wounds healed.

Valerius, however, leaned shakily against a wall, his breath belabored, his skin covered in sweat. In battle, he'd been fearless, flawless, merciless. His enemies would never have guessed he was so weak he could barely stand.

But now that the fight was over, as the adrenaline rush subsided, the Fallen warrior could barely lift his head.

Their mission had been a miraculous success. Dalair was in the process of transporting Sophia back to the Shield. Through their ear pieces he'd updated them briefly about her condition—she was safe, whole and soundly asleep.

But the sacrifices...

Aella said a silent prayer for her fallen comrades Leonidas, Alexandros and Orion. For Eveline's speedy recovery and for Seth's safe return.

And for Valerius and Rain.

As if conjured by her thoughts, the pattering of racing feet echoed closer from one of the tunnels feeding into the large central arena.

A moment later, the Healer herself burst through the entrance, followed closely by Ayelet, who huffed by way of explanation, "Couldn't keep her back. She insisted on following him here."

Rain flew to Valerius the moment she saw him, just as his legs could no longer support his weight and he slid heavily down the wall into a half sitting, half lying heap on the ground.

Without a word to the others, Rain concentrated solely on the Protector and held his beloved face between her pale palms. Immediately, she began to transmit healing energy from her palms through his skin.

With his last remaining strength, Valerius swiped aside her hands and speared her with a glare.

Furiously, he bit out, "No! I didn't see you restored to your vitality for you to waste your energy on me now. You know this is futile!"

Ignoring his growl, Rain calmly placed one hand back on his face and thrust something in his fist with the other.

The handkerchief. She'd saved it.

Valerius locked his fingers around the precious gift, the one thing that had comforted him, helped him endure the past ten years of being so close to his heart's desires but never close enough. She had given him strength all along, he realized. She'd been healing him since the moment they first met.

And this was how he repaid her. Not even able to Serve out the full course of the Cycle.

Rain pressed both hands against his cheeks again and closed her eyes. Her long, almost completely black hair lifted in a dark halo around her, stretching from roots to their needle-like ends in undulating waves.

"Get her off me!" Valerius barked out to their audience, who stood surrounding them in a semi-circle, watching with breaths held.

No one moved an inch at his command. Ayelet shook her head at him silently.

This was between Rain and him. Their friends would not interfere.

Valerius could feel his life force drain, even as Rain sent bursts of energy into his helpless body. His heart had begun to slow, and his lungs could no longer provide the oxygen he needed. He couldn't feel his limbs, couldn't lift his hands to stop her, had no more voice to speak. The energy she fed into him was not nearly enough to stem the outflow of his life force.

She was killing herself for a dead man!

All of her *zhen* had inserted into his pores, some deeper still through his skin into his muscles, and even deeper into his internal organs, forcefully pumping hot white energy into his system, even as his soul was already in the process of lifting away from his corporeal form.

Don't do this, he silently beseeched her with his mind. *Let me go.*

Never, she answered him through the connection of their bodies, *if you go, then I will go with you*.

Don't do this, he continued to beg her. *I am not worth sacrificing your life.*

Rain gingerly bent her lips to his cold, lifeless ones and sealed their mouths in a shatteringly sweet kiss.

You are everything to me, she responded. *You are my eternity.*

A sudden blast of energy erupted from their bodies, a blindingly bright light radiating outwardly from them in a protective cocoon.

Ayelet and the others had to step back from the expanding orb of light as electrifying sparks shot out from its center, singeing anything and anyone in its way.

Within the center of the cocoon, Rain's hair slowly began to lose color from inky black to transparent crystal, starting at the needle ends that were inserted into Valerius and gradually up along each silken strand to the roots.

Valerius gasped as his heart began to accelerate and his breath began to quicken. Every nerve felt as if it were on fire, a welcome pain compared to the deathly numbness before.

Meanwhile, Rain's consciousness began to fade. Her eyelids became too heavy to keep open, and her pulse began to slow. Though she maintained the seal of their mouths, her hands slipped limply from the Protector's face.

Before long, she was surrounded by a familiar white light.

As if in a dream, she heard a woman's warm, kind voice, one that she had not heard since the last moment of her human life.

"What is it you wish for, my child?" the voice inquired of her. "If you could have anything, be anyone, what is your one true desire in this next life?"

Rain answered her without hesitation.

Whatever the consequences, whatever the sacrifice, she would accept anything and everything if she could have her deepest desire.

For eternity.

*** *** *** ***

Though it was only three in the morning when the Dozen returned to the Shield, it felt like an eon had passed.

Weary and sore, saddened by their losses, but also infused with new hope, especially at Valerius and Rain's Mating, they each retired to their chambers to rest and recover for the ceremonies that night.

First there would be the mourning of their fallen comrades. Then there would be the Mating Ritual and celebration.

Many questions remained unanswered, many mysteries unresolved, not the least of which was the fact that their nemesis was still at large.

But there would be time to evaluate, consider and plan. The time now would be dedicated to paying their respects to their friends' sacrifice as well as the bond of love between two Soul Mates.

Unlike the others, Valerius and Rain slept not a wink, too energized and too joyful to close their eyes. For hours into the first rays of dawn, as reflected within the ever-changing wall mural of their Enclosure, they made love. Urgently at first, desperately. Then leisurely, languorously. Always passionately.

They washed each other in the shower and thanked the Goddess that the Enclosure had been untouched by the invasion of the previous night, mere hours ago. They fed each other fruits and cheese and laughed and teased like carefree young lovers in the first bloom of youth and innocence. They murmured long hidden feelings and thoughts. And simply listened to each other breathe.

Valerius shuddered in ecstasy as another orgasm jolted through his deliciously aching body, and Rain's answering release milked him voraciously with her surprisingly strong inner muscles. Hot on the heels of his climax was the rapturous infusion of energy from Rain's core, as she funneled into him waves of pure spiritual bliss wherever their skin touched, and most of all, where they were intimately joined.

Her long sigh of pleasure sounded like a feline purr, and she nuzzled him affectionately as she burrowed her face into his neck, daintily licking the thick vein in his throat from which she'd fed repeatedly.

"Love you," she said happily, exuberantly, as if all the floodgates had been opened and she held nothing back. "Have I told you that lately?"

Seventeen times in the past four hours, Valerius reflected. He treasured every word.

"And I you," he answered without hesitation, stroking his fingers lovingly through her long, white hair.

As he brought a lock of silken tresses before his face, inhaling her faint feminine scent, a pang of regret speared through him.

She had relinquished everything for him. Her role as the Healer. Her very Gift. Even her original beauty. She would never grow back her luminous black hair.

"But I have you," Rain said, reading his thoughts.

Now that they were Mated, they shared the mental, emotional and spiritual connection that were reserved only for Soul Mates.

"And you are all I'll ever need or want."

She took his hand in hers and kissed his knuckles, noticing that he still wore his Tiger's Eye Consort ring. When she started to tug it off his finger, Valerius stilled her efforts.

"I'd like to keep it," he said, entwining their fingers.

Pure ones did not exchange matrimonial bands like most humans did during the Mating ceremony. The Phoenix Rite required the token as a declaration to others of their race that a particular male was taken, but only for the duration of the Cycle. To Valerius, however, the ring had come to mean much more.

"It's a symbol of our joining, that I belong to you. In the beginning it..." he paused to swallow and closed his eyes.

Speaking his heart was something in which he had no practice, but this was Rain, he reminded himself. As his Mate, she could read his thoughts, his feelings, even more clearly than himself. He wouldn't be able to hide from her. He didn't want to any more.

"In the beginning it pained me," he continued quietly, "it was a constant reminder that I was merely your Consort, that the love I felt was one way."

Rain stirred at those words, but Valerius squeezed her hand to hear him out.

"In the back of my mind was the knowledge that many males have worn this ring in the past and many more would wear it in the future. It... hurt."

He took a shuddering breath and tried to even his breathing. Even the memory of the pain made his heart ache now.

Rain wrapped herself more tightly around him, trying to infuse him with the warmth of her love and devotion. Though it killed her to stay silent, she forced herself to be still, be patient.

He needed to speak freely. He was slowly unfettering his heart.

Her face in the crook of his neck, she couldn't see his expression, could only hear his voice, feel his body's shivers of pain, his Adam's apple bobbing as he swallowed once more.

"I know a few of the past Consorts. I know what kind of men they were. They were kings, generals, princes, noblemen. I-I was nothing... a...a sex slave."

He inhaled deeply and plunged on before his throat closed up entirely, "But even as such, I didn't know anything about the act. It was never my choice."

The last he said fiercely, his voice deep and vibrating with anguish, sorrow, and fury.

Tears leaked out of Rain's closed eyes and ran silently down her cheeks. She bit down on her tongue to keep silent, to prevent the sounds of her shattering heart from escaping.

"I was nothing, and even after eleven years of *training*," he all but hissed out the word, "I knew not the first thing about pleasuring a female. I only knew how to receive and inflict pain. I knew that among all of your Consorts, I was the least worthy."

After a long pause, Valerius whispered, reverence and disbelief in his voice, "But still you chose me. The ring became a symbol of that choice. I...never imagined you could... care for someone like me."

Even now, even after hearing her confession of love for him seventeen times, he could not bring himself to accept it.

In a voice so low and guttural she could barely hear, he said brokenly, "I thought for a while that my blood wasn't strong enough for you, that maybe it was... contaminated. I thought I was... defective. I feared I would poison you with the demons inside."

"But for some reason, you seemed to want me—I mean—my Nourishment," he quickly amended, lest she thought he was too full of himself.

I want you, she shouted in his mind, unable to keep silent at least in that regard. *I love you!*

Goosebumps rippled across Valerius' skin as he heard her words in his heart, in his soul. Like a soothing balm, they cooled the feverish wound of his self-doubt.

"And now, I will be the last to wear this ring."

He said it almost as a question, as if he still couldn't believe the truth of it.

Rain vigorously nodded her head in affirmation. There would never be another for her. And even though Valerius might not understand or accept the fact, yet, there was never another for her even in the past.

She had only ever truly loved *him*. Nothing else compared.

She didn't even realize that she'd voiced her thoughts aloud, until he shivered in response and murmured in a tortured, half disbelieving-half hopeful voice, "You don't have to say that."

It would take time to heal him completely, she knew. Even now, he doubted. Not so much her love for him, but whether he deserved it, given his past, his demons. But they had an eternity to love each other.

Rain did not take one moment for granted, however. To prove her immeasurable desire and love for him, she snuggled closer and took his swollen length even deeper inside with a graceful twist of her hips.

Valerius gasped and flexed his buttocks in reaction, grinding the engorged head of his penis against her pleasure spot.

Rain tilted her head back and gave into the steadily building pressure within. As he continued to flex into her slowly and methodically, she struggled to maintain coherence.

"I have not lost all of my Gift," she said as her hair flowed silkily over their bodies like caressing hands.

"Like I said, they have a mind of their own."

She smiled at the sound of his helpless moan when her *zhen* found and inserted into his erogenous zones.

"You don't play fair," he whispered huskily beside her ear, nibbling gently on the lobe. "How can I ever please you as much as you please me?"

She stroked his broad back as he slowly shifted until she was directly beneath him, her legs twined about his hips.

"But your pleasure is my pleasure," she sighed when he began to quicken his thrusts.

"I can feel everything you feel as if it were my own body through the connection of the *zhen*. Right now your heart is beating faster, as is mine. Your blood is pumping vigorously through your veins, especially here."

She brushed the place where they were joined, smoothing the pad of her thumb against the root of his staff as he pumped powerfully in and out. The exquisite friction of her touch and the internal clench of her hot, wet core pushed Valerius ever closer to the edge. But he used his iron control to hold back, prolonging both their pleasure.

"I can feel your testicles draw tight," she continued to whisper against his throat and reached one hand to cup his sacs, wrenching a guttural groan from his lips.

"I can hear your blood singing, your temperature rising, your pulse quickening."

She clenched her thighs in time with his thrusts, magnifying the friction, the devastating sensations tenfold.

Kneading his testicles with just the right amount of pressure, in the most perfect places, she continued inexorably, "Your seed is pulsing in Nourishing waves through them, into your manhood, making it even thicker, longer, harder... and then—"

She sank her fangs into the vein at his throat and sucked hard.

Into me.

Valerius shouted involuntarily as his body clenched tight and shattered on her command, filling her with his blood, his life force in unending gulps.

He quaked so hard from the mind-blowing orgasm he thought he could hear his bones breaking, his tendons snapping.

But there was no pain. There was only the unimaginable bliss of his surrender. And it seemed to go forever, waves after rolling waves of ecstasy. All the while, she squeezed him tightly, caught in her own release, funneling white hot energy into him. The pleasure she returned upon him was just as devastating, and he absorbed it all greedily.

When the shudders and tingles finally subsided like ebbing tides after a tsunami, Valerius rolled with her until she was draped like a blanket over him. She refused to let him leave her body, however, and squeezed her thighs together to keep his length within her. Despite the bone-deep exhaustion and heavy soreness of his muscles, especially that particular muscle, Valerius gladly obeyed her will.

He could deny her nothing. Not ever again.

She eased away from his throat and licked the two small puncture wounds closed. Levering up a little, she leaned over to kiss his mouth sweetly, leisurely, darting her tongue inside, nibbling on his full, wide lips.

Valerius cupped the back of her head with one large hand and deepened the kiss. Despite having just climaxed, and for the umpteenth time besides, he wanted her again with an urgency and passion that astounded him. He couldn't get enough of her. He would never get enough of Rain.

"You will be the death of me," he murmured against her plump, wet mouth, "but it will be a wonderful way to go."

Rain giggled in delight and wriggled playfully against him, making him hiss at the spike of pleasure, sharpened by the soreness of his sex.

He began to stroke her long, silky hair again, marveling at the shimmering mass. Again, he thought of all that she had lost, despite her admonitions to the contrary.

"Will you resent me one day for your sacrifice?" he blurted out despite himself, then wished immediately that he could take his words back.

She raised her head on her arms to gaze down into his eyes, full of vulnerability and self-blame.

"I did not make a sacrifice," she answered solemnly, firmly. "The Goddess gave me a choice: continue as the Pure Ones' Healer, alone without you, or take you as my Eternal Mate. It really wasn't a choice. I love you far more than any calling, any Gift. And anyone I've ever known, Valerius."

She kissed him tenderly and longingly to make her point, and he kissed her back with all the love and fierceness in his heart.

"And besides," she said, pulling back slightly to catch her breath, beaming down at him with her Mona Lisa smile, "I can still be a healer if I choose. The knowledge and experience I've accumulated would make me arguably the world's premier physician. I intend to keep my clinic and study surgery."

"There was no need to learn human medical procedures before—my *zhen* took care of everything. But I'm beginning to realize that human surgical advancement has progressed further than I ever thought possible. With microbes and lasers and optic fiber treatments similar to what I used to accomplish with my *zhen*, perhaps we don't really need an official Healer in the traditional sense. Perhaps we could have several healers trained on Pure Ones' physiology and human technology. Perhaps I can even help with the training while learning new techniques myself."

Valerius was astounded and impressed beyond words at his Mate's passion and drive. She was the most incredible, amazing, beautiful being he'd ever known. She'd soothed his pain, physical, emotional, spiritual. She'd saved his life with her courageous love.

She was cleansing, rejuvenating, joyful rain.

His pure, healing Rain.

"What did you tell the Goddess when she came to you?" Valerius couldn't help his curiosity.

Rain snuggled close and let her limbs turn liquid against the heat of his body.

Inhaling deeply his musky, intoxicating scent, she murmured as she began to drift off to sleep, "That is between me and the Goddess. Suffice it to say that you are stuck with me for the rest of Eternity, my *airen*."

Epilogue

It's been almost three months since we pitted forces against the "evil ones."

Whoever they might be.

I've finished my final exams and am on my first day of winter holidays. I think I aced all of my classes, except the statistics class from my required curriculum.

How I hate math.

I'll be thankful if I pass. No ambitions for a high score there. I'm not delusional about my numerical abilities, or lack thereof.

Please Goddess, let me pass! I really don't want to endure another semester of the same type of torture. After all, if I pass, I'll have financial accounting to look forward to. Isn't that punishment enough?

Lots have happened over these months.

We've moved the Shield to a brand new location. Can't tell you where. I'd have to kill you if I did.

But here's a hint, we're hidden in plain sight, in the most beautiful crystal tower in Boston city. No more underground tunnels this time. Our last location took ten years to build properly, secretively, expensively from afar, while we still lived abroad.

Thankfully, Cloud's stallion is not afraid of heights, for it seemed none the worse for wear during the long flight over here and finally settled into its stables forty stories above ground. It has taken a distinct dislike to Valerius' Hayabusa, however. We often find piles of manure near the wheels and what I can only deduce to be horse spittle on the seat.

I think the stallion views the Hayabusa as competition.

Their masters, by contrast, seem perfectly at ease with one another. You'd have thought they were bosom buddies the way Valerius banters with Cloud like he's never done with any of the other Elite.

But the Protector has changed quite dramatically overall. He's more easygoing with all of us, more affectionate too. I've been surprised with a few hugs myself, probably because I'm the easiest one to sneak up on.

At first I thought he was trying some abbreviated Heimlich maneuver on me or maybe a new way for training me to escape enemy clutches by enveloping me with those unyielding steel bands he calls arms. But then I realized he was just hugging me. Sometimes for no reason at all.

I gotta tell you, I *adore* this side of Val.

Didn't I peg him for being too high-strung and tense from lack of sexual release? See how a little bump and grind finally loosened him up?

And now that he has infinite access to sex and orgasm and spiritual energy in his Soul Mate, Val is a whole new man.

Sure took him and Rain long enough to get together though. Geez!

Speaking of the ex-royal Healer, I'm slowly getting over my awe of her. Of course, I'll always be astounded by her beauty and intelligence and talents—she's like a real life *xian nü*, a mythical fairy of the Heavens in Chinese folklore.

What I mean is, I'm getting to know her better, so I don't feel like an ocean of distance separates us; she, a heavenly creature, me, a lowly earthling.

I've been helping her study for her MCAT, the medical school admissions test. Not that I know anything about medicine, but I know how to study for standardized tests. With my rambling educational background and mix of home school, private and public schools, I've had to get pretty good at faking through admissions tests.

Rain is so smart, she passed the MCAT with flying colors on the first try. Well, I guess two thousand five hundred years of healing did come in handy somewhat. She's going to start at Harvard Medical School just across the river from me in the Spring.

These days, she and Val are inseparable. Maybe it's the Honeymoon stage, but I somehow doubt it. Whereas Tristan and Ayelet have an easy-going, affectionate relationship, Valerius and Rain have an intense, passionate bond.

I guess true love takes many different forms for different couples.

Wan'er has her hands full keeping up with the booming clinic in Chinatown. She and Rain are sharing duties for the Pure Ones' clinic in our new base. With so much to do, she doesn't seem to miss her previous role as a handmaiden.

But I must say, she almost seems a little too obsessed with work. Out of everyone, she took Xandros' death the hardest, shutting herself away for days. I won't venture to guess what happened between them—she hasn't shared her grief with anyone.

We're still searching for leads on our nemesis, the beautiful vampire who caused so much destruction and devastation, but it's as if he/she has disappeared into thin air.

Honestly, I don't know what to call the vampire. I still don't know whether it's a male or female. Apparently, no one does, especially after Dalair added to the confusion by sharing that he witnessed the creature transform its figure into different people.

We have no idea who or what we're dealing with. It's practically unheard of that a vampire or a Pure One would have such abilities. I wish Orion was here to help us confirm, but as it is, Eveline has been taking over his duties, trying to build a rudimentary knowledge base of our race's long, *long* history. What's worse, a quarter of the tomes in the library have been destroyed in the attack.

Eveline is also tasked with finding Orion's replacement. Not surprisingly, she's been dragging her feet on that one. We are in no hurry. She will find the right person when the time comes.

Meanwhile, Seth is still MIA. We don't know his location or when he'll come back. Besides the occasional news from his projections, he doesn't stay in regular contact.

Well, we kind of guessed where he is. Or rather, whom he's with.

The Vampire Queen wouldn't send her personal guard to our aid for nothing. Seth is the best negotiator we know. He can bargain tears from a stone. But I'm pretty certain Jade Cicada is no pushover.

I wonder what the Consul agreed to give in return for her support...

We continue to wait patiently for his return. None of us want to contemplate that he won't. Ayelet is half-heartedly running through the motions of looking for his backup, but she finds fault with each potential candidate even without a thorough background check.

We chalk it up to her hormonal surges, for wonders upon wonders, the Guardian is pregnant!

Frankly, I didn't even know Pure Ones can have children. There are rumors, and a few have been documented in the Zodiac Scrolls, but I mean, with so few Mated couples and a precise balance of Pure souls that enter and leave this world, conception is so rare it's become a myth.

Maybe the Goddess is balancing our losses—the losses of our race as a whole in recent years—through this miracle. It's only one soul, one person, but the joy he or she will bring will lift us all. It also gives Valerius and Rain hope that they too could have their own little one.

Lots of sex going on in our new Shield, I can tell you that much.

I wouldn't be surprised if Aella and Cloud are next. Even I, with my virginal teenage innocence, can tell that my best friend is hankering to get a piece of the warrior hunk. She's been dogging his heels pretty relentlessly over the past few months.

Aella is like a whirlwind (hence her name, which means exactly that). I pity the man who tries to refuse getting swept up by her passion and energy. She doesn't take no for an answer.

Sigh. If only I had my own affairs sorted out.

Ere left a note in my locker at school the Thursday I returned to class. He was off on some research stint again, this time to Siberia of all places. And he wouldn't return until the New Year.

For my Christmas present, he left me the keys to his apartment and an invitation for me to stay there whenever I wanted, whether to read books from his massive library or just to get a little privacy, a bit of personal time away from my "roommates."

I am grateful beyond words. I wish I told him how much I'd miss him the last time we saw each other in class. Oddly, I don't feel lonely. Sometimes, I even talk to him in my mind. It's as if I'm carrying part of his spirit inside of me, as if we're connected no matter where we are in the world.

In contrast, my relationship with Dalair continues to deteriorate. He's taken himself completely out of my guard rotation, even though there are only five Elite right now.

Aella is working with Ayelet to recruit the sixth. But it's been tough going because the war with the vampire demon had turned and sacrificed so many Pure Ones of warrior class. It may be easier to train a hundred new recruits than to find another ancient warrior like Cloud.

Dalair is obsessed with finding the vampire demon that captured me. He's like a man possessed, going out early in the morning, returning late at night, hunting for leads, picking fights. Because we've ceased the nightly hunt for vampire rogues for the time being (it's been pretty quiet these days with the North End Horde eliminated and our erstwhile nemesis defeated), he has no outlet for his pent-up fury and burgeoning need for retribution.

He reminds me of a wounded animal on the edge of insanity from its unbearable pain.

I don't know how to help him—he never lets me near him anymore. We barely exchanged two words in the past few weeks. I wish with all my heart that I could ease his pain. I feel sorry for every ungrateful, mean thing I've ever said to him.

But he's become unreachable. Perhaps even more unreachable than Valerius once was. I wish I knew his story. I wish I knew his past. With that knowledge, maybe I can begin to understand more about this mysterious, haunted warrior.

But you know what they say...

Be careful what you wish for.

Other Books in the Pure/ Dark Ones series:

Dark Longing **Book 2**
Dark Desires **Book 3**
Dark Pleasures **Book 4**
Pure Rapture **Book 5**
Dark Redemption **Book 6**
Pure Awakening **Book 6.5**
***Pure Ecstasy* Book 7**

51546218R00201

Made in the USA
Middletown, DE
03 July 2019